SHADOW OF POWER

By Steve Martini

TRADER OF SECRETS
THE RULE OF NINE
GUARDIAN OF LIES
SHADOW OF POWER
DOUBLE TAP
THE ARRAIGNMENT
THE JURY
THE ATTORNEY
CRITICAL MASS
THE LIST
THE JUDGE
UNDUE INFLUENCE
PRIME WITNESS
COMPELLING EVIDENCE
THE SIMEON CHAMBER

STEVE MARTINI

TRADER OF SECRETS

A PAUL MADRIANI NOVEL

HARPER

An Imprint of HarperCollins*Publishers*

This is a work of fiction. The events described are imaginary, and the characters are fictitious and not intended to represent specific living persons. Even when settings are referred to by their true names, the incidents portrayed as taking place there are entirely fictitious; the reader should not infer that the events set there ever happened.

HARPER

An Imprint of HarperCollins*Publishers*
195 Broadway
New York, NY 10007

First Harper premium printing: January 2012
First William Morrow hardcover printing: June 2011

HarperCollins® and Harper® are registered trademarks of Harper-Collins Publishers.

Printed in the United States of America

Visit Harper paperbacks on the World Wide Web at
www.harpercollins.com

10 9 8 7 6 5

To my daughter, Meg

ONE

Most of the blood left on the concrete floor of the garage in Washington belonged to the big black investigator working for Madriani, the man named Herman Diggs, but not all of it.

Liquida could feel the tight constraint of the large gauze bandage covering the searing wound under his right arm. Every bump in the highway brought pain as the motion tugged on the metal staples holding the wound closed. It made his eyes water. Still, the pain kept him awake and on course.

What kept Liquida going was his hatred for Madriani and an unquenchable thirst for retribution. The firm of Madriani and Hinds had caused him to lose a small fortune, enough money for Liquida to retire. That was before the lawyers' investigator carved up Liquida's back with a knife, but not before Liquida had dealt the man a deathblow. As the bastard lay dying on the concrete floor, Liquida twisted the knife by telling him that he knew where the girl was and that she was next. Now he intended to make good on the promise.

His right arm hung limp in a sling as he steered with his left hand. Liquida struggled to keep his eyes on the road, periodically holding the wheel with his knees as he sipped fluids, alternating between coffee and orange juice. He refused to consume the pain pills given to him by the physician for fear they might dull his senses; not until the girl was dead.

The doctor had told him to change the bandages daily and to remain quiet for at least a week to allow the stapled sutures to heal. The all-night clinic was a seedy place in a dingy area just outside D.C., one of those surgi-centers where, for enough cash, usually they would remove a bullet or stitch up an open wound, no questions asked. Liquida was in and out in less than an hour.

He had no intention of remaining quiet for ten days. Madriani's daughter would not wait that long on the farm in Ohio. Once she was told what had happened in Washington, she would bolt for another location to hide out, or join her father. Either way it would be much more difficult to find her again. Liquida knew he had to act and act quickly. Before he murdered Madriani, he wanted the lawyer to know that his daughter had died under Liquida's knife.

He made the four hundred miles from D.C. to Groveport, Ohio, in a little under eight hours. Liquida napped just briefly in a small motel a short distance from the farm where the girl was staying. He knew that with every minute that passed he ran the risk that Sarah Madriani and her father's law partner, the one they called Harry Hinds, might pack their bags and make a run for it. But Liquida had no choice. He was in no condition to plan and carry out a killing against a well-guarded location without at least a few hours' rest.

He changed the bandage on his wound. It was a painful exercise, twisting around and using his one good arm, trying not to pull the sutures or tear the skin around the wound as he wrestled with the tape. He set an alarm for two hours and collapsed onto the bed to sleep.

TWO

Joselyn Cole and I spent most of the night locked up with the FBI and the Metropolitan Police, each of us in separate rooms being interrogated about the events leading up to the bombing near the Capitol.

Joselyn and I have been an item now for the greater part of six months. She is, you might say, my better half, especially if intellect, moral values, and judgment count for much. During a time when I have found myself increasingly tossed about by waves of chaos, Joselyn has become my outrigger, that extension of life, the flotation of love that keeps me upright.

In terms of philosophy, she is my opposite number, the positive to my own negative political electrical charge. She is a dreamy-eyed liberal whose self-appointed mission is to get the nuclear genie back in the bottle with the cork on tight. Joselyn is the chief instigator and lobbyist for an organization known as Gideon Quest. We met six months ago in the turmoil following an attack on the naval base in Coronado. She arrived at my front door looking for information. The rest, as they say, is history.

Thorpe and the FBI grilled us into the wee hours, recording our statements and getting all the details, everything we knew about the device that landed in the rail yard just outside Union Station in Washington, D.C., how we got involved, and what we knew.

The twisted tracks and thirty-foot hole in the ground have screwed up the local rail system bigtime, though this was not the intended target.

A little after two in the morning they turned us loose, at least long enough to get a few hours' sleep. By six A.M. we were back catching catnaps from chairs near Herman's bed in the intensive care unit at George Washington University Hospital. The prognosis is not good. But if Herman regains consciousness at all, I don't want him to wake up in a strange room with no one there.

Herman's sister is due in from Detroit this afternoon to join the bedside watch.

In the meantime, Joselyn and I are being chaperoned by the FBI. If we are not in custody, it's as close as you get. After I had a brief phone conversation with my daughter last night, the FBI lifted our cell phones. They don't want us talking to anybody about the events until they know more. We are now incommunicado, their favorite couple it seems, at least until they finish pumping us dry of any useful information.

Agents check into the ICU every so often to see if Herman is awake and able to talk. No doubt they want to check his story against ours, trusting people that they are. Still, considering all the media parked outside, satellite trucks around the block and 24/7 cable coverage of the big bang in the rail yard, coming and going through the hospital basement in a darkened FBI van is not the worst way to travel.

Joselyn is slouched in the other chair with her eyes closed. Her little snoring sounds punctuate the noise of the ventilator forcing oxygen into Herman's lungs. I decide to take a walk.

Outside the room I nearly run into a nurse carrying a fresh IV bag and a bottle of clear liquid.

"What are you doing here?" She glances at her watch.

"I'm a friend of the family."

"Only family are allowed in ICU."

"He's all right." The voice comes from behind me, a uniformed cop planted on the bench a few feet away. "He's allowed. Check the list. The doctor put their names on it, both him and the woman inside the room." The cop doesn't look up at her. Chewing gum, he's studying a tattered copy of *Field & Stream*.

The nurse doesn't like interference with her authority, which upsets the hospital pecking order. But she suffers it and slips by me into the room.

"How's he doin'?" The cop is still looking at the magazine.

"Same."

I see Zeb Thorpe down at the end of the hall talking to one of the agents. What he is doing here at this hour, I'm not sure. Thorpe never seems to sleep. It's the price you pay for being head of the FBI's National Security Branch.

Thorpe has become our chief jailer. The man is a

brick, an ex-Marine with a flattop straight out of the '50s. He looks the part of the original Jughead, but he has moments of inspiration. He is dogged once he gets on the scent, though at times he can be slow to pick it up.

Thorpe has posted security all over the hospital and limited press access to the lobby downstairs.

Last night during the interrogation, one of his people let slip with a comment that caused me to think that the rail yard bombing may not be the only iron Liquida has in the fire. There is no telling what other mischief the Mexican may be involved in.

Thorpe is hoping to talk to Herman to find out if he got a good look at Liquida. So far the authorities have a pseudonym, "Muerte Liquida," with no face. They are streaming the videos from every security camera near the garage where Herman was knifed, hoping to find pictures of the mystery man. So far, from what I am told, they have had no luck.

The killer who cut his teeth working for the Tijuana drug cartel, Liquida, aka "the Mexicutioner," is a ghost with no record on file, either here or in Mexico. He has now branched out and gone global. By all accounts he has slipped the bonds of narco-terrorism to move on to the wider world of clients with larger weapons and deeper pockets. In doing so he has grabbed the attention of Homeland Security and the FBI.

Thorpe eyes me over the shoulder of the other agent, finishes the conversation, and heads my way.

He sidles up close, looks me in the eye. "How's he doing?"

I shake my head. "No change."

"You know, if you're tired, you and the lady can go back whenever you want. I'll have one of my guys drive you."

"Back to the government pad?"

"Where else?"

"That's OK, you don't have to wait for us. We can find our way," I tell him.

He gives me a tight-lipped smile, all dead in the eyes, and switches the subject. "The doctor's changing out the medication in his IV, lightening up on the sedatives."

"Do me a favor. Leave him alone," I tell him. "If he's gotta die, let him do it in peace."

"What?" He holds his hands out palms up, looking at me as if to say, What did I do? "Doctor's just changing out the meds, that's all."

"Right."

"If he does come around, you will let us know?" he says.

"What good will it do? Herman can't talk with the tube down his throat."

"Yeah, but he can point. We got a man with a laptop and Identi-Kit software waiting in the hall outside. If Diggs saw Liquida, we'd like to get a shot at a sketch if we can."

"Why not? You can just put your man with his computer and the software in Herman's coffin and see what develops."

"I don't like this any more than you do," he says. "But I've got a job to do. It may not be pleasant, but it has to be done."

"I take it your people ran up a dark hole after Liquida left the garage? No leads?"

"We're still looking."

"That means he's had, what . . . ?" I look at my watch. "Eleven hours' head start to lose himself."

"We'll get him," says Thorpe.

"When?"

"I don't know. He's probably gone to ground until he can recover. We'll get him."

"Always the optimist."

"According to forensics, your investigator must have done a pretty good job on him. He left a small river of blood getting out of the garage."

"Not enough to satisfy me," I tell him.

"They tracked the trail through a back entrance and half a block before it disappeared. Either somebody picked him up out on the street or he had a car stashed. We're checking all the hospitals and clinics."

"Call me when you catch him. I have a daughter and law partner who would like to go home, and a life I would like to resume."

"Tell that to your investigator," says Thorpe.

Touché!

"You're sure there's nothing else you can remember?" he asks.

"We told you everything we know. I've gotta get back inside." I turn to walk.

"Thanks for your help. I mean it. You will call the minute he wakes up?"

"Yeah. Maybe. We'll see how he's doing." I leave him standing there as I disappear back into the room with Herman.

The nurse has already changed out the IV. She leaves and I settle into my chair.

"What's going on?" Joselyn is half asleep, roused by my entry into the room.

"Thorpe appreciates everything we've done for him."

"That's grand. Tell him I can die a happy woman," she says.

"Go back to sleep." I settle back into the chair and close my eyes.

How long I slept I am not sure, but it must have been deep REM because a rasping noise invades my subconscious for some time before it becomes clear that it is the sound of someone choking.

I open my eyes and Joselyn is gone. Her chair is empty.

I turn and see Herman's eyes wide open, his hands clawing at the tape around the tube at his mouth and nose.

I am out of the chair in a flash, grabbing his wrists to keep him from yanking on the tube.

"Herman! Herman, relax. It's me. It's Paul. You're all right. They've got you on a ventilator. Leave it alone."

His arms pull against me, struggling to reach the tube in his mouth. The trauma of the last day is etched across his broad face like a death mask. His eyes are staring at me in stark terror. Herman is in a state of panic, fighting the device that now controls his breathing.

He tries to move his mouth as if he wants to say something.

"Don't try to talk. They got a tube down your

throat. There was some lung damage. You're gonna be OK," I lie to him. "Doctor says you're gonna be fine. Just rest." I want to reach for the call button to get the nurse but can't let go of Herman's hands without running the risk that he'll pull the tube.

He eases up a little with his powerful forearms. Herman forces a pained smile, as much as the tube down his throat and the mass of tape around his mouth will allow. He swallows hard. His eyes open wide as he chokes a little.

"That's better. Don't fight it. That's it. Just relax and let the machine breathe for you. I know it's hard."

He nods gently. His head settles back into the hollow of the pillow once more.

I don't tell him that, according to the surgeon, he flatlined twice during the four-hour operation. For much of the time he was on a heart-lung machine as they struggled to repair the damage to his right lung. Liquida had nicked a main artery. An inch more and he would have severed it. Herman would have bled out within seconds at the scene.

I hold each of his arms near the wrist, trying to avoid any contact with the IV needle going into the vein at the back of his hand. If he continues to strug-gle, they will have to tie his hands off to the railings on the bed. Knowing Herman, I'm sure he would tear the bed apart.

He lifts his head off the pillow once more and calls up a moaning sound from somewhere deep inside. His chest rises suddenly as if a million volts have been run through his body.

"Herman! Herman! Stay with me," I tell him.

"Joselyn!!" I yell at the top of my voice. I look over my shoulder, hoping either the nurse or Joselyn will come into the room.

When I turn back, Herman is trying to sit up. "No, no. Just stay still. Lie back." He looks at me sternly in the eye as if maybe this is the last image his brain will ever register. He wants to say something, but he can't. Herman's most serious expression. Whatever it is, it's important; at least it is to Herman.

I could kill Thorpe for having the doctor reduce the sedatives.

"Are you in pain? Lie back and I'll get the nurse." I can't tell how much of what I am saying he understands.

He shakes me off. That's not it.

"Relax. Let me get the nurse."

He shakes his head again, this time more violently.

The cop steps into the room.

"Get the doc," I tell him.

He leaves on the run.

Herman grabs the sleeve of my coat to keep me from leaving. Then he reaches up with both hands, wincing in pain as he motions in pantomime, his right hand scribbling on the palm of his left. He wants something to write with.

Frantically I look around, but there is no pencil or paper in the room. The best way to quiet him is to give him what he wants.

"I have a pen in my pocket. If I let go, you won't pull on the tube? You promise?"

He gives me a quick sharp nod, anger in his eyes.

I release his wrists and fish the pen from my inside coat pocket. I find a couple of loose business cards in the side pocket. "Sorry. Best I can do," I tell him.

He turns one of the business cards over and scribbles quickly on the back. With the needle inserted and taped to the back of his hand, the scrawl is barely legible. "Liquida?" He points at it with the tip of the pen.

"You got him good," I tell him. I am hoping this news may calm him. "The cops found blood all the way out of the garage and onto the street. He won't get far. You may have killed him. He may be dead for all we know."

Herman shakes his head violently. He glares at me from under furrowed brows. He's trying to tell me something, and I'm not getting it. He grabs the business card from my hand and starts to work the point of the pen over it again.

I move up a little toward the head of the bed to watch as he writes. The word *Sarah* and then *farm*. He stabs the last word with the point of the pen.

"Yes, Sarah is still there. She's OK. I talked to her last night."

Herman shakes his entire body this time, bellowing through the tube so violently that I'm afraid he is going to rip it from his throat. Suddenly the sensor on the monitor over the bed goes off, a screaming tone that fills the room.

"Herman, stay with me." I pull away as if to get help. Where the hell is the doctor?

Herman grabs my sleeve once more. As I turn back, he points to the words on the card *Sarah, farm*, and then the word *Liquida*. It is as if he is struggling to deliver one last message before the grave closes over him.

The revelation suddenly seeps into my brain. "Liquida knows about the farm?"

Herman's stark eyes stare at me as he gently nods.

"He knows where Sarah is?"

He drops the sleeve of my coat and nods once more as his body collapses onto the bed, his head slumped onto the pillow.

THREE

Liquida motored slowly down the country road in front of the house, checking his watch as he drove. The place was dark inside, just a porch light and one of those bright yellow vapor lamps high on a pole near the barn. It lit up much of the front yard and cast an eerie glow out toward the road.

He drove on three hundred yards or so, turned off his headlights, then swung a quick U-turn and headed back the other way.

It wasn't a working farm or by this time they would be out milking the cows or feeding the animals. No signs of life. He knew from earlier observation that, unless they were into eating dogs, it was a hobby farm. They raised guard dogs.

It was what most gringos knew about farming. Food came out of a can or grew in plastic bags and cartons on grocery store shelves. All you had to do was add water and zap it in a microwave. If it had to be picked or killed, they didn't want to do it or see it being done. It was how many of the twelve million Mexicans they now called illegals came to be living in the States.

The gringos had borrowed all the money there was from foreign governments. Now they wanted to send all the Mexicans home. If they kept working at it, they could become the first empire in history to starve to death with bumper crops in the fields and feedlots full of cows and chickens, all dying of old age.

He pulled off and parked along the side of the road behind a line of bushes where the car couldn't be seen from the house. It was the area near the berry bushes where he had seen the girl the last time, near the edge of the property. In his present state, Liquida didn't want to have to go far to get to his car if something went wrong. If they tried to run, Liquida, with the car parked as it was, would be in a good position to follow them. When it became light, he would move the vehicle to a less visible lo-cation, then watch and wait.

He grabbed the binoculars from the passenger seat, stepped out of the car, and quietly closed the driver's-side door. He went to the rear of the vehicle and opened the trunk. He leaned over as he fished with his one good hand inside an open zippered bag. He pulled out a cloth bundle about fourteen inches long. It was rolled and closed with laces that were stitched to the fabric and tied in a bow. It looked like a storage roll for silverware, which was, in fact, what it was.

Liquida untied the bundle and rolled it out flat in the bottom of the trunk. Slipped into narrow pockets stitched into the fabric were a dozen textured metal handles, each one machined with a fine cross-hatch design etched deep into the steel. This made for a better grip. It also prevented fingerprints from being lifted from the surface of the handle.

Liquida slipped a leather glove on his one good hand, his left. Then he pulled one of the stilettos from its cloth pocket and examined the edges of the blade. They were razor sharp. The stilettos were made in a small machine shop in Tijuana, no wood or plastic, just a single piece of high carbide steel sharpened to a point, a five-inch handle with a nine-inch double-edged blade. The blade was very thin all the way to the needlelike point. It was designed for probing and piercing vital organs and slicing major blood vessels. In the hands of an expert, it could kill almost instantly or exact excruciating pain from its victim as the person twisted and squirmed in agony on the long spike of the blade.

Liquida laid the stiletto on the floor of the trunk and rubbed both sides of the metal with a piece of cloth, making sure that any prints that might be on it were either smudged or polished clean.

Now that the FBI had the other stiletto, the one he had dropped on the floor of the garage in D.C., the one Liquida used to kill the investigator, he would leave this one near the body of the girl as a calling card. Liquida wanted to leave no doubt as to who killed her, not that there should be any question.

He slipped the stiletto into the fold of the sling supporting his injured arm and quietly closed the lid on the trunk.

*   *   *

To the east, the Ohio horizon began to take on the hazy blue glow of a midsummer morning even as the last stars struggled to stay in the sky.

Sarah Madriani slipped out of the house, easing the rickety screen door closed behind her so that no one inside would hear. They were asleep. It was four thirty in the morning and still dark outside.

Today she was feeling a little better. Last night she had talked to her father on the phone, the first time in several days. The farm was isolated. She didn't even have access to a television, no cable. And they wouldn't allow her to get near a Wi-Fi signal for fear she might send an e-mail disclosing her location.

To save her sanity, Sarah had taken to running with one of the dogs, a Doberman named Bugsy. Each morning before the crack of dawn, without anyone knowing, she would turn off the security alarm at the control keypad in the kitchen, unbolt the front door, and head out.

She worked with Bugsy for a week around the farm and they bonded. There was nothing else to do. The dog gave her a sense of security and someone to run with. She needed a little exercise without being under Harry's gaze or the watchful eye of her aunt and uncle. Harry Hinds was her father's law partner.

The two of them had been stuck on the farm for two weeks. Sarah was climbing the walls. She was tired of it, and so was Harry, though he took pains not to show it.

Fearing for her life, her father had shipped her off to her Aunt Susan and Uncle Fred. Fred was a gun enthusiast with an arsenal in his basement and contacts with the local police, some of whom seemed to live on the farm. They were always there. The place felt like the county honor farm. The couple bred and raised Dobermans. Her father figured she'd be safe here. Safe was one thing, imprisoned was another.

For almost a week now, Sarah and the Doberman had gone for a morning romp through the fields past the berry bushes and the fence line, well beyond view from the yellow wood-framed house owned by her aunt and uncle. At a good clip Sarah could do a mile and a half out and back before any of the lights came on in the house. She would reset the alarm in the kitchen, head up to take a shower, and no one was the wiser.

She wore a pair of running shoes, shorts, and a jersey along with a light fanny pack strapped around her waist. The pack contained an aluminum water bottle she had purchased during the trip east with Harry. Sarah wasn't used to the elevated humidity in Ohio. Depending on how far and how fast she ran, she might swallow a little water or spit it out along the way.

This morning she skipped down the porch steps, kicking up pebbles along the gravel path as she headed for the dog run. A light morning breeze ruffled the frizzy tendrils of hair that framed her face. At least for a few minutes she would be free.

FOUR

Liquida couldn't believe his eyes as he tried to focus the binoculars. She was halfway down the path before he even looked up. There in the yellow glow of the vapor lamp was a young woman. She was in running shorts and a top, moving quickly toward the barn. He checked through the field glasses. Same hair. Same build. Her height looked right. It was her. It had to be. Liquida recognized her from his earlier stakeout of the farm, when he had lain in wait but couldn't get close enough. That was before he was called to Washington to deal with Madriani and his investigator.

Now suddenly the girl was alone in the darkness with no signs of life in the house. Liquida couldn't believe it. He had been perched behind the bushes along the road for less than ten minutes, and here she was as if served up on a platter.

The thought settled on him. It was too convenient. If the house was under surveillance, they would have seen him when he drove up. They could have called the house to set the trap. Maybe they were waiting for him.

He swung around with the binoculars half expecting to see the gumball lights of police cars screaming in on him from both directions along the road. He looked ahead as far as he could peer into the darkness, cutting through it with the field glasses, searching for any hint of headlights. There was nothing. He looked behind him, toward the parked car. The road was dark for as far as he could see. There was only the cool still air of the night, broken by an occasional breeze rustling through the branches of the trees. If it was a trap, they were using night vision, and the girl as bait, waiting for him to make his move.

She could be a policewoman, someone fitted out to look like Madriani's daughter. If so, the minute he made a move she would shoot him, or a police tactical unit would have their snipers cut him down from a distance. The thought played on Liquida's mind that he might not even hear the crack of the shot that killed him.

He aimed the binoculars back at the girl. It could be a double. Still, from what he remembered it looked like her. She was still moving toward the barn. Liquida had to make a decision, either cut and run, head for the car and try to escape, or make his move now.

Forty yards out Sarah could see Bugsy behind the chain link as he started to jump in the air, anxious to get out of his cage. He had come to expect her each morning at the same time. It was as if he had a clock.

The first day he had barked twice before she could get to him to keep him quiet. Sarah was sure somebody in the house would hear him. If they did, they never looked out. The side of the barn where the dog run was located was lit up like a prison yard by the overhead vapor lamp.

Since that first morning Bugsy hadn't made a peep. When he saw her, he would jump up, six or seven feet, his head soaring over the top of the gate. Inches away, he never once hit the chain link. It was all he could do to vent his excitement. Somehow the dog knew that the two of them were engaged in a conspiracy of silence. How he knew it, Sarah wasn't sure. As if by osmosis he absorbed it from the secretive ether in the atmosphere around them. Sarah had no way of training him. The dog seemed smarter than many of Sarah's friends, including almost all of the guys her age that she dated.

She reached the run and lifted the metal latch on the gate. The dog quivered with excitement on the other side as the gate swung open. He rushed out and rubbed himself against her, his long lean body wiggling and squirming like a fish out of water. Sarah felt the warm wetness as he licked her hand and tried to nibble on her fingers with his sizable teeth, the big canines up front. Bugsy was almost three years old. He had the build and bite of an adult Doberman, but he was still a puppy at heart. His docked tail was missing; otherwise he would have beat the hell out of the open gate, making enough noise to wake the dead.

Sarah was hunched over him with her back to the barn and facing the house, trying to calm him, when suddenly she saw the light in the upstairs guest bathroom come on.

Harry was out of bed. She wondered if somehow he heard the gate open or the commotion outside the dog run. She didn't want to wait to find out. Sarah grabbed the dog by the collar and pulled him around the corner of the barn toward the shadows and the darkness of the barn door yawning open. Quickly she disappeared inside, into the darkness with Bugsy in tow.

There was nothing she could do now but wait and hope that Harry wouldn't look out the window and see the open gate on Bugsy's cage. She was praying he would go back to bed, that the bathroom light was nothing but an urgent call of nature. Harry didn't usually get up before seven, though her aunt and uncle were usually up and about by six thirty.

She waited several minutes, then peeked out through the open door. From where she stood she couldn't see the bathroom window. She crept along the front of the barn, pulling Bugsy along with her until she reached the corner of the building. When she looked up, the bathroom light was out.

Sarah breathed a deep sigh. She unsnapped the dog's collar to free him from the underground electric fence and turned him loose. She sprinted toward the open field and the barbed-wire fence beyond, with Bugsy running out ahead of her.

* * *

Using the binoculars, Liquida surveyed the girl's movements through a bald spot in the bushes as he huddled along the side of the road. He watched every detail, the dog and the chemistry of chaos that went on outside the gate when she let him out. For a second he thought the animal might make love to her.

This was not your usual disciplined German Nazi dog, the kind of Doberman Liquida had learned from long experience to treat with respect. He liked to keep an impenetrable fence between himself and the snarling doggy breath and bared foam-covered fangs. A good Doberman was smarter than your average Jurassic Park raptor, and almost as lethal.

This dog was young and not well trained. Liquida was betting that within forty yards, he'd be off on a frolic after a rabbit or rolling in the alfalfa stubble trying to kill the smell and the sting in his eyes from that weird cat with the stripe down its back. By the time Liquida got to the girl, the dog would be off in the next county.

Liquida saw the light come on in the window upstairs. He watched the girl's reaction as she grabbed the dog and slinked around to the front of the barn where they both disappeared inside.

She didn't come out again until the light went out. When it did, she checked it. Then she turned and ran the other way as if it was a prison break. It told Liquida all he needed to know.

The girl had given her protectors inside the house the slip, including Madriani's law partner.

Why, Liquida didn't know, but it didn't matter. The only thing important now was that she was out in the field without backup, moving farther away from the house with each stride, and no one inside the place knew it.

FIVE

arah jogged out toward the open field on the other side of the barn. She was moving at a good clip. The dog bounded out ahead of her, taking detours from time to time into the bush to check out new smells or to chase birds.

It had become part of his routine. He would dart here and there, picking up scents and following them. He usually came back, racing to catch up only to pass her again. She figured that during her three-mile run, Bugsy probably covered five or six times that distance. Trapped in his cage the animal needed to burn off energy.

On their very first run, the dog hung close and was highly cautious as they approached the barbed-wire fence. It was here that the underground wire had been lain that triggered a warning followed by a low amperage but painful shock through the dog's collar if the animal approached too close. Through this device Bugsy had been conditioned not to get near the visible fence line. Once he realized that without the collar he was free, the dog went wild, streaking off into the distance to explore the unknown world. Since then he didn't even slow down at the fence. He would slip under the bottom strand of barbed wire and be gone, as he did this morning.

Liquida settled in behind the steering wheel. He could hear gravel popping under the tires through the open driver's-side window as the rental car, headlights out, rolled slowly down the road, keeping pace with the girl out in the field. If the road wasn't so flat, he would have used gravity rather than the motor to keep the noise down. He was sure that she hadn't noticed the slow-moving car out on the road. The girl was a good hundred yards away, out in front of him with her back to the vehicle as she ran.

He watched the Doberman taking off across the field well out ahead of her. There was just enough budding light on the horizon to see the two of them, dark silhouettes moving across the freshly mowed ground, the scent of alfalfa still in the air.

Within seconds Liquida watched as the dog came to an abrupt stop. The animal sniffed the ground. Then with the speed of a greyhound he suddenly took off in another direction. The girl ignored the Doberman and continued on her way. Thirty yards on she jumped the wire fence and headed toward a long line of trees in the distance. The trees flanked a slight depression in the ground, what appeared to be a creek that meandered across the girl's line of travel.

Liquida pressed on the car's accelerator. Within seconds he was out in front of her, rolling silently at speed down the dark road until he crossed the bridge over the creek. He pulled off to the right alongside the road and turned off the engine. He stepped out, crossed the road, and made his way down the embankment and toward the line of trees along the creek. Liquida moved swiftly, staying just above the bank and periodically checking his quarry through the binoculars. He kept moving until it appeared that the girl was running directly toward him from the other side. She was maybe seventy yards away. The question was whether she would cross the creek. If not, Liquida was going to have to get his feet wet.

In the distance he could see the farmhouse. Except for the porch light, the house was still dark. He lowered the field glasses, letting them hang from the strap around his neck. He was about to move toward the water to try and cross when he glanced to his right and noticed a sodden wooden plank jutting out into the creek from the other side. He moved around a patch of reeds and saw that the board, maybe twelve feet long, spanned the creek. It was supported by three large rocks, a makeshift footbridge.

Along the creek bank on both sides was a tangle of heavy brush and chest-high reeds. There was a narrow path through this foliage leading down to the plank on each side. He stepped to high ground and checked through the field glasses one more time. She was making her way directly toward the path across the creek. Liquida knew instantly that he had his spot. By the time she reached this point, she would be winded and tired, the lactic acid building up in her legs, making the muscles burn.

If Liquida had the use of both arms, he would have taken her from behind, but as it was, he couldn't.

If things went sour and it turned into a wrestling match, even with his arm in a sling he would have a fifty-pound advantage over her, the element of surprise, and the fact that he was fresh. He moved toward a line of reeds no more than five feet from the near end of the wooden plank and settled in behind the natural blind to wait.

The tug of the fanny pack bounced against her hip as she jogged toward the tree line.

There was no sign of Bugsy. He had disappeared. He would usually cross the creek through the water and turn up on the other side, wet and sometimes muddy. If he got too dirty, Sarah would have to hose him off at the barn before putting him back in his cage. She had done this a couple of times in the last few days.

She stopped for a moment, checked her pulse, and took a swig of water from the aluminum bottle in her pack. She was beginning to work up a good sweat. Sarah checked her watch. She would have to keep moving if she was going to make it back to the house before the lights came on. She screwed the top back on the bottle, dropped it in the pack, and zipped it closed. Then she slid the fanny pack around to her front. Bouncing around with the heavy water bottle inside, it was beginning to chafe her hip. She started off once more, this time at a faster pace, edging toward the county road and making a beeline for the wooden plank across the creek.

SIX

Liquida could now hear the faint padding of her running shoes as the soles slapped the harder ground leading toward the opening in the brush. A second later he picked up the sound of her labored breathing. Crouched down behind the reeds, he inched toward the path until he was no more than two feet from the well-worn ground of the trail.

He reached into the sling with his gloved left hand and felt the handle of the needle-sharp stiletto. Slowly he drew it out and held it down low, close to his body, parallel to his left thigh.

If he timed it right, he would spring up from behind the reeds just as her leading foot cleared the end of the wooden plank on this side of the creek. When he jumped, his sudden movement would cause her eyes to be instinctively riveted on his face. She wouldn't notice the blade until her own forward momentum carried her body onto the point as Liquida thrust it upward under her rib cage. It would be over in an instant.

Liquida dipped his head low as he heard the rustle of brush on the other side of the creek. A second later the footfalls slowed as she negotiated her way carefully down the embankment; then came the first flat thud as the sole of her shoe landed on the wooden plank.

He could see her through the reeds. Two more hollow drumbeats followed as she raced across the narrow wooden bridge over the water.

She was close enough now that Liquida could smell her. He waited half a beat, then launched himself up onto his feet. He took one quick full stride forward directly into her path, closing the distance between them before the girl realized what was happening.

I am out of Herman's hospital room like a bullet racing for the telephone at the nurses' station. The doctor with a crash cart is working over Herman.

"What the hell's goin' on?" The cop is out in the hall again after getting the doctor.

I turn back and skip sideways as I yell to him, "Call Thorpe. See if he's still in the building. If not, get one of his agents up here—now. Tell him it's an emergency."

"What's wrong?"

"Just call him."

By the time I reach the nurses' station and the phone, I realize that I don't have the number, and the phone number at the farm is unlisted. It's in my cell phone, but Thorpe or one of his minions has that. God knows where it is, probably back at their office in a lockbox with other property.

I head for the elevator just as Joselyn steps out of the ladies' room.

"Where are you going?"

"Liquida knows where Sarah is."

"What?"

"They're working on Herman!" I point to the room. "Liquida must have told him just before he went unconscious." I am hammering the button on the elevator over and over again. The doors can't open fast enough.

"Call the farm," she says.

"I don't have the number. It's in my phone."

"Shit!" says Joselyn.

"I got him," says the cop. He's talking into a handheld radio from his belt. "He's in the building. He's on his way."

"Are you sure?" says Joselyn to me. "Maybe Herman doesn't know what he's saying."

I shake my head. "He wrote it out."

"It's not too late," says Joselyn. "It would take Liquida a while to get there."

"Not if he left yesterday."

"Oh, God!"

A second later the elevator doors open. Just as I'm about to jump in, Thorpe steps out. "What's going on?"

The abrupt motion startled Sarah. She saw him flash in front of her. The evil in his eyes caused the blood to drain from her head. The fleeting electric impulse of having flushed some homeless vagabond living along the creek instantly evaporated. In the split second before they collided, Sarah knew she was in trouble.

She reached up with both hands toward his shoulders, trying to ward off the collision as she screamed, but it was too late. His clenched hand came up fast from underneath, catching her low in the abdomen, driving powerfully up into her stomach. The blow collapsed her diaphragm, forcing the air from her lungs.

The impact of his punch stopped her forward motion in midstride. He pushed again, another shot, jammed up under her ribs, leaving her feet to grapple for traction in the soft mud along the edge of the water. Sarah stepped back with one foot, turned it on a rock, and fell backward into the creek.

SEVEN

The instant the blade went in, Liquida knew something was wrong. The sharp point hit a hard surface as if it had glanced off a bone. It penetrated maybe two or three inches before the blade stuck as if it were caught in a vise. He pulled back and the stiletto moved as if it were free, but it wouldn't come out.

His upper body was up against the girl's. He couldn't look down to see the blade. He was in too close.

Instinct flexed his right arm in the sling as he tried to reach out to hold her in place so he could force the stiletto up into her body. But the burning pain under his arm reminded him not to do that. He punched again with the handle, this time harder.

The girl stepped away from him, lost her footing, and tumbled backward into the creek. As she fell she ripped the stiletto from Liquida's grip, taking it with her into the water.

Liquida took one faltering step toward her when he heard barking in the distance.

The girl was crawling on her hands and knees in the water, whether wounded or stunned he couldn't tell.

He retreated a few steps up the embankment so he could see over the top. Two hundred yards away the Doberman was coming this way across the open field, devouring the ground ahead of him like a jet on afterburners. He must have heard the girl's scream. Puppy or not, he had sharp teeth.

Liquida looked back at Sarah Madriani. She was lying dazed in the water. She was defenseless. A couple of shots with a heavy rock and he could crack her skull like a walnut.

By the time Liquida looked back, the Doberman had closed half the distance to their location on the creek. He considered the equation for a nanosecond, then turned on his heels and ran.

I catch Thorpe as he steps out of the hospital elevator. I tell him about Herman's message that Liquida knows the location of the farm and that Sarah is there. Before I am finished, Thorpe has his cell phone out.

"Do you know the area code for the farm?" he asks.

I give it to him. "But the number's unlisted."

"Relax." He punches in the area code and the number for information. "What's your brother-in-law's name?"

I tell him and give him the rural mailing address.

In less than a minute, Thorpe has a supervisor on the line. He identifies himself and a few seconds later has the number at the farm. He dials it.

"Hello, is Sarah Madriani there? My name is Zeb Thorpe. I'm with the FBI."

He listens for a moment. "Is she all right? Why can't she come to the phone?" He lifts the phone away from his ear for a second. "What's Hinds's first name again?"

"Harry . . ." My heart is pounding so hard it feels as if it's going to penetrate the wall of my chest. "Here, give it to me." I rip the phone from Thorpe's hand. "Hello—who is this? Fred, this is Paul. Is Sarah there? Is she OK?"

Before Fred can answer, Harry is on the line. "Where the hell have you been?" he says. "We've been calling your cell, but there has been no answer."

Sarah was conscious of movement behind her, thrashing in the brush, and the shallow water washing around her body. She was able to breathe again. She rolled over. The shock of the ice-cold water on her back sharpened her senses. The tight pain in her stomach began to ease.

She came to just as Bugsy streaked past her, shot across the creek, and up the embankment on the other side. In the flash of an eye he was gone, heading at the speed of light toward the road.

Sarah struggled to her feet, stumbled around the rocks in the creek half dazed, and slowly made her way up the path in the direction of the dog. When she reached the top, she saw Bugsy in the distance.

He was racing toward the embankment leading up to the road.

Before he reached it, a small sedan parked on the other side started up, turned on its lights, and skidded in the gravel along the shoulder as it pulled away. Sarah watched as the car's taillights disappeared around a bend. When she looked back, Bugsy's lean militant body stood silhouetted in the middle of the highway.

Only then did she look down and notice the steel handle and the narrow blade of the stiletto dangling from a hole in her fanny pack. She unzipped the top of the bag and found the point of the blade embedded in the aluminum water bottle. Like a cork on the tip of a knife, it had saved her life.

"Liquida paid us a visit," Harry says, "earlier this morning."

"Sarah . . . ?"

"She's all right, shaken up, but no serious wounds. She had a very close call. She was lucky. If she had nine lives, eight of them are gone now. I'll tell you what happened when we see each other. If you have a god, you'd be wise to thank him tonight," says Harry.

"Liquida?" Thorpe is over my shoulder.

I nod.

"Is she all right?"

I nod again.

"How long ago?" says Thorpe.

I shake my head. I don't have a clue.

Thorpe grabs the phone from the nurses' station

and dials a number. Within seconds he is talking to someone on the other end.

"Liquida is in Ohio, a place called Groveport." He gives them the farm address. "He hit the place earlier this morning. He's on the run again. Contact the nearest field office. It's probably Columbus. Tell them to get some agents out there ASAP. If they need to use a chopper, do it. Get whatever information they can. Put out an APB. Just a second."

I am listening to Harry with one ear and Thorpe with the other.

Joselyn is back from Herman's room. She leans in over my shoulder and whispers in my ear, "The doctor has stabilized him."

I look at her and nod.

"Do we have a vehicle description, license number, anything?"

"I don't know. . . . Harry, listen, can you put Sarah on the phone?"

"She's pretty upset. Shaking like a leaf," he says.

"I understand."

"Did she get a good look at him?"

"Yeah. One she's not likely to ever forget," says Harry.

"Did she get a good look?" says Thorpe.

I nod.

Thorpe's back to the other line. "Tell the agents to take a laptop with Identi-Kit software with them. They need to talk to the girl, Sarah Madriani, and work up a good computer-generated photo. . . . What about any vehicle?" He is talking to me again.

"Did she see a car?" I ask Harry.

"Only from a distance. No license plate or vehicle description," says Harry. Harry's voice drops almost to a whisper. "He did leave a knife, however. A wicked-looking thing."

"Where?"

"You don't want to know," he says.

"What do you mean?"

"I'll tell you when I see you."

"She is all right?" I ask.

"Yes. Physically she's fine, a few bruises and scrapes," says Harry.

"Can I talk to her?"

"Right now she's in the other room with Susan. I'd give her a few more minutes and call back. Let her get herself together. She's pretty upset."

"I understand. Are the police there?"

"Sheriff's deputies crawling over the place like ants," says Harry. "He won't be coming back, not here, not if he's smart."

"How did it happen? How did he get to her?"

"I'll tell you later," says Harry. "It's a sore subject with Sarah. You might want to go easy. She made a mistake."

"I see." A few seconds of silence pass between us on the phone.

"Harry?"

"Yeah."

"Tell her I called. Tell her I love her. Tell her that I'll call back in just a few minutes and that I am making arrangements to get the two of you out of there and here to D.C. as quickly as possible." I look directly at Thorpe as I say this last bit.

He nods. "Can do," says Thorpe.

"Got it," says Harry.

"And Harry, don't let anyone touch that knife in case there's prints," I tell him.

Harry laughs a little. "I don't think they'll find any. But it is true what they say, that the fruit never falls far from the tree."

"What do you mean?"

"I mean with all the hysteria, the fact that Liquida came within a hairsbreadth of killing her, your daughter had the same thought, to leave the knife where it was, all the way back to the house. It took some courage," says Harry.

EIGHT

Lawrence Leffort was tall and slender, six foot two, a hundred and sixty pounds. Built like a pencil. At forty-two he showed not even the slightest bulge of a paunch or love handles.

Ever since he was a kid he'd worn spectacles thick as bottle glass, only now they were darkly tinted with circular wire frames, like the ones John Lennon used to wear. An astrophysicist with an advanced degree from MIT, he sported a ponytail that dangled to the center of his back. The hair, which was thinning, and the glasses were part of the metamorphosis from his milquetoast period—a midlife crisis that hit him like a runaway train two years earlier.

In that time Leffort had gone from horn-rimmed academic to avant-garde edgy man at NASA's Jet Propulsion Lab on the campus of Caltech in Flintridge.

Leffort was a researcher having little contact with the undergraduates, a couple of lectures a year and that was it. If he wanted to grow hair down to his ass and play an air guitar on his own time, the people in the department didn't care as long as he got his work done.

They might have taken more interest had they known about Larry's darker side. Since emerging from his shell at forty Leffort had discovered women. The ones he dated liked to abuse their bodies, and Larry liked to help. Most of his ladies were tattooed like sailors and pierced like punch cards. For a man who never dated before the age of forty, this was a novelty he couldn't seem to resist.

With his new friends as tour guides, Leffort had taken to visiting private dungeons in West L.A. where he developed an Olympic-class appetite for bondage and sadism. He liked to sample the chemicals brewed by the warlocks in these places, mostly meth. After getting high, he would play Grand Inquisitor with women on the rack, or experiment by using some of the other exercise equipment. Larry learned about heightened awareness and experienced firsthand how Dr. Pepper's lonely heart got poisoned. Whatever inhibitions he had, melted. In little over a year he cultivated a secret nightlife to rival Jekyll and Hyde.

This afternoon, about nine days after the attack on Sarah Madriani, Leffort sat behind the wheel of his car in a parking lot on Foothill Boulevard a hundred yards from Starbucks sipping an iced latte as he listened to Raji tell him all the reasons they shouldn't be doing what they had already done.

"We need to think about this some more. There's no reason that we should be in such a rush. What if we missed something?" said Raji. "Some small detail . . ."

"We haven't missed anything." Leffort kept looking out the windshield, watching for any telltale signs that Fareed might have been followed to their offsite meeting. They didn't dare discuss it in the office. There was no telling who might be listening. There were security cameras and microphones everywhere, with ID cards that limited access to restricted areas.

"How can you be so sure we haven't made a mistake?" Raji Fareed was a veritable engine of angst. On a normal day, his fret level usually ran a thousand degrees hotter than Leffort's. During the last two weeks, his anxiety quotient had been off the scale.

Fareed was born in Iran. Now in his early forties, he had come to the United States as a kid with his family. He worked for NASA as a computer programmer and had been thrown into the mix, assigned to work with Leffort on the Thor Project. The two men had been working together for almost a decade and at times rubbed each other raw.

Raji designed programs to crunch numbers. Using supercomputers, he could craft software to solve complex equations and formulas that might otherwise take a couple of hundred lifetimes to work out on a chalkboard. Once he designed a program and loaded it into a computer, a thousand-line equation could be worked out in anywhere from seconds to minutes, and with near-perfect precision.

"Trust me, everything's covered. The only things left are the guidance programs. Did you bring them?" Leffort had been after Raji to produce the final guidance programs for almost a month. They were the key to terminal targeting. Without them, they had an incomplete package and nothing to sell.

"I've got them," said Raji.

"Good."

"But I still think we ought to wait."

"Wait for what?"

"So we can slow down a little, and think," said Fareed. "Right now everything's just going too fast."

"Yeah, well, that's what happens when they decide to throw you under the bus," said Leffort. "They don't usually step on the brakes until after it runs over you."

After more than a decade of research, rumor had it that the Thor Project was about to be scuttled. With the economy on the skids and Washington looking for ways to cut costs, NASA was being chopped to pieces. Not only were the manned space programs being canceled, any item considered non-essential to national defense was on the block.

"Fuckers would probably try and sell the moon to the Chinese if they thought they had a chance," said Leffort.

Theoretical programs were high on the hit list. At a meeting three months earlier, Leffort had tried to convince NASA that what he and Raji were working on was far more than mere theory. It would work. When the meeting was over, Leffort didn't need a crystal ball or a cipher to tell him that he'd failed. Their research grant, with its five remaining years, was about to be shifted to other higher priorities. The smell of pink slips was in the air. It was then that he and Fareed started moving ahead with the plan.

"We agreed we would go during the Paris conference," said Leffort.

"We did, but I figured by now we'd know whether they were going to pull the grant. We still don't know. Maybe they've decided to leave it alone. If so, there's nothing special about being in Paris. And there's no reason to run."

"Yeah, there is. We're outside the country. And that's where all the data is, parked on a server in Paris, remember? Besides, after the conference it may be much harder to slip away. If they pull the plug and can us, you can bet they're gonna be watching us, at least for a while," said Leffort. "Anybody with a high security clearance who's out of work is going to be seen as a potential risk in terms of classified information. You try to leave the country, you're liable to find yourself on a no-fly list."

"You think they're gonna be watching us?"

"Yep."

"Why, if nobody else knows what we've done? I mean, nobody else knows, right?"

"I don't know," said Leffort. "You tell me."

"What are you saying?" Raji glared at him. "You accusing me? You think I told somebody?"

"I don't know. You seem awfully nervous lately. I thought we were both committed. Now you want to slow down, take your time. What am I supposed to think?"

"Hey, I don't need this." Raji reached for the door handle, ready to get out and hoof it to his own car.

"Hey, relax. Calm down." Leffort put a hand on

Fareed's arm. "Don't get mad. I didn't mean anything. You know me, I shoot from the hip. I'm just tired, strung out. And like you, I'm getting a little nervous."

"That's no reason to accuse me," said Fareed.

"I know. It's just that we're both under a lot of stress right now. And the longer we have to hang here under the gun, the worse it's gonna get. That's why the sooner we can leave, the better," said Leffort.

"I never gave you any reason not to trust me," said Raji.

"I know that."

"For all I know, maybe you told somebody."

"Why would I do that?"

"I don't know," said Raji. "But you don't trust me, why should I trust you?" He was back to the door handle again, only this time Leffort could tell Raji wasn't serious. He was fondling the handle either for more sympathy or for leverage.

"Who said I didn't trust you? I never said I didn't trust you. I'm just wondering why you're having all these second thoughts. Especially now, when we're almost home. Hey, buddy, listen. Look at me."

Raji was still turned, looking out the passenger window, leaning in his seat toward the door.

"Come here." Leffort leaned across the seat and grabbed Raji to give him a hug, something he'd never done before. "We've been together too long to let something like this come between us." He needed Fareed, at least until he got his hands on the final guidance programs. After that, fuck him.

He got Raji turned toward him, put his arms

around him, then squeezed and patted him in a male bonding moment.

The move made Fareed very uncomfortable. Two guys sitting in a car hugging—Raji kept his hands to himself, out in the open where anybody looking in could see them. "Hey, come on. Cut it out. OK. I forgive you."

Raji tried to pull away, but Leffort wasn't having any part of it. He was busy smoothing Fareed all the way down to the small of his back, feeling around for any small cord, bumps, or little boxes that the feds might have taped to his body if Fareed was wearing an electronic wire.

"I know it's been tough on both of us. We need to learn to trust each other," said Leffort. "After all, we're in this together. We just need to calm down and relax. Everything's gonna be fine." Leffort sat up, dragging his hands up and down both sides of Raji's torso inside of his outstretched arms as if he were trying to warm him up.

"That's enough." Raji finally pushed Leffort's hands away. "You worry me. You're getting strange."

"You have to learn to be tolerant," said Leffort. "We're all different. Don't be so uptight. Thing to remember is that in a month you and I are gonna be up to our eyeballs in money. We'll be sitting on a beach somewhere counting it all and wondering why we worried about any of this. So where's the guidance programs?" Having finished with the frisk, Leffort was back to the important stuff. "Why don't you give 'em to me so we can get 'em on their way."

"I think I know why I'm worried," said Raji.

"Why is that?"

"It's all this 'we' shit. *We* have never loaded any-thing onto the computer. Come to think of it, I don't even know where the computer is, the one you've been using to send all the data to Paris. And the server you keep telling me about. I don't have the slightest idea where it is, or whether it's leased or owned or what."

"It's leased, I told you that. We'll download ev-erything out of it when we get there. It's gonna take one hell of a big SATA drive to hold it all. You think you can get ahold of one? I'll leave that to you. There, you see?"

"In the meantime, I still don't know where any-thing is," said Raji.

"So what are you saying? That you don't trust me? That I'm trying to cheat you?"

"No, it's just that you have control over every-thing and I have none."

What Leffort wasn't telling him was that he, Leffort, had made the decision to bail out at NASA more than a year earlier. He had been sending stolen program data to the overseas buyers for more than two years, and taking money for it. He knew from the responses he was getting and the tech-nical questions they asked that the people on the other end were well staffed with technicians and scientists who knew what they were doing. And they were much further along than anyone could have guessed. Whoever was backing them had deep pockets. The buyers were already geared up, having built a test site with a massive antenna array. They were getting ready to do a dry run, tracking objects and doing computer simulations. All the things that

Leffort had encouraged NASA to do, but they refused. If Raji knew how far along they were, his cold
feet would have turned to blocks of ice. He would
back out, and Leffort would be unable to deliver the
rest of the program. Leffort was in far too deep for
that. Unknown to Raji, Leffort had already piled
up a significant stash of cash, salted away in a numbered account down in the Cayman Islands. If he
could get his hands on the software programs for
the final targeting sequence, Raji's work would be
done. Leffort wouldn't need him any longer. He
would still have to take Raji to Paris, though, if only
to keep him quiet until Leffort could disappear or
figure out what to do with him.

"If you don't trust me, just say so," said Leffort.

"It's not that." Raji always shied away from a
frontal confrontation. It was cultural as much as
anything else. "It's just that if we're going to be
partners, at least until the money is divided, then
I need to know everything you know. So why don't
you tell me once more how the deal works, how we
get our money and when?"

"We've been over all that. It's still the same.
Nothing's changed."

"Help me out. Refresh my memory."

Leffort wasn't nearly as upbeat now. He was wondering if he was still going to get the final guidance
programs. "Payment is on delivery to a numbered
Swiss account. I told you that."

"Do we have a name for the bank and a number
for the account?" Raji took out a pen and a small
notepad from his pocket.

"What, you expect me to memorize the account

number? I have it at home. I'll get it for you, next time we meet."

"What else?" said Raji.

"We won't know where the data is to be delivered until we get to Paris."

"And you say you don't know who these people are?" asked Raji.

"Not the end buyers, no. But as I told you before, we're dealing with a middleman who has an international reputation for brokering these types of matters. He is for real. I've checked him out. I've spoken to him on Skype, got a good video cam image of the man, compared it to a known photograph. It's him, all right."

"So, hopefully, at least we're not dealing with the FBI on the other end," said Raji.

"No. Not to worry," said Leffort. "The way I figure it, it could only be one of two, or possibly three, foreign countries, emerging nations that would have the missile and rocket technology to take advantage of Thor."

Raji had come to the same conclusion.

"The telemetry stuff we deliver will give them a quantum leap," said Leffort. "It will allow them to close the gap with the major powers in months instead of years. The rest is up to them. In return, they give us twenty million euros, ten for you, ten for me. The broker is making his own deal with them for a finder's fee."

"It's a lot of money," said Raji. "Still, it doesn't seem like that much when you look at everything we're giving them. NASA is already into the program for more than half a billion dollars."

"You can't expect them to pay that. Besides, it's unproven technology," said Leffort. "If NASA or the air force had already tested it and we could verify that it worked, then you're right. We could get a lot more. But as it is, they'll be using our data to invent the wheel. Question is, will it roll? As far as you and I are concerned, it won't matter. We'll be set for the rest of our lives."

"OK, so after we do all of this, they get the data, we get the money, what then? Where do we go?" said Fareed.

"As part of the deal, the broker will provide new passports, not forgeries, the genuine item, as well as all the necessary documents to fashion new identities. The man has connections."

"Passports from where? You can't get far with something from North Korea," said Fareed.

"That's what I've been telling you. I've taken care of all the details. The passports will be from a Western country, one of the member states of NATO. Not to worry."

"Then what?"

"After they transfer the money into our Swiss account, we do a couple of wire transfers out. You're gonna want to set up an account under your new passport name as soon as you get it. I'll have to do the same. One transfer to you, one to me. We take the passports, the money, and disappear. You go wherever you want. You have a new identity and, depending on exchange rates, something north of thirteen million U.S. dollars. I'd say that's a pretty good nest egg to make a fresh start."

Raji just sat there in the passenger seat thinking, mostly about all the things that could go wrong.

"You have to admit it's better than an unemployment check." Leffort looked over at Raji. "You don't look happy. Do you have some problem living like royalty?"

"Hardly," said Raji. "That's not even as much as some state lotteries."

"Yes, but our chances of winning are much more certain. The money is clean, there's no way to trace it. And you're a very smart guy. Turn your skills to the investment markets, and in a few years—I know you—you'll double it. Especially in Asia. China is booming. Southeast Asia is not far behind, and Brazil. So smile."

"I'll smile when I see the money," said Raji.

Leffort's biggest fear, though he didn't tell Raji, was that NASA might cancel their trip to Paris. With unemployment edging toward double digits, it didn't look good having two guys who worked for the agency jetting off to the city of lights.

If NASA called off the trip, he and Raji would have to run for it and hope they could slip out of the country before somebody wised up and stopped them at the airport.

The European Space Agency Conference had been scheduled for more than a year. The money for the trip was already budgeted and accounted for. This was probably the only thing saving the junket, that and the fact that it was probably their last hurrah before they were cashiered and put out on the street. He was sure this was what the administrators at NASA were thinking. Leffort was thinking they were leaving the gate open, his last chance to get out of the country before the roof caved in.

"The critical thing is, we have to hold to the original timetable," said Leffort. "We have no choice. The Paris conference. All we have to do is keep our heads for a few more days and we're out of here, winging our way to France. Otherwise the deal's gonna be off the table. We will have done it all for nothing."

"What if NASA doesn't cancel the grant?" said Raji.

"What difference does it make? Either you're in or you're out. You want to spend the next thirty years of your life chained to a desk with your nose glued to a computer screen, fine. Just remember, you're never going to get an opportunity like this again."

"I know. Still, we could always go to Paris and come back. If they don't pull the grant, we could finish the project, trash the copied data, and nobody would ever know. Think about it. We could write our own ticket, get any grant we wanted. When they realize who we are, that we did the NEO . . ."

"You forget, it's classified," said Leffort. "Nobody's ever gonna know. They'll take our work and bury it on a shelf. They'll sit back and hope that the Russians or the Chinese or some third world tyrant doesn't figure it out. Sooner or later some other country is going to wake up and realize what's out there, see the potential, only to rediscover it on their own. I don't know about you, but if that's gonna happen anyway, I'm for getting paid," said Leffort.

"I don't know." Now that the time was drawing near, it looked as if Raji was having difficulty coming to grips with the thought of being transformed from a word-a-day programmer in an office to a criminal on the run, even a rich one. Unlike Leffort, he didn't mind the routine of his life.

Leffort realized that the carrot wasn't working. Now he tried the stick. "Lemme ask you a question. What if we go to Paris and come back and NASA decides to do a program audit on Thor? What then?"

"What do you mean?"

"What if they call you in and start asking questions?" said Leffort.

"Why would they do that?"

"It's standard procedure when they cancel a grant. They'll do a closing audit. What are you gonna say when they call you in and ask why certain data files are missing?"

"But nothing's missing. Right? That was the deal." Raji suddenly looked worried. "I thought we copied everything and put it back."

"We did. But you can bet that after ten years, a program like this, that something's going to be missing," said Leffort. "It would have to be a fucking miracle if every slip of paper and all the computer files are all in the right place."

"We can't be responsible for that," said Raji.

"That's not the point. If they call us in one at a time and question us across a table piled with files, even if it's something trivial, something that's not our fault, it won't matter. They'll test what you say against what I say. We'll end up making a mistake, inventing some stupid excuse that they'll know is a lie. It's what happens when somebody starts tugging on a thread; things come unraveled. They won't have to catch us. We'll bury ourselves." Raji's forehead was beginning to sweat. This was only a precursor of what might happen if they trapped him in an audit. Raji would drown everybody in the room. "I don't want to stick around and wait for an audit. Do you?"

"No." Raji got religion fast. He didn't even hesitate.

"That's what I thought. So why don't you give me the guidance programs so we can get this thing done?"

Fareed reached for the door handle. This time he opened it and stepped out. He leaned back into the car. "Like you and the number for the Swiss account, I don't have them with me right now."

"Where are they?"

"I've got 'em; they're safe. I'll get them to you the next time we meet." Raji closed the door and headed for his car.

NINE

When Liquida failed to kill Madriani's daughter, he knew instantly that he was operating on borrowed time. No doubt, the lawyer had already informed the FBI that Liquida was connected to the D.C. bombing. With the news of the attack at the farm, federal authorities would waste no time throwing up checkpoints in Ohio and the surrounding area. State patrols would be watching for him, a lone driver in a late-model sedan, dark hair, probably Hispanic. The description would become more detailed the longer Liquida waited.

The girl had gotten more than a good look at him. From the evident shock on her face, Liquida's image was probably seared into her psyche like a woodcut engraving. The cops would have a solid description of him the minute they could shake her out of her catatonic trance. He now had a reason to kill her other than vengeance: his own survival—but it would have to wait.

Instead of driving west on the interstate where

authorities would most likely be fanning out in their search, Liquida made a snap decision. He turned around out on the main highway and headed like a comet for the outskirts of Columbus less than twenty miles away. He made one stop at a hardware store just two miles from the airport. There he purchased a roll of plumber's lead tape and headed for the restroom.

Fifteen minutes later, Liquida abandoned his rental car in a parking space at the airport, bought a ticket at the counter, and checked his luggage, including the rolled-up collection of stilettos from the trunk of the car. He killed a few minutes waiting outside the TSA security area watching people pass through the metal detector, a few of them being wanded as they set off the detector's alarm.

He got in line; took off his shoes, watch, and belt; and emptied his pockets into one of the plastic trays. He pushed the tray along with his overnight bag toward the conveyor belt and waited his turn.

A few seconds later, the tray and the bag disappeared into the metal box housing the scanner. Liquida was directed to pass through the metal detector. He held his breath and walked through. A minute later he had his shoes on, his belt through the loops in his pants, with the bag over his left arm headed for the gate.

Plumbers use lead tape under hose clamps to tamp down vibration where it's a problem. Golfers and tennis pros paste the stuff to their rackets and club heads to weigh them down and straighten out their swing. Liquida applied his lead tape to the area under his arm to prevent the surgical staples from tripping the alarm on the TSA metal detector. If they wanded his back and it buzzed, they would pat him down. And when they felt the staples and the puffed-up wound, they would invite him into the little room and tell him to take off his shirt. Even TSA staff could recognize a knife wound once they saw it.

Liquida caught his flight to Atlanta, where he scanned the departure boards inside the security area for the quickest exit out of the country, somewhere safe. He was burning money like kerosene. Soon he would have to start using stolen credit cards, something Liquida never liked to do. It only heightened the risk of detection.

He used his last set of foreign travel documents, a Spanish passport that was tucked away in the lining of his overnight bag. He purchased a ticket and boarded a Delta flight for the United Arab Emirates. It was a long trip, the longest of his life, at least in terms of stress and anxiety. He was under the gun of the FBI. Liquida didn't relax entirely until he landed and made his way through customs and into a taxi outside the airport in Dubai.

He had the driver take him to the Royal Meridien Beach Resort, where he booked a room and took up residence as a vacationing Iberian businessman. The place was expensive, more than Liquida wanted to spend, especially now. But he had stayed there before, in better times when he was financially flush, and he knew the place. On the run Liquida had learned that there is an element of safety in surrounding yourself with the rich. A foreign national staying in a flophouse always drew more attention from the local authorities, especially in a conservative country like the Emirates. They were certainly more likely to roust you and ask questions. That was the one thing Liquida didn't want.

The Royal Meridien and its grounds were the size of a small city. It was an easy setting in which to remain anonymous. The resort was crowded with wealthy tourists—Europeans, Asians, and Arabs— all cloistered in their own separate tribes lounging around the pools.

The next morning Liquida walked to a small convenience store just outside the resort. He purchased a dozen Etisalat prepaid cellular SIM cards from the clerk. Then he returned to the resort and found a quiet area near the edge of one of the pools. He ordered a drink from the wandering waitress and went to work.

Using a four-band unlocked cell phone and the stack of SIM cards, Liquida began collecting his messages.

Timing himself with the sweep second hand on his watch, he ended each call at three minutes on the dot whether he was finished collecting his messages or not. The Americans had a nasty way of using their listening posts in the sky to turn cell calls into party lines. After three minutes, he would remove the SIM card from the phone and grind it under the leg of the metal chair he was sitting on. When he was satisfied that he had destroyed the card's miniature circuitry on the abrasive concrete of the pool deck, he would pick up the card, smudge any prints that might be on it, and drop it into a trash can just behind his chair. He would then slip a new SIM card representing a new telephone number into the phone and pick up where he left off.

It was a laborious process, but Liquida was paranoid when it came to the perils of government and the seductions of technology. Combine the two and get a good glimpse of hell. Too many of his friends were either dead or sitting out their lives in maximum-security dungeons, casualties of the digital disease.

Having won the Cold War and toppled the Evil Empire, the American government had now become what it had destroyed. Its political class was busy using technology to digitize its citizens into slavery. There was nowhere left for people to hide. Babies were registered at birth and given Social Security numbers like cattle with ear notches so that power-hungry politicians could track them throughout their lives and harness them as taxing units. The government was everywhere, listening to private telephone conversations, reading people's mail and e-mail, watching them through cameras built into their laptops. They could turn on your cell phone and use it like an undercover wire to listen in on private conversations, all of this while they tracked you with GPS and filmed you from cameras on every light pole. In less than ten years, the United States, the leader of the free world, had become a prison without walls. Liquida was starting to feel like everybody else. He wanted the government off his back. The critics were right. They were killing the economy. In a world like this, how could any small businessman, someone like Liquida, make a decent living?

Liquida was of the old school, the world of the Unabomber and Osama bin Laden. There was a lot to be said for a cave in the mountains or a shack in the forest where lighting was by candles and conversation consisted of an occasional grunt, where messages were written on rice paper so the words could be quickly eaten when you were finished reading.

He worked the small cell phone, crushing and replacing SIM cards as he went, always keeping one eye on his watch. He rang up several message services, one in Spain, another in the States, one in Thailand, and a fourth one in Rio, in Brazil. He listened intently to his messages while he jotted down notes in a small pocket pad.

When he was finished, Liquida sat up straight, adjusted his dark glasses, and sipped a little of the mojito from the tall glass on the table in front of him. He set the glass down and slowly licked his lips, savoring the flavor of the rum as he studied the last entry in the small notepad.

It was a message from Bruno Croleva, a Chechen who in the last two years had risen in Liquida's eyes to become his favorite rainmaker.

Business from Bruno had lifted him from the squalor of Tijuana and the limited possibilities of the cartels, where retirement usually came in the form of a bullet.

Bruno had connections with Islamic militants as well as other injured and angry ethnic and religious groups. These were people highly committed to killing their enemies, which at any given time might include half the world's population, mostly Westerners.

The clients were well funded and paid far more than the chump change offered by the cartels. Prices of a good assassination in Mexico had been driven to rock bottom by an army of itchy-fingered teenagers possessing no proper sense of values. Best of all, the foot soldiers used by Bruno's clients were willing to die for their beliefs. This was an extremely efficient arrangement. It left many fewer tongues to wag when the job was done. Liquida didn't have to dirty his own blade arranging for the sounds of silence. These were his kinds of people.

According to the message, there was forty thousand euros in cash in a drop box belonging to Liquida, delivered there by Bruno's courier as final payment for a job Liquida had completed several months earlier.

Liquida had almost forgotten about it. He had given up on the money, thinking he would never see it. He assumed that Bruno was angry with him and that he might never hear from the man again. The last two ventures had not gone well, though it was not for want of trying on Liquida's part.

Bruno was now paying up. What's more, according to the message, he was offering Liquida another job and dangling a very tempting commission. The details, along with the money, were in the drop box.

For Liquida the money couldn't have come at a more opportune time. He was low on cash and he needed the work. You might have thought that Liquida would be happy, but he wasn't. His first response was caution.

Ordinarily he would have called the courier service and made arrangements to have the stuff in the box collected and delivered by giving them a temporary forwarding address, someplace where Liquida could move in and out quickly and safely.

But things were now much more complicated. The U.S. government had put a price on his head. Liquida had seen it earlier that morning, using one of the guest computers in the hotel lobby to check the FBI's website. It was something he did on a frequent basis. It wasn't there yesterday. But this morning he turned up, not on their most wanted fugitive list, but instead, on their terrorist site. There was no picture or sketch, at least not yet. But they were offering two million dollars for tips that would lead authorities to a man known only under the alias of "Muerte Liquida." There was other information, some of it accurate and some of it not. That was the thing about government; they had a hard time getting things right. If Liquida could have figured a way to stay safe and collect on the reward, for that kind of money, he might have called in a tip or two himself.

Now he had to worry about Bruno. In Liquida's line of work, two million dollars could turn an associate into beef on the hoof in less time than it took to say the word *tip*.

His natural paranoia was telling him that the stuff in the drop box could be a trap. He looked at the date on the message. It was two days old. Unless Bruno somehow knew about the reward before it was posted on the FBI's site, he could not have known about it when he sent the message. In which case it might not be a trap at all. Or else . . . Liquida's mind searched for the hook and its jagged barb.

What if the message wasn't from Bruno at all? What if the FBI had somehow found the box? Liquida had been using the drop box for about seven months. That was too long. It was time to get a new one, to find a fresh location. But it was too late to think about that now. If the message was real, then the money was there. But if the FBI knew about the box, they could know about the messaging service as well. They might be using the box as bait.

TEN

How many times do I have to tell you? I just want to go home," said Raji. "This is not going to work. That's all there is to it."

"It will work if you help us," said Bruno.

"I already told you, no. I made a mistake. I admit that. I should never have come to Paris."

"It's too late for that," said Leffort. "There's no way back. They already know. The authorities will be looking for both of us by now."

"I'll take my chances," said Raji.

"Unfortunately, that is no longer possible." Bruno Croleva was an equal opportunity merchant of death. There was no cause he would not fuel with guns or munitions. He was totally nonpartisan in the same way politicians are who take donations from all sides on every issue. Bruno was in it for the money. Warm bodies or cold steel, it didn't matter to Bruno. If there was a profit to be made, he would deliver it.

"You know what I think?" said Bruno.

Raji sat on the edge of the bed with his head in his hands. "No, but I'm sure you're going to tell me."

"I think you are a little homesick, is all. Maybe you have someone waiting for you back there. A nice woman perhaps?" Bruno wrinkled an eyebrow at him with the delivery of this diagnosis.

Raji looked up at him and winced, as if to tell Bruno that he had an air bubble trapped somewhere between his ears. "No. You're wrong." Raji shook his head.

"No need to be embarrassed." Croleva fancied himself a mind reader, a delusion fostered by the fact that most people were sufficiently terrified of him that any semicivil suggestion from Bruno was generally followed by the word *yes*.

Larry Leffort sat on the couch against the far wall in Raji's Paris hotel room. He knew that playing twenty questions with Bruno could end with piano wire being used to make something other than musical notes.

"Listen to me," said Raji. "You don't understand."

Bruno's forced smile compressed the furrows above his eyebrows. The no-man's-land between there and the shiny bald dome up top looked like a crooked plowed field. "Tell me. What is it that bothers you? Why do you want to go back?"

"I just want to go home, that's all."

"There is nothing there for you," said Bruno.

"I want my life back. Can't you get that through your head?" Raji was afflicted more by anger than fear at the moment. "I know that coming here was a mistake. We all make mistakes. I'm sorry if I caused you problems. But now I just want to go home.

That's all there is to it. Understand?" Raji looked up at Bruno, all three hundred and sixty pounds of him and gave the man an annoyed expression, like what part of no don't you understand.

"I knew it," said Bruno. "It is a woman. I can see it in your eyes. You miss her. You are in love. Admit it. Dat's only natural. Young man like you. But soon you will be a rich man. You must learn to cast your net into the open sea, where there are many fish." Having divined the problem, Bruno's brain didn't allow for conflicting messages even from the patient. "You want a woman, I get you one. Beautiful woman. No problem."

"I doubt he's ever been with a girl," said Leffort.

"Fine. You want a boy, I get you . . ."

"No!!!" Raji glared up at Bruno and shouted. "You're not listening."

"OK, OK. You want more than one woman? I can do that."

Raji just sat on the bed, looking up at the ceiling and shaking his head.

"How many can you get?" asked Leffort. "Women, I mean." Leffort knew there had to be piercing and tattoo parlors in Paris. Just think what he was missing.

Bruno shot him a harsh glance that crossed the room like a bolt of lightning. The two Americans were driving him crazy. He couldn't wait for Liquida to arrive so the Mexican could take them off his hands.

"You, outside!" Bruno gestured to Leffort. "You stay here. I'll be back in a minute," he told Raji.

Croleva and Leffort stepped from the room into

the hallway outside. Bruno said something in Russian to the man seated in the chair at the end of the hall. They had already bolted the window in Raji's room closed so that he couldn't crawl out on the ledge and try to escape.

Leffort and Bruno walked a short distance down the hall, out of earshot of Bruno's thug sitting in the chair.

"We are going to have to put something in his food to sedate him," said Bruno.

"You think that's necessary?" said Leffort.

"Yes. And you will have to keep an eye on him."

"Why me?"

"Because you are his friend. He trusts you."

"Right," said Leffort.

"And because, if you had done your job, you would already have the rest of the materials, in which case we wouldn't need him any longer." Bruno was talking about the final targeting programs. "You are certain that he has them?" Croleva watched Leffort's face closely as he asked the question.

"Yes. Absolutely. He has them. I know it."

"How do you know?"

"Because he told me. And because he ran the programs and plugged in the targeting data for a computer simulation the day before we left. And it worked."

Bruno studied Leffort's eyes for any hint of deception.

"He completed the programs three weeks ago." Leffort couldn't afford to show even the slightest equivocation on this. If Bruno thought for a moment that Raji didn't have the final targeting software,

he would kill both of them now and make whatever excuses were necessary to his clients. Without
that software the rest of the project materials were
worthless, and both Leffort and Bruno knew it.

"You say he loaded them into a computer for the
simulation? Then why couldn't you get them from
the computer?"

"Because he deleted the software the moment the
test was done. He's no fool," said Leffort.

"Then where are they? We have been through
his luggage. They are not there. At least not that
we could see. You have checked his working papers
and you say they are not there. I have had my people
scan everything from his laptop. There is nothing
there. So maybe he left the programs behind. That
could be the reason he wants to go home. He knows
he cannot deliver when the time comes."

"No, he either has them or he has access to them
at some remote location online," said Leffort. "He
would never have gotten on that plane otherwise.
I'm sure of that."

"So where are they?"

"I don't know, but I'll find out," said Leffort.

"You had better," said Bruno. "I cannot allow you
to leave Paris until I am certain that you have them.
Do you understand?"

Leffort nodded.

Liquida had two more tasks to complete before
leaving Dubai. The first was done using one of the
hotel's guest computers. He typed up an anonymous letter addressed to the U.S. Embassy in

Dubai. It was one of Liquida's "white-glove specials," for he always wore gloves when he printed them out. Fingerprints on the paper were a no-no. It was an anonymous tip to law enforcement. He used them occasionally to take down competitors or to drop sand in the gears of a client who failed to pay. He sealed the letter in a blank envelope and delivered it to a private courier service in downtown Dubai. He paid for the delivery in cash, used a pseudonym to set up the account, and left firm instructions that the letter was to be held in their offices until he called. At that time he would give them the delivery address. Liquida didn't want to give them the address now in case they screwed up and delivered it early, in which case it would be his ass in the flames.

The second task was more painful. Back at the hotel, Liquida downed some of the pain medications given to him by the doctor in D.C. He used the sharp point of one of the stilettos to spread the ends of each of the thirteen surgical staples. Then, gritting his teeth, he plucked them out one by one from the pursed-up wound under his right arm. Liquida found it difficult maneuvering the sharp point of the blade with his left hand. He stopped periodically to steady himself and to dab the bleeding pinholes around the wound with tissue from a dispenser on the bathroom counter.

As he moved the blade, Liquida dripped venom while bargaining under his breath with the evil imps that inhabited his heart. He haggled for the soul of the dead black bastard who did this so that Liquida might staple his spirit to the hottest rock in hell. By the time he pulled the last wicked little piece of wire from his flesh, he was a quivering mass of sweat. Liquida looked at himself in the mirror. Even to his own eyes he appeared the hideous image of Gollum.

He rested for an hour and then showered. When he was done patting the wound dry, he checked the towel to make sure that the tiny pinholes from the staples were no longer seeping blood. He dressed, putting on a pair of tan slacks and a loose-fitting Egyptian cotton white shirt with an open collar and black buttons down the front. He left the bottom of the shirt outside his pants and slipped on a pair of loafers with no socks, the casual Spanish squire on holiday.

Liquida spent the rest of the day relaxing, sitting under an umbrella by the pool and reading newspapers to catch up on the evil others had done while he was on the run, hiding and plucking sharp pieces of wire from his body.

He was two days early removing the staples, but he had no choice. Bruno's offer wouldn't wait. It was now or never. If Liquida didn't reply and do so soon, the offer would be gone.

While the better half of his brain told him it was a setup, his weaker side didn't want to believe it. Besides, he had no option. He was running out of money. He needed the cash in that box. And if Bruno had a job for him, a big one, there would likely be money for expenses. Bruno was hip deep in people who could supply top-notch passports and create new bulletproof identities, all the resources that Liquida needed for cover. It would buy time.

He could use it to stay out of the clutches of the Americans.

He wanted to believe that it was all there in the box. The problem was, there was only one way to find out.

ELEVEN

Harry, my law partner, gives me a sleepy stare from tired, heavy-hooded eyes. It's almost noon and Harry just fell out of bed. He and Sarah came in late last night in a two-car caravan, large dark SUVs with all the windows blacked out, driven by the FBI.

This morning Sarah is out working with one of their computer techs in the ongoing effort to refine an Identi-Kit portrait of Liquida, at least as much as she can remember. It is likely to be the only image they have since Herman, who was taken from behind with the knife, says he never got a clear look at the man.

"Paul, listen. I don't know how else to say it. I'm sorry." Harry is looking at me sheepishly, wiping the sleep from his eyes. "I was supposed to be watching her and I blew it."

"It's not your fault."

"Yes, it is. I should have been watching her more closely. You trusted me and I let you down."

"You did what you could. Besides, it was my job. I'm her father. I should have been there."

"You couldn't be everywhere," says Harry. "We agreed I would be the one responsible for keeping an eye on her and I failed. Simple as that."

"Let's not talk about it," I tell him. "The important thing is, she's alive."

"No thanks to me."

Harry and I are seated in the two tufted wing-back chairs in the living room of a safe house in Washington, D.C. It is a high-rise condo courtesy of Thorpe and the FBI. At the moment none of us knows how long we'll be here. The place is decked out with rented furniture and contractor-painted eggshell-white walls. With all the blinds drawn it has the ambiance of a whitewashed cave.

"Any idea how Liquida found the two of you on the farm?" I ask.

Harry nods. He's gazing down at the floor, still half asleep. "They think he used an electronic tracking device. The fucker's devious," says Harry.

"I thought Herman had the cars all swept. He found the one attached to your car and had it removed," I remind him.

"He did. Liquida mailed another small tracking device to Sarah at the house, figuring she probably left a forwarding address with the post office. The FBI found the tracking device in one of the drawers in her bedroom in Ohio. The note with it said it was from you, that you'd explain what it was the next time the two of you talked on the phone. When you talked, Sarah forgot to mention it. All Liquida had to do was read the tracking information on his computer. It led him right to the farm."

"Son of a bitch."

"She didn't tell me about it because the note said it was a surprise for me." The craggy gray lines down Harry's face appear like ravines on a mountainside. He seems to have aged five years since I saw him last in Coronado. That was less than a month ago.

Our law practice in California is now a shambles. Neither of us has been in the office for weeks, forced into hiding by Liquida. No doubt clients are now complaining to the state bar that their phone calls are not being returned. Before long the bar will be trying to punch our tickets to practice. Harry and I can take down the shingle and start selling pencils out on the street. Our lives are unraveling.

"Coffee's ready." Joselyn sticks her head through the open doorway to the kitchen.

"Be there in a minute," I tell her.

"You two need to stop talking about this. Dredging up all the little details isn't gonna make it go away. What's happened has happened. The more you pick at it, the worse it's going to get." She's been listening through the open door.

"So what are we supposed to do?" I turn and look at her.

"Get off your ass and come get something to eat." Before I can say anything more, she disappears back into the kitchen.

"Yeah, I can see how she could be good for you," says Harry. He looks up at me and winks. "How's Herman doing?" He changes the subject.

"They moved him out of intensive care yesterday." We get up and start walking toward the kitchen. "He'll be on the mend for a while. But he's starting to get irritable."

"That's a good sign."

"The doctor's telling him six weeks to two months before he can do any heavy lifting."

"Take bets," says Harry. We enter the kitchen. "Give you three to one Herman's back out on the bricks in less than a month."

"At death's door one day, fighting to go home the next. Herman's always been a quick healer," I tell him.

"More power to him," says Joselyn. "Either one of you would be laid up for a year."

"You see what I have to put up with? What a hard-ass." I look at Harry and smile.

"Yes, and it'll be a long time before you touch it again with that kind of an attitude." Joselyn has her back to us as she works at the counter slicing some small sandwiches and stacking them on a plate. "He's been in the dumps since he first heard about what happened to Sarah."

"Yeah, well, it's pretty hard when your daughter comes within a whisper of being murdered," I tell her.

"Yes, but she wasn't. You have to let it go and move on," says Joselyn.

"On to what?"

"You can pour your own coffee. Cups are in the cupboard over there." She gestures with her head. "Sugar and cream are on the table. Silverware is in the drawer. Help yourself." She turns and sets the dish of sandwiches in the center of the table. "Napkins, I don't know. You'll have to use your sleeve. I forgot to put 'em on the list the last time they went for groceries."

"The FBI does our housekeeping," I tell Harry.

"So what's the gig this time? Protective custody, witness protection, or are we under arrest?" He looks at me.

"It's not entirely clear," I tell him. "I don't think we're in custody. As far as I understand it, we're just cooperating with their investigation. For the time being, they're happy to provide security, at least while we're here and on their terms."

"What's Thorpe saying?"

"He's suggesting we stick around, at least for a while. This thing with Sarah rattled him. They squeezed Joselyn and me for information, whatever we knew. They questioned Herman as soon as he could talk. Now they're working on Sarah."

"They talked to her at the farm," says Harry. "Questioned me as well. They lost interest when I told them I hadn't seen or talked to either of you in almost a month, that I'd been hanging out on the farm in Ohio since we split from California. I couldn't tell them anything. Didn't even see Liquida. They trampled all over the farm looking for anything that might give them a lead. They would have grilled the Doberman but his English wasn't that good."

"Sarah tells me the dog saved her life," says Joselyn.

"If he'd been just a few seconds faster, the FBI could be doing DNA on a hunk out of Liquida's ass, I suspect," says Harry. "She's quite attached to him. The dog, I mean. He's been sleeping at the bottom of her bed ever since it happened. He's getting spoiled. Kibble and bacon bits out of her hand. I take it you met him last night?"

"Lie down with dogs, wake up with fleas," I tell him, "but that's one animal I'd kiss. I'm glad she has him. At least for the time being."

"Which reminds me," says Harry. "Where is he? You didn't lock him in the bedroom, did you? Cuz he'll chew the carpet off the floor. He doesn't like to be locked in a room where he can't see out. And he tends to get antsy when he's separated from her."

"Sarah took him to her meeting at the FBI office," I tell him.

"They let her do that?" says Joselyn.

"It's hard to say no when you have a snarling dog with his nose in your crotch," I tell her.

We pour coffee, settle into chairs around the table, and start to eat.

"Thorpe give you any idea as to whether they have any leads on Liquida?" Harry talks with his mouth half full.

"They're looking. But without a name or something else to track, it's difficult. All they can do is print a sketch, put it on their website, hang it in the post office, circulate it to local law enforcement, and hope somebody calls in."

"I would think that after the bombing near the Capitol he's going to draw a pretty high number on their wanted list," says Joselyn.

"Depends whether they put him on their terror list or regular most wanted list. They put him on the terror list, there's no way he's going to get near

the top. There's too many big names already," I tell
her.

"The last time I checked, bin Laden was still
number one. And that's going on ten years now,"
says Harry. "And, of course, while they're looking,
we don't have a life. Can't go home cuz Liquida may
be waiting for us."

"Yeah, well, I've thought about it. I can't speak for
either of you, but I don't intend to sit around growing old, waiting and hoping that somebody snags
the crazy bastard before he kills me or murders my
daughter." I look at both of them. "He came within
a breath of killing Herman. He's made one attempt
on Sarah's life and murdered one of her friends."

Liquida killed Jenny, one of Sarah's girlfriends,
after following the two of them to a club in San
Diego. It was Liquida's twisted way of sending a
message that my family and I were next.

"So you think he'll try again?" says Joselyn.

"Hell, yes," says Harry. "Unless he dies of cancer
or gets hit by a truck."

Harry, Herman, and I had become entangled
with this psychotic as a result of a case that turned
out to have connections with terrorism south of the
border. Ever since then Liquida has been crossing
our path with the constancy of an orbiting death
star, making it crystal clear that he has declared war
on us even if we refuse to realize it.

"It's cultural," I tell her. "Liquida has his roots in
the Mexican cartels. These are people to whom vengeance is a religion. Only heretics allow the flame of
revenge to go out."

"What did you do to him?" she asks.

"I don't know. But it wouldn't matter even if I knew. Assuming I could undo whatever it was, it would make no difference to Liquida. He has no sense of proper proportion. Look at him without genuflecting and he'll kill your entire family, shoot your dog, and burn your house. When he's finished, he'll dig up your ancestors and grind their bones to dust for fertilizer. He may have gone upwardly mobile and branched out to service the international terror trade, but his instincts come from the cartels."

"So what do we do?" says Joselyn. "Stay here? Hope the FBI will provide protection? Pray they'll catch him?"

"For how long?" says Harry. "We've been through this before. Hiding out in an FBI safe house. You weren't with us."

"Harry's right. And when we came out into the open, Liquida came back. He killed Jenny. While we were looking for him he was busy hunting down Sarah. He's smart and he's very patient. He knows sooner or later we have to surface again. He'll simply wait. When we feel safe, when we get into the routine of life with the illusion of security, that's when he'll hit us. And this time we may not be so lucky."

"I can't disagree with your logic, but it still doesn't answer the question of what we do," says Joselyn.

"Simple, we find him before he finds us," says Harry.

"Unless you have a better idea," I tell her.

"We tried that; it didn't work, remember? Herman very nearly got killed," says Joselyn. "It's too dangerous. We don't have the resources. Look around the table. There's three of us. None of us has a gun or, for that matter, knows how to use one. Herman was your only real backup in terms of security and he's down. Let the FBI do it."

"We could die of old age hiding out in this hole," says Harry. "The FBI's got a full plate, and Liquida probably doesn't even show up on their list of hors d'oeuvres. We could be here for years. I'm not that patient. You want to know the truth, I'd just as soon be dead."

"If you go after him, you probably will be," says Joselyn.

"I don't intend to go toe to toe with Liquida. But if I can find a lead, hand it off to Thorpe, or let the local police take him down, I'll settle for that," I tell them.

"Only if they lock him up at Supermax and I can swallow the key," says Harry. "On the other hand, there's nothing more permanent than death."

"Listen to him," says Joselyn. "Dirty Harry wants to kill him?"

"Why not? He wants to kill us."

"Harry is a different kind of criminal defense lawyer," I tell her.

"And how would you go about this?" asks Joselyn.

"Well, I wouldn't try to take him in a knife fight, if that's what you mean," says Harry. "But then, this isn't a duel, and Liquida doesn't necessarily get to choose the weapons."

"So what's it to be, water pistols at twenty feet?" she asks.

"Show me where he hides his coffin and I'll rent a cement truck, fly it through his window, and run over him in his sleep," says Harry. "That way I can take my time driving the stake through his heart."

"Listen to this man." Joselyn thinks he's joking.

The fact is, Harry is one of the few people I know whose capacity to kill I would never question, not if the motivation was sufficient. And knowing Harry, he wouldn't lose a lot of sleep after he did it.

Harry has what you call a hair trigger. Some might call it an anger management problem. Rub him the wrong way and there's no way of telling what might come out of the barrel. More than once I have had to pull him off someone before he did serious damage. I have seen Harry kick the crap out of drunks in bars who got in his face thinking it might be fun to push the guy in the rumpled suit with the bow tie. He once pounded the shit out of a client using a casebook off his shelf when the guy started slapping his wife around in Harry's office. The fact that the man was there on a manslaughter rap didn't even enter the equation. Not to Harry. It was all in a day's work.

It's not that Harry brawls. But if you push his button, he can go crazy all over you. His victims are often stunned and defenseless in the same way you might be if you stepped on a pit viper you thought was a common variety garden snake.

In a crowded room Harry is the guy you never notice, the one holding the smoking gun.

If I got a phone call in the middle of the night telling me that my partner was in the clink on a homicide charge, it wouldn't exactly shatter my image of who Harry is.

"Fine, now that we know how we're going to kill him," says Joselyn, "how do we find him? What about that address in Thailand?" She looks at me.

"What address?" says Harry.

"Herman and I found a notepad in a hotel room in Puerto Rico when we were trying to track down Thorn. You remember, Liquida's client in the D.C. bombing."

"Yeah?"

"The note was from an impression left on the inside cover of a notepad. It mentioned something called 'Waters of Death' with an address in Thailand. It was something Thorn had jotted down. To me it looked like a contact address for Liquida."

"Was it?" says Harry.

"We don't know. I turned the information over to Thorpe. He had two of his agents from the U.S. Embassy in Bangkok check it out. A few days later he told me they struck out. The address was for an office in a place called Pattaya. Thorpe told me his people found the office, but it was locked up and dark. There was nobody inside. There was nothing on the door or anywhere else in the building with the name 'Waters of Death.'"

"Maybe they got the address wrong," says Joselyn.

"No, according to Thorpe it was the right address. The one on the note. It even had the suite number. They had the local police check with the landlord. The office was on a year-to-year lease.

The tenant was a Thai businessman. The local authorities told the FBI agents that the guy had no apparent criminal history. The cops found him, and the agents talked to him. The man told them that he used the office only to store business records. He said he never heard of anything called Waters of Death. He had no idea what it was."

"He could have been lying," says Harry.

"Chances are, if he had dealings with Liquida, it would have been under a different name," I tell them, "an alias."

"God knows he's used a few of those," says Harry. "All of his banking records here were under aliases, remember?"

"And, of course, they couldn't show him a picture of Liquida," said Joselyn. "The FBI was still working on that."

"You're right."

"Do you know, did the agents actually get inside the office to look around?" says Harry. "Any kind of a search of the premises?"

"I asked Thorpe. He said he didn't know, but that it was difficult sometimes to get local authorities to go along with a search unless there were formal documents."

"What does that mean?" says Harry.

"He didn't say. I'm assuming maybe a search warrant from a judge in the States, an affidavit, maybe something from the State Department by way of an official request."

"Or maybe crossing the palm of the local cops with some coin," says Harry. "But whatever it takes, it sounds like they didn't do it. So the fact is, they don't know any more about what's in that office than we do."

"It sounds like all they know is what the tenant told them," I say. "Thorpe told me he'd have his people at the embassy keep an eye on the place. No round-the-clock surveillance—they don't have the manpower over there—but they'd check back in a while. I looked on Google Earth. It's a long way between the embassy in Bangkok and Pattaya. I'm guessing maybe two hours by car; that's if the highway is good."

"We know what that means," says Harry.

"They think it's a dead end," I tell him.

"And they're not likely to waste their time," he says.

"No."

"Do we have anything else?" he asks.

I shake my head.

"So it looks like we either sit tight right here . . ."

"We're not going to waste a lot of money, take a chance, and fly off to Thailand?" says Joselyn.

"No, we're not. I was thinking more along the lines of Harry and me," I tell her. "Somebody has to stay here with Sarah."

"Don't look at me," she says. "Besides, Harry already has experience in that field."

"And you saw how much good it did," says Harry.

"Yes, but you know her. You're almost family. I'm just a stranger."

"Maybe she'll listen to you," says Harry. "An older woman and all."

"Watch it! Those are fighting words," she tells him.

"I'm afraid I'm going to need Harry with me."

"That's fine. Then that'll make three of us. Cuz if you go, you're not leaving me behind."

"That means I've got to bring Sarah."

"The plane's going to be crowded," says Joselyn. "You, me, Harry, Sarah—and the dog," she says.

"Shit! I forgot about the dog. We can't take him with us," I say.

"Why not?" says Joselyn. "From all accounts, he's the only one of us qualified to deal with Liquida."

"You can't take a dog overseas. They'll impound him. Probably want to hold him ninety days, maybe six months," I tell her. "And if they don't take him going over, U.S. Customs is sure to hold him coming back."

"Not if he has all his shots," says Joselyn.

"Over there they'll probably want to eat him," says Harry.

"Unless he eats them first," says Joselyn.

"Cut it out," I tell them. "This is serious. I'm going to have to deal with Sarah, and that's not easy."

"One thing's for sure," says Harry. "You can't take Sarah and leave the dog. He'll tear the place apart and then eat the help when they come to clean it up."

"You're right. We'll have to leave Sarah and the dog. The question is, who's going to tell her?"

"Sounds like a father's duty to me," says Harry.

"Yeah, I know, but how?"

"If we move quickly, get over there and back in three, maybe four days," says Joselyn, "perhaps you can talk Thorpe into having Sarah remain here.

And she'll have the dog. You'll have to explain to her that that's the reason she can't come with us. There really is no other way. Unless she wants to put the dog in a kennel."

"And I suppose you'd want to draw straws to see who gets to talk to the dog about doing time in a kennel?" says Harry.

"OK, you sold me. Sarah stays here," I tell them.

"Now you just have to convince her and the dog. I hope she keeps him on a short leash when you're discussing all of this," says Harry.

"And you think Thorpe is going to let us go, just like that?" asks Joselyn.

"Not if I tell him we're going to Thailand. I'll tell him Harry and I have some pressing business to take care of back in Coronado. Something that can't wait. We'll be back in three or four days. We'll be very careful. We won't stay at the house. We'll stay in a hotel."

"What about me?" says Joselyn.

"I'll just tell him you're coming along."

"Good, then let's hope he buys it," she says. "Cuz if he doesn't, I'm telling him you're going to Thailand."

"You don't trust me?"

"In a word—no," she says.

"And what if he wants to take our passports or assign agents to accompany us to California?" says Harry.

"Then I suppose the urgent business in Coronado is somehow going to resolve itself, avoiding the need for any travel. It's worth a shot."

"There's a Wi-Fi hot spot in the lobby downstairs," says Joselyn. "I saw it on my cell phone when we were down there yesterday. If you loan me a credit card, I can book the tickets in the morning. Right after you talk to Thorpe."

TWELVE

By the time Bill Britain got to Thorpe's office on the fourth floor of the FBI building, he was running late. Thorpe's secretary had called him away from a staff meeting. She told him to drop what he was doing and come up immediately.

"Go on in, they're waiting for you." Thorpe's secretary gestured toward the closed door.

Britain opened the door and stepped into Thorpe's office. "What's going on?"

"Close the door," said Thorpe.

Britain knew it was something big the minute he saw Herb Llewellyn closeted inside with his boss. Britain was the head of the FBI's Counterterrorism Division. Llewellyn headed up the FBI's Weapons of Mass Destruction (WMD) Directorate.

"Take a seat." Thorpe picked up the receiver to the phone on his desk and punched a button. He waited for a second. "Nancy, I don't want to be disturbed. Hold all my calls and clear my calendar for the rest of the morning. I'm not sure when I'll be available. Good." He hung up the phone. "What I'm about to tell you doesn't go beyond the confines of this office, is that understood? I am told that any other assistance that we might need has to be cleared by the White House."

Llewellyn and Britain glanced at each other and then nodded toward Thorpe. "Must be pretty bad," said Britain.

"Less than an hour ago I received a phone call from the White House. I was told that a weapons program, something that DARPA has been working on with the air force and NASA for a number of years, now appears to have been compromised. We don't know the full extent of the damage yet. NASA and DARPA are still doing an assessment."

"When you say compromised, you mean information has found its way into the hands of a foreign power?" asked Britain.

"We don't know for sure, but it's a possibility," said Thorpe.

"The White House wouldn't get involved in something like this unless there was a top-of-the-line national security breach or the prospect of some lethal political fallout," said Llewellyn.

"In this case it may be one and the same," said Thorpe. "They wouldn't give me any details, especially over the phone, other than to emphasize the magnitude. I was told that if there has been a complete breach of the program in question, the damage to national security could be on the order of the Soviet's penetration of the Manhattan Project."

"So it's nuclear?" asked Llewellyn.

"No. I asked them that," said Thorpe. "That's the only thing they would tell me. It's not nuclear."

Llewellyn issued a subtle sigh and settled back into his chair, as if suddenly he was off the hook.

"According to what I was told, it could be much worse. What they said was that the loss of the information in question could be catastrophic."

"What the fuck are they working on over at DARPA," asked Llewellyn, "a doomsday device?"

DARPA was the Defense Advanced Research Projects Agency, the technologic black-ops tool designer for the Pentagon. It had been on the cutting edge of every advanced weapons system from the stealth bomber to the latest generation of aerial killer drones. DARPA possessed classified futuristic projects on its drawing boards and computer screens that made Star Trek look obsolete. It might have been fiction, except that the agency had a track record for making sci-fi dreams come true. It was through DARPA that the United States maintained its edge of technologic superiority on the battlefield.

"According to the phone call, the project was right down DARPA's alley. They simply wanted to get a handle on it before somebody else did. That's what I was told, and that's their job," said Thorpe. "We've got a big bull's-eye painted on our ass. So if it's that dangerous, whatever it is, we better find it, get it, and keep it. Otherwise somebody's gonna use it to put an arrow in our butt."

"Point taken," said Llewellyn.

"Here's what we do know," said Thorpe. "Two NASA researchers scheduled to attend a conference at the European Space Agency in Paris failed to show up. They never checked into their hotel, and nobody knows where they are. They've been missing for two days now."

"Maybe they're off having a frolic," said Britain.

"Yeah. That's what I said. But it gets worse. NASA has information that somebody has been downloading data from the project. There's only a handful of people with clearance to access the data. The two missing researchers were cleared since they were working on the project on a daily basis. They don't know how long the unauthorized downloads have been going on, so they can't be sure how much information may have been taken. DARPA had NASA install some security software on the system. From what I gather, this was fairly recent. Immediately afterward, the software indicated that data was being copied, downloaded to an unauthorized device. NASA figured it was probably a glitch in the new security software. They thought they'd take a look at it and test it before they got all excited. It wasn't a glitch. The data was downloaded to a device connected to a computer on the desk of one of the two researchers who is now missing."

"Any chance these guys might have fallen prey to foul play?" asked Britain.

"Anything's possible," said Thorpe. "I'll get more information, names, and backgrounds later this morning. I'm scheduled to be in briefing at the White House in an hour. I'll bring back as much as I can. But from what I gather, they're going to be tight-lipped. I have a feeling it's going to be on a need-to-know basis, and I'm afraid they're going to be operating on the basis that we don't need to know."

"Find out if these two missing guys are critical to operations of whatever the device is. See if it's just the data they're worried about or if the two researchers could be part of a package," said Llewellyn.

"Do we know whether either of them has any kind of ideological bent, political, philosophic, religious?" said Britain.

"I don't know. I'll try to find out," said Thorpe. He made a note.

"And try and see if they'll tell you anything about the nature of the device itself," said Llewellyn. "If we don't know what we're looking for, we're going to be terribly hobbled trying to guess who might be in the consumer pipeline."

"That's why you're here," said Thorpe. "From the telephone conversation, I got the distinct impression that that's the one thing they're probably not going to want to talk about. For whatever reason, unless we run into a brick wall. And by then it may be too late. I was wondering if perhaps I could get enough information as to the background on these guys, where they got their education, their field of study, maybe a résumé if we get lucky, do you think you might be able to piece together some clue as to what they were working on?"

"It's possible," said Llewellyn. "But it's probably a long shot. I mean, they're gonna have science backgrounds of some kind. You can be sure of that. It depends how much information they're willing to give you."

"I'll try to get as much detail as I can," said Thorpe.

"Get it," said Llewellyn, "and I'll see what I can do."

"Beyond that, we do have one lead. What's the latest information we have on Bruno Croleva?" Thorpe looked to Britain for a response.

"Last time I looked he was still near the top of our hit parade. We don't know where he is, if that's what you mean. Probably in the Middle East somewhere," said Britain.

"Who's Bruno Croleva?" said Llewellyn.

"International arms merchant," said Britain. "Supplier of merchandise to needy warlords and aspiring terrorists."

"Bruno Croleva is an upwardly mobile jack-of-all-trades," said Thorpe. "If you check his jacket in the file, you'll find that at one time, in another life, Bruno trafficked in drugs. He had extensive connections in Colombia and North Africa as well as in Marseilles in the south of France. Narcotics is where he got his start. It was from his connections there that he moved into arms sales. A lot of his early deals were to the cartels in Colombia."

Thorpe had a file on his desk containing two intelligence reports from the CIA. Together with the sparse information given to him over the phone from the White House, he was beginning to connect the dots.

"Bruno is becoming a regular rainmaker of violence," said Thorpe. "He's been slipping into the middle of some really big international transactions and making himself indispensable."

"In what way?" said Britain.

"He's no longer just selling guns, bullets, and explosives. He's now peddling some major ordnance. Just before you came over here today I pulled a couple of intelligence reports. It seems Bruno was partnered up with Victor Soyev."

"Soyev peddled the thermobaric device that landed in the rail yard at Union Station," said Britain.

"Right. When we took Soyev down, Bruno inherited the entire business," said Thorpe.

"Now, do you remember the Mexican assassin, the one the cartels called Liquida?"

Britain had to change gears for a second to think. "Yeah, I remember. We kept wondering why his name was popping up around the fringes in the two terrorist attacks. The one in Coronado, at the naval base, and the aerial bomb that hit the rail yard here."

"Liquida is always around the edges," said Thorpe. "Never in the middle. We were wondering what a contract killer for the cartels was doing involved in the two terror attacks. The answer is Bruno Croleva," said Thorpe.

"According to the intelligence reports, Croleva has done business with the FARC in Colombia," Thorpe went on. "He has connections in Cuba where he has sold weapons as well as in the Middle East, in Iran . . ."

"And we know he had a connection in North Korea because that's where Soyev got the thermobaric device," said Britain.

"Correct," said Llewellyn.

"All the places where weapons were used in the last two terrorist attacks were either obtained or transited during their shipment to the United States," said Thorpe. "And it seems that in addition to peddling blockbuster ordnance, Bruno has become a major talent agent. He doesn't just sell the weapons. If you require it, in a pinch, he can rent you the services of specialists who can wield them and do so with great discretion. According to the CIA, one of his principal artists in this field is a professional assassin known only by the alias 'Liquida,' which in Spanish means 'water.' In other words, if you've got a deal going down and suddenly somebody's getting ready to drop sand in the works, Bruno can commission Liquida to lubricate the gears with blood."

"OK, I understand all that," said Llewellyn, "but how does that give us a leg up on whatever it is that has the White House in such a shit storm?"

"That's the thing about information," said Thorpe. "Whoever has it possesses power. In this case, the power to know more. During the telephone conversation, the White House let it drop that apparently the National Security Agency has no file on Bruno."

"I don't understand," said Britain.

"The NSA managed to track some Skype traffic, Internet telephone communications, and apparently a chat line message left by one of the missing researchers from NASA to someone named Bruno Croleva. They wanted to know if the bureau had anything in its files on a man by that name. I'd suggest that gives us two leads, not one, Croleva and Liquida. And we'd better find them fast," said Thorpe.

THIRTEEN

Five hours out over the Pacific and my body is beginning to cramp up in the tight coach seat. We are thirty-two rows back in the big 767, and not even halfway to Taipei. There we have a two-hour holdover before we fly on to Bangkok, another three and a half hours in the air.

Harry, Joselyn, and I flew directly from Washington to L.A., not even going near San Diego. We booked a midnight flight on EVA Air, the national airline of Taiwan. I can't begin to calculate the number of time zones we will cross, let alone the international date line.

By the time we arrive, we will be the walking dead, talking in our sleep, terminally jet-lagged with no chance to get over it before our scheduled return flight in three days.

The lights are out in the cabin, and the shades are all pulled. Most of the passengers are in various states of disarray. Some of the pros brought bed-clothes, loose sweats or shorts to sleep in. There are bodies under rumpled blankets, some of them hugging pillows. The guy behind me is slouched in his seat snoring like a foghorn with his knees buried in the back of my seat. The interior of the plane has the mood of an opium den but without the benefit of the drugs.

Joselyn's head is tilted on my shoulder. She is snoring gently in my ear, making harmonics with the foghorn behind me. Harry is just across the aisle. He is snoozing when he can, but like me he is having trouble finding the sandman.

He looks at me and sees my eyes open. "Who was the Sherlock who thought this one up?"

"You wanted to come," I whisper to him.

"What's the time difference in Thailand?" says Harry.

"I think it's fourteen hours ahead of the clock on the West Coast," I tell him.

Joselyn begins to stir. She lifts her head from my shoulder and stretches. "You still awake?"

"I can't sleep."

"Take a pill," she says. "Want an Ambien? I've got some up in my bag in the overhead."

"No. I want to try and keep my head clear."

"For that you need sleep," she says.

"I keep thinking about Thorpe," I tell her.

"What about him?"

"He let us go way too easily."

"I was thinking the same thing," says Joselyn. "Could be he just realized he couldn't hold us any longer."

"No. He didn't even try and argue when I told him we were going. Instead he tells me to be careful and gives me the name and number of the agent in charge of the FBI field office in San Diego. Told me to call him if we had any problems. That's not the Thorpe I know. The question is, what's he up to?"

Thorpe showed us the composite computer sketch of Liquida, the one they had been working on with Sarah before we left. He gave us a copy in case we needed to study it more. I didn't say anything to him, but my daughter is not the only one who has seen the man. The sketch was a good likeness of the face I saw that night in Costa Rica, now nearly two years ago. It is not a face I am likely to forget.

I turn around in my seat and glance down the aisle behind me, stretch my upper body, and check to see who's sleeping and who's awake. I turn back to the front. "I'm betting he put a tail on us."

"Who?" says Joselyn.

"Thorpe."

"For our sake, I hope you're right. Do me a favor. If you're able to identify him, ask him to come up and sit here so I can sit in his lap."

"You don't think I can protect you?"

"In a word . . ." She sticks her fingernails under my rib cage, causing me to jump. Then she giggles.

"Cut it out."

"Don't be so uptight."

"You're right, I shouldn't complain. Thorpe allowed Sarah to remain in the condo."

"After what happened in Ohio, I'm sure he'll have his people keep a close eye on her," says Joselyn.

"Unless she pulls a slip on them the way she did with Harry," I say.

"Why would she do that?"

"Sarah wasn't happy about being left behind. You don't know my daughter."

"She can be that willful?"

"Willful isn't the word for it. Having the dog was the only thing that kept her from forcefully boarding the plane with us."

"She perked up when you told her Herman was getting out of the hospital tomorrow."

Joselyn was right. The thought that she could play nurse to Herman, someone she likes, made Sarah feel more useful. Herman will be bunking in the condo for a period of convalescence. Still, I am itching to get back as quickly as possible before Sarah's mind turns to thoughts of home.

"I contacted the embassy and gave them the airline and the flight number. I told them that the plane should be on the ground shortly before noon their time." Bill Britain was looking tired, jowls down to his ankles. Thorpe looked almost as bad. It was nearly three in the morning, Washington time. The two of them had been at it for nearly twenty hours. Thorpe didn't plan to go home until Madriani and his party were safely under surveillance.

"I'm wondering if I gave in a little too easily," said Thorpe. "I mean, just letting them go like that. They're not stupid."

"Not to worry," said Britain. "Two agents will meet the plane at the gate. We sent copies of their passport photographs so our people will recognize them. We've got three cars, and we've brought in backup from the embassy in Jakarta."

"Good. You're sure they got on the flight?" said Thorpe.

"Checked it and double-checked it," said Britain. "L.A. field office saw them get on and watched the plane until it took off."

"I should have detailed two agents to stay with them all the way across," said Thorpe. He was looking a little worried.

"Why? What could happen to them on the plane?" said Britain.

"We don't know where Liquida is," said Thorpe. "He could be anywhere. For all we know, he could be on the fucking airplane with them."

Britain had no comeback for this.

"Liquida now knows we have a witness, somebody who can identify him. He's gotta figure we'll have a pretty good description. He's wounded and on the run. If you were in that situation, what would you do?" said Thorpe.

"I'd go to ground," said Britain.

"Right, but where?"

"Someplace where I'd feel safe, probably outside the country. Someplace where our reach does not extend."

"He has to know the longer he waits, the harder it's going to be to get out," said Thorpe. "His face, or a pretty good likeness, is going to start circulating with TSA at the airports, security at the train stations, and bus depots. He's going to be feeling antsy about renting a car, figuring we'll be sending any sketches to rental car agencies along the main routes between Ohio and the Mexican border."

"He'll run for Mexico," said Britain. "It's obvious."

"Yeah, well, he has a habit of doing things that are not obvious, not until after they're discovered. And by then it's usually too late," said Thorpe.

"Mexico is Liquida's home turf. It's where he's going to feel most comfortable, at least until the heat's off. If I was gonna hide, that's where I'd go to do it," said Britain. "Especially given the current situation."

He was referring to the veritable civil war currently going on between the cartels and the Mexican government. During the last year, more people were killed by violence in Ciudad Juárez and Tijuana along the U.S. border than in Iraq and the Afghan war combined. Not only was this familiar ground for Liquida, but the chaos in Mexico made it highly unlikely that local or federal Mexican authorities would have the time or the inclination to look for him. They were too busy trying to stay alive.

"So tell me," said Thorpe. "If we're so right and Liquida is headed for Mexico, why are Madriani and his friends jetting off to Thailand?"

"Because they're crazy," said Britain.

"I'm not so sure."

"You told him the address in Pattaya was a dead end. Our people checked it out. There's nothing there."

"Madriani asked me whether our agents actually went inside the office at the address in Pattaya, whether they looked around. Did they?"

Britain glanced at him with a dubious expression. "I don't know. I'm not sure."

"Why don't we find out?"

"You want to know what I think? I think Madriani's off his nut. He's finally cracked. Let's assume for purposes of discussion that there's something in Thailand that shows the way to Liquida. Or maybe the man himself, perhaps he's there, though why the hell he would go there instead of Mexico, which is much closer and which he knows like the back of his hand, is a mystery, you have to admit. But let's assume that he's there. Why would two lawyers and a girlfriend . . ."

"Three lawyers," said Thorpe. "Joselyn Cole is also a lawyer, though she doesn't practice anymore."

"Fine, three lawyers," said Britain. "Why would three lawyers in their right minds want to go off searching for Liquida, especially after they saw what he did to their investigator? I mean, this is a guy who looks like he could coldcock a charging bull in rutting season, and Liquida carved him up like a turkey."

Thorpe took a deep breath. "They're desperate, that's why."

"There's a difference between being desperate and having a death wish," said Britain.

"From where they're standing, they're running out of time," said Thorpe.

"What do you mean?"

"We're not walking in their shoes. Spit out the government teat for a second and think. Twice now, over a span of more than a year, Liquida has forced Madriani and company to take up residence under a rock. Both times they had to stay there for extended periods. Their law practice has to be drying up. They're probably on the verge of losing everything they own. Liquida has tried to kill Madriani's daughter, and he managed to kill one of her friends. He took down their investigator, the man you say could slay a bull. So unless somebody gets a collar on the Mexican and does it soon, as far as they're concerned their lives are over. They may be breathing, but it's the economic and social equivalent of death. What do you do when you're desperate? You chase the only lead you have. The Thailand note, as thin as it is, is probably the only thread they have left that, in their minds at least, would seem to lead to Liquida."

"Yeah, but it doesn't," said Britain. "They're chasing a rainbow."

"Well, fine, then at least they won't get hurt," said Thorpe. "You have to remember they don't have access to our intelligence reports."

"Thank God for little favors," said Britain. "I understand everything you're saying. I feel sorry for them. But they're better off staying here where they're safe. I wish they would just let us do our job. Let us find Liquida. It's what we do."

"They probably would," said Thorpe, "if they had some idea how long it was going to take. But they don't, and we can't tell them because we don't know. Do me a favor; check and see if our agents in Bangkok got a look inside that office."

"Will do," said Britain. "In the meantime, let's hope to hell nothing happens to Madriani or his friends. We may have a lot of explaining to do if Liquida kills one of them."

Britain was right. With the high profile that Liquida had assumed since the meeting at the White House, the theory that he might be involved, it would look very bad if the bureau were seen as trying to lure him out using three American civilians as bait.

"Make sure your agents stay on top of them when on the ground in Bangkok," said Thorpe. "Whatever you do, DON'T lose them!"

"Understood." Britain left the office, closing the door behind him.

Thorpe sat at his desk, the fingers of both hands teepeed under his chin as he considered the consequences of what he had done. That Liquida was stalking Madriani and his clan out of some psychotic soul-searing thirst for vengeance was clear. What was problematic for Thorpe was the fact that he had let Madriani and the others go, knowing that they were headed for Pattaya in Thailand.

What Britain saw as a long shot, Thorpe saw as a fertile fishing ground. Pattaya was a city with a reputation as a fugitive's Mecca. Like Port Royal during the age of piracy, it was one of those places that offered instant camaraderie, often without any questions. Split-second friendships were formed over a bottle of local Thai-brewed beer and the assumption that if you were bold enough to be there, then you belonged.

The unnumbered constellation of outdoor bars and the neon confusion of Pattaya's nightlife presented a kind of analgesic refuge for anyone on the run, whether it be from the law, life, or a nagging wife. All poisons were treated with the same remedy, and it almost always came out of the long neck of a bottle. It was precisely the kind of place where Liquida could go and feel completely at ease. The kind of community where you could relax on the beach and recover from a wicked and obvious knife wound, and no one would notice, and if they did they would never ask questions. Old bullet wounds and knife scars were so plentiful in the shirtless atmosphere of Pattaya that most people never even bothered to look.

Thorpe visited Pattaya for the first time as a young man, during Vietnam when he was in the Marine Corps. Then it was an R&R center, rest and recuperation from the stresses of combat. Since then the city had grown up, with high-rise thirty-story condos, glitzy restaurants, and a shopping mall that was first world. But still the city had a reputation to defend, and "wild" was its name.

If things went wrong, anyone examining Thorpe's conduct later might easily conclude that he had been trolling for Liquida in the waters of Pattaya, and that he had used Madriani and his friends as bait.

But Thorpe had begun to realize that there was another dimension to this equation. He had observed Madriani and his movements now for more than a year, particularly as they pertained to Liquida. Madriani and Liquida seemed to be caught in a death spiral. Ever since the murder of Jenny, Sarah Madriani's friend, the lawyer seemed to operate under the influence of some invisible force, at least as far as Liquida was concerned. Not unlike gravity, it seemed always to place Madriani in the orbit of the psychotic Mexican. This was true even at times when Liquida wasn't stalking him. In fact, a casual observer might have viewed it as the other way around. At times it seemed as if Madriani could pick up Liquida's scent half a world away, and home in.

If Madriani thought Liquida was in Thailand or that there might be information there that could lead to finding him, who was Thorpe to question one of the invisible forces of nature? The problem was that the lawyer and his friends were becoming increasingly careless. And with Liquida that was a quick path to the grave.

Ever since the Tuesday morning meeting at the White House, Thorpe was himself becoming increasingly anxious. He needed Madriani to sniff out Liquida or the other way around. It didn't matter to Thorpe, as long as he had enough agents in place to prevent any harm. The critical point was he couldn't afford to wait. From the little bit they told him, time was of the essence. He had to find Liquida, and he had to find him soon.

FOURTEEN

From the air, the international airport in Bangkok looks like a huge copper dragon with hackles of white scales erupting from its back. Up close it is a soaring modern complex of buildings, the fifth largest air terminal in Asia.

The concourses are long, encased in curving walls and arched ceilings. Looking down from the confines of the international arrival gallery, we can see the public areas below. The cavernous halls are festooned with shops and restaurants, and dotted with stunning artwork. There are statues of Vishnu and an entire array of giant-size figures cast in what appears to be porcelain; the entire work is half a football field in length, all painted in striking colors. It seems even more surreal because I am half asleep.

Harry, Joselyn, and I are dying on our feet, exhausted from jet lag. We do the quarter mile to immigration trudging along the hall like zombies auditioning for parts in *Night of the Living Dead*.

It takes a half hour to clear immigration, gather

our bags at customs, and make our way out to the main terminal. There we agree on a division of labor. Harry and Joselyn head off to the window that says "Currency Exchange" to get some local cash while I make arrangements for ground transport.

It takes only a few minutes to hire a car and driver. We follow our bags as they are rolled out of the terminal and into the garage, where the pungent odor of petrol fumes mixes with hot humid air.

Harry and I take off our jackets as the luggage is loaded into the trunk of a low-slung sedan.

"I don't think we dressed for this." Harry wipes the perspiration from his brow using the long sleeve of his shirt. "I didn't even bring any shorts."

"We're not going to be here that long," I tell him. "Hopefully we'll be back in the States before we can adjust to the difference in time."

"Right now I just want to be here long enough to sleep for a day or two." Joselyn is looking as if she's about to drop.

Outside the light is bright. Heat waves ripple the air beyond the confines of the garage. Our driver, a slight, small-boned Asian man wearing a coat and tie, is looking sufficiently cool to make me wonder if this is winter in Thailand. He looks at the paperwork given to him by the girl at the counter inside. He glances up at Harry and me, then says: "We go Pattaya?"

"Right, we go Pattaya," says Harry. "How long?"

The guy looks at him, scrunches up his mouth a little. "Ninety minute, maybe. You sleep." He gestures toward the car.

"Do I look that bad?"

"Naw, you're beautiful," says Joselyn. "Take the bamboo shoots from under your eyelids and get a few years of sleep and you'll be fine."

She and I collapse into the backseat while Harry sprawls in the left-hand passenger seat up front. You might swear the car was filled with laughing gas. As soon as the driver starts the engine and begins to roll, the three of us are asleep. The driver could have dragged me behind the car and I would have slept right through it. The only sensation is some vague awareness of sweeping curves and the rumble of the tires on the road at high speed. At some point I feel a series of rolling rhythmic bumps that jar my body. It feels as if the car is porpoising along the highway. But I'm too tired to wake up and complain about it.

Some time later, I don't know how long, I become aware of voices. When I open the slits that are my eyes, Harry is talking to the driver.

"What's the problem?" My speech is slurred.

"He wants to know what hotel we're going to. I told him the Marriott, right?"

"Right."

Harry reconfirms it with the driver as the car moves to the left onto what appears to be an off-ramp. I'm in that middle place where the brain is debating whether to sample another slice of death or wake up. The car takes a broad sweeping turn to the right. We cross over the top of the main highway and onto another road. It is lined with palm groves and low brush. There are several large buildings that look like factories off in the distance to the right.

Behind us the landscape erupts in occasional sharp jutting hillsides, an indication that maybe this is volcano country. Ahead of us the lay of the land is low and flat for as far as I can see, and the sky has that kind of ethereal edge to it that makes me wonder if it might be kissing the sea. If I had to guess, I would say we are moving toward water, a shoreline somewhere off in the distance.

"How much longer?" I ask.

"He says maybe ten minutes," says Harry.

I look at my watch. At the airport I had changed the time to Bangkok time. It's just after one in the afternoon. I decide to rouse myself so that I can move enough at least to get to the room.

"What time is it back home?" says Harry.

"I don't have the slightest," I tell him. My leaden brain is not up to those kinds of calculations, not at the moment anyway. Joselyn is sprawled across the backseat, her head on my lap. She is out cold. I am wondering if I can wake her or if we're going to have to roll her inside with the luggage.

Within minutes the traffic begins to thicken. Occasional small motorcycles, some of them spouting sidecars mounted with smoking braziers, begin to propagate along the sides of the road. Soon there is a growing herd of two- and three-wheeled traffic. Like a line of motorized wildebeest they hug the edges of the road with the riders bent over the handlebars as the cars and trucks speed past them using the main traffic lanes. As we draw closer to civilization I notice that some of the bikes are carrying four and five passengers, a few of them with small children clutching the handlebars and standing up front between their momma's knees. None of them are wearing helmets. It looks like the motorbike equivalent of the family minivan.

Doing sixty miles an hour you'd have trouble slipping a playing card between the grip on the handlebars on some of the bikes and the side of our car. How our driver is missing them is a mystery.

"Damn!" says Harry. "This could be an ambulance chaser's paradise."

"Maybe they don't get that much for an arm or a leg off over here," I tell him.

"You think?" says Harry.

"Not everybody has a jackpot tort system like ours. Why do you think all of our manufacturing jobs moved over here twenty years ago?"

"I figured that was because of the thirty-cent-a-day minimum wage."

"That too," I tell him.

"Pretty soon I suppose the doctors will figure out a way to do intercontinental robotic surgery. Then we won't be able to reach them anymore. And the way Washington wants to tax the rich, they'll all be picking up and moving over here. Pretty soon there won't be anybody left to sue. So why should we bother going home?" says Harry.

"I don't know. You got me."

We pass under a high gold arch that spans the road. A short distance farther on, the road swings to the left. Here there are multiple lanes in each direction separated by a wide grass-covered median strip. We travel on this road for a few miles, moving at high speed. There are commercial buildings and businesses on both sides of the road, and traffic is starting to get heavy. It looks as if we're getting close to the center of town.

We come to a stoplight. The driver maneuvers into the far right lane, getting ready to cross traffic and make a turn. The light turns green; we go a couple of blocks and find ourselves stopped in bumper-to-bumper traffic. The sidewalks here are crowded with pedestrians, vendors selling fruit, fish, chicken, anything you can eat from the sidecars of parked bikes. Now the slower two-wheel motorbikes get the upper hand as they stream between the stopped cars. They jump to the front of the line at each stoplight.

"How much longer?" says Harry.

"Not far. Maybe ten minute."

"That's what you said a half hour ago," says Harry.

"You give tip?" says the driver.

"I give tip if we get there today," says Harry.

The driver maneuvers into the left lane and a few feet farther up he turns into a narrow alley and starts to move. We twist through a maze of backstreets, dodging kids and dogs, Asian women with pushcarts selling food, and potbellied white men in tank tops and T-shirts hanging out in the beer bars, some of them tattooed like scrimshaw.

A few more minutes and two more turns and we find ourselves on a broad four-lane one-way street with shops and businesses on both sides. Here the traffic is heavy once more. There are vendors all along the street and beer bars on every corner. "Seccon Road," says the driver. "Marriott." He gestures with his head up the street.

Harry turns to glance at me from the front seat.

I'm looking out the window to see if I can catch any street numbers. According to the note, the office for "Waters of Death" is somewhere along Second Road.

"I don't see any numbers," I tell him.

"Don't worry about it. We can check with the front desk when we get to the hotel. Show them the address. I'm sure they can tell us where it is," says Harry. "I don't know about you, but I'm gonna get some sleep before I go anywhere."

I look at my watch. "It's a quarter to two. Hope to hell our rooms are ready."

"They better be," says Harry. "Otherwise I'm gonna crawl over the counter and kill the clerk."

FIFTEEN

Liquida sat in a chair near the window of his room on the third story of the small hotel and listened to the prattle of motorbike engines, watching the traffic as it streamed by on Second Road.

He had arrived in Bangkok, Thailand, three days ago and had been planted in the city of Pattaya ever since.

He settled into the hotel because of its location. For a few extra Thai baht, he was able to get a room with a good view of the building across the street. It was the place where the lockbox was located.

The old charm of the block-long cream-colored colonial facade with its small curved balconies and masonry balustrades had become buried behind a vast picket of painted metal business signs. These jutted out over the sidewalk in such a bewildering array of sizes, colors, and shapes that it was almost impossible to focus on any single message. A thick tangled vine of black wires and cables meandered across the front of the building until the messy snarl reached over the sidewalk and snared the wooden power poles along the street out in front. The building sported corrugated metal add-ons on the front and the roof, where the penthouse looked like a flattened-out army Quonset hut.

At ground level the building housed small retail shops, restaurants, and a grab bag of other businesses, some of them open air, others sealed behind the comfort of air-conditioned walls. On the sidewalk out near the curb, street vendors reduced the normally broad walkway to a narrow path, setting up business under canvas awnings or sheets of plastic to peddle their wares.

Through all of this confusion, Liquida's attention was riveted on a single green-painted wooden door. It was situated across the street about half a block south of the window in his room.

The green door was located between a Pakistani tailor shop and a small pharmacy. It seemed almost invisible set against the harried sea of commerce taking place on the sidewalk in front of it.

But every once in a while someone would either come or go, entering or leaving the building through the green wooden door. Whenever they did, Liquida would use his field glasses to study them closely. He looked at their faces to see if they were Asian or if they looked Caucasian, what the Thais called *farang*—foreigners. If they were leaving the building, he watched to see if they talked to anyone out on the street. He examined them for bulges on their ankles, heavy fanny packs on their sides, or coiled wires growing out of their ears.

He had been doing this for two days. So far he had seen nothing unusual. There were no obvious signs of surveillance. Which only meant that if they were doing it, they were doing a good job. And, of course, the whole point of surveillance was not to be seen.

Once we got up, got dressed, and got out, it took Harry, Joselyn, and me only a few minutes to find the right building. The concierge at the Marriott was able to give us some pretty fair directions and by 3:30 we found the place.

It wasn't an office building in the sense that I had envisioned. There was no main entrance with double glass doors and street numbers over the top. From the outside it looked as if the upper three stories could have been either apartments, condos, or commercial office space. Across the front of the building, French doors opened onto small balconies. But from where we stood about a block to the south on the other side of the street, it was impossible to tell what kind of furnishings might be inside.

After watching for several minutes and by process of elimination, we concluded that the way in had to be a single door tucked away between two stores on the ground level.

"Unless they put the main entrance in the back of the building," says Harry.

"Why would they do that?" asks Joselyn.

"Look at the place; they've tacked on everything else, why not that?" says Harry.

The privacy of the single lonely door unnerved

us a bit. There was no way to tell what might lie beyond it without going in.

"There could be security," says Harry.

"Or worse," says Joselyn.

"Or it could be locked," I tell them. "So what do you think? Should we try it?"

Beyond the green portal, up on the second floor, was another wooden door, this one with a translucent glass panel on top. There was no lettering or name on the glass other than the number 208.

Liquida had seen the inside of the office only one time, the day he first established the account with the company known as TSCC Ltd. Some people used it as a place to store business records or other private papers that for one reason or another they didn't want to keep at home or in their office. For others, including Liquida, it was an address of convenience.

For a reasonable fee, TSCC, like any other private parcel service, would take receipt of packages or letters addressed to clients and hold them in a locked box or, in this case, the steel drawer of a filing cabinet assigned to the client. Unlike other parcel services, TSCC distinguished itself by not being particularly scrupulous in checking to see whether customs declarations and clearance documents accompanied packages coming in from abroad. This was particularly true when an item was hand-delivered by special messengers, otherwise known as mules.

The company's fee schedule also offered additional services, including use of its automated voice-mail system. This allowed gift givers and recipients to leave messages for one another; a message that a present was on the way and a verbal thank-you from the happy beneficiary were often well received. Clients and their friends were usually careful to employ obscure terms when communicating their largesse or happiness in these matters.

Best of all, TSCC maintained its own courier service to forward items on to those clients who, for reasons of survival, preferred not to pick up their own mail. For this purpose, the company maintained a complete stable of global mules able to travel to the ends of the earth to deliver private parcels. You could get overnight service to your cave in Afghanistan if you wanted it. Depending on the paranoia of the client, TSCC's couriers were also adept at sleight of hand, magic acts, and games of chance, this to entertain any government workers who might be watching for the handoff at the time of delivery. They could play "package, package, who has the package" all over the New York subway system if you had the time, inclination, and money to pay for it.

Liquida had a key to the office as well as the locked cabinet drawer inside. But he was never stupid enough to use them, not in his line of work. He always used the forwarding courier service, and he never had anything delivered to the same place twice.

SIXTEEN

Herb Llewellyn generally had a pretty good handle on the science of weapons systems. As head of the FBI's WMD Directorate, an office created after the 9/11 attacks on the Twin Towers, Llewellyn had become Thorpe's go-to guy whenever an investigation involved questions of science or technology.

The problem this time was that Llewellyn had run into a wall erected by political and policy operatives in the White House, and neither he nor Thorpe knew why.

"Nothing," said Llewellyn. "I can't get a thing out of anybody at NSA or the Pentagon. People who usually talk to me, the minute they find out why I'm calling, are no longer taking my calls. Suddenly I'm Typhoid Mary. The two who did talk told me they were out of the loop. One of them, a fellow I used to work with, warned me not to ask too many questions."

"Did he say why?" Thorpe sat behind the desk in his office hoping for answers.

"He wouldn't talk on the phone. We met for a drink after work. He claims he doesn't know anything, only that the strings on this thing are held so high that nobody below the level of the Joint Chiefs has a clue as to what's going on. He warned me to be careful. According to him, partaking of the fruit of the tree of knowledge on this one could be dangerous."

"In what way?" asked Thorpe.

"Whether he meant physical as in dead or just a career killer wasn't entirely clear. But he warned me off and told me not to call him again. Not on anything having to do with the two missing NASA scientists, anyway."

"So they got the lid on tight," said Thorpe.

"All over town."

"So how are we supposed to find these guys? Unless we have some idea what they were working on, we don't even know who the opposition is," said Thorpe. "They could turn up in Moscow or Beijing on the morning news, the latest defectors from the land of liberty, and we'd be the last to find out."

"I know."

Thorpe turned in his chair, opened the top drawer to his desk, and pulled out a pack of cigarettes. He tapped one out and lit up.

"I thought you quit," said Llewellyn.

"I did. Tell it to the president." The building was off-limits to smokers. Thorpe used the open drawer as an ashtray. "Anything on the background for our two missing scientists?"

"One tantalizing tidbit maybe. Nothing we can really get our teeth into."

"What's that?"

"One of them, Raji Fareed, was born in Tehran. He came to this country with his parents as a kid, age eleven. His father was Iranian, deceased. Died of a heart attack about ten years ago. The mother is Jewish."

"That must have been difficult," said Thorpe.

"Difficult while the shah was in power, impossible after he fell," said Llewellyn. "After the revolution, the family escaped. His father was a functionary in the government, nothing major, but apparently enough to get political asylum from the State Department."

Thorpe blew a smoke ring and picked a speck of tobacco from his tongue with his fingernail. "You think the kid's a throwback?"

"It's possible," said Llewellyn. "He could have been radicalized locally. Or he could be a sleeper, though I doubt it."

"Helping out the mother country," said Thorpe. "The father could have poisoned him before he died."

"It's a possibility. I've got the L.A. field office checking it out, seeing if Fareed hung out at the local mosque, who his friends were. State Department is looking to see if they can find any relatives in Iran that he might have been in contact with."

"Good," said Thorpe. "Anything else?"

"We know that the two men boarded the plane to Paris. They cleared French immigration and customs, but they never showed up at their hotel.

It's possible they may have met with foul play, but there's no evidence of it. They simply vanished."

"Any indication at all as to what they were working on?" said Thorpe.

"That's a deep dark hole," said Llewellyn. "Personnel records are sealed. NASA won't give them to us. They're under executive seal. Orders from the White House. What we know is that the two men . . ." Llewellyn looked at his notes. "Raji Fareed and Lawrence Leffort worked at NASA's Jet Propulsion Lab near Pasadena in California. The people at the lab aren't talking."

"Great," said Thorpe. "That helps."

"All they would tell us is that the Iranian, Fareed, was employed as a software engineer. The other one, Leffort, holds a degree in astrophysics. Ph.D. from MIT, bright guy. He's listed as a principal research scientist by NASA, but as to what programs, we don't know. The last public information was eleven years ago. He was involved in a short-term project having to do with particle physics, short-impulse force fields."

"In English," said Thorpe.

"Fringe science," said Llewellyn. "Star Trek stuff. Tractor beams and teleportation theories. Credible scientists generally steer clear of it. You get a bad reputation among your peers if you spend too much time trying to figure out how to transport yourself from a phone booth in Pasadena to the moon."

"That's what he was doing?" said Thorpe.

"No. They probably had him in a holding pattern, paying him from funds on the particle physics project until they could work out funding for the mystery project they recruited him for. There's a million ways to hide that money—black box projects, CIA, military budgets, DARPA, defense research projects. You can forget trying to trace any of that. You want my guess as to what he's doing now, off the top of my head, given his background, the high level of classification, I'd say rail guns, lasers, something geared to star wars," said Llewellyn. "Antiballistic missile systems. God only knows what's going on there."

"I wish he could tell us," said Thorpe. He made a note.

"NASA moved Leffort out of the particle physics project early on, before it ran out of money. Congress cut it off after pouring eighty million down a rat hole."

"Who says they're stupid," said Thorpe. "Maybe this Leffort could find some way to teleport Congress to the moon. Now that would be worth a grant. I'd give him my pension. Anything else?"

"Well, yeah."

The way Llewellyn said it Thorpe knew it wasn't good news. "Give it to me."

"It seems science wasn't the only thing on the fringe for our man Leffort."

"Go on."

"He had a kinky nightlife."

Thorpe's head snapped toward Llewellyn. His eyes opened wide as he held the smoking cigarette off to the side. "You're gonna tell me he fell in with some Russian belly dancer," said Thorpe.

"No. At least I don't think so. You can read the details tonight before you go to sleep." Llewellyn flipped a copy of a document onto the desk in front of Thorpe. "I'd recommend you take a cold shower first. It's Leffort's last fitness report for his security clearance."

"Cut to the chase. What's in it?" said Thorpe.

"More to the point, you might want to ask who did the investigation and wrote it up."

"Who?"

"The National Security Agency," said Llewellyn.

"Why not us?" This was normally something done by the FBI.

Llewellyn made a question mark out of the expression on his face. "You'll find some large portions of their report are redacted. Anything and everything having to do with the project Leffort was working on, as well as some other things. According to the report, they had their eye on him all the time."

"Then why don't they tell us where he is?" said Thorpe.

"Good question. To read it, they were getting ready to cancel his security clearance, dump him from the project, and castrate him; that is, if you believe what's written on those pages. Of course, NSA never got the chance. It was a matter of unfortunate timing according to them."

"Leffort rabbited," said Thorpe.

Llewellyn nodded. "It makes for interesting reading, but if you're smart, you don't want to be sitting upright in bed when you open it. Cuz all that self-serving crap inside, it's gonna spill out all over you and make for a damn mess," said Llewellyn. "You want to know what I think?"

"That's why we're talking here," said Thorpe.

"I think that report and the investigation that goes with it were both done after the fact."

"You mean after Leffort disappeared?"

"Exactly. You can read it for yourself. Form your own conclusions," said Llewellyn. "NSA is trying to cover their skirts. They redacted the names of all the witnesses they talked to, including the women Leffort had trysts with. You have to wonder why."

"Maybe Leffort was into pillow talk about the project?" said Thorpe. "Classified information."

"To read the report, the only classified information any of these women had was as to the location of warts on Leffort's tallywacker. There's not the slightest hint that any of them knew squat about Leffort's work. Nor is there any indication that any of them were extorting him for classified information. First thing I thought of was spies," said Llewellyn. "But there's nothing there. Not even the slightest whiff that any of them were in the employ of a foreign power. NSA doesn't even bother to raise the specter. So why withhold their names?"

"You tell me," said Thorpe.

"Because NSA doesn't want us talking to them," said Llewellyn. "They deleted the names because they knew we'd get the cart back behind the horse. They knew we'd find out that they didn't interview the witnesses until after Leffort disappeared."

"I don't get it," said Thorpe.

"You will in a moment, all nine yards," said Llewellyn.

Thorpe didn't like the sound of that.

"It explains how they found out somebody was

lifting information from the NASA computers. After the fact. When Leffort was already gone. The same way they got the names of the women. This guy was running wild on a top-secret, highly sensitive program and they had no clue. And now the shit is about to hit the fan, and everybody in town, except us, is looking for a rock to crawl under."

"The White House and the brass at the Pentagon are looking for somebody to blame," said Thorpe.

"Right," said Llewellyn. "And NSA is a little too close to home to crap in that particular backyard. So they're looking for someplace else to take a dump."

"Us," said Thorpe.

Llewellyn nodded.

"Next you're gonna tell me that NSA had lead responsibility for security on this mystery project," said Thorpe. "Whatever the hell it is."

"No, not just lead responsibility," said Llewellyn, "exclusive responsibility. Everybody else was cut out, all the defense intelligence agencies, protective services, security management at NASA—they were all cut out of the loop. That should give you a hint as to what's going on here. It's why we weren't asked to do the security background update on Leffort."

"And NSA blew it!" said Thorpe.

"Yep."

"I knew it. I knew it. This thing smelled the minute I got that call from the White House." Thorpe got up out of his chair, waving the cigarette around like a torch. "So now they dump it on us to find these guys, and if we fail, it's our ass in the flames. And if that's not enough, they want to play hide the ball. They can't tell us what it's about. Son of a bitch," said Thorpe. "Damn it!" He stood there, face full of fury, tendrils of smoke surrounding the shadow of his head on the wall, the fumes appearing as if they emitted from his ears. He swallowed hard. It was one of the few times that Llewellyn could remember ever seeing signs of fear on his friend's face.

Thorpe took a deep drag on the cigarette and sucked it into his lungs to quell the anger. He held the smoke for a long moment and then expelled it toward the ceiling.

"That shit's gonna kill you," said Llewellyn.

"What, this?" Thorpe held it up in front of his face and looked at the cigarette. "This is therapy. It's the fucking National Security Agency's gonna kill me."

SEVENTEEN

"What are they doing now?"

Two FBI agents from the embassy in Bangkok stood in a room on the third floor in the office building in Pattaya. They were two stories above the green door, the entrance to the building, watching Madriani and the two people with him.

"They're standing out on the sidewalk looking at the door from across the street. Can you beat it? Travel halfway around the world, then stand there with your thumb up your ass." One of the agents looked through a spotting scope set up in the vacant third-floor office.

They had used a credit card to slide the cheesy lock open on the door and established a blind inside. They set up the spotting scope far enough back from the windows that with the interior lights out anyone looking in from the outside would see nothing. From here they got a bird's-eye view of everything on the other side of the road. To cover this side, an agent in shorts and a tank top, looking like an expat, was camped out in a shop across the street. Another was in the Thai restaurant downstairs.

The radio crackled in the agent's ear. "Do you see 'em?"

"Charlie One to Charlie Three, stay off the air if you can. They're still on the street. We'll let you know if they move."

The problem was that the call for assistance from Washington had come without sufficient advance warning so that the embassy was unable to coordinate their actions with local Thai authorities. Consequently, the agents were on their own, using a communication channel that they couldn't be sure wasn't being used or monitored by the Pattaya police. Their instructions were to watch and report, to provide protection if necessary for the three U.S. nationals, and to watch for the man named Liquida, though they had no photographs, only a rough description.

We stand there on the sidewalk, parting the waters with throngs of pedestrians flowing around us as we watch the naked door across the street and debate what to do.

"Why don't we go round back?" says Harry. "See what's there."

Looking at the door, not knowing what is inside, neither Joselyn nor I want to argue with him.

We walk down the sidewalk to the south, half a block closer to our hotel, and cross traffic where a narrow lane intersects Second Road on the other side.

It looks like more of an alley than anything else. But it must go somewhere. Cars and motorcycles are moving on it in both directions, so we follow it. A little farther on, maybe fifty yards, Joselyn stops. Harry and I keep walking.

"What about right there?"

Harry and I turn to look at her. She is pointing off to the left toward a narrow walkway between two buildings.

"It looks as if it might go through," she says.

I take a peek. The walkway looks as if it passes between the buildings and widens out into a parking area behind the building with the green door.

"Let's try it." We start walking single file toward the narrow passage.

"Charlie One to Charlie Four, you got 'em?"

"No. This is Charlie Four. Give them a minute." The agent was sitting in a restaurant next to the pharmacy just two shops down from the green door. He had a perfect view of the three Americans across the street. He watched them as they crossed over until they got too close to the sidewalk on this side where he couldn't get an angle any longer. He was sure they were coming this way, heading for the entrance to the offices upstairs. If he panicked and raced out, he'd run right into them coming the other way.

"Charlie Four, do you have them?"

"No."

"Where are they?"

"I don't know. They could be hanging on the corner. Give 'em a couple more seconds."

"Can you see them?"

"No, but I'm on it. Moving now." Charlie Four tossed some Thai money at the waitress to pay for his iced tea, told her to keep the change, and hoofed it out onto the sidewalk. There was no sign of them at the corner. He looked south down Second Road against the direction of traffic. He couldn't see them, though. The sidewalk was crowded. In running shoes and shorts, he'd have no difficulty catching up with them—if he only knew which way they went. "Got a problem here," said Charlie Four. "Need help. They either went south on Second, in which case they're probably headed back to their hotel. Or else they went down the side street. It's Soi . . ." He looked for the street sign. There wasn't one. "I'll take the side street."

"I got Second Road," said Charlie Three.

Charlie Four turned left and headed down the narrow side street. There was no sign of the two men or the woman. Like everything else, the side *soi*s were getting crowded as people caught up in the rush hour looked for alternate routes.

There were cars and pedestrians, motorbikes and vendors with their pushcarts, all moving and jostling for space on the narrow side street. The agent caught a lift, jumped on the back of a moving baht bus, and tried to use the elevated height to see if he could find them in the crowd. The bus found an opening and headed down the street with the agent on the back, his eyes scanning the distance for the three Americans.

* * *

Liquida had no intention of going anywhere near the green door or the locked box upstairs. Nor did he want to take a chance on the company's courier service, not now. One thing was certain; it was Bruno's voice he had heard on the telephone message he picked up in Dubai. The question was whether the FBI had their hand up his ass playing puppet using the Chechen to try and hook Liquida and reel him in. If that's what was happening, any deliveries from Bruno would be made by a courier with a government pension and a badge. Still, Liquida desperately needed the money that was in that drawer, assuming it was there.

He looked at his watch. It was after four. Traffic was beginning to thicken up out on Second Road. In a few minutes the street in front of his hotel would be a parking lot. He had things to do. He got up from the chair, slipped out one of the stilettos from the rolled cloth pack, and dropped his pants. He taped the long straight weapon to the inside of his left calf using a foot and a half of vet wrap. It was an area of the body that, unless police saw some bulge, they often didn't frisk all that carefully. A piece of steel like the thin stiletto could easily slip by. He pulled his pants up and checked to make sure that nothing showed.

Then he grabbed a white canvas beach bag that was lying on the bed. The bag had two sturdy strap handles and was big enough to hold a couple of fair-sized phone books. He had purchased the bag earlier that day from an outdoor display on Beach Road, a place called Mike's Department Store.

Liquida headed out of the room and down the stairs. He passed through the small lobby in front of the clerk at the desk and stepped out onto the sidewalk, which was teeming with pedestrians. He instantly lost himself in the sea of people moving quickly around the corner onto one of the side streets.

Ten feet farther on, two Thai teenage boys, motorbike taxi drivers, lay lounging on the long seats of their bikes while a third one sat perched in a low beach chair up on the sidewalk. They were all wearing worn and soiled green vests with the name of a local beer bar on the back. This was their turf, the corner where they hung out hoping to pick up fares. For a few baht they would give you a thin plastic helmet, let you hop on the back of their bike, and deliver you anywhere in the city. That is, if you could hang on and if you didn't mind the occasional near-death experience.

EIGHTEEN

The narrow walkway between the buildings delivered Harry, Joselyn, and me into the middle of a parking area directly behind the building with the green door. In the back was a small loading dock, and on the elevated concrete pad was a steel overhead door that was closed. Next to the loading dock was a set of cement stairs leading to a heavy steel door, only this time the door was open.

Harry and I look at each other. "Listen." I turn to Joselyn. "Why don't you stay here? If we're not out in, say, ten minutes, go see if you can find a local Thai policeman and tell him where we are."

"I got a better idea. Why don't you stay here and I'll go in?" Joselyn doesn't wait for me to answer. Instead, she takes off like a greyhound for the open door, Harry and me trailing along in her wake.

Inside the door is a large storage area, a stack of fifty-gallon drums against one wall and what looks like part of a motorized rack for hanging clothes in a commercial laundry. We don't loiter. Instead, we

pass quickly through another door and find ourselves in an open hallway. We move down the hall
toward the front of the building; the smell of food,
chicken broth and steamed noodles, fills the air.

"I'm gettin' hungry," says Harry.

"You want to stop and eat?" asks Joselyn.

"Not now, but when we're done, yeah," he says.

We reach the front of the building and end up at
the foot of a staircase leading up to the second floor.

"According to the note, it's upstairs, second floor,
room 208," I say.

Harry is already climbing, two steps at a time. We
get to the top and start checking off the numbers on
the doors. The place is a rabbit warren of small businesses, some white collar, others providing support
services for some of the shops on the ground floor.
We pass by one and see several women inside working sewing machines, stitching jackets and slacks,
probably for the tailor's shop downstairs. The next
door is all the way open, swung back against the
wall. I very nearly pass it when Joselyn taps me on
the arm. She points to the open door, the numerals
208 reversed on the translucent glass on the upper
panel of the open door.

"Maybe we got lucky," she says.

We peek inside. I am guessing that the room is
maybe twenty feet deep by thirty feet wide. There
are no windows or desks, just filing cabinets arranged in neat rows with narrow passageways between each row. I count six rows. There is a man in
the far corner standing on a tall ladder up against
the ceiling. His back is to us. He's changing out flu-
orescent tubes in one of the light fixtures.

Before I can stop her, Joselyn dips down low and slips through the open door. She scurries into the aisle between two of the rows of cabinets, keeping low so the guy on the ladder can't see her.

"What's she doing?" Harry whispers in my ear.

I shake my head.

When I see her again, she's on her hands and knees peeking around the corner of the end cabinet, crooking her finger at me to join her.

The guy on the ladder is almost done. He is replacing the long plastic cover, clipping it into place on the light fixture.

I lean toward Harry and whisper: "Stay here and keep an eye. Warn us if anybody comes."

The guy is halfway down the ladder. Before Harry can say a word, I slip down low and cross the open space between the door and the cabinets. I end up in the aisle between the first and second row of cabinets, huddling up close next to Joselyn down on the floor.

She is giggling silently, a single finger to her lips shushing me to be quiet. We hear the tall aluminum ladder being folded up and a second later the clatter of metal as it hits up against some of the cabinets while the guy makes his way down the long aisle. He is four rows over. I am praying he has no more lights to fix. I glance up. The fixtures overhead appear to be fine.

We press deeper down the aisle as he approaches the open door. We have an angle of defilade unless he actually steps into our aisle. A few seconds later the lights go out. Then we hear the door close.

Joselyn and I sit on the floor in silence for a few

seconds as we listen to the clatter of the ladder being carried down the hallway until we can no longer hear it.

"Now we look," she says.

"How?"

"You think it would be safe to turn on the lights?" she asks.

"Not with that glass door. Gimme a second." I fish in my pocket for keys. I don't know why I'm carrying them halfway around the world from my house and car. I suppose it's habit. On the key ring is a tiny Maglite powered by a single triple-A battery. I'm hoping it's not dead. I twist the end of the little flashlight and we get a beam.

"That's handy," she says. "Let me see."

I focus the light and hand it to her.

She stands up and shines the narrow beam of light down the row of cabinets, five drawers on each one.

"That's strange."

"What?" I say.

"Usually a cabinet has a single lock at the top. It locks all five drawers. Look at these."

She is right. Each of the cabinet drawers has its own small brass push-button lock. There is a printed label slipped into the label holder on the face of each drawer. Some of them are in English, others in a script that I assume is probably Thai. From the ones I can see, some of the labels appear to bear the names of businesses or companies, while others are for individuals.

"Let me see the flashlight."

Joselyn hands it to me.

Each label appears to be printed on a standard

form. In the upper left-hand corner of the label, in smaller twelve-point type printed in green ink, are the letters "TSCC Ltd." Underneath this, also in green ink, are two lines of Thai lettering, each one followed by Arabic numerals on the same line. Beneath that in English is an "Office Telephone Number" and under that something called "Client Messaging System" with a different phone number.

"The drawers look like they're all locked. Even if we could get into them, we wouldn't know where to begin looking," says Joselyn.

"Let's start by going up and down the aisles. Check and see if anything jumps out at us."

"You mean 'Waters of Death'?"

I nod.

"Charlie Four, can you hear me? Come in, Charlie Four."

"This is Charlie Four."

"Any sign of them?"

"Negative. But I'm still looking."

"Charlie Three, do you read?"

"HELLO! HELLO! THIS PATTAYA POLICE DEPARTMENT. WHO IS THIS?"

Charlie One took his finger off the button on the wireless mike. "Shit!" He stood in the abandoned office on the third floor above the green door looking at his compatriot. "What do we do now?"

"Why don't I drop down, take a quick look, make sure they didn't come into the building some other way."

"Do it," said Charlie One.

"Be back in a sec." The other agent raced out the door and headed for the stairs.

Charlie One hesitated for a second, then pressed the button on the mike once more. "Charlie Three, come in! Are you there? . . ."

"THIS PATTAYA POLICE. WHO IS THIS!"

"This is Charlie Three."

"Do you have them?"

"N . . ." All of a sudden there was a screeching sound in the agents' ears as somebody else toyed with the squelch on the band.

"Damn." Charlie One jerked the earbud from his right ear. He put his finger in and wiggled it around a little trying to relieve the pain. Then he held the bud up to his ear without putting it in. "Repeat. Charlie Three. Do you read?"

"Nothing yet. I'm almost to their hotel. I'll check there and let you kn . . ."

"THIS IS LIEUTENANT CHATNGEON, PATTAYA POLICE. THIS OFFICIAL POLICE BAND. WHO IS THIS? IDENTIFY YOUR-SELF!"

Charlie One released the button on the mike. He pulled out his cell phone and started to dial just as the door opened behind him.

"Quiet as a tomb downstairs," said his partner. "I took a peek from the stairwell. 208 is locked up tight, lights out as usual. I checked all the way down to the ground level. There's no sign of them in the building. Who you calling?"

"The embassy. If any of those three get them-selves killed, Washington's gonna have our scalps."

"What can the embassy do?"

"If we don't find them soon, we're gonna need help. The Pattaya police aren't gonna be feeling terribly helpful when they find out we've been working their turf without notice."

"And?"

"And so we may need a royal dispensation," said Charlie One.

NINETEEN

Liquida talked for a minute or so to the motorbike taxi boy sitting in the beach chair up on the sidewalk. Body language indicated to Liquida that of the three kids lounging at the taxi stand, this one was probably the boss. After conversing for a while, he took out his money clip, peeled off a few bills, and handed them to the kid. The biker got up and followed him across the narrow alley of a side street where the two of them climbed a couple of high steps onto the tiled floor of an outdoor beer bar. The place was already starting to rock with loud music. By nine you wouldn't be able to hear yourself think.

They sat down at a table, and Liquida ordered two beers. He talked to the bar girl who delivered them. After a few seconds, she pointed to one of the other women who was working the bar.

The other woman was wearing a tight white dress with large burgundy flowers printed on the cloth.

Liquida paid the barmaid for the beers and gave her a generous tip.

She walked over and talked to the woman in the flowered dress and then gestured toward the table where Liquida and the taxi driver were seated. The woman in the tight dress walked over to Liquida's table.

"What can I do for you?"

"The other lady says you speak good English," said Liquida.

"Yes?" She studied the pockmarks on his face.

"This is my friend," said Liquida.

She glanced at the taxi driver seated next to him. The kid was hunched over the bottle of beer, his eyes cast down at the table. There was enough road grit on his face to know he probably hadn't showered in two days.

Liquida leaned toward the bike driver. "What's your name?"

The kid looked up and said, "Kee."

"This is my friend, Kee," said Liquida. He wanted to make sure that the next time the girl saw him she would recognize him, so that there would be no problems. "If I get busy, sometimes Kee takes care of things for me."

"I see him before," she said. "Over there." She gestured toward the taxi stand where his friends were still hanging out.

"Yes, well, I have a problem, you see. I wonder if you would mind doing me a favor? There are some papers I have to pick up in an office just across the street. Right over there." Liquida pointed lazily in the direction of Second Road. "I have a conflict, you see, and I cannot go over and get them right now. It's helpful to have someone who speaks such good English. I wonder if you would mind walking across the street and picking up these papers for me?"

She turned and looked back toward the street, the direction where Liquida had pointed. This was not the usual request from one of her male customers. "I don't know. I'm not really supposed to leave, not unless I am bar-fined out," said the girl. A bar fine was the amount of money a customer paid to take a girl out of the bar.

"I'd be happy to pay you if that's the problem," said Liquida.

"How much?"

"I don't know. . . . Say five hundred baht?"

She flexed her eyelids, jerked her head back just a bit and smiled. "You going to pay me five hundred baht just to walk across the street, pick up some papers, and come right back?"

"Yeah." The way she looked at him, Liquida knew he'd stepped in it. He tried to do some quick calculations and realized that he had just offered the girl fifteen bucks for a quick two-minute stroll across the street. This was probably two days' wages working in the bar.

The money was too easy. Now she was suspicious. "Why can't you get it yourself?"

"The problem is I'm supposed to meet a friend. He should be here any minute." Liquida regrouped instantly. "If I'm not here when he shows up, he's liable to leave thinking I decided not to come. And he doesn't have a cell phone, so if I miss him I may not be able find him later. So you see, I have to stay here. And when my friend gets here, we have to leave immediately for a meeting and we need the papers. So you would be doing me a big favor."

"Why can't he do it?" She looked at the biker.

"He's waiting for a fare; guy went up to get something in his room, said he'd be right back down," said Liquida. "He can't leave. Listen, if it's too much trouble, don't worry about it. I'll find somebody else."

"Let me talk to my boss," said the girl.

"Sure, no problem. Go ahead. We'll wait here."

She walked away and disappeared around behind the bar. Liquida sat waiting, thumping his fingers on the table to the beat of the music as the taxi boy sat drinking his beer.

A few seconds later the girl came back. "My boss says I can go so long as I am back in five minutes."

"No problem. I'll show you where it is. It's just right across the street." Liquida got up and told the taxi boy to sit tight. He picked up the beach bag and escorted the girl to the front corner of the bar where it bordered the sidewalk on Second Road. From here they had a good view across the street and to the south about a quarter of a block. He told her about the green door just beyond the tailor's shop, next to the pharmacy. He waited for a break in the stalled traffic that was now bumper to bumper until they got a glimpse of the door. He described the interior of the office and told her the filing cabinet she was looking for should be in the second row from the right, about halfway down. Liquida hoped they hadn't moved it since that first day when he set up the account and they gave him the tour.

Then he grabbed one of the bar napkins, took a pen from his pocket, and wrote something on it. He handed her the napkin.

"There will be a label on the drawer that will look just like this. It will have this typed on it in big letters. You can't miss it. Just go ahead, take everything out of the drawer; there shouldn't be that much. Drop it all in the bag and bring it back here. That's all you have to do." He handed her the beach bag and the keys and told her which one was for the office door and that the other was for the cabinet drawer. He gently took her arm and eased her toward the sidewalk. He thanked her and then watched as she slowly threaded her way through the stalled traffic toward the other side of the road.

Harry was wondering what in the hell was taking so long. At first he was worried that something might have happened inside. He was tempted to knock on the door, but as he got up close to the translucent glass he saw the faint flicker of a light inside. They must have found some kind of a flashlight. He left them alone and checked his watch.

He felt a little obvious standing outside the door, so he wandered down the hall toward the restrooms forty feet away. Just as he got there Harry heard footsteps coming down the stairs behind him. They were coming fast. There was no time to go back and tap on the glass. Besides, whoever it was was moving so fast they were probably on their way to the ground floor and out of the building, unless it was a call of nature.

Harry figured he could hide in one of the stalls. He opened the door to the men's room and stepped inside only to discover that the room was a single-holer, one commode. Good news was, there was a latch on the door.

He waited to lock it to see if whoever it was would go on down the stairs. They didn't. The footfalls suddenly stopped. Harry eased the door open just a crack. There was a guy, six feet tall, Caucasian, in slacks and a polo shirt standing just outside the stairwell. He was looking at the door to room 208 as if he was in a trance.

The thought suddenly hit Harry that perhaps there was a motion sensor inside the room. If so, the janitor who fixed the lights might have reset it when he locked up, in which case it may have triggered a silent alarm. They needed to get the hell out of here.

The guy in the polo shirt walked away, down the hall in the other direction. Just as Harry started to take a deep breath, the man came walking back, headed straight for the bathroom. Harry closed the crack and locked the door. Six seconds later he heard the door handle jiggle, and somebody pulled on it.

If Harry had known the Thai word for *busy*, he would have used it. But he didn't. So he just held his breath and hoped the guy would go away. A few seconds later, he heard footsteps going the other way, and then elephant feet on the stairs again, all the way down to the ground floor.

Harry waited a couple of seconds, lifted the latch on the door, and peeked out. The coast was clear. He walked quickly down the hall toward the dark office. It was time to leave. Just as he got there, elephant foot was back. Coming up the stairs two at a time. Harry knew he was screwed. He stood there frozen, waiting for his fate. The guy was close enough that Harry could hear him breathing. Any second the man would step out of the stairwell and into the hall and Harry would be standing there in front of the dark door. That is, until he realized that the sound of the thudding footfalls was now coming from overhead. The guy had gone on up to the next floor.

Harry let out a deep sigh. He was standing there catching his breath when he heard them. Much slower and lighter this time, a tapping patter on the concrete steps. High heels. The place was getting busier than Union Station. Harry turned around and rapped on the glass. "Come on!"

The patter of the footsteps was getting closer. They seemed to be slowing as they approached the second floor. Harry skated on the balls of his feet down the hall as fast as he could. He grabbed the door and slid into the men's room. He held the door open and caught his breath as he peered through the crack.

The woman entered the hall from the stairwell. She didn't even slow down. Instead she walked right up to the dark glass in the door and slipped a key into the lock.

TWENTY

Traffic was thick as cement. It was approaching the peak of rush hour. Cars and tall tourist buses were parked in the lanes on Second Road. The little blue baht buses, light pickup trucks with stainless steel tops and benches in the back for passengers, were stacked up all over the shoulder of the road picking up and dropping off fares.

Liquida watched the gal in the flowered dress as she threaded her way through the stalled traffic, checking between lanes so that she didn't get creamed by a motorbike riding the lines.

As soon as she disappeared, Liquida went back toward the table in the beer bar. He snapped his fingers, and the taxi bike kid got up from the table. He left his beer, and together the two of them headed back to the taxi stand where the bikes were parked. Liquida gave the kid a five-hundred-baht banknote. "You know what you're supposed to do?"

The kid nodded.

"Sabai, comprende?" said Liquida. "You understand?"

"Yeah, yeah. Soi 2."

With that Liquida turned and headed quickly back toward Second Road. When he got there, he turned right. But he didn't go into his hotel. Instead he walked past it and kept going south along the sidewalk. He looked across the street to see if there was any sign of the girl. He didn't see her. By now Liquida figured she must be inside the building.

He picked up his pace and kept walking. He glanced over as he passed the green door on the other side of the street. He walked another fifty yards and stopped near the curb. Liquida took one last look around and then stepped off the sidewalk. He used a key from his pocket to pop the seat on one of the motorbikes parked at the sidewalk. He grabbed the helmet from under the seat and put it on. Then he fastened the strap under his chin and closed and latched the seat.

Liquida took a deep breath, put the key in the ignition, threw his leg over the bike, straddled it, and began to roll it backward out onto the shoulder of the road. He turned the handlebars to the left and worked the bike back and forth a little with his feet until it was parallel to the stalled traffic and just a few feet off the road.

Cars and buses were creeping forward, inches at a time. Liquida turned the key and pushed the starter button on the bike. The little Suzuki Hayate started up instantly, its engine purring almost silently as it idled.

Liquida had rented the motorbike the day before. He used it the previous night to scout out the area behind the office building looking for signs of surveillance. He didn't see anything, but he still wasn't convinced. It was the reason he had lived this long.

Joselyn and I take turns working high and low, using the small flashlight to quickly scan the labels on the filing cabinets and hoping the single battery in the Maglite lasts.

We get to the bottom drawer at the end of the last aisle. Joselyn looks up at me. "That's not it. So either there's nothing here, in which case we've wasted a lot of time and a good deal of money, . . . or else it's the one we saw back over there."

None of the labels on any of the cabinets bear the words *Waters of Death*.

"That would explain why the fellow who leases the office—I assume he owns TSCC limited, whatever that is—why he told Thorpe's people that he never heard of anything called Waters of Death," says Joselyn.

"Do you remember where it was?" I ask.

She gets to her feet and starts walking along the back wall past the end of each aisle until she comes to the second row of cabinets. Using the Maglite, she flashes it up and down the face of each cabinet. "It was around here somewhere."

"As I recall it was up high, first or second drawer," I tell her.

She moves forward a few more cabinets. "Here it is." She holds the light on the label. In the center of the two-by-three-inch label is the word *WOD* in large block letters, all capped. It is printed on the same form as every other label, with the three large black letters just under the smaller green print showing "TSCC Ltd." and telephone numbers.

Joselyn reaches up and grabs the handle on the drawer and pulls, but it is locked. You can see the small brass cylinder lock jiggle in its setting just a speck each time she jerks on the handle. "Any ideas?"

"No. Last time I saw one of these locked up like that, it was in our office. Somebody lost the key. We had to call in a locksmith. It would take a crowbar to pry it open, and then we'd probably make enough noise to bring the whole place down on us."

Something catches my eye on the top right corner of the cabinet. "Here, let me see that." I take the flashlight from Joselyn and look more closely.

It's an old decal about an inch long, pasted to the corner of the steel frame right at the top. It's old and worn, very nearly scraped off the metal, but I can make out enough of the letters to piece it together.

"What I said about prying it open with a crowbar . . ."

"Yes?"

"Forget it. It's military surplus stuff. See that?" I touch the old decal. "It says 'U.S. Army Signal Corp.' It's probably left over from the Vietnam War. Thailand was a big R & R center, rest and recuperation for the troops. If I remember right, they had a big air base around here somewhere. That's probably where it came from."

"So?"

"So the U.S. government doesn't buy cheap stuff. You're probably looking at a twenty-thousand-dollar filing cabinet—to go along with their forty-thousand-dollar toilet seats and their fifteen-thousand-dollar hammers. And even if they overpaid, that's heavy-gauge steel. You won't find that in Office Depot."

"So where's the nearest locksmith?"

Just as she says it, there's a tap on the glass at the door. I turn and look over the top of the cabinets. I see Harry's silhouette backlit against the lights out in the hall. "Come on, we better go."

"What's the matter, getting nervous?" says Joselyn. "You don't like the idea of doing time in a Thailand jail?"

"We can try and figure out something tomorrow," I tell her.

Joselyn and I start to move toward the door when I look up and see Harry's shadow receding like a sprinter away from the glass. "Hold on a second!"

"What's wrong?"

"I don't know."

As we are standing there, another shadow approaches the door. This one is much smaller than Harry, with a feminine form.

I twist off the Maglite. Joselyn and I retreat back down the aisle as fast as we can. We reach the end of the row just as we hear the key in the lock at the door.

It opens as we slink around the corner behind the end cabinet. I am down on one knee with Joselyn behind me. She has a hand on my shoulder, breathing in my ear as the lights in the room suddenly flash on.

The unexpected brilliance blinds me. I hear the door close and then the click of high heels as they cross the linoleum floor and head down the aisle directly toward us.

I push back against Joselyn, trying to retreat. Just as I do, the woman slows down. She takes a few tentative steps and then stops. For a few seconds I hear nothing, then the jiggle of keys. It's followed by a slight metallic *click*, and an instant later a drawer slides open.

I can't resist. I ease my head toward the corner of the cabinet until my left eye just clears the edge.

The woman is standing in the aisle maybe ten feet away with her back to me. She is leaning over an open drawer removing papers and a few envelopes, putting them in a bag.

Joselyn taps me on the back. She wants to know what's happening.

I shake my head, wave her off.

A second later the woman closes the drawer. She pushes the lock back in, turns the key, and removes it. She straps the bag over her shoulder and heads for the door.

I slowly settle back against Joselyn.

The door opens, the lights go out, and then the door closes behind the woman.

Joselyn lets out a long deep sigh. "That was close. Now it's time to get out of here," she says.

"No! You stay here in case we need to get back in." I twist on the flashlight and hand it to her as I get to my feet and head down the aisle.

"Where are you going?"

"She just cleaned out the drawer," I tell her.

"You mean WOD?"

"Yes."

TWENTY-ONE

Liquida saw the girl coming out of the building as he sat on the bike with the engine purring. She had the white canvas bag, carrying it with the straps over her shoulder. He could tell there was something in it from the way it drooped.

She walked a short distance up the sidewalk on the other side and then slowly began to cross over. Liquida watched her as she carefully threaded her way through traffic.

He looked to see if anyone was following her. It was possible they could be watching her from a distance. If they were, all hell was going to break loose in about twenty seconds.

She reached his side of the street and headed down the sidewalk in front of Liquida's hotel. Just as she stepped off the curb across from the beer bar, the kid on the taxi bike pulled out of the side street directly in front of her.

They talked for a second as Liquida watched. Then the kid handed her the five-hundred-baht note. She took it, and a second later handed the bag to the boy on the bike.

The kid took off like a shot, turned north onto Second, and screamed along the shoulder of the road, streaking past the stalled traffic like lightning.

It happened so quickly that Liquida barely had time to react. He slapped the face mask down on his helmet, twisted the throttle, and took off after him. He tried to gun it and glanced down at his speedometer just as the flailing form darted out from in front of the stopped bus. He jerked the bike to the left. The guy did a toreador move to the right, hips and ass in reverse. Liquida screeched by him, shaving the front of the guy with the right side of the bike and the hot muffler.

He didn't bother to look back. Instead, Liquida twisted the throttle all the way over. The bike shrieked along the side of the road, leaving all of the commotion behind. Liquida raced along, trying to catch a glimpse of the kid, but the taxi bike was gone.

By the time Harry sees me coming out of the office door, the woman with the bag is halfway down the stairs.

He steps out of the men's room. "Let's get out of here."

I put a finger to my lips.

"What's up?" he whispers.

I motion for him to join me at the stairwell. We wait until I hear the wooden door downstairs open and then close again.

"Come on!" We head for the stairs.

"What the hell's goin' on?"

"The gal with the bag . . ."

"Yeah."

"She may be delivering to Liquida," I tell him.

We hustle down the stairs into the hallway on the ground floor. We stop just inside the door that leads out to the street. I open it six inches or so, just enough to see out.

"There she is."

She is off to the right, walking up the sidewalk away from us. The loud flower print of her dress and the oversize bag over her shoulder make her easy to track even with the glut of pedestrians at rush hour.

"Let's go." Harry tries to push by me.

"No, no. I can see her fine from here. Give her a second. See where she goes. She's starting to cross the street."

"What, you're gonna let her get away?" says Harry.

"No, but if Liquida is out there somewhere watching her, he's gonna bolt the minute he sees us. We may not get another chance."

I watch her as she crosses over. I am getting a little nervous. If she jumps into the back of one of the little blue trucks, the ones they use as buses, and heads down a side street, we could lose her.

"What's she doing now?" says Harry.

"She's over on the other sidewalk. Let's go. . . . No, hold on! She stopped. She's talking to somebody."

"You think it's Liquida?"

"I don't know. I don't think so. . . . Oh shit!" I am out the door before Harry can move, running for the street. I hurdle a vendor out on the sidewalk and weave between the cars stopped on the road. I cross three lanes when I run smack into the side of a large white tourist bus that pulls up. His air brake hisses as he stops. I hear the high whine of the motorcycle engine over the heavy rumbling diesel as I race toward the front of the bus.

Out under the bus's massive windshield, I look to the right searching for the woman and the man on the motorbike, praying that she is still there and has the bag.

As I run out from in front of the bus I get only a flashing glimpse of the oncoming rocket through the periphery of my left eye. Throwing my body back, I feel the end of the handlebar as it carves a path across my lower stomach, followed by scorching heat on my left shin. I land on my ass in front of the wheel of the bus, stunned and praying that the driver sees me and doesn't lurch forward.

Up on the third floor, Charlie One wasn't even looking through the spotting scope. He had his hands full fielding orders from the U.S. Embassy in Bangkok. They instructed him to notify the Pattaya police as to their location and to wait there until the police arrived. The embassy was busy making apologies to a higher authority.

"What should we do about the three U.S. citizens?" He listened over the cell phone as they gave him instructions. Then he ended the call.

"What do they want us to do?" said his partner.

"Punt."

* * *

Up ahead, two parked baht buses had the shoulder blocked. Liquida found an opening, moved to the right, and started streaming through the groove between the stalled vehicles. He rode the line, easing off whenever he approached a blind spot. He stopped at a red light and glanced skyward to see if there was anything moving overhead. It looked clear.

He was certain that nobody could have followed the kid on the ground. It would have been impossible on anything but a bike. And if motorcycle cops had gone after him, Liquida would have seen them.

The light turned green. Within seconds the twenty or so bikers at the head of the line took off down Second Road headed for the Dolphin Circle and the roundabout a mile away.

Liquida hung back and allowed some of the traffic to pass him. A minute and a half later he approached Big C, a large shopping center off to the right. He drove in front of it and stopped at the curb directly across from the intersection of Soi 2. He sat there for a few seconds looking down the narrow side street as traffic moved past him.

About a quarter of the way down there was an empty parking lot on the left side of Soi 2. It was in front of a nightclub that Liquida knew did not open until at least nine at night. Sitting in the parking lot on his bike wearing his grimy green vest was the taxi kid. Liquida could see the white beach bag hanging from the handlebars of the kid's bike like a trophy.

He looked to make sure there were no other vehicles in the lot. There was nothing moving on Soi 2. Liquida waited for a break in traffic on Second Road, then swung across the lanes and onto the narrow side street. He went straight to the parking lot next to the taxi bike, peeled off a thousand-baht note, gave it to the kid, and took the bag.

The kid pocketed the money and took off, heading down Soi 2 for Beach Road and back to the taxi stand.

Liquida didn't waste any time. He scooted over near a trash can in front of the nightclub and quickly went through the contents of the bag. He opened the envelopes and examined it all. Anything not important he tore up into little pieces and tossed into the trash can.

He ripped open the large insulated brown envelope and found four packets of wrapped five-hundred-euro banknotes, each bound with a brown paper wrapper. He also found a printed note from Bruno Croleva giving him the initial details of the new job, the where and when of Liquida's next travels. He looked closely at the mark on the bottom of the page. Bruno never signed anything. Instead he used a signet ring like the ancient Roman consuls. He would use an ink pad and punch his seal on the bottom of the page. A signature on incriminating documents was hard to deny. A signet ring could always be melted, and yet to those who knew it, the mark was unique—an arrow with crossed serpents.

Liquida didn't bother to count the money. Instead he tore off the wrappers, tossed them in the trash, and then flexed the bills carefully in small groups, bending them to see if any of them were unduly stiff. He looked for any notes that might be glued together. The cops now had tiny radio-emitting wafers thinner than a credit card and not much bigger than a postage stamp. These were tracking devices that, if you didn't find them, could lead authorities right to your front door. When he was finished, he tossed the insulated envelope into the trash, keeping only the money and Bruno's note.

In less than two minutes, Liquida buzzed out of the parking lot headed for Beach Road. He was feeling relieved and rather pleased with himself. There was no reason to worry after all. The drop box in the office was perfectly safe. He would change it soon, but for now it was good. It was also the only way to contact Bruno, the lockbox in conjunction with TSCC's messaging system. Liquida would have to notify him that the job was accepted. And he would have to do it soon; otherwise Bruno would hire someone else.

Liquida glanced at his watch, checking the date. Almost a week had passed since Bruno's original offer. If Bruno didn't hear from him soon, Liquida would lose the job, and with it any gold-plated passports and new identities.

He stopped the motorbike before he reached the end of Soi 2. He pulled off to the side and grabbed Bruno's note from the bag. Liquida reached for his cell phone, flipped it open, and dialed a local number using the Thai SIM card he had purchased the day before.

He keyed in Bruno's extension on the Thai messaging system and, when prompted, left a message: "This is WOD." Liquida liked the acronym. It even sounded like a Thai name. "Payment retrieved. Job offer accepted. Confirmed. Will arrive Hotel Saint-Jacques Monday A.M. Will require usual documents, at least three sets." The last was code for passports and identity papers. Bruno's operation excelled at this.

Liquida pushed the end button on the phone and flipped it closed, another chore done. He fired up the bike and headed back to the hotel to pack.

TWENTY-TWO

By the time I scrape myself off the pavement in front of the bus and get to my feet, the girl in the flowered dress and the man she was talking to on the motorbike are nowhere to be seen. There is a growing cluster of people around me. One old lady touches my torn left pant leg below the knee. I glance down. The frayed threads look as if they are singed.

The bus driver has set the air brake, turned off the engine, and come down out of his seat through the open bus door to see what has happened. Harry is right behind him.

"You OK?" Harry pushes his way around the driver.

"I think so." I am leaning over, feeling around to make sure my leg is still there. "Did you see him?"

"See who?" says Harry.

"The guy on the bike."

"I saw him," says the driver. "Guy's crazy. Run right over you."

I ignore the driver, talking instead to Harry. "No, I don't mean the guy who hit me. I mean the other one. The guy on the bike, the one she was talking to."

"I couldn't see a thing. I was on the other side of the bus," says Harry.

"You didn't see him before the bus pulled up? When she was standing there talking to him."

"Oh, you mean when we were back there in the doorway?"

"Yes."

"All I could see was the back of your head," says Harry. "How the hell am I supposed to see anything when you're in the way? Next time get a glass head," he tells me.

"Damn it!"

"What difference does it make? They're gone now."

"Right, and one of them has the bag, the stuff from the drawer." I am looking over the crowd to see if the girl is gone. "I couldn't tell if she got on the bike or if she just gave him the bag."

"What drawer?" says Harry.

"Never mind. I'll fill you in later." I hear sirens in the distance. "Let's get Joselyn and get the hell out of here."

Harry and I slip back inside the building. We climb the stairs and I tap on the dark glass. "Open up!"

A few seconds later Joselyn opens the door.

"Let's go." I tell her.

"What happened?"

"I'll tell you later."

Just then we hear footsteps coming down the

stairs. Joselyn, Harry, and I head toward the back of the building. We leave the way we came, out the back and down the steps next to the loading dock. We cross the parking lot and escape through the narrow gap between the two buildings.

Charlie Three got to the Marriott and called Madriani's room using one of the house phones. He was prepared to hang up if anybody answered. No one did. He tried the partner's room and got the same result.

He stood in the lobby debating whether he should call the bad news in to Charlie One using the radio, or if it might be wiser to switch to the cell phone. Just as he reached for the phone on his belt, a silver lining appeared over the hotel's main entrance.

He pulled out his phone and turned his back so they wouldn't get a good look at his face as he pushed a single button and did a quick dial to Charlie One. The phone rang three times before it was answered.

"Yeah!" He didn't sound happy. Charlie One was yelling into the phone over the din of background noise. He was obviously under some stress.

"Thought I'd let you know the three of them just walked into the hotel," said Charlie Three.

"You just made my day. Are they all right?"

The agent looked over his shoulder and took a peek at the three Americans as they walked by him toward the elevator. "They look fine to me." There was music and crowd noise on the other end of the phone, then a quick siren punctuated by a buzzer. "What the hell's goin' on over there?"

"You don't want to know," said Charlie One.

"You want I should call Charlie Four and we can pick up the three of them over here and put 'em on a plane in the morning? I don't want to have to go through this again," said Charlie Three.

The agent in charge thought about it for a second and then said: "No. All we were asked to do is to follow them and provide protection. If they're OK, leave 'em alone. Just stay there and make sure they don't leave the hotel again unless you're on them like second skin. Understood?"

"Got it."

"Call Charlie Four and tell him to get over there and provide some backup. And stay off the radio. Whatever you do, don't come back over here."

"Why not?"

"I'm afraid we're gonna be here for a while."

"Got it."

Charlie One ended the call and was about to slip the phone into his pocket when a hand reached around from behind and took it away from him.

"I will keep this for now."

When the agent turned around, he saw the uniformed Thai policeman standing there in front of him. He could tell this was no ordinary cop. The man was maybe five foot eight, tall for a Thai, and very fit. He was wearing a military-style five-point hat with a shiny visor. The starched uniform bore captain's bars and looked as if it was molded to his body. "We will have that as well." He took the hand-held radio and handed both the cell phone and the radio to the officers standing behind him.

By now there was a good-size crowd forming out

on the street in front of the green door, all jostling for position to see what was happening. Two police cars and a police pickup were parked on the road, blocking traffic in the first lane, their light bars flashing red, blue, and gold.

"Your friend tells me you are the one in charge."

"Lucky me."

The cop smiled. "Are you armed?"

"No." The two agents inside the building had enough sense to lock up their .40-caliber Glocks along with the extra clips and the fanny pack holsters in the embassy car before they radioed in and told the Pattaya police who they were and where they were located. Charlie One produced his FBI credentials and then handed over his passport.

The cop glanced at the ID and handed it to one of the other officers, who made notes while his boss looked at the passport. "I see. I take it then that you are assigned to the legal attaché in Bangkok?"

"That's correct."

"And your friend here?"

"Same, same," said Charlie One.

"You will find that I speak fluent English. Would you like to try Thai?"

"I'm sure that your English is better than my Thai," said the agent.

The officer considered his options, which were now much more limited. The agents had diplomatic passports and hence diplomatic immunity. He could take them into custody, but to do so would cause a big stink. "Would you mind telling me what you're doing here?"

Charlie One didn't say anything.

The cop lowered the passport and tapped it against his thigh for a moment. "Are there any more of you?"

"Here, you mean?"

"Yes."

"No," said Charlie One. Of course, that all depended on how you defined the word *here*.

"Do you mind my asking why, if there are only two of you and you're both standing here together, why do you need radios to communicate?"

"Certainly you can ask." Charlie One had no intention of telling him anything, not now, not with the three Americans safely back in their hotel. The agent didn't know much, but what little he knew he was fairly confident Washington would not want disclosed. Besides, the three Americans were running out of time. According to the information from bureau headquarters, they were scheduled to be back in D.C. in two days. They would either have to leave in the morning or catch a red-eye the following night. By then they would be somebody else's problem.

"So I take it you're not going to tell us anything?" said the officer.

"I'm sorry, but at the moment I'm not at liberty."

"I see. Well . . ." The cop took a deep breath and stood there for a moment. "Since we can't arrest you and since you're not willing to cooperate, I suppose there's not much we can do, is there?"

The agent didn't want to rub it in. Instead he stood there trying to look sufficiently rebuked so as not to make the man feel bad. He was, in fact, sympathetic to the cop's position. Guests in their country and brothers of the badge, they had needed help many times from the local authorities. The agent knew that it was inevitable that in time they would once again need the help of the Pattaya police.

"Do you mind telling me how long you have been on assignment in Thailand?" said the cop.

"Six years," said the agent.

"Do you like your duty here?"

"Very much."

"Then I would advise that in the future it would be wise to inform us before you do something like this again. Whatever it was you were doing."

"Understood," said the agent.

"Good," said the cop. "I will take your radios. Kindly ask your other agents not to use them. You can inform your embassy that a report of this matter will be filed by my department with the Ministry of Foreign Affairs. If your ambassador wishes to get his radios back, he can check with the ministry."

"I suspect they probably belong to you now," said the agent.

The officer looked at them appraisingly. "Nice radios. You wouldn't happen to have any vehicles around here, would you?"

The agent didn't say a word.

The officer smiled at him. "In the meantime, try not to get in any more trouble." He handed the passports and the FBI credentials back to the agent, turned, and said, "Give them back their cell phones."

TWENTY-THREE

I'm sitting on the edge of the bed in my underwear as Joselyn tries to clean the burn on my lower leg with a damp washcloth from the bathroom as Harry looks on.

"Two days, a lot of money, and a long trip, and we've got squat," I tell them.

Harry is sitting in a chair in the corner. "How do we know the drawer was even the right one? I mean, just because the letters line up with a note you found in Costa Rica . . ."

"Puerto Rico," I tell him. "Waters of Death, same address as on the note, and the only thing in that room that matches it is . . . Ow, that hurts!"

"Don't be a wuss," she says.

"Easy for you to say. It's not your leg."

"A few more inches, and it wouldn't have been yours anymore either," she says. "That bike did a pretty good job on you. Didn't your mother ever tell you to look both ways?"

"Problem was I was looking the wrong way on a

one-way street. Yeah, that's clean enough," I tell her. "Here, let me have the towel."

"You should put something on that," she says. "There's a pharmacy across the street."

"I'll get something later."

"You want to lose your leg, it's up to you," she says. "You sleep in the other bed tonight. I don't want that bloody stump next to me."

"It's not bloody."

"Look at the towel," says Harry.

"Well, OK, so there's a little blood. But it's no stump."

"Give it time," says Joselyn.

"Listen, both of you, just leave me alone. I've got to think."

"About what?" she asks.

"About that drawer and what might have been in it."

"Yeah, well, good luck on that," says Joselyn.

"We had her in our grasp," says Harry.

"We never got that close to her," I tell him.

"Of course not. Sherlock here thought it would be a good idea to let her get just a little farther ahead of us," says Harry. "Then suddenly she and her bag take a ride on a rocket bike."

"OK, so I screwed up."

"Well, there you go. Admission," says Joselyn. "The first step in every idiot's recovery."

"God, but you're cruel," I tell her.

"You're not the one who got left behind in the dark room."

"I thought you would be safer there."

"Always thinking of me," she says.

"I did leave a flashlight."

"What can I say? Thank you. And if any words of mine ever cause you any real pain, would you like me to tell you how to ease the agony?"

"I'm afraid to ask."

"Just stand up and run your lower leg into the side of a bed."

Harry doubles over in laughter from his chair.

"OK, OK. I get it. You're angry."

"Not at all," she says. "If I was angry, you would know it. This is my reaction to a minor annoyance."

"God help me."

"Maybe he will, maybe he won't," she says.

"In the meantime, we're back where we started," says Harry.

"Not entirely," says Joselyn.

"What do you mean?" I look at her.

"While you two were jousting with motorcycles and buses down on the street, I was busy doing a little research."

"On what?" I ask.

"I figured that if the drawer was empty, I may as well take the label."

"You mean WOD?"

"Uh-huh."

"Why?" says Harry.

"Because I didn't have anything to write with," she tells him. "And my memory is not that good."

Harry looks a little baffled.

"The label had more than just the three letters printed on it," I tell him. "There was the name of a company, TSCC Limited."

"We assume the company rented the office space

and in turn rented out the boxes to their clients," says Joselyn. "There were also some telephone numbers, contact information for TSCC printed on the labels."

"Ahh," says Harry.

"So I suppose we can start there in the morning," I tell her. "See if we can get a lead on Liquida by going through the company."

"But that's not all," says Joselyn. "That's what was on the front of the label. On the back were some numbers." She stands up and reaches into her pocket. "By the way, I've got your keys and your flashlight." She hands them to me and then unfolds a small piece of paper. It's the label that was on the drawer. She shows it to me.

Sure enough, on the back are the numbers "00088" printed in the same font as the three letters on the face of the label, only smaller.

"And that's not all."

"What else?" says Harry.

"I checked some of the other labels on the other drawers. Every one of the labels I checked had numbers printed on the reverse side, all of them with five digits, and all starting with zeros."

"What do you make of it?" I ask.

"I don't know. I thought the two of you might have some ideas."

"You know what it sounds like to me," says Harry. "The place is nothing but an old-fashioned drop."

"What do you mean?" says Joselyn.

"I thought it was something that went out with high button shoes," he says. "The numbers rackets used them back in the 1920s to collect cash and receipts from their street runners. Drop it all in the box, and a bagman would go around and clean out the boxes and take it all to the central counting house. That way only one guy knew where the counting house was. Concept is simple. It's just a way of keeping the world at a distance," says Harry. "The OSS put a twist on it during the war. They realized you didn't need a box. Anything could be a drop—the underside of a table in a public restaurant would do if you had some tape. You stick a message there, and as long as the people you're working with know which table is being used, they can collect it and nobody ever has to meet. They drop some colored chalk on the sidewalk out in front of the restaurant and crush it underfoot, white to let people know that the drop was loaded and pink to let the world know the message was received; you didn't even have to know who the people were you were working with."

"What happens if the other side finds out about the drop?" says Joselyn.

Harry arches an eyebrow. "In the case of the OSS, you got trapped, tortured, and when they couldn't get anything more out of you, you probably got hung with a piece of piano wire."

"So what you're saying is that Liquida is a throwback to another age," says Joselyn.

"In a word," says Harry. "He's using a war surplus filing cabinet to collect his mail. The problem is he has it, and we don't."

"But you notice he didn't come and get it himself," I say.

"That would defeat the whole purpose of the drop box," says Harry.

"And you can bet that the people sending mail to him, the ones hiring him, they've never been near that box either. Let me see the label again," says Joselyn.

I hand it to her.

"TSCC. What do you think it stands for?" she says.

"We could Google it. But if Liquida is typical of their clientele, I doubt they're advertising on the Internet. More likely to be word of mouth," says Harry.

"Let me see," I look over Joselyn's shoulder. "We could call the number. It's after hours. Maybe they've got a tape."

A quick consensus that we have nothing to lose finds me with the receiver to the room phone in my hand. I dial for an outside line, a local number, and punch in the eight digits.

I take up the pen and pad by the nightstand and listen for a few seconds as I make a note. "Trident Storage, Courier and Communications," I tell them.

"That sorta covers the field," says Harry.

"Sounds like they will forward your mail if you want it," says Joselyn.

"Except that woman didn't look like any kind of courier I've ever seen," I tell her.

"This is a different kind of courier service," says Harry.

"Did they mention any office hours on the tape?" she asks.

"No. Just push number one if you're calling to have your mail forwarded. Number two if you want to make arrangements to rent a box and three if you want to cancel service."

"Which makes you wonder if they actually have an office," says Harry.

"I think we've seen the office," I tell him.

"So where does that leave us?" Joselyn looks at the two of us.

TWENTY-FOUR

L iquida parked the motorbike in a sea of other bikes at the curb along Beach Road, at the intersection of the narrow alleylike soi that ran along the side of his hotel. He put the bike helmet under the seat and dropped the keys in with it, then locked the seat down. He wouldn't need the bike again.

He walked up the narrow side street. It connected with Second Road, but Liquida didn't go that far. Instead he entered the hotel through the garage and went in the back way. He wanted to avoid any possibility of running into the taxi bike kid at the stand or the girl from the beer bar on the corner across from it. By morning when the car and driver came to pick him up and Liquida checked out, both the girl and the kid would be long gone, catching up on z's for the next night's work.

Liquida climbed the back stairs, slipped into his room, and dropped the beach bag on the bed. He sighed and stretched out on the mattress, relishing the day's work. He realized just how well things had gone. Liquida had not had this much good fortune in months; in fact, not since helping himself to the stash of gold coins from the house in Del Mar near San Diego more than a year before. In the end, that whole episode was soured by the lawyer and his partner, who put the feds onto Liquida's safe-deposit box where the gold was stored.

He noticed that the maid had already been to his room. She had turned down the bed, pulled the blinds, and closed the curtains. He was snug as a bug in a rug with the money, his bags almost packed. But he was tired. He had a few more things to do before he could sleep.

He used the room phone and called Air India. He booked a one-way ticket, business class, on an early morning flight from Bangkok to Paris with a con- nection in Delhi. He used a credit card under the Spanish passport name to hold the ticket and told the ticket agent that he would pay for it with cash at the airport counter.

Next he called the car service and arranged for a vehicle and driver to pick him up at the front of the hotel at 5:15 the following morning. It would give him plenty of time to get to the airport ahead of the 8:55 flight. He called the front desk and asked them to bring up his bill so that he could settle it before he went to bed. Liquida didn't want to go down to the desk. The lobby of the hotel was too close to the taxi stand where the bikers hung out. He didn't want to take the chance that one of them might walk by and see him.

When the bellhop delivered the bill, Liquida paid

with cash using a five-hundred-euro note. When the bellhop returned with the change, Liquida gave him a good tip.

He took a shower and packed the last few items into his luggage. Turning off the lights, he got ready to crawl into bed, then decided to get some fresh air by opening the window.

Liquida drew back the curtains and pulled the cord on the blinds. The traffic on Second Road had thinned considerably. Vehicles were now rolling freely over almost the entire road so that his attention was fixed on the animated motion rather than the one blocked lane on the far side. Liquida turned and took a step toward the bed before the image fully registered in his brain. When it did, the heat that erupted out to the tips of his ears made him feel as if the blood in his veins had become a cauldron of molten lava.

He whipped his head back toward the window. For several seconds he stood there slack-jawed, staring at the light bars on the two police cars and the pickup truck across the way.

They were parked blocking the number one lane on the other side of the road—directly in front of the green door, the entrance to the building where Liquida's box was located.

There were cops everywhere, too many uniforms for Liquida to count. They crawled over the sidewalk in front of the shops on the other side of the street like ants. He watched as three more cops pulled up on motorbikes, parked them, and joined the growing crowd.

Liquida turned and did a double take on the

beach bag near the foot of the bed. He pounced on it like a leopard, dumped all the currency on the bed, and began poring through it all over again, this time more carefully. In a panic, he ripped two of the bills in half before he realized that they were not actually glued together. A thousand euros gone, but Liquida didn't care.

He very nearly grabbed his luggage and ran, leaving the money behind. But a thin seam of logic settled his nerves. He regrouped and began to think. If the euro banknotes housed a tracking device, the cops would already be at his door.

He scooped the money back into the bag and stepped toward the window again. He could see no indication that the cancer of lights and uniforms had spread to this side of the street. If the cops had a lead on him, it was possible they were just starting with their search. If he moved fast, he still had time.

Liquida threw on his clothes, keeping an eye on the spectacle across the street as he buttoned his shirt and buckled his belt. He slipped his feet into the loafers, not bothering with socks. His mind was working all the angles as he did it.

He picked up the phone next to the bed, checked the number, and called the driver who was scheduled to pick him up in the morning. When the man answered, Liquida identified himself by the name on his Spanish passport. He asked how much it would cost to take him to the airport in Bangkok immediately, tonight.

When the man quibbled and said he was already off work, Liquida offered to pay him an additional five thousand baht if the man picked him up in fifteen minutes. The driver told him he could be there in ten.

"Just one change," said Liquida. "Pick me up at Beach Road, the intersection of Soi 13. You will see me. I will be at the corner on the sidewalk with my luggage. Good. See you there. Ten minutes."

Liquida grabbed the white beach bag with the cash inside and stuffed it into the large suitcase. He was taking a chance. Customs generally limited the amount of cash transported across international boundaries to ten thousand dollars unless the funds were declared. Liquida couldn't declare the money without explaining where it came from. He had no choice. He would have to run the gauntlet and hope they didn't look in the bag when he arrived in Paris.

Once there he could use several bank accounts that he maintained in Europe and make deposits through ATM machines. If he spread the funds among several accounts, it would draw less attention. By the time he flew out of Paris, he would no longer be carrying large sums of cash.

He checked his watch, then grabbed the binoculars from the suitcase and took one last look out the window. Liquida couldn't figure how the cops might have gotten onto him. It was possible that they simply stumbled on the drop box. If so, Liquida's timing was impeccable. But he didn't believe in either religion or chance.

He looked to see if either the woman from the bar or the taxi bike driver were among the throng of cops across the street. It was possible either one or the other might have taken his money and then called the police if they were suspicious. If they were being questioned, that would explain it.

He scanned the crowd, looking for the woman's bright-colored dress. He didn't see it. What he did see were two tall Westerners, what the Thais refer to as *farangs*. As he surveyed the crowd, the swirl of commotion, the two Caucasians seemed to be in the eye of the storm. One of them was talking to a Thai cop who looked to be in charge. Liquida didn't have to wait long for confirmation. The cops handed documents back to the two men, what looked like passports and two blue credential cases, the kind used by Interpol, the police, and the FBI. Liquida had seen enough.

He pulled the cord on the blinds and stepped quickly across the room. He repacked the binoculars, grabbed his shaving kit from the bathroom, stashed it in his luggage, and dropped the room key on top of the nightstand. He zipped up the suitcase, grabbed the overnight bag, and stepped out the door, headed for the back stairs.

TWENTY-FIVE

What does that give us?" says Harry. "We have 'T' for Trident; 'S' is storage. Presumably those are the locked drawers themselves, unless there's another storage location we don't know about. The first 'C' stands for courier and the last is communications. The courier I think we know. So what kind of communications you think they're offering?"

"I'm guessing it's probably the client messaging service, the other phone number on the label," says Joselyn.

"I'm for calling it," I tell her.

"Let's do it," says Harry.

I pick up the phone and dial. Joselyn is over my shoulder listening with her ear next to mine. She picks up a notepad and pencil from the nightstand. Two rings and a digital voice answers. "To collect or leave a message, enter the extension number followed by the pound sign. To delete or change messages left on any of your assigned extensions, enter your code." I wait for a second and there is a beep.

I hang up.

"We need to know the extension number to leave or collect messages," I say.

"Back where we started," says Harry.

"Not necessarily." I dial again. This time I wait for the beep and enter the five numbers printed on the back of the WOD label: 00088. Then I punch the pound sign. I wait a few seconds and the system hangs up on me. I try again, only this time I drop the three zeros. I get the same result. The system disconnects. I get a dial tone. I try a three-digit extension and a four-digit extension, dropping one of the zeros on the first call and two on the second. I strike out each time. "Now we're back where we started," I tell them.

"Let's think about this. The instructions on the phone indicate more than one extension per client," says Joselyn. "And Liquida would want more than one."

"Why?" says Harry.

"Because he would need a separate extension for each of his clients. He's not going to want client A listening to the messages he leaves for client B, or for that matter the messages they leave for him, not in his line of work."

Joselyn is right. Liquida would want to keep it all straight. He would want to limit each message to as few ears as possible.

"The instructions on the phone mentioned something else, called a code." She is looking at notes she made on the small writing pad.

"Yeah, I know. I already thought about it," I tell her. "But the only numbers we have are the five digits on the back of the label. I've dialed them in every combination I can think of. If that's Liquida's code, it should have connected, and it didn't."

"Yes, but you didn't dial the right way." She's looking at her notes. "You entered the pound sign. The instructions didn't say anything about a pound sign for the code, only for the extensions."

I dial again, all five digits—00088. This time I omit the pound sign. We wait. A second later, we hear the digitized voice once more.

"Press one for extension 13. Press two for extension 47. Press three for extension 76. Press four for extension 128. Press five for extension 343."

I press one. "There are no messages." I do the same with the second and third extensions. There is nothing on either of them. When I press number 4, the mechanical voice says: "There are two messages. Press one to hear the first message." I do it. We hear a voice.

"This is WOD."

The small hairs on the back of my neck rise with the sound of his voice. I am holding the phone out so that we can all hear it. Joselyn pens a note as quickly as she can, just the essentials: "payment," "job accepted," "Saint-Jacques," "Monday A.M." Then the voice says: "If you wish to delete this message, press seven." The call ends. "Press one to hear the next message." I hit one.

It's another male voice, somebody by the name of Bruno. "The payment for the last job was sent three days ago. Sorry for the delay. I have another commission for you if you are interested. It's a big one. Six-figure fee. Details are with the money. Advise as to availability." And then a click as the man hangs up. "There are no other messages. If you wish to delete this message, press seven." I hang up.

Joselyn heads to her laptop already set up on the desk near the television.

"Where the hell is the Hotel Saint-Jacques?" I ask.

"Gimme a minute," she says.

"There is no clue as to where Liquida is calling from," says Harry. "He could be anywhere."

"My guess is he's here," I tell him.

"Why, because of the girl with the bag? I wouldn't count on it. The contents of that bag could be anywhere by now. They could be shipped overnight halfway around the world by morning."

I look at my watch. "Friday. We have three days. One thing we do know is where he will be come Monday morning. We need to get ahold of Thorpe. Call it in to him."

"Your watch is wrong," says Harry. "When you changed the time, you forgot to change the calendar. We lost a day. We crossed the international date line, remember?"

"You're right."

"It's Saturday night," says Harry. "Twelve hours' difference between here and the East Coast. Opposite ends of the earth. That means it's Saturday morning in Washington."

"Oh, hell," I tell him.

"Thorpe's office is closed," he says. "We could leave a message."

"He'll get it Monday morning," I tell him. "It'll be too late."

"So we call the FBI, one of their field offices," says Harry. "They gotta be open on weekends."

"Where?"

"I don't know," says Harry. "Not here. In the States."

"They won't know us from Adam," I tell him. "By the time they check us out and get on top of it, Liquida will be gone."

"Hotel Saint-Jacques. It's in the Latin Quarter, Left Bank. It's Paris," says Joselyn. "He's headed for Paris."

Liquida zoned out in the back of the limo on the way to the airport. For ninety minutes he drifted in and out. His only worry now was whether the Thai authorities at the airport might have a description of him, or worse, a sketch provided by Madriani's daughter.

If they had the Spanish name from his passport, they probably would have nailed him at the hotel in Pattaya. The hotel had taken a copy of the passport. Liquida had to assume that the passport was still good. He would get a new one the minute he connected with Bruno.

"Oh, shit!" With the name Bruno, it hit him right between the eyes.

"A problem?" said the driver.

"No, no, everything's fine." The message Liquida had left for Bruno was still on the tape. With the cops drilling out his locked box it wouldn't take long before they discovered the message system. That is, if they hadn't already found it.

Liquida whipped out his cell phone and started dialing. He waited for a moment while the instructions played out, then keyed in the code. He listened to his own message and took solace from the fact that the system was still up and running. The message was still there. If the FBI had found it, Liquida was guessing that after listening to the messages, they would have taken the system down and hauled the hardware back to their lab for analysis.

He waited for the message to Bruno to end. The moment it did Liquida pressed seven. "Message deleted." He went on to Bruno's original message left for him and erased that as well. "There are no messages on your system."

He wondered if the eggheads at the FBI would have any way to retrieve deleted messages. If so, by the time the lab sorted it out, he would be gone. Liquida made a mental note to keep his stay in Paris brief.

TWENTY-SIX

The doorbell rang in the D.C. condo. Sarah turned the dead bolt, unhooked the chain, and opened the door without hesitation. She already knew who it was.

"Hello, Ms. Madriani?" The man was in his mid-forties, with short gray hair cut military style and parted neatly on the left. In a blue worsted suit he could have passed for an Iowa banker, but for the FBI credentials he was holding with the flap on its leather case hanging down.

"You must be Agent Ellison." Sarah spoke without looking at the agent or his credentials.

"So they tell me."

Sarah's gaze was stranded on the Olympic-class eye candy standing behind him. By the time she forced her attention back to Ellison, he was already smiling.

"That's OK. I'm getting used to it. Being a potted plant, I mean."

"I'm sorry." Sarah smiled and felt her face glow red.

"The good-looking one here is Mr. Adin Hirst," said Ellison. "Don't feel bad. You should see the secretaries in my office. He leaves in a few days. The place is going to look like a wake when he goes."

"Yes, well, your office called earlier. They told me you would be coming by." She tried to change the subject. "Please come in."

The two men stepped inside. Sarah closed the door behind them. Ellison gave her a business card and told her he was with the Bureau's International Operations Division, training section.

No matter how hard she tried to fix her attention on Ellison, Sarah couldn't help but sneak another glance at the younger one. Six two, dark wavy hair, brown eyes, and tawny complexion. She guessed that the James Bond of the FBI couldn't have been more than mid to late twenties.

She was overjoyed to have company, any company, so this was a pleasant surprise indeed. After four days alone, with only the dog Bugsy for companionship, Sarah was going stir-crazy in the cloistered apartment.

"The handsome one is here for training," said Ellison.

"Gimme a break." Adin blanched. "Don't listen to him. He's been giving me a hard time since we met."

"I can imagine." Sarah looked up at him and smiled coolly.

"Nice to meet you." He reached out and shook her hand.

Sarah had always wondered if such smoking exterior looks routinely spoiled whatever was on the inside. She had never been close enough to find out.

"They told us you had a dog?" Ellison was looking around. "A Doberman?"

"You mean Bugsy," said Sarah. "Not to worry. I locked him in the back room. He's a little skittish around strangers, especially men. I figured you probably didn't need that. Why don't we go in the living room." Sarah led the way. "Go ahead and have a seat. Can I get you some coffee? Something else to drink?"

"I'm fine," said Ellison.

"How about you?"

"I'm good," said Hirst.

The two men planted themselves on the couch like bookends.

Sarah took one of the wingback chairs across from them.

"How are you doing here alone?" said Ellison.

"I'm OK," Sarah lied.

"You know, we have offered to have one of our female agents come and stay with you until your father and your friends get back. It's not a problem."

"I know, but it's not necessary," said Sarah.

"What about counseling?" said Ellison. "I know they've talked to you about having someone from our behavioral science unit come by. We have mental health people on staff. They're not generally into therapy, but they do have training . . ."

"I know, but I think I'm OK."

"OK, but if you change your mind, I want you to call me."

"I will."

"You've got my card," said Ellison.

She looked at the business card. "What, ah, what exactly is the International Operations Division, training section?"

"Back to business," said Ellison. "How much did they tell you on the phone?"

"Nothing," said Sarah.

"IOD has to do with overseas operations. In addition to doing investigations stateside, the FBI also maintains agents in various U.S. embassies around the world. They provide a liaison with law enforcement from other countries. We exchange information, and in that regard we do a fair amount of training. That's where my office comes in."

Sarah nodded as if she understood.

"To make a long story short, you've become part of today's training exercise. That is, if you're willing to do it."

"Sure, why not? I have nothing else to do," said Sarah.

"Adin says that someone from his agency overseas sent him an inquiry last night about getting whatever information he could on witness protection as well as the bureau's safe-house operations. Did I state that correctly?" He looked at Hirst.

"Dead-on."

"So we thought we would start with a tour of the facility. Your name came up, so we thought we'd start here."

"How did my name come up?"

"That was my fault," said Adin. "Someone told

me that your father and his partner and someone else had left . . ."

"That would be Joselyn Cole," said Sarah.

"I figured it would be easier if we were disturbing fewer people. Since you were here alone, you became the guinea pig."

"I see. Well, I'm delighted. So where's home?" she asked Adin.

"I'm afraid I can't tell you that. If I did, I'd have to kill you." The instant he said it, Adin made a face. "Forget I said that."

"That's OK." Sarah smiled.

"Good move, Adin. You get twenty points deducted for lack of tact," said Ellison. "Want to try for more?"

"I'm sorry."

"It's all right, really."

"Adin sometimes works undercover. Though how he manages it with moves like that, I'm not sure," said Ellison.

"Undercover I leave the levity at home," said Adin. "The only time I screw up is when I'm myself, in a bar with a girl."

"Foot-in-mouth syndrome?" said Sarah.

"You've seen this with other stupid guys, I take it," said Adin.

"A few times." She laughed. "So is Adin Hirst your real name?"

He made a face, like maybe yes, maybe no.

"I don't want to be killed. So I won't ask any more questions," said Sarah. "What is it you need from me?"

"I have a short questionnaire. A couple of pages," said Hirst. "If you can fill it out at your leisure and send it back through Agent Ellison's office, that would be a big help."

"Sure."

"When, ah, when are your father and his friends going to be back?"

"I'm not sure."

"Where did they go?"

"I can't tell you that. If I did, I'd have to kill you." Sarah smiled at him.

Hirst laughed. "Touché."

"You speak French, you must be from France."

"Funny you should say that. All the girls I kiss tell me the same thing."

"Oh, you're bad," she said. "I'll bet that's not on your résumé." She looked at Ellison, who was red to the tips of his ears. "Did you know you had a professional tonsil hockey player on your team?"

"Now you see, you're wrong," said Hirst. "With me it's only a hobby."

"I think maybe . . . I think we should, ah . . ." He looked at Sarah. "You're not on sound surveillance here, are you?"

"God, I hope not."

"I think we should look around a little. The unit itself, the apartment," said Ellison. "And maybe talk to you a little about your experiences here."

"This is about the best one I've had since I got here," said Sarah.

All three of them cracked up. Sarah thought Ellison might have a heart attack. He was laughing that hard. When he finally regained his composure, he opened his notebook as he wiped a tear from his eye. "Let's try to get serious here for a moment. Let's start with a critique of security, starting with the front door," said Ellison. He looked at Hirst.

"Good point," said Adin. "Let's see. Why did you open the door?" He looked at Sarah.

"What do you mean?"

"It's a simple question. Why did you open the door?"

"Because you rang the bell."

"How did you know who it was?" said Hirst.

"Because your office called. I told you."

"I have no doubt somebody called," said Adin. "But how did you know it was the FBI?"

"Because that's what they told me. Who else would have the number to this condo? It's unlisted. The place is run by the FBI," said Sarah.

"All of that is true," said Ellison. "Still, what Adin is saying is correct. It's possible that an unlisted number, even one issued to the bureau, can be discovered by an outside party. If so, they can call the number and identify themselves as anyone."

"I assume that perhaps you've given the number out to relatives?" said Hirst.

Sarah nodded a little sheepishly. "Just my aunt and uncle back in Ohio. No one told me I couldn't."

"That's why the FBI has to keep changing the numbers," said Adin.

"So when your office called . . . I assume it was your office?"

"It was," said Ellison.

"So what was I supposed to do?"

"As soon as they identified themselves," said Adin,

"you should have taken the name of the person calling, and the division or office they were calling from. Get all the information and details you can, write it all down. If they want to give you a phone number, fine, but don't call that number. As soon as they hang up you call downstairs to the duty desk and give the agent all the information. He or she will call the division, check it out, and get back to you."

"And until they do, you don't open the door when someone shows up," said Ellison.

"I see. I thought the place was safe," said Sarah.

"It is, but because of the people we house here, it's also a target. Precautions are in order," said Ellison.

"I screwed up," said Sarah.

"How could you know? You came in late, and you're here alone. I'm sure your father and the others were given an orientation, brief as it might have been. They no doubt assumed whoever was on the duty desk would do the same with you. They didn't." Ellison took out a small pad and made a note. "What else did you see?"

"Me?" said Sarah.

"No. The hockey player here. He's the one being graded," said Ellison.

"When she opened the door, the chain was off," said Hirst.

"Right. That door is steel, and it's imbedded in a steel frame," said Ellison. "The bolts fastening the safety chain are three inches long. They are threaded all the way through the steel frame and into the masonry wall. Same with the hinges. The chain itself is titanium, three-eighths-inch links.

Somebody tries to kick that door open, they're going to break their foot. The same with their shoulder. Of course, none of that works if you open the door without the chain on. That's what it's for. What else?" said Ellison.

"The credentials," said Hirst.

"What about them?"

"She didn't look at them, and even if she did, it wouldn't have mattered," said Adin.

"How do you know she didn't look at them?"

"Because she was looking at me."

"OK, we won't dwell on that one," said Ellison. "What should she have done?"

"Assuming she had confirmation of our visit from the duty desk, she should have opened the door with the chain on, taken the credentials through the opening, and made sure that the name on the credentials squared with the name from the duty desk."

"And if not?" said Ellison.

"Slam the door on our fingers and call the duty desk," said Adin.

"Maybe we should start over so I can practice," said Sarah. "You can go outside the door. I can put the chain on, and you hand me whatever you want through the crack." She stared at Adin.

"I don't think I want to do that. Not with that look in your eye." He smiled.

"And the dog," said Ellison. "For the time being, until your father and his friends get back, do yourself a favor and don't lock him up. Especially if someone you don't know comes to visit."

"Got it," said Sarah.

"Good. Then we'll give Adin a tour of the unit, let him see the layout, ask any questions. Perhaps we'll let the Doberman growl at his groin and we'll go," said Ellison.

TWENTY-SEVEN

Liquida cleared French customs at Charles de Gaulle Airport in Paris and stopped to purchase a few quick items, four separate French SIM cards for his unlocked cell phone and a small pocket French/English dictionary. He grabbed a cab and told the driver to take him to the Hotel Saint-Jacques on the rue des Écoles.

In the backseat of the cab, Liquida slipped one of the SIM cards into his phone and then checked the dictionary. He had the driver get the telephone number for the hotel's front desk from taxi dispatch. Liquida then called the number and asked to speak with Monsieur B. Merchand. It was an alias Bruno had used before; the B for Bruno, with the surname "Merchant" translated into the language of the country he was residing in at the moment.

A few seconds later he heard the familiar voice on the other end: "Hello!"

"WOD here."

"Ah, good to hear from you. I got your message. Where are you?"

Liquida was both relieved and disturbed to learn that Bruno had retrieved his message from the Thai messaging system before it had been removed. He wondered if anyone else had. He quickly conferred with the driver, then back to the phone and Bruno: "We are about twenty minutes out." Liquida checked his watch. "We should be there by eleven. I assume you have the documents?"

"I do," said Bruno.

The Spanish passport Liquida had been using since his flight from the States was burning a hole in his pocket. He wanted to get rid of it as soon as possible. French immigration would show airport entry of the Spanish businessman at Charles de Gaulle. Of course, Liquida was not so foolish as to list his residence in Paris as the Saint-Jacques on his entry immigration card. Instead he wrote down "The Ritz," one of the few Paris hotels he could recall off the top of his head. Now Liquida would use the Spanish passport to send the FBI on a wild-goose chase.

"Is there a café where we can meet before I check in? Perhaps you can bring the documents?" asked Liquida.

Bruno got the message. Liquida was on the run, as usual. "There is a coffee shop directly across the street. La Petite Périgourdine. You can't miss it." They exchanged SIM card phone numbers in case Liquida got lost.

"I will see you in twenty minutes." Liquida hung up.

*   *   *

The two men sat at a quiet table at the back of the café, Liquida's rolling luggage next to him as he examined the three new passports Bruno delivered to him. The photograph on each was the same, a stock shot Bruno maintained just for this purpose.

"Good." Liquida checked the entry and exit stamps, looked at the dog-eared pages, a few of which were suitably stained. All three of the passports were well worn. He noticed that one of them, the Italian passport, bore an entry stamp for the Charles de Gaulle Airport dated that day. "Very good. What about departure? Will it clear the French immigration computer?"

"There is no need to worry," said Bruno. "You will not be going out through immigration. We have arranged private transport, a Gulfstream from a secluded runway near Marseilles. The plane belongs to the client. It's long range. From there to Morocco for refueling and on to Mexico. Only one stop."

To Liquida this was sounding better and better. "When do we leave?"

"When the job is done here."

Liquida sipped an espresso from the small cup as Bruno gave him the details on the two NASA defectors. "There is only one problem," said Bruno. "We cannot move forward until we get the missing data from the Iranian. His name is Raji Fareed."

"You would think he would want to cooperate," said Liquida. "Can't you appeal to his patriotism?"

"We tried that. It seems that his family fled when the shah was toppled back in the seventies. He went to the States as a young boy. We're not sure what's going on. Perhaps he doesn't like the current regime. If so, he's not saying. He says he has the software, but he doesn't want to deliver it. He wants to go back to the States."

"That's not going to happen," said Liquida.

"No. We thought perhaps he just wanted to re-negotiate the deal. We tried that. It didn't work. At this point, it's neither here nor there. Bottom line is, we have to get the information and we have to do it quickly."

"What about the other one? Maybe he can help," said Liquida.

"You mean Leffort? No. There is bad blood be-tween the two of them. Fareed seems to think that Leffort is getting a better deal. More money. It seems Leffort antagonized him before they even arrived."

"Is he?"

"Is he what?" said Bruno.

"Getting a better deal," said Liquida.

"I don't know. I don't care. Leffort is highly edu-cated, very smart, lets you know it all the time. A real asshole, if you know what I mean. I suspect he has been playing mind games with the Iranian for some time. Telling him one thing, doing another. Keeping secrets, as well as most of the advance pay-ments from what I gather. It's been going on since before they left the States. By the time they arrived here, the two of them were barely talking. If it were up to me, I would have you cut both their fucking throats. Unfortunately, according to the client, we need to get the information from the Iranian, and Leffort is necessary to the project," said Bruno.

"Which is?"

"Making money." Bruno looked at him as if the Mexican had just walked on sacred ground. "I don't ask. I don't care as long as they pay me. And these clients pay very well. There is a bonus for all of us if we deliver the data and the necessary personnel to Mexico by the due date."

"How much?" said Liquida.

"To you, two hundred and fifty thousand dollars, U.S."

"When is the deadline?"

"Five days from now."

If Bruno was telling him a quarter of million to expedite delivery, Liquida knew that Croleva was getting three or four times that much.

"Which takes us back to the Iranian," said Bruno.

"There are ways to make a tongue wag," said Liquida.

"Yes, I know, electrodes and car batteries. The problem is that here we are talking sophisticated computer software programs. Something you and I would not know from a Chinese anagram. Once we torture him, we alienate him. The man, Raji, he is no fool," said Bruno. "Beyond that, he is Persian."

"What does that have to do with it?"

"His pride has already been injured. He is feeling insulted because of the way Leffort has treated him. If we torture him, he may decide not to talk and force us to kill him."

"Of course, I don't know the man," said Liquida, "and all of his body parts might not be working so well anymore, but I'm pretty sure I could persuade him to cooperate before he takes his last breath."

"In which case he may give us something worthless," said Bruno. "With these clients you don't want to jam a piece of software in their machine and find out you have the original version of Pac-Man."

"The other one, this Leffort. He wouldn't be able to look at it and tell us?" asked Liquida.

"No. He says he won't know if the final software is good until he is able to test it at the facility in Mexico."

Liquida liked to work alone. It was how he had stayed alive this long. Strip Bruno's chitchat to the essentials and the message was clear; the two guys from NASA were the walking dead. The minute their jobs were finished, so were they. Liquida didn't want to be standing around them when it happened. It could be contagious. A call to do the wet work on them wouldn't have twitched a brow on his forehead. But not this. To Liquida this sounded like an invitation to a funeral—his own. Although he didn't like it, at the moment he didn't have much choice. "One thing I don't care for here is the location. You have them set up in the hotel across the street, right?"

"What's wrong with it?" said Bruno.

"It's just that the Latin Quarter is a tourist area. The Iranian gets away from you here, you're going to have your hands full. There are too many prying eyes and nosy sightseers," said Liquida. "Let me take them out to the suburbs." Liquida wrinkled an eyebrow at Bruno. He was talking about neighborhoods to the northeast where angry Arab immigrants burned hundreds of cars each night, whenever they felt a grievance coming on. "Let the Iranian see what's going on out there. It may loosen his tongue."

"No time for that," said Bruno. "Besides, there are too many police and French intelligence out that way. My people are already set up in the hotel. Just keep your knife in its sheath and use your head. A little finesse. That is what is called for here. I am sure you can do it. I have confidence in you."

"Whatever you say." The reason Liquida wanted out of the hotel was not because it was a tourist site. He had left the name "Hotel Saint-Jacques" on the message machine in Thailand. Liquida began to sweat, wondering if the FBI might already have the place under surveillance. With a fresh passport and another hotel, Liquida would have had a new lease on life. Time to figure out what to do. Now he would have to cross the street and walk into the hotel with his luggage and hold his breath as he did so.

On the way in from the airport, after talking to Bruno on the phone, Liquida had made one more call. This one was to the private courier in Dubai, the dispatch service that was holding his anonymous letter. He told them to deliver it and gave the address of the U.S. Embassy in Dubai, Office of the Legal Attaché.

Liquida had checked on the hotel computer in Dubai just before leaving. His FBI poster on their website was now updated with a sketch. This had to be courtesy of Madriani's daughter. It wasn't a very good likeness. He felt it failed to properly display the strength of character in his face. It looked like a picture made by a machine. Still, it was one more fly in the ointment, something to contend with whenever he flew commercial.

Liquida's anonymous letter was in reference to

the FBI's most wanted website, not the old one used for gangsters, but the new one on terrorism. In the letter Liquida claimed to be a physician in Dubai. Liquida had postdated the letter by two days, knowing that he would be out of the country by then. He withheld his name, explaining that he could not take the chance of publicly assisting the American FBI since he resided and worked in such a dangerous region of the world. He explained that a foreigner had come into his office requesting medical attention. The man claimed to be a guest staying at the Dubai Beach Resort. He wanted the doctor to remove some surgical staples from what he claimed was a wound under his arm. While the doctor was happy to assist, he recognized the injury as a knife wound and immediately became suspicious. Later after the man left, he checked the few sources available to him online and discovered a wanted poster on the FBI website showing a sketch that looked very much like his patient. One of the aliases posted under the sketch was the name "Liquida."

If the FBI found anything in Thailand, Liquida was hoping to send them in another direction, back to Dubai. By the time they checked out the lead in the Arab Emirates and discovered that the Spanish passport had moved from there in the other direction, to Thailand and then on to Paris, Liquida planned to be long gone, under a different name and on a different continent. He hoped that by then the Americans would be hooked on the Spanish passport. Liquida had plans for that as well.

He didn't dare tell Bruno that the FBI was breathing up his ass and that the Paris hotel might be compromised. Bruno would pull out of the Latin Quarter all right, but only after one of his henchmen pumped a bullet into Liquida's brain and dumped his body in the Seine. The only way out now was to work and work fast, to get out of Paris and back to Mexico where he knew the lay of the land. Perhaps it was all a matter of perspective, but for Liquida, suddenly the old cartels were not looking nearly so bad.

TWENTY-EIGHT

Waiting for our flight from Bangkok to Paris, I borrow Joselyn's laptop. She is an Apple user. I am not. She sets up the e-mail for me, and I send two quick e-mail messages.

The first message goes to Thorpe telling him about the Hotel Saint-Jacques and Liquida's message on the tape along with the number code to get into it. I tell him that we are on our way to Paris, hoping that maybe he will have someone there to meet us. The second e-mail I also send to Thorpe but with a request that it be delivered to Sarah. I tell her we are headed to Paris, but I give her none of the details. I tell her not to worry, that we hope to be back in just a few more days.

I would have called Thorpe's office, but since it is the weekend, and with a twelve-hour time difference between Bangkok and Washington, all I would get was his voice mail.

When I finish with the laptop, Joselyn takes it back and treats us to the mysteries of Earth Google and Google Maps. Within less than a minute she shows us the street view of the Hotel Saint-Jacques in Paris using Google Maps. Moving the camera's perspective she is able to glide in front of the place, adjust the angle of view to look at the hotel from the ground level to the roof, and move down the side streets as if we were there. Cars on the road and pedestrians on the sidewalk are all stopped in freeze-frames as if frozen in time.

"How did you do that?" Harry is mesmerized.

"I'm sure you've seen this before," she tells him.

"I've seen maps," says Harry. "But not like that."

"Watch." She does it again, zooms in from the satellite view to the bubble that appears on the street and from there to the sidewalk view. "It's easy," she says.

"Maybe for you." Harry is leaning over her shoulder looking at the screen. "How often do they update the pictures?"

"I'm not sure," she says.

"Maybe if we watch long enough, we can catch Liquida coming out of the building," says Harry.

Joselyn stops moving her finger over the tracker and looks back at him with big round eyes. The smile spreads across her face as she laughs. "You have a good poker face." She turns back toward the screen. "For a second I thought you were serious."

Harry shoots me a dense look.

"Even the village idiot knows the satellite over-head and ground photos are not in real time," says Joselyn. "And, in answer to your question, they probably upgrade the photos every few years."

"Wouldn't want you to think I'm some techno-bozo with a bone through my nose," says Harry. "But are there any programs out there that give you pictures in real time?"

"Not unless you have an office at Langley with the CIA," she tells him. "I wanted to take a look at the area around the Hotel Saint-Jacques so we can see the lay of the land. Maybe we can scout out a place to stay. Somewhere safe."

She has a point.

Joselyn moves back to the map page and starts typing in a search for other hotels in the area.

There is no one from the FBI to meet us at the airport in Paris when we arrive. I suspect Thorpe may not have received the message.

By the time we approach the Hotel Claude Bernard, it is dark. The street outside looks nothing like the daytime pictures we saw on Joselyn's computer nearly twelve hours earlier.

The incandescent lights in the restaurants and bistros combine with the eerie glow from the brighter lights of central Paris to give the neighborhood a fairy-tale-like appearance. Based on the map, the Bernard is about three hundred yards west of the Hotel Saint-Jacques and on the same side of the street, the rue des Écoles.

According to the computerized map, there are two other hotels that are closer, but the Bernard appears, to us at least, to be safer because of the distance. There is not much chance of running into Liquida by accident unless we get careless; that is, assuming he is booked at the Saint-Jacques. It is at times like this I miss Herman and his streetwise instincts for knowing how heavily, and where, to tread. The fact that Herman, who lives in the dark crevices of tracking and surveillance, was ambushed by Liquida in a dim garage in Washington is not lost on any of us.

Businesses crowd the sidewalks on both sides down the rue des Écoles, mostly small shops, restaurants, and other boutique hotels. Our taxi pulls up and stops at the sidewalk in front of the hotel. Harry, who is up front with the driver, speaks pidgin English and does sign language gesturing for him to get our bags. The guy sits there with a cigarette dangling from his lip. He seems not to understand a word of English other than the name of our hotel.

The Claude Bernard has a redbrick façade on the ground level with five stories above, including the penthouse. Wrought-iron-railed balconies reminiscent of those in New Orleans wrap the building on three of the upper floors.

Harry spies a boulangerie behind us and just across the street, kitty-corner to the hotel. He has his taste buds set for coffee and a pastry. It has been a while since our last meal on the plane. Riding in coach, we didn't get much.

"Later," I tell him. "We need to get off the street and up into the rooms." Though we are a good block away from the Saint-Jacques, it wouldn't do to have Liquida cruise by and see us.

The driver is out, getting the bags from the trunk. Joselyn and I collect our belongings from the backseat of the taxi. "Seeing as none of us speak French, how do we pay the guy?" says Harry.

"Hold out money," says Joselyn.

"What, and let him take what he wants?" says Harry.

"The price of cultural ignorance," she tells him.

"So we shouldn't come to France unless we speak French, is that it?" he says.

"In a word, yes."

"It's that kind of attitude that's gotten American tourists speaking English in Paris turned into spittoons," says Harry. "Why don't you and I get the luggage?" He looks at me. "I'll deal with the driver. Qué quantos euros?" says Harry.

"Your Spanish is as bad as your French," says Joselyn.

"Tell you what, why don't you get the rooms?" he tells her. "The desk clerk will be less likely to spit on a woman." Harry hands Joselyn his credit card and smiles at her. "You might want to wear a raincoat."

"Fine." She grabs the credit card from his hand. "No problem. Should we put both rooms on this one or do you have a card you'd like to give me as well?" She looks at me, all pissed off.

"What did I say?"

"Do you have a credit card or not?"

"It all comes out of the same pot," I tell her. Harry and I are using business credit cards, and the business is very nearly drained.

Joselyn gets out of the car and slams the door like she is trying to break the window.

"Here," Harry hands me some euros. "You deal with the driver. I'll get the bellman to get the bags."

Before I can say anything, Harry is out of the car, following Joselyn toward the entrance.

I get out on the driver's side and stand pressed against the side of the car as traffic passes by.

The driver tosses the last bag onto the sidewalk. It's a good thing we aren't carrying glass. He closes the trunk and comes around to the driver's side.

"How much?" I hold up the euros.

He gives me a face. I get the sense that he understands every word, but he's not going to say it, not in English anyway. He flashes five fingers with his right hand and one more with his left, cigarette ash dripping down the front of his tweed coat. He wants sixty euros. I don't know if this is correct or not, but I pay him. When the last ten-euro note hits his hand, he takes it with the other and stands there with his hand still out waiting for more. He wants a tip. I give him five euros. He looks at it as if it's shriveling in his palm and turns his nose up. For a moment I think perhaps he is going to give it back to me. Instead he pockets it, looks at me with disgust, and flips what is left of his cigarette. It hits my shoe. He does this with such accuracy that I suspect it is well practiced. He gets into the taxi, slams the door, and pulls away. He nearly runs over my toes as I stand in the street.

Harry is out on the sidewalk with the bellman. They have the bags stacked on a cart. I follow them into the hotel. By the time we get there, Joselyn is engaged in animated conversation with the desk clerk, a young man she seems to have charmed.

"What did I tell you?" says Harry. "Send a pretty woman to deal with a Frenchman, you get smiles and French bullshit. You and me, we just get the bullshit."

As we approach, Joselyn turns and says: "Hi, guys. I'd like you to meet Michel."

"Bonjour!" says the guy behind the desk. "Comment vous appelez-vous?" He looks at me, waiting for a reply.

I stand there like a potted plant.

He looks at Joselyn, then back at me. "Parlez-vous français?"

I shake my head. "No."

"No parlez-vous?"

"No."

The clerk rips up the registration card he had already started and throws it at me.

"Now you've done it," says Joselyn.

The clerk sprays us with a stream of French I suspect is laced with profanities. Then he points toward the door. "Sortez! Get out!" He motions for us to take our bags and leave.

I stand there like a jackass, foot in my mouth.

"All he wanted was your name," says Joselyn. "Tell him your name, stupid!" Joselyn is staring at me, hands on her hips.

"Enough of this shit," says Harry. "Let's get out of here."

"PAUL, my name is Paul. Paul Madriani." I'm ready to genuflect, crawl on my hands and knees. All I want is a room.

The clerk looks me up and down, weighing whether to toss us into the street or try again. Slowly he pulls another card as he looks at me with contempt. He writes something on it. I'm guessing it's my name.

"You better answer the next question correctly or we're going to have to start all over again looking for another hotel," says Joselyn. "I don't know about you, but I'm tired."

"You didn't tell me you spoke French."

"I don't. Mike here is from Colorado. He attends the university in Boulder."

I look at her.

She starts to laugh.

The clerk starts to break up.

A few seconds later the two of them are belly laughing all over the counter.

"Very funny!" I tell them.

"You catch the look on his face?" She is pointing at me, talking to the clerk, tears running down her cheeks, she is laughing so hard. "I thought he was going to pee in his pants."

The clerk nods. "Sorry, mister, she made me do it." He speaks in perfect American English. He is still laughing.

"OK, so I've been had." I start to join them.

"Mike is touring Europe, working for a stint to earn money." Joselyn is wiping her eyes; looking at me, she starts to crack up again. "Consider yourself spit on," she says.

"I was ready to walk out," says Harry.

"You can if you want, but I'm staying the night," says Joselyn.

"Sorry," says the kid. "She put me up to it. I couldn't resist." He laughs.

"She would." I smile at him and shake his hand. "How long have you been working here?"

"Two months. I took a year off school to travel. Studied French in high school and college. Actually my French is not that good."

"Could have fooled me."

"He did," says Joselyn. She looks at Harry and slaps him on the shoulder. "See, not everybody in Paris spits on you."

"Easy for you to say. You still have your toes," I tell her.

"What's that supposed to mean?"

"I'll tell you later. What do we have for rooms, Mike?"

"He's upgrading us, third floor, street view with balconies," says Joselyn.

"Excellent!"

"Let him piss on us again, maybe we can get the penthouse," says Harry.

"Sorry, but it's already booked," says the kid.

"Is it possible to get two adjoining rooms?" I ask.

"Let me see. I think I can do that." He checks the computer. "Yes."

"Good. You get a bigger tip than the taxi driver," I tell him. "Even so, I doubt if it will probably take you far in this town."

"If you mean it's expensive, you're right. But then I don't live in the Latin Quarter."

"Where do you live?" I ask.

"I've got a small flat out in the suburbs. Place called Rosny-sous-Bois. And a roommate to share the cost."

"Another American?" says Joselyn.

He nods. "A friend from Colorado."

"How long you gonna be here?"

"Another few weeks, then we're off to Italy. How about you guys, on holiday? Vacation?"

"Not exactly," I tell him.

"Here on business, then."

"You could say that. Do you work the desk every day?" I change the subject.

"I'm on nights this week. But you won't have any trouble with the language if that's what you're worried about. The house operator speaks perfect English, as does much of the staff. Just tell them Mike sent you. That you're friends of mine. They'll treat you very well. Parisians are actually quite friendly once you break through the veneer."

"I know. It's just getting through that diamond veneer that worries me," says Harry. "Guy could die on the street looking for directions."

"It's not that bad," says the clerk.

"Not if you speak French," says Harry.

The clerk hands one key to me and the other to Harry, then slaps the bell on the counter for the bell-man with the luggage cart to take us to our rooms.

"Any chance of renting a car for a few hours tomorrow?" I ask.

"It can be arranged. Just call down to the desk. Phillippe is on tomorrow. He will take care of you."

A car could be handy. It provides a place to hide out if we want to watch the front of Liquida's hotel, especially at night, and a fast way to escape in a pinch if we need it.

I hand the kid behind the counter a fifty-euro note and watch his face as it lights up. "Oh! Merci beaucoup!" he says. "That means thank you."

"The show was worth it," I tell him.

"Thank you for everything," Joselyn says to Mike as she takes my arm. "Now I am afraid to go up to the room with them."

"If they give you any trouble, just call the front desk," says the kid. "I'll send up our chef, Marcel, with a butcher knife."

"I'll keep it in mind," she tells him.

We turn and follow the bellman toward the elevator.

"Maybe you could call down later and get Marcel's phone number," I tell Joselyn.

"Or we could just lead Liquida to the kitchen," she says.

"I'd rather do takeout," says Harry. "Call Thorpe and tell him his man's in the frappé."

TWENTY-NINE

The shadow moving across her Nook reader caused Sarah to glance upward. She found herself looking into angel eyes staring down at her.

"Hello," he said.

"What are you doing here?"

"Seems that we are now neighbors." Adin Hirst was standing there with a cup of coffee in one hand, a bagel in the other, and a smile on his face. "Mind if I sit?"

"No. Help yourself." Sarah closed the cover on her reader. She had taken to spending a few minutes each afternoon in the small coffee shop on the ground level of the FBI's condo complex.

"What are you reading?" Adin set the plate with the bagel and his coffee cup on the table, and then sat down across from her.

"Oh, just rereading some of the things I had to read in college. Doing it for enjoyment this time." Sarah was going nuts up in the apartment, she and the dog climbing the walls. She had an hour every other day in the company of one of the FBI agents to walk the dog. That was it, her only foray out of the building.

"Can I look?" Adin gestured toward the reader.

She handed it to him.

"I've seen these, but I've never held one." He hefted it in his hand. "It's very light, isn't it?"

"Yes."

He opened the cover. She hadn't turned it off. "*Gatsby*. You're a Fitzgerald fan," said Hirst.

"You've read it?"

He nodded. "Wonderfully written, not a word wasted. Cuts to the soul of his characters like a knife. How many books will this thing hold?"

"They say fifteen hundred, but I'm not sure. It probably depends on the length of the books."

"That's amazing. So what do you do, download the books through your computer?"

"No, it's 3G. Has its own chip. You just go online into their library and order what you want, pay with a credit card, and it downloads in about sixty seconds. I have a Kindle upstairs, same thing, but a different library. That way I get a broader selection of books."

"Incredible," said Hirst. "What will the Americans think of next? I'm going to have to look into it." He smiles and hands it back to her.

"What's this about being neighbors?" said Sarah.

"I'm now living in the building." Adin took a sip of coffee. "Whew, that's hot!"

"Since when?"

"Since yesterday." He wiped his lips with a napkin. "The lease on my apartment was up. I tried to renew for a short time and couldn't, so the bureau offered to put me up here until the program is over."

"I see. What floor?"

"Eight. Same as yours."

"You are close."

"Just around the corner." He smiled at her and nibbled around the edges of the bagel. "How is your dog?"

"He's fine. But he needs more exercise. He's starting to give off gas in the evenings. Lies on the carpet and issues forth with silent clouds of death, if you know what I mean."

He laughed. "If you like, I can take him out and give him a run."

"That would be good. The only problem is, I need exercise too."

"I'm not sure they'd let me do that," said Adin. "I mean, take you for a run."

"I knew what you meant." Sarah smiled. "They let us out every other day. Just for an hour, under the gaze of a friendly agent. It's like being in prison."

"Actually most prisoners get more yard time than that," said Adin.

"I don't mean to complain, but I can't wait to get home, back to a normal life."

"And when's that going to be?"

"I don't know. Hopefully when my father gets back, I'll know more."

"Where are they?"

Sarah almost told him, then hesitated. "Right now I'm not sure. They should be back in a few days." Sarah knew they were in Paris, for how long she wasn't sure. She had received a printout of an e-mail message from her father. It was delivered to her by the FBI, but there were few details. "I should have some company in a day or so. Herman, my dad's PI, is going to be staying with me in the condo . . ."

"PI?"

"Private investigator. My dad's a lawyer. He and his partner have a firm in Coronado near San Diego. Herman investigates cases for them. He was injured here in Washington."

"I see."

"He's recovering. They decided to put him up in the condo rather than a skilled nursing facility where they'd have to provide security. His sister who had been visiting him in the hospital had to return to her job in Detroit. They'll have a nurse on call as needed in the condo. I told them I'd be happy to prepare his meals. It will give me something to do."

"You probably shouldn't be telling me all this," said Hirst.

"Why? Are you going to print it in the newspaper?"

"No. It's just that it's best sometimes to keep everything on a need-to-know basis."

"Need-to-know basis—what's that, spy talk?"

"No. Well, maybe. Sometimes. But not between you and me."

"Good. It seems I never get a chance to talk to anybody. The only one I can talk to is Bugsy, and except for the noxious fumes, that's a one-way conversation."

"I see," he said as he smiled.

"Lately I've started talking to myself."

"I'm told that's not a serious problem until you start answering yourself."

"And I've done that a few times," she told him.

"The crazy lady in 805," said Adin. "That's OK; it'll be our secret. I won't tell a soul. Just speak into my lapel."

"You know, I have wondered if they have cameras and microphones in the rooms," said Sarah.

"Oh God, I hope not!" Adin said it with a stark look in his eyes. They both laughed.

Sarah liked his face. She liked everything about him. It was hard not to. There was a strange kind of calm about him, something understated that made him seem older than his years. "So tell me about yourself."

"What, for example?"

"How old are you?"

"Thirty."

"You don't look that old."

"I can cut off a leg and show you the rings if you like."

She laughed. "That won't be necessary. Where are you from?"

"Another land."

"Yes, I know. You already told me that. Which one?"

"I'm an extraterrestrial from Delphi X," he says. "I left my pointed ears out in the car."

"Give me a break," she says.

"I'm not supposed to say."

"I see; so you're a national security secret, is that it?"

"Not exactly."

"You could at least be a gentleman and give me a clue."

Adin held up the bagel, turned it over in his hand, and examined it. Then he looked at her through the hole in the center. "Are you any good at pantomimes?"

"Spyglass?"

He gave her a look of failure and shook his head. Then he licked the bagel, looked at it covetously, and took a bite.

"Bread?"

He gave an angry expression and pointed at the bagel.

"Bagels."

He didn't nod, but he smiled.

"Jewish. Israel?"

"I didn't say anything."

"You're Israeli! I had a friend in college who was from Israel."

"Did you like him?"

"He was a she."

"Ah. Did you like her?"

"I'm not sure how you mean that."

"I mean, were you attracted to her personally, or was it her personality?"

"Personality." Sarah gave him a scolding sideways glance.

"Now that that's settled, I wonder . . . do you think it would be worthwhile if I had my room scanned for hidden mics and minicams?"

"I don't know. Do you play with yourself at night?" said Sarah.

"No, but it sounds like I'm going to be." He snapped his fingers.

She laughed.

"You know, I think it's going to be very difficult to bring women into this place. I mean, with agents at the front desk and all."

"You should have thought about that before you moved in."

"I did, but it's not working out." He winked at her, and they both laughed.

THIRTY

NASA had hung Raji out to dry. When he had talked with Leffort in the car back in California and told him that he had the final targeting software and that it was tucked away in a safe place, Fareed had lied.

For some reason there had been a delay. The software that was supposed to have been completed by the work group a week earlier was in fact not completed until the very morning of their departure for Paris.

Fareed barely had time to download it from his office computer to the flash drive and tuck it away before Leffort was on him, pushing him toward the car and the airport so they could get away. Since then he had not been out of Leffort's sight long enough to transmit it.

Now Raji was a prisoner, trapped in his room in the Hotel Saint-Jacques. A guard sat in the hallway outside his door. The window was bolted shut, as were the French doors that led onto the small balcony outside his room. All of his meals were delivered by the guard. The telephone had been disconnected, and the Wi-Fi, the wireless signal to the Internet that Raji had glimpsed just briefly on his laptop upon arrival, disappeared within seconds after they locked the door.

They ransacked his computer and found nothing. They gave it back to him and told him that if the software was stored somewhere online that they would be happy to connect him so that he could download it. Raji knew they would stand over him the entire time, watching his every move the second they turned on the wireless connection. He told them he needed to think about it.

The bald one, the man they called Bruno, visited him several times each day bargaining with him, cajoling him, doing everything possible to extract the final software that they needed, and that only Fareed possessed.

On one occasion they sent Leffort in alone to talk with Fareed in hopes that maybe he could convince Raji to give up the data. Again Raji put him on hold.

Fareed realized quickly that the story that he merely wanted to go home wasn't working. Bruno was not the sort who could get his head around notions of homesickness. He dealt in a world of money and greed. So Raji gave him something he could comprehend. In their next meeting, he told Bruno that Leffort had cheated him on the deal for the sale of the data, and that if Bruno would transfer the agreed-upon sum into a numbered account of Fareed's choosing and make acceptable arrangements for his safety and freedom, Raji would transmit the software back to him.

While it was a naive proposal, the motivations behind it were at least something Bruno could understand, money and survival.

Bruno smiled, slapped Raji on the shoulder, and told him they would have to talk some more.

Fareed knew they had no intention of letting him go. He was playing for time.

This evening Bruno arrived and tried to tempt him with bits of information. At one point he repeated his original promise that they would all be moving on, including Raji, the minute he delivered the missing software. He went so far as to take Fareed into his confidence, tantalizing him with vague bits of information as to where they were going once they left Paris.

Bruno showed him pictures of the facility, a large metal building with a massive antenna array, large satellite dishes already up and waiting. If it was true, if they were already this far along, then the money wasn't the only thing that Leffort was lying about.

From what Raji could see in the photographs, the facility was in a tropical area of jungle. Bruno told him there was a swimming pool and comfortable bungalows. He guaranteed Raji that he would have the run of the place, no more locked rooms, and freedom to move around and go into the city if he liked.

When Raji asked what city, Bruno just looked at him and smiled. He told him he would have to stay only until the mission was completed, at which time they would pay him everything they promised and

Raji would be free to go. He promised that Leffort would not be permitted to cheat him again. All of this through Bruno's smiling crooked teeth.

Raji wondered if at some point they planned to kill Leffort as well. He told Bruno it all sounded good, except that he needed more specifics as to how he would be paid and what assurances could be made for his safety once the software was delivered. They were back to square one.

Bruno was reaching the point of frustration. Thus far, he had taken pains to avoid direct threats of violence, though it didn't take much to decipher fury from the beads of sweat flowing over the wrinkles on the fat man's forehead. He said good night, turned, and walked out of the room.

Time was running out for Raji, and he knew it. As long as they believed that ultimately he would deliver, they would keep him alive. The minute they realized there was no hope, Bruno would turn to the dark side. When torture failed, they would kill him. Fareed took consolation in the fact that at least he had a means at hand to avoid the pain of torture. When the end came, it would be quick, though probably not a bullet, not in the hotel anyway. For now he was looking for an opening, some way to transmit the data. All he needed was a few minutes alone with access to a high-speed Internet connection, and it would be done.

Since being confined to the room Raji had wondered if they were watching him through hidden cameras. Minilenses and microphones could be concealed anywhere. He had searched the room with care, but the little devils that were on the market now were so tiny they could be easily missed—a fly-speck on the wall, a crack in the paint. He couldn't be sure.

As a precaution, each time he loaded something new into his notes, Raji went through the same involved procedure. He donned his sport coat and took out his glasses. They were an oversize pair of spectacles with heavy tortoiseshell frames attached to a woven lanyard so he could hang them from his neck when not in use. He put them on, sat down in front of the computer, lifted the screen, and waited for it to light up. He checked to see if perhaps there might be an Internet connection.

There was none.

He assembled some papers off to the right side of the laptop, a couple of pieces of hotel literature that he propped up to cover the USB port on the side of the machine. This was his cover, thin as it might be.

Raji reached under the left lapel of his jacket and felt for the small rip in the seam. As soon as his finger found it he opened it up a bit, and then pinched the other end of the small flash drive, squeezing it out through the opening in the seam. He grabbed the tiny thumb drive, concealing it in his hand. The entire gesture looked as if perhaps he had merely reached under the jacket's lapel to scratch himself.

He placed his closed fist under the papers along the right side of the computer and carefully slipped the flash drive into the USB port. A few seconds later it registered on the screen along the left-hand margin, popping open under the title "No Name." It appeared just below the one that read "Specs."

"No Name" was Fareed's insurance policy against

pain. If forced to do so by torture, he would deliver it to them.

Raji hit the drive entitled "Specs," then selected the file called "Intel Notes" and opened it. He went right to the top of the document. It already contained several pages. He hit the Caps Lock key and moved the cursor to make the letters bold, then typed the words: "**IMPORTANT – VITAL**."

Quickly he typed in the information given to him by Bruno concerning the facility in the jungle. He described the pictures showing the antenna array, giving the number and estimating the size of the satellite antennas. He also described the large metal building and then typed the following: "Assuming the information to be true and accurate, mission appears much further advanced than current estimates. Project may be nearing completion. From photographs observed, based on vegetation and foliage, estimate facility to be within tropic zone, fifteen degrees north or south of the equator."

Raji didn't waste any time. He quickly saved the notes and ejected the two drives. As soon as he was done, he pulled the flash drive from the USB port in the side of the machine. Then he scratched himself under the lapel one more time. When his hand came out, it was empty.

He took off his glasses, folded them, slipped them into the case, and put it in the drawer of the nightstand next to the bed. Then he took off his jacket and hung it up.

Raji kicked himself for not thinking ahead. Instead of bringing the flash drive, he should have tucked away one of the new international wireless broadband devices. They used cell band phone frequencies for connection to the Internet. They were not much bigger than a thumb drive and could easily be hidden in the lapel of his coat. While the connection was slower than high-speed Internet, he could have attached the software along with his notes to an e-mail. The entire package would have been on its way and out of their grasp within a few minutes. Fareed would have been free to throw a chair through the window and if need be, jump for it.

Instead he was playing for time, hoping for more information and praying that somehow he would find a way to get it out.

THIRTY-ONE

Just after three in the afternoon Bill Britain, head of Counterterrorism, knocked on the door to Thorpe's office.

"Come in."

The second Britain opened the door Thorpe looked up from his desk and said: "Did you get ahold of Madriani?"

"I did."

Thorpe issued a sigh of relief and leaned back in his chair.

"But he wasn't easy to find," said Britain.

Thorpe was relieved. He was also angry and frustrated with the lawyer and his two companions. "How the hell did they get away from our people?"

"I don't know," said Britain. "I didn't want to tell them they'd been under surveillance."

"Probably just as well." Thorpe had taken a huge risk by letting them go. If anything happened to them, he would be answering questions for the next several years. They had lied to him about going to

San Diego on business, though Thorpe knew from the inception that the story was a ruse. The FBI had used them as bait to try to trap Liquida. This was something absolutely forbidden, using civilians as possible targets. Thorpe had never done it before. He did it now only because of the importance placed on the matter by the White House. Using them as bait was a long shot. It failed. Now Thorpe wanted them back.

Instead, Madriani had slipped the bonds of the FBI's operation in Bangkok. He had skipped out of Thailand, sending Thorpe an e-mail as if it were a picture postcard, telling him they were on their way to Paris. Worse yet, they claimed to be hot on Liquida's trail. Then in all the excitement, they failed to give Thorpe the name of the hotel where they were staying in Paris. Thorpe handed the crisis off to Britain, who had been up half the night trying to run them down.

"Got ahold of Madriani at his hotel early this morning," said Britain.

"I hope you woke him up," said Thorpe.

"It was early afternoon their time," said Britain.

"Too bad."

"The good news is they're OK."

"Are you sure?"

"I talked to all three of them."

"I have half a mind to have them picked up. The question is, how? We'd have to cut paper to satisfy the French authorities, and I don't have any charges. Did you tell them to get their asses back over here now?"

"I did."

"And what did they say?"

"Madriani wants us to send in the troops," said Britain. "He claims Liquida is booked into a hotel just down the street from the one they're staying in. A place called Hotel Saint-Jacques."

"That's what he said in the e-mail," said Thorpe. "Sit down."

Britain took a seat. "I don't think they're in any danger."

"What makes you say that?"

"I think they're chasing rainbows," said Britain. "When I pressed Madriani over the phone, asked him whether they'd actually seen Liquida, he said no. Though he probably wouldn't know what he looks like."

"You're wrong," said Thorpe. "Madriani has seen him, at least we think so, at least once, in Costa Rica a little over a year ago."

"So be it," said Britain. "He admitted they never saw him in Thailand or in Paris. But he's sure he's there."

"How does he know?"

"All the stuff he told us in the e-mail, except none of it pans out," said Britain. "I had our people in Bangkok go back out and check the office in Pattaya, just in case there was something to the lead Madriani gave us, the thing about Waters of Death."

"Yeah?"

"The embassy wasn't particularly happy to be doing this. Seems they're still putting out fires with the Pattaya police, but they did it."

"And?"

"There is nothing anywhere in that office referencing Waters of Death, or anything close to it," said Britain. "Just a lot of filing cabinets. We also ran a check on the telephone messaging system, the one Madriani told us about. It does exist."

"Well, that's something," said Thorpe.

"Yes, but there's nothing on it. At least not using the code he gave us. I had our people dial in, and according to them, the voice on the tape said there were no messages. There was no reference to anything called WOD or any mention of a hotel in Paris. You want my opinion, I think Madriani and his pals are smoking dope."

"Could be somebody erased the message," said Thorpe.

"It's possible," said Britain. "But if I had to guess, I'd say Madriani is looking in all the wrong places."

"What do you mean?"

"This." Britain slid a file across the desk. "It came in yesterday morning, a report from our legat in Dubai. Take a look at the photocopy of the letter on top."

Thorpe opened the file and read. A few seconds later he looked up: "Did anybody check it out?"

Britain nodded. "We got a copy of the sealed indictment on Liquida and wired it over to our embassy in Dubai late yesterday. Our agents got the local authorities—including some armed military, they weren't taking any chances—to visit the Dubai Beach Resort. The Spaniard under the passport checked out four days ago."

"Was it him?"

"Take a look underneath the letter," said Britain. "There's a copy of the passport photo from the front desk at the hotel. The quality of the copy is not great, but you can judge for yourself."

Many hotels overseas are required by law to copy the passports, the entry stamp, and the photo page of all foreign registered guests.

Thorpe looked at the photograph and compared it to the sketch of Liquida from the FBI's wanted poster, a copy of which was also inside the file. He took out a magnifying glass from the center drawer of his desk and looked at the photo more closely and back to the sketch. "I'd say it's a pretty fair likeness. Have we checked with Spanish immigration?"

"The embassy in Madrid checked overnight. We're waiting for an answer back."

"Probably stolen or lost."

"And of course he wasn't about to leave any forwarding address at the hotel in Dubai," said Britain.

"So he's either still in the Emirates or he's left the country."

"Our people from the embassy are checking with their immigration department as we speak."

"Knowing Liquida, he probably has another passport, in which case he could be long gone and we wouldn't know it," said Thorpe.

"No way to know until we hear back from immigration. In the meantime, what do you want me to do about Madriani? You want me to have somebody from the Paris embassy go babysit?" said Britain.

Thorpe thought about it for a moment. "If Liquida was in Dubai four days ago, I suppose it's possible he could have flown on to Paris or . . . via Thailand to Paris. But you say none of the information Madriani gave us regarding Liquida's connections to Thailand panned out?"

"Correct. After I hung up from him this morning, I got the report back from Bangkok," said Britain. "None of the information in Madriani's original e-mail to you checked out."

"Did you call him back?"

"I tried. There was no answer in either of the rooms. They must be out."

"And yet Madriani claims to be tracking Liquida from Thailand to Paris." Thorpe looked across the desk at Britain.

"That's what he says, but he admits he has absolutely no visual ID on Liquida, nothing in Thailand or in Paris. That much is clear."

"So it sounds like he's working on faith," said Thorpe.

"Liquida could be on the other side of the moon based on what we know from Madriani," said Britain.

"We can't afford to waste any more time," said Thorpe. "Listen, have my secretary prepare an e-mail. Tell her to send it out over my name. Send it to Madriani. Use the e-mail address he used to send his last message to me. Tell him that if he and his two friends are not back here in D.C. within forty-eight hours, I'm going to put their names and passport numbers on the international no-fly list. Tell him that the only way home after that will be on a MATS flight, military air transport, direct to Andrews Air Force Base. They can come back bundled up like freight. Let's see if that puts a kink in their chain."

THIRTY-TWO

I assume that's not him," says Joselyn.

I open my eyes. A fat guy with a bald head has just come out of the front door to the Hotel Saint-Jacques.

"No." I start to close my eyes again.

"You're going to have to stay awake if we're going to do this," she tells me.

"Give me a break. I got almost no sleep last night." With thoughts of Liquida running through my head, I kept wondering why the FBI hadn't sent someone to meet us.

"That's not my fault," says Joselyn. "I don't know what he looks like. You do."

It's late afternoon. Joselyn and I are camped in the front seat of a small black Renault. We rented it through the front desk at our hotel this morning. She is behind the wheel. I'm in the passenger seat. We are parked across the street and about a half block down from the front entrance to the Hotel Saint-Jacques.

It is a European-style boutique inn with a single entrance on the main street shaded by a maroon canvas awning. There is not a lot of foot traffic in or out. On the corner it looks as if there is an attached restaurant or bar.

We are at a loss to figure out how to confirm whether Liquida has checked into the hotel or not. It would be senseless to call the front desk, since it is certain he would never register under the name Liquida. Joselyn called looking for the other name left on the Thailand message system—the name "Bruno." The desk told her there was no one there, either under the Christian name or surname of Bruno. We're batting zero for two.

"Tell me what he looks like." Joselyn is talking about Liquida.

"He's got black hair." My eyes are closed again, but I can see him. "You have to remember it was more than a year ago. His hair looked like it might have been slicked down. His face is pockmarked. Childhood acne would be my guess." The minute I say it the mental image is blocked. The concept of Liquida as a child is a non sequitur, like describing Satan when he was a kid.

"How tall is he?"

"I'm guessing average build, but I don't really know. He was seated behind the wheel of a car when I saw him. It was quick, nighttime, and I only got a glimpse. But I won't forget the face."

"Why not?"

"He was dead in the eyes, if you know what I mean."

"No. Tell me."

"How do I explain it? Ever seen any mug shots?"

"A few."

"Luciano and Dillinger, you look at their eyes?"

"Yes."

"That doesn't cut it, not with Liquida. I've thought about it. The only picture I can ever recall seeing that comes close is Dillinger's postmortem shot, the one they took after the feds shot him. The lids half open but no spark of life whatever. That's Liquida."

"Now you're freaking me out," she says. "Could it be that's why you couldn't sleep last night?"

"You asked."

"OK. So tell me more."

"That's it."

"No, you said his eyes were dead—why, what's your theory?"

"It's no theory. Go to San Quentin, take a look through the yearbook. You can always tell the ones who like to kill from the rest. You don't need any training. You can see it in their eyes. Like a vampire looking in a mirror. There's nothing there. I'm not just talking about the nutcases in the adjustment center. I mean the ones who crave killing. The ones who, if you let them out, will kill again before sundown, not because conditions force them, but because they're addicted. It's their narcotic of choice."

"You really think there are people like that?" Joselyn is a romantic. She likes to believe that wherever there is life, there is some goodness.

"I know there are. And Liquida is hooked. He may not be a bloodsucker, but he mainlines on death. Look in his eyes and you'll get a glassy, dead stare, as if whoever made him forgot to light the candles. If his pupils are moving, it's only because he's measuring you for a box, or a fifty-gallon drum if he can fold you up neatly enough to fit."

"Now I'm not going to be able to sleep tonight."

"If you see him, you'll recognize him. Trust me. So maybe I can catch a few winks now."

She waits about ten seconds. "I don't get it," says Joselyn. "We send a message to Thorpe, tell the FBI what we found, and we get nothing. You would think they have connections in Paris. The law enforcement fraternity. Why don't they call somebody with the Paris police and have them come out?"

"Probably for the same reason we don't."

"Why is that?" she asks.

"There's no hard evidence that Liquida's inside. Britain, Thorpe's man on the phone—the only thing he seemed to key on when we spoke was the fact that none of us—you, Harry, or I—have seen Liquida in the flesh. Not here and not in Thailand. The minute I told him we had no visual confirmation, he told me to drop it and get back to D.C."

"Why didn't you tell us that back in the room?" says Joselyn.

"Because I didn't want you to lose hope." I open my eyes long enough to wink at her. "If I tell Harry that, he's gonna want to go back. And once we go back, that's it. Thorpe's not going to let me out of his sight again. And if you recall, Harry was not in favor of this trek to begin with. And don't you go telling him what Britain said. There's enough to deal with right now without having to do a pitched battle with Harry."

"Maybe he's right," says Joselyn.

"You heard the voice on the tape. Tell me you don't think Liquida's inside that building." I nod toward the hotel across the street. "He said he'd be in Paris Monday. That was yesterday."

"If in fact it was his voice," says Joselyn.

I look at her.

"OK, so perhaps he's there. We can't prove it unless we see him."

"That's why we're sitting here."

"It is possible the FBI might know something we don't."

"Like what?"

"I don't know," she says.

"You're starting to sound like Harry. Give them time. I am confident that Thorpe will come around the minute he hears Liquida's voice on that tape."

"If you say so."

"What time does Harry spell us?" I ask.

"Six o'clock, why?"

"I need to call Sarah at the condo as soon as we get back to the room. I told her we'd be back in four days. Knowing my daughter, she's going to be mad as hell."

THIRTY-THREE

Knock, don't ring the bell," she told him. "Herman's trying to sleep." Sarah hung up the phone and went to stand by the door. She waited until she heard the slight rap and then opened up.

Adin was standing there.

"Come on in."

"You're sure it's a good time? I mean if you're busy . . ."

"No, not at all. Herman is resting."

All of a sudden the dog started to bark.

"Damn it! Or at least he was," said Sarah.

"Who is it?" Herman's deep voice bellowed from somewhere down the hall.

"It's OK, Herman. It's just a friend."

Bugsy started to bark again.

"I'm gonna kill that dog," she said.

"Why don't you bring him out?" said Adin.

"Are you sure? He's not terribly friendly around men. He tolerates Herman only because he's in bed.

He drove the visiting nurse, this young guy, right up against the wall in Herman's room this morning. I had to go pull him off. That's why he's locked up."

"Go let him out," said Hirst.

"I'll put him on a leash if you want to meet him." Sarah headed down the hall. A few seconds later she came back with the Doberman on a heavy leash. There was a choke chain that looped around Bugsy's neck. It tightened every time he pulled. Even with this the dog dragged her from the hallway out into the living room.

"Put water wings on him and you could ski behind him," said Adin. "He's beautiful."

"He thinks so," said Sarah.

"Let him go."

"I don't dare."

"Sooner or later we're gonna have to meet," said Adin.

"Are you sure?"

"Yes." Adin got down on one knee. "You can mop up the blood if I'm wrong, but I don't think he's going to attack me."

"It's your funeral," said Sarah. Gently she released the strain on the leash.

"Go ahead and take it off," said Adin.

"No. No. You don't know him. I need to be able to haul him in if I have to." The minute she let go of the leash, Bugsy stopped.

He looked at Adin, one knee down on the floor ten feet away. The dog and the man were at eye level.

"Come on." Adin coaxed him. "The secret is no sudden moves. Come on." He allowed his voice to rise just a little. With the rest of his body perfectly still, he slowly raised his right arm, keeping his hand limp, palm down, with his fingers curved a little and open.

Bugsy moved slowly across the floor, sniffing the air as he went. A step at a time he slowly glided across the carpet until he was no more than three feet from Hirst. The dog moved cautiously to his right as if circling.

Adin didn't move his hand. He left it where it was.

Bugsy came in from the side and slowly sniffed the back of his hand.

"That's a good boy." He allowed the dog to sniff as long as he wanted.

Slowly the dog moved in closer to Adin's body. He picked up the scent off his chest and his face. By the time dog and man were nose to nose, the nub of Bugsy's docked tail was wagging like the stylus on a Richter scale in a tremor.

"I don't believe this. He's never done that before with anyone, even the trainers on the farm," said Sarah.

"It's all a matter of trust. They can smell fear, and they can sense danger. The reason he went after the nurse is probably because the man panicked. You start backing up and instinct tells him to go after you, to close the distance. You have to remember that his only real weapon are those pearly white teeth. And to use them he has to move in. Maintaining close contact is his only defense. And with a Doberman, the best defense is a good offense. It's in their breeding." Adin slowly drew his right arm in, keeping the palm away, with the back of the hand toward Bugsy.

"How is it you know so much about dogs?"

"I used to work with them, in another life," said Adin. He slowly scratched the dog's head, carefully slid his hand down and petted the feltlike hair on his snout.

Bugsy sat down, ears straight up, the nub of a tail wagging behind him.

"Good thing you're not a burglar," said Sarah. "If he was a cat, he'd be purring."

"I don't think we need this anymore." Adin removed the leash, unclipped the metal collar, and removed the choke chain from the dog's throat. "That's better." Slowly he stood.

Bugsy got up, walked around behind him, and sat again as if he was heeled on a leash waiting for a command. "Whoever trained him did a good job."

"They didn't think so," said Sarah. "That's why they gave him to me. He flunked training."

"He outwitted them," said Adin.

"Trust me, they raise Dobermans, my aunt and uncle. They've been doing it for years."

"And I'm sure they know their business. But Bugsy may be the Einstein of Dobermans for all we know." Adin walked over to the couch and sat down.

As if to prove the point, the dog walked half a foot behind him all the way as if they were tethered. When he got to the couch, he sat on the floor right next to Hirst, ramrod straight between the couch and the coffee table, and didn't move.

"I think I've lost my dog," said Sarah.

"No. He'll be back to pulling you down the hall again the minute I leave."

"Why?"

"Be glad he doesn't speak English. If he did, he'd have you on a leash. I'd say this is one smart animal."

"Then why did he give the people on the farm so much trouble?"

"The dumb kid in class," said Adin. "Failing every subject, always in trouble, until you test him and find out he has an IQ of a hundred and eighty. I'd say Bugsy learned everything in the first two days, got bored, and spent the rest of his time training his masters."

"They told me he came from the shallow end of the gene pool. He was worthless. Pet quality is what my uncle called him."

"Don't look now," said Hirst, "but who's off the farm living in a condo? I'll bet he sleeps on your bed at night. Give him time and he'll have all your pillows."

Sarah didn't answer. She didn't have to.

"And you love it there, don't you?" Adin petted his head and the dog wiggled.

"Yeah, well, he's sleeping on the floor tonight," said Sarah.

The phone rang, and Bugsy flinched as if he was going to take off.

"Heel!" said Adin.

The dog froze.

"First time he hasn't torn the place to pieces when the phone rang or the door chimed." She reached for the receiver and picked it up. "Hello. . . . Dad, where the hell are you?" She turned her back, cupped her hand over the mouthpiece, and lowered her volume.

"You guys were going to Thailand. You were gonna be back in three days, remember? Now I get a message from Thorpe's office, you're in some swank hotel on the Left Bank . . . Yeah, yeah, I know." She waited for a moment to let him get a word in. "Well, I hope you're having a good time, because I'm here wrestling the dog with one hand and juggling Herman with the other. . . . I know the dog was my idea. That's not the point."

"Who is it?" Herman was calling from the back room.

"It's Dad!"

"Tell him I want to talk to him."

"In a minute," said Sarah. "Did you find him?" She listened for a long while as Adin sat on the couch, petted the dog, and watched her. At one point she wrote something down on a pad lying on the counter to the pass-through in the kitchen. "Listen, when are you going to be back because I'm not going to stay here forever. . . . OK, tomorrow night? What time are you going to call? . . . My time, right? . . . OK. Yes, I will be here. Where else would I be? Hold on a minute. Herman wants to talk to you." She laid the phone on the pass-through next to the note and turned toward Adin. "I'm sorry. Give me a second."

"No problem."

Sarah headed down the hall toward Herman's room.

"Stay!" Adin quickly got up off the couch.

THIRTY-FOUR

After the first night in the hotel, Liquida began to relax, if only a little. He settled in, buoyed by the notion that if the FBI was going to batter down his door, they would have already done it.

The next morning Liquida got up early. He had a busy day ahead of him. He slipped down the back stairs of the hotel, grabbed a taxi, and told the driver to take him to the Gare du Nord, the train station in North Paris.

The Gare du Nord is one of six main train terminals serving the Paris area. There Liquida purchased a one-way ticket on the Eurostar, the Paris-to-London run through the Channel Tunnel for later that day. He used his old Spanish passport to buy the ticket.

The trains ran every hour. The trip on the high-speed rail took two hours and fifteen minutes.

Liquida pocketed the ticket and then took a taxi out into the northern suburbs. These were neigh-

borhoods of desperation housing thousands of immigrants, mostly from countries in North Africa. A
good portion of these were asylum seekers from re-
gimes of repression. Many were living in France il-
legally, constantly under the hammer of the French
immigration service. For many of these people, de-
portation to their homeland meant torture or worse.

A few years earlier the French government an-
nounced a crackdown, threatening to repatriate any
and all immigrants who lacked proper documentation to be in the country. Within days vast fires
raged through the northern suburbs. Each night
scores of cars were torched as rioters rampaged
through the streets.

The government got the message. It eased its
immigration policy, and the riots stopped. But the
subterranean tensions between immigrants, most of
whom were young, and the French government remained. Many began to look for other lands of opportunity, places where permanent political asylum
might be easier to obtain. One such place was Britain.

Some stowed away on boats and ships; others
looked to the Channel Tunnel. They hoboed on
freight cars and buried themselves in the cargo on
trucks. Some even tried to cling to the undercarriage of the high-speed Eurostar. At least a dozen
paid with their lives. French and British authorities
tried to put an end to it. The French constructed a
double fence along the tracks at the tunnel entrance
near Calais. They made efforts to cordon off the rail
assembly yards. And while the numbers were down,
the most desperate among the asylum seekers continued to try.

Liquida knew that to the right buyer a Spanish passport and a one-way Eurostar ticket to London would be an irresistible offer. He was prepared to make a generous sacrifice regarding the price, on one condition: that the ticket and the passport were used today. He would even provide transportation back to the northern rail station by way of his own taxi. All he needed was a candidate with a compelling itch to test the waters of asylum in Britain and a passing resemblance to his photograph on the Spanish passport.

This was easier than it might seem. It was a category of passport fraud generally known as "imposters." The most common were stolen travel documents with a photograph close enough in appearance to the thief to be ambiguous. In Liquida's case, many of the asylum seekers in the suburbs were Iranians with dark hair and a complexion similar to his own.

A good portion of passports, depending on the country of issue, could be anywhere from five to ten years out of date. At times Liquida had used passport photos showing a full beard and mustache, long hair down to his shoulders, only to stride through immigration clean-shaven with his hair cropped short. The inspecting officers never said a word. They saw what they wanted to see—an aging hippie gone straight, the holder of a valid passport walking by in front of them.

The introduction of holograms, intended to tighten up on passport fraud, only made it worse. Now the immigration officer had a toy to rely on, the ultraviolet light. Either the hologram was there or it wasn't. Once it was caught in the light, it provided the false assurance that the passport was valid, when in fact the identity and the information on it might well be false. The hologram that was intended to detect manufactured passports became the center of attention and reinforced the notion that the picture was irrelevant.

Only fools used manufactured passports. Liquida wouldn't even touch "stolen blanks," passport documents taken from official stock or purchased from corrupt bureaucrats and completed by somebody else.

He used only the best, genuine passports issued by government agencies using false identities, usually people who were dead. This was what the Spanish passport was. Except for the fact that the FBI now had it on its radar screen, the Spanish document was triple-A rated. With it you could enter the United States without a visa, as Liquida had on two occasions.

Because the passport numbers were actually entered into the computer system of the issuing government, the fraud, the fact that everything written on it was false, was virtually undetectable.

It was why Liquida liked to use Bruno's services. His people had corrupted half the passport offices in the Western Hemisphere, Europe, and Asia. Give him a day, and he could get a genuine passport from any member nation of the UN displaying your picture along with the name and vital statistics of Michael Jackson. You could moonwalk through immigration.

By noon the Spanish passport in Liquida's pocket

would show an exit stamp leaving France through the Chunnel with a matching record in its immigration computer. A corresponding British entry stamp verified by its computers would follow.

Where the passport went after that, Liquida didn't care. If he got lucky, it might end up at the North Pole with the bearer disappeared under the ice cap, though Liquida wasn't counting on it.

He had actually considered two other possibilities; one, going to London himself on the Spanish passport and coming back on the new one that Bruno had given him. But he couldn't because the new passport would be missing the British entry stamp. The minute he tried to leave he would be picked up at immigration. The second alternative was burning a body in a car in the suburbs and leaving the partially charred passport as the only identification. But the convenience of that plan was a little too symmetrical for the FBI to swallow. A living, breathing, moving passport was better. It would buy him time, which at the moment was all he needed.

THIRTY-FIVE

The moment Sarah came back into the room, she heard the tinny voices coming from the telephone receiver. Herman was in the back bedroom talking to Sarah's dad over the phone in Paris. She remembered the receiver was still off the hook and hung it up. "Sorry."

"That's OK," Adin said. "You're busy." Bugsy, Sarah's dog, and Adin were still camped at the couch, a budding love affair. "Maybe I should come back some other time."

"No, that's all right. You don't have to go."

"Actually I do," Adin started to get up. "I was headed to the range to do some targets. I thought perhaps you might want to come along."

"You mean shooting?"

"Yeah."

"I'd love to. But I don't know if I can get away." She glanced down the hall toward Herman's room. "I need to put together something for his dinner.

And I'm not sure I should leave Herman alone with the dog."

"Who, this guy?" Adin looked down at Bugsy. "He's a pussycat."

"Yeah, with you. If he gets frisky and jumps on Herman, I'm not so sure."

"How bad is he?" Adin lowered his voice so Herman wouldn't hear.

"He's going to be fine. Doctor said he should rest, no heavy lifting for at least six weeks. Let me see what I can find for dinner." She turned toward the kitchen. "Where do you shoot? Is it a long drive?"

"I walk. It's two blocks. It's at FBI Headquarters. They have an indoor range downstairs. Pistol loads only. But you can do some full automatic stuff if you want, MP5s and the like."

"Really? What's an MP5?" She looked at him from the kitchen, brown eyes big as she pulled a pan out from under the counter. "Would you like something to eat? Sorry, I should have asked earlier."

"No, I'm fine."

"Something to drink?"

"No, really, I should be going."

"You didn't answer my question."

"I said I wasn't hungry."

"Sit down," said Sarah.

"If you insist." Adin slumped back down onto the couch, sprawled his tall, lean frame against the sofa, and draped his arm over the back. Bugsy took the move as a signal to relax and dropped his chin across Adin's knee.

"You were going to tell me what an MP5 was."

She hustled about in the kitchen getting dinner ready.

"Oh. It's just a light submachine gun," said Adin. "Used mostly for breaches, hostage situations, close encounters. It has a short barrel. Some people think it's kinda fun to shoot. There's not much recoil. I usually just fire the sidearm."

"Which is?" Sarah wanted to keep him engaged. She was still weighing the idea of going to the range; that is, if she could get dinner ready and lock Bugsy in one of the extra bedrooms.

"It's a bureau-issued Glock 22. They loaned it to me while I'm here. I don't usually carry, but I can."

"Where is it? Do you have it with you?"

"No, it's back in my room."

"What's back in the room?" The sound of Herman's voice caused Bugsy's head to whip around.

"Heel!" When Adin looked up, he saw a big black guy, maybe six foot four, standing in the entrance to the hallway. He was wearing a white terry cloth robe that was at least four sizes too small for him.

"What are you doing up?" said Sarah. "The doctor said you're supposed to be resting."

"Yeah, well, call the doctor, tell him to come over and get flat on his back in bed for three weeks," said Herman. "I'm fine. I'm feelin' pretty good." He looked back toward Adin on the couch. "You gonna introduce me to your friend?"

"Oh, I'm sorry," said Sarah. "This is Adin Hirst; he lives just down the hall. Adin, this is Herman Diggs. Herman works for my dad."

Adin started to stand.

"Don't get up," said Herman. "I may be feeling pretty good, but I don't need a face full of dog. Haven't seen that animal that relaxed since I moved in."

"I think Adin slipped him some Valium," said Sarah. "I've almost got dinner ready; are you hungry?"

"Eat a horse," said Herman.

"I'm sorry I don't have that, so how about some chicken stir-fry?"

"Sounds good. How about you?" Herman looked at Adin.

"I've already eaten," said Hirst.

"How'd you come to live in the building?" Herman knew that the condo complex was held by the FBI as temporary housing for witnesses in high-profile cases, some of them being slugs on the run.

"I'm here on a training program with the bureau."

"Ah, local law enforcement?"

"Not quite."

"Don't ask him anything more," said Sarah. "If he tells you, he's going to have to kill you."

"Oh, it's like that," said Herman. "Well, stamping me out when I'm looking like this is not gonna get you many points. You do better hittin' a bag lady in a crosswalk. Now gimme a few weeks and maybe I can give you a run for your money."

"I bet you could. I don't think I want to go there." Adin smiled. "Notice how she likes to create conflict? Just like a woman." He winked at her.

"What do you mean?" said Sarah.

"Get two people who don't even know each other in a fight. Only a woman can do that."

"I didn't do anything."

"Yeah, but I notice in all the patter I still ain't heard where you're from," said Herman.

"I see what you mean, Sarah. He's a very good investigator. Once he locks on the target, he's hard to shake off."

"And kissin' my ass ain't gonna work either," said Herman.

"I'm here on an overseas foreign training program," said Adin.

"Yes?"

"I'm not supposed to say anything . . ."

"Adin was just about to go get his gun," said Sarah.

"Not on my account, I hope," said Herman.

"He's going to the range. He asked me if I wanted to go. Dinner's ready." She moved the pan toward a plate on the countertop and scooped the stir-fry into it. "You want to eat in bed?"

"No, I'll eat out here. Watch a little television."

"Would you mind terribly if I went? To the shooting range, I mean," said Sarah.

"You sure you're supposed to leave the building?" said Herman.

"I'm with Adin. He's got a gun. I think I'll be all right," said Sarah.

"Yeah, but Adin here ain't givin' me no references," said Herman. "And in the absence of your father, I'm what you might call a chaperone."

"It's true, we are going to go shoot some guns," said Sarah. "But I guarantee you I won't be coming back pregnant, if that's what you're worried about." She looked at Adin. "Maybe you'd like to chime in and second that?"

Adin was now standing, the dog sitting on the

floor right next to him. "I, ah, I don't know what to say." He held up two fingers. "Scout's honor?"

"Do what you want," said Herman. "But I was gonna teach you how to shoot, remember?"

"We can still do that," said Sarah.

"How long you gonna be gone?" Herman didn't like it.

"We're only going a few blocks. The FBI building. I'm guessing we'll be back in, what?" Adin looked at his watch. "Maybe ninety minutes? Two hours tops," he said.

"You got a cell phone?" said Herman.

"I do."

"Gimme the number."

Adin gave it to him as Herman grabbed the pencil from the pass-through in the kitchen and found the pad. "What's this?"

Sarah glanced at it. "Oh, that's the information Dad gave me. The hotel where he's staying and the phone number."

Herman shook his head and tore the page off the pad. "You don't want to leave that lying around. Gimme the number again."

Adin gave him the cell phone number once more.

Herman wrote it down, then plucked the receiver off the phone and punched buttons. A few seconds later, the phone on Adin's belt began to hum. Then it played Mozart. Herman hung up. "Just wanted to make sure I wrote it down right."

"I'm putting your dinner on the coffee table," said Sarah. "You want something to drink?"

"I'll take care of it," said Herman. "You guys go so you can get back."

"Maybe I should lock Bugsy up in the back room," she told him.

Herman was grabbing a beer out of the fridge. "No, leave him out. He'll be fine." He looked at the dog.

Bugsy was sitting up tall next to the coffee table, sniffing the steam coming off the plate of stir-fry.

"But you might want to warn him. He eats my dinner and I'll eat him," said Herman.

"He really is a nice dog," said Adin.

"Yeah, I'll bet he'd taste real good." Herman moved with a sullen stride toward the couch. "Move," he told the dog. And Bugsy did.

Sarah got her coat and purse. She and Adin headed for the door. "We'll be back as quick as we can," she told Herman as she turned. "And don't worry."

"I ain't worried," said Herman. "I ain't the one goin' out."

"See you later." Sarah smiled and closed the door behind them.

Out in the hall she told Adin: "I'm sorry about that. Herman can be a pain sometimes. It's just that he's not terribly trusting."

"Trust isn't his job," said Hirst.

"Still, it's insulting."

"Nonsense," said Adin. "He's looking out for you. I'm not sure I would trust me."

She laughed.

"It's just that since he's been laid up he's gotten worse. You have to understand, Herman is a very physical guy. He's not used to being down. He doesn't know what it is to be really sick. I know that sounds stupid for a man who was near death three weeks ago. But to Herman it's simple. You just over-come something like that by sheer will, like flipping a switch. Problem is, when it doesn't come fast enough to suit him, he takes it out on the people around him."

"I can tell," said Adin. "How old is the injury?"

"Two weeks ago he was on a ventilator. Now he's walking up and down the hall threatening to eat my dog."

Adin laughed.

"If you want someone like Herman to rest, there's only one way. You're going to have to drug him and tie him to the bed," said Sarah.

"Given what he's been through, he bounces back well. I'll give him that."

"We better pick up the pace, get your pistol, and get out of here. Otherwise he'll be doing push-ups before we get to the elevator," said Sarah.

THIRTY-SIX

D o you remember me? I am Joaquin," said Liquida. He shined a flashlight in Raji's eyes and woke him up.

"Oh God, not again. Yes, I remember you."

"Get up. We need to talk."

"What time is it?" said Raji.

"You can sleep later." Liquida turned on the lamp on the table and cocked the shade a little so that the light would hit Raji in the eyes.

Fareed threw his legs over the side of the bed and sat up as Liquida pulled over a chair and sat down just a foot or so away from him.

Sleep deprivation had now become part of their tactic. Working like a tag team, Bruno and this new man who called himself Joaquin kept Raji awake all hours of the day and night. They would wake him up every hour with inane questions about the targeting software. Some of the inquiries were technical, things that Bruno and this man would never understand. Someone was feeding them information. Fareed suspected it was Leffort.

"I have been asked to talk to you once more because your situation is becoming very dangerous. The people I work for are running out of time, and unfortunately so are you. We are all running out of time."

Raji wiped the sleep from his eyes as he looked into the face of this man who spoke so earnestly to him. They were close enough that in the light of the lamp from the table the pocks on the man's left cheek bore an eerie resemblance to the craters of the moon.

"I want you to understand the seriousness of what I am about to say. Your life now rests in your own hands," said Liquida. "If you act quickly, make the right decision and are truthful with us, no harm will come to you. On the contrary, when you are finished, you will depart a rich man.

"We know that your friend Leffort cheated you. It is possible that your anger toward him may have clouded your judgment. This is unfortunate, for it has poisoned the pool of trust that might otherwise exist between you and the people I work for. Mr. Leffort deceived everyone. He also cheated my employers."

Fareed tried to shake the sleep from his head to comprehend what the man was saying.

"Leffort's theft was discovered some time ago. He tried to cover his tracks, but we caught him. It is for this reason that I come to you now. My employers decided then that they could no longer move forward with Mr. Leffort. He simply could not be trusted. This was unfortunate but necessary. His services are being terminated."

"What?"

"You heard me," said Liquida.

"Is he dead?"

"The only thing you need to worry about right now is whether you will be alive in the morning," said Liquida. "I am going to ask you some questions on two very important issues. I expect straight answers. No stalling and no lies. If you do, you will die. Do you understand?"

Fareed did not respond verbally. Instead he nodded.

"Good. First I need to know if you have the required targeting software, yes or no?" said Liquida.

"Yes."

"When you say yes, I assume you mean that you have it physically in your possession?"

"Effectively, yes," said Raji.

"Here we go again. Playing with words," said Liquida. "Effectively, yes. What does that mean— effectively, yes."

"It means that I can deliver it to you immediately," said Raji.

"Are you sure?"

"I am."

Liquida was puzzled by this. They had searched Fareed's room thoroughly and everything in it. He was dying to ask him where it was hidden.

"What guarantee do I have that after I give it to you, you won't kill me anyway?"

"None," said Liquida. "I can guarantee you that if you don't, you will be dead within minutes. But what good is it for you and me to sit here making threats?" Now that Liquida had shown him the stick, it was time for the carrot. "We need to talk about the second item. Remember I told you I had questions on two issues?"

"Go on."

"You may feel a bit more comfortable once we talk about this one. Let's assume for purposes of discussion that Mr. Leffort will no longer be joining us. My employers have asked me to ask you whether or not you are familiar with . . . ahh, whatta they call it? . . . something like pre pro. Target pre something."

"Pretargeting protocols?" said Raji.

"That's it." Liquida pointed a finger at Raji and gave him a toothy grin. "I told them you would know all about it. Right now they're a little upset."

"That was Leffort's department," said Fareed.

"Yeah, I know. But you and I both know what kind of an asshole he was. The man had a very bad attitude," said Liquida.

"So what happened?"

"First he takes their money. Payment for some stuff he didn't deliver. The scientists have to sort it out. When Bruno goes down to talk to him about it, fucker won't open the door. He's smokin' dope and watching porno movies in his room. Last night he calls an escort service and has two women shipped in. The guy outside is asleep so he misses the two ladies comin' in. This morning one of the women's got bruises all over her body. She's threatening to go to the police. So Bruno has to give her a ton of cash to keep her quiet."

None of this surprises Raji. He had been around Leffort long enough to know about his dark side.

"So they tell me to go down and visit him, give him some lessons in pain, sweat him a little and find out where the money was he took from them. I go to his room, he won't let me in. I have to get a passkey from one of the maids downstairs. When I get in, I ask him a question, where the money is, he tells me to get out of the way. I'm blocking his view. He can't see the people humping up on the screen. When I don't move, he starts giving me a bunch of crap. How he's this big-time brain, got all these letters after his name, diploma from this school, honors from that school. Tells me no skinny little wetback is gonna put a hand on him . . . how he's going to kick my ass if I don't move. Then he throws an ashtray, hits me in the head. What kind of society will you have if you put up with that kinda shit? You either have rules or you don't. One thing led to another. Things got a little out of control. Leffort tried to breathe through a pillow and found out it didn't work," said Liquida.

"You smothered him with a pillow?"

"There was nothing else handy," said Liquida. "I wasn't supposed to kill him so I didn't have a knife. Like I told you, the man was an asshole. Let me ask you a question. You worked with him for a long time, right?"

"Yes."

"So it would be expected that he might share some of his secrets with you, I mean like these protocols."

"The pretargeting protocols were his responsibility," said Fareed.

"That's not what I want to hear," said Liquida. "It's not healthy for either one of us right now. Think about this. Right now these people are worried about it, that with Leffort gone they got a hole in the program. If I go back and tell them you know about the protocols, there's no problem. It makes you more valuable. You turn over the software, and you move on to Mexico."

Liquida glanced quickly over his shoulder as if someone might be listening outside the door, then turned back to Raji and lowered his voice to a whisper. "I am not supposed to tell you this but the facility is in Mexico, in the Yucatán near Coba. They have been set up there now for over two years. They have several of these people, scientists, what you call, you know the thing what was Leffort . . ."

"Astrophysicists?" said Raji.

"Yes. They have several of them working there. From what I hear, this is an easy one for you. They probably did most of Leffort's work for him already." Liquida spoke quickly. He was still leaning in close, whispering. "I heard one of them say that Leffort had been sending information down to Coba for the last two years. So how much could be left to do? If you give us the software and tell me that you can help out even a little with these protocols, they'll be happy and you will live. Do you understand? Don't be a fool."

Raji wondered if any of it was true. But what difference did it make? If it was part of an elaborate lie devised to gain his trust, that meant they were going kill him anyway, the minute he turned over the targeting software. Fareed had nothing to lose. "I know a little about the protocols."

"You want to be careful not to undersell your-self," said Liquida.

"OK. I am very familiar with them. I know a lot."

"That's better." Liquida leaned back in the chair. "That leaves only the first item. The software." He arched an eyebrow at Raji.

"I would need a few minutes and an Internet con-nection."

"So you don't have them here?"

"They're online at a remote site. And they're encrypted. The decryption software is in my com-puter."

"So you must download it, is that it?"

"Correct."

"That can be arranged. It may take a few min-utes. Don't go anywhere." Liquida smiled, stood up, and pushed the chair back against the wall. He turned toward the door, started to walk, and then suddenly stopped. Like an animal who had picked up the scent of prey, he looked down at Raji. For a moment he gave him a cold dark stare as if he were sniffing the air for signs of deception, trying to read what was going through Fareed's mind. "You would not be so foolish as to lie to me, would you?"

"No!"

Liquida walked over and rapped twice on the door. Bruno's man outside in the hallway unlocked it. A second later Liquida was gone. The door closed, and the key turned in the lock once more.

Before it was even shut, Raji stood up from the bed, opened the laptop on the desk, and grabbed his glasses from the drawer in the nightstand. He got his jacket from the armoire that served as a closet and sat down in front of the computer ready for his ritual of transferring notes onto the flash drive.

It could all be a lie. Nevertheless, Raji was desperate to get the information about Mexico onto the hidden drive—the Yucatán near Coba, the two-year lead time. If it was true, the information would rock them to the core. He had no idea where Coba was. But he knew they would find it in minutes once he got the information to them. Satellite overflights would tell them the rest. All that mattered now was to get it embedded onto the flash drive and to do it fast before Joaquin came back.

Raji knew they would never leave him in the room alone with the Internet up and running. Still, there might be a way. After all, in order to download the data they wanted, he would have to do a handshake online with a remote site. They would expect this. If instead of downloading, Raji was transmitting the information from the flash drive in the other direction, would Joaquin or whoever was with him know the difference? It was a long shot. But it was the only chance he had.

Sitting in front of the screen, Raji assembled the paper tent over the port to the flash drive at the side of the machine. He put on his glasses and scratched under the lapel of his jacket once more. In less than ten seconds, the two drives showed up on the margin of the computer screen. He started typing as fast as he could.

If Joaquin came in now, Fareed was dead.

THIRTY-SEVEN

Some people have a natural gift for hand-eye co-ordination. Sarah Madriani was one of them. Adin was surprised how well she had done on the FBI's indoor firing range.

He thought that the triple-burst recoil on the short-barreled MP5 would intimidate her, but it didn't. She sucked it up, held the muzzle down, and, with a thirty-round clip, blew out the target, chest high, center mass.

It was with Adin's handgun, the Glock, that she seemed most comfortable. With it she was able to punch intersecting holes in several of the targets, something a first-time shooter almost never did.

Adin was impressed. Of course, shooting paper targets was a lot like playing golf. Nobody was firing back. A novice with nothing to lose could afford to be relaxed. A single muzzle flash in their direction and the heart rate would jump threefold. The conscious brain would turn to jelly. It was why the tips of the spears, the international badasses who faced fire for a living—the Navy Seals and Delta Force in the States, Special Air Service in Britain, and Shayetet 13 in Israel—often required that each of their members put a million rounds downrange in training situations each year. In the field, under fire, the only part of themselves they wanted to bring to the game were their hair-trigger automated motor skills.

"Can we stay a little longer, just a few more rounds?" Sarah was like a kid, smiling, glad to be out of the condo. She was wearing one of the official FBI baseball caps the range master had given her when she and Adin first arrived.

"I wish we could, but we can't," he told her. "I have to make a phone call." Adin looked at his watch. "And I'm already late."

"Hot date?" She looked at him and winked.

"No. Actually, it's business."

"OK, then I guess we can go," she said.

They cleared the firearms, released the empty clips, and opened the chambers to make sure there were no live rounds inside. Adin held up the MP5 for the range master to see. The guy waved him over and Adin placed the submachine gun back in the rack. He put his Glock in his side pouch empty, though he had two fully loaded clips in the zippered pocket. They headed out.

"I want to thank you," she said. "I haven't had that much fun in a long time."

"Perhaps we can we do it again."

"You think so?"

"Sure, if we can find the time. Look at your schedule, and we'll see if we can set it up."

"Yeah, right," said Sarah. "I'll just call my secretary and have her check my calendar. You know, I don't think you realize how lucky you are."

"In what way?"

"You have a job, a career that takes you all over the world."

"I have to admit, at the moment, as you Americans might say, 'life doesn't suck,'" said Adin.

"But I'm left here to worry about my father, who is off someplace God knows where and for God knows how long. I'm left in a helpless position totally powerless to do anything. Everyone treats me like a child, and I'm not. I'm left to sit with Bugsy, the only one who seems to understand me. I want my father back. I want my life back."

"You have to admit, the dog's pretty nice," said Adin.

"Well, thank you. I'll tell him you said so. And Herman was worried about what you might do to me. Now I know. You're just using me to get to Bugsy. You just want to kidnap my dog."

"Now that you mention it."

"Well, thanks. That certainly reinforces my self-image."

"I'm just kidding."

"For that you owe me at least another two hours at the range."

"Duly noted. I'll mark it down," said Adin.

They headed for the door. By the time they got outside, it was dark, the ebbing tide of rush hour in Washington, the red taillights of cars streaming down Pennsylvania Avenue.

They walked on talking and laughing. By the

time they covered the few blocks to the condo, Sarah wondered where the time had gone. Minutes later they stepped off the elevator upstairs. She glanced up at him and said, "So what does your schedule look like tomorrow?"

"You're worse than a child at Christmas," he told her.

"What do you mean?"

"You can't wait to go back and shoot."

"Or you could loan me your pistol and some bullets and I could set up targets in the hallway of the condo. After all, it would make Herman feel better if I spent a little time with him shooting."

Adin laughed.

"You didn't answer my question. Are you busy tomorrow? After work, I mean."

"Why?"

"Why don't you come to dinner, say about seven? I've got some steaks in the fridge, and I do a wicked salad."

"Do you think it would be all right with Herman?"

"Once you two get to know each other, it'll be fine," said Sarah.

He looked at his watch. "It sounds like a date," said Adin. "Tell Bugsy I'll see him tomorrow night."

She gave him a sideways glance and smiled.

"Sorry, I'm late. I gotta run." Adin started to move backward down the hall toward his room. "See you tomorrow night."

"You like rice or potatoes with your meat?" she asked

"Whatever you have will be fine," said Adin.

"I have dog kibble."

Adin laughed. "See you."

"Bye."

He disappeared around the corner.

Sarah turned the other direction and walked back toward her condo.

Once inside the apartment Adin wasted no time. He went to the bedroom and tossed the fanny pack with the empty handgun onto the bed. He would clean it later.

He reached into the closet, lifted the empty sports bag off the hook, then changed into his running togs, shorts, a T-shirt, and a pair of Nikes.

Adin opened the top drawer of the desk and grabbed the phone inside. He disconnected the charging cord and connected the earbuds with the small, wired mic. He dropped the phone and the wired mic along with his wallet and ID into the sports bag and left the apartment.

Downstairs he nodded and smiled to the female agent at the front desk. He watched as she made an entry in the log showing the time of his departure. Besides the ubiquitous security cameras, those residing in the condo complex were checked in and out by the security staff. Adin had had to sign the register and agree to provide security for Sarah before she could accompany him to the range.

He stepped out onto the sidewalk and began to jog back toward the FBI building. He crossed Pennsylvania Avenue and ran toward Constitution and the Mall.

Hirst didn't stop until he reached the area near the Tidal Basin, where he took a seat on one of the benches. He unzipped the sports bag and opened the top wide. He didn't take out the black phone. Instead he propped it up so that the stub antenna would have a clear, unrestricted line of sight into the open heavens above the Mall.

Adin plugged the two small buds into his ears and left the tiny mic dangling on the wire just below his chin. He reached in the bag, got his wallet, and retrieved a small folded piece of paper from the section of the billfold. Then he punched a series of numbers on the phone. The first was a code to power up. The second, only two digits, was a quick-dial number to the party on the other end.

The satellite telephone operated behind two levels of encryption, one provided by the manufacturer and a second layer of algorithms added by the people who had modified the phone and given it to Hirst. It was set up to dial a single number.

Adin waited for almost a minute while the signal worked its way to the satellite in low orbit 485 miles above Earth.

He listened anxiously for the three-second high-pitched tone. When he heard it, Adin waited until it stopped. Then he spoke, not in English or Hebrew, but in Farsi, a single word: "Redwing!"

The magicians who modified the phone had installed safety mechanisms. Both the password and the digitally confirmed voiceprint of the person saying it were required before the satellite would allow the signal to be transmitted to the party on the other end. Anyone finding the phone, even if they could power it up, would never be able to complete the connection or trace it to its ultimate destination without the password delivered in Adin's voice.

It took another seven seconds for the call to reach its destination. When it did, it was answered in a crackling tone, again in Farsi: "Hello, Redwing. Thrush here. Ready for data burst."

Adin waited a few seconds so that he wouldn't step on any words coming the other way. There was always a delay on the satellite. "No burst. Request voice trans." He waited again. Adin did not have time to prepare a keyed-in message that would allow him to send the information in the form of a high-speed data burst. This was the preferred method of transmission since the time of exposure to interception was always much less.

A few seconds later the response came back: "Voice trans authorized. Ready . . . Transmit." They had turned on the audio recording device.

He waited again, and then spoke: "Cover intact. Contact made. Leopard in Paris. Repeat, Leopard in Paris."

Zeb Thorpe had bought into the cover story that Adin Hirst was employed by the Israeli Security Agency, Israel's counterpoint to the FBI. The ISA was responsible for Israeli internal security. The FBI swallowed the cover because it had been carefully laid.

The FBI had checked with Tel Aviv in the hours after Adin arrived and requested confirming documentation. This was standard procedure. They were blinded by the fact that everything, right down to Adin's picture, squared with information on file in Israeli records.

Adin had been sent out by his handlers soon after word leaked that the White House was beginning to panic over two missing NASA scientists. And Adin knew why. They were trying to put the cork back in the bottle, but it was too late, unless Madriani screwed up the works again.

He looked at the small folded piece of paper from his wallet. It was a quick, nearly illegible note in Adin's hand, a copy of the message left on the kitchen pass-through written down by Sarah on the phone as she spoke with her father.

Adin talked slowly and clearly into the tiny mic below his chin. "Current location, Hotel Claude Bernard. Repeat, Hotel Claude Bernard. This is urgent. Employ immediate dispatch. Use all available methods. Message ended." Adin pushed a button on the phone and terminated the call.

Newspaper accounts that were now nearly a year old had mentioned Madriani by name in connection with the failed attack on the U.S. Naval Base at Coronado in California. Rumors persisted that the Coronado attack involved a radioactive device. The government denied it. The feds had sought to discredit the rumor by publishing it in thousands of conspiracy-riddled comments on nut sites across the Internet. American intelligence had learned that the fastest way to hide the truth was to soak it in paranoia and hang it out on the web for the world to see.

But when Madriani's name popped up again, this time in connection with the failed Washington bombing, even the legitimate press began asking questions. They wanted to know if the two attacks were linked. If not, how did the FBI explain Madriani's presence in both cases? What was the connection? The government's response was to put the lawyer and everyone around him who might know the answer under the FBI's protective wing. In that way anyone with questions couldn't get to them. Only the bombers knew the answer.

When Adin found out that Thorpe had allowed Madriani and his friends to leave Washington, he knew something was up. He put his ear to the ground, trying to find out where they had gone and why. They had not gone home to California. One of their other operatives working with Adin's people had checked. The law office was closed and the house was empty.

Adin couldn't get near Thorpe, and even if he could, it wouldn't have done him any good. The man was tight-lipped. So were his chief lieutenants. When you want information, you go to the bottom. In this case one of Britain's female assistants.

Over drinks in a bar she decided to charm Adin with her inside knowledge. She let it drop that Thorpe was in a cold sweat. The White House was flogging him hourly over two missing American scientists. They were desperate for the FBI to find them, though the woman didn't know precisely why.

What she did know was that there was a middle-man, someone on the FBI's most wanted list, named Liquida, who was somehow connected to the earlier two events, the attack in Coronado and the bombing in Washington. It was Liquida who had tried to kill Sarah Madriani in Ohio and who was believed to have some connection to the two scientists.

Liquida was the missing link.

She told Adin that Thorpe was frantic because he had used Madriani as bait in an effort to lure

Liquida into the open. He was hoping that Liquida would lead the FBI to the two missing men.

Without appearing too interested, he asked her if she knew where Madriani was. She told him that no one knew except her boss and Thorpe, and possibly Madriani's daughter.

Adin knew he had to act and act quickly. The next morning he went to see Jim Ellison, head of the bureau's International Ops training program, with the story that got him into Sarah's condo.

The fact that he liked her made no difference, not to the people Adin worked for. Once he realized she was the key to finding her father, Sarah Madriani became a player. Whether she knew it or not, she was now fair game.

THIRTY-EIGHT

ow'd it go?" asked Bruno.

"I'm not sure," said Liquida. He was standing on a small footstool, peering through a tiny pinhole high on the wall as he looked down into Fareed's room. It was one of several peepholes they had drilled, all of them up high so that Raji wouldn't find them.

"What did you tell him?" Bruno was huddled up close behind Liquida's legs as the Mexican stood on the stool.

"He thinks we are getting him an Internet connection."

"Are we?"

"Not yet," said Liquida. "Not yet." He watched for several seconds as Raji performed the ceremony of the glasses and the coat. "That's strange."

"What?"

"Would you say it was cold in that room?"

"No. If anything, it's stuffy with all the windows closed," said Bruno.

"So why is he putting on his jacket?"

"You know, we noticed that the other day," said Bruno.

"What is this?" As Liquida watched he could tell, even from behind, that he was being treated to a display of some sleight of hand. "You say you searched the room?"

"Thoroughly," said Bruno.

"What about his jacket?"

"What do you mean?"

"Did you check it?"

"Of course. All the pockets, everything. We turned them inside out. There was nothing."

"Are you certain?" said Liquida.

"Absolutely."

Liquida watched for a few more seconds, then leaned back away from the hole. "Listen, I want you to go outside his door. Talk to your man in the hallway and speak to him in English so that Fareed can understand. Make sure you can be heard inside the room. Tell your man they are bringing up some food for Fareed."

"What, at this time of night?" Bruno looked at his watch. "It's three thirty in the morning."

"Don't worry about it. If your man says anything, tell him it's coffee and some desserts. It's necessary because we're going to be working for a while. Also tell him that we are going to have to take Fareed to another room so he can connect his computer to the Internet. Then knock on the door, but don't open it and tell Fareed we're going have to move him to another room. You got it?"

"Yes."

"By then I will join you." Whatever Fareed was typing, he must have finished. By the time Liquida got his eye back to the hole Raji was sitting there reading whatever it was he had on the screen, his right hand dallying under the papers that lay along the side of the computer. If Liquida thought for a moment that Fareed had a gun, that's where he would start looking, under those papers.

Bruno's booming voice just outside the door made Raji jump as if someone put a few thousand volts through his body. The Chechen would never make it as an actor. He was speaking loud enough for Fareed's dead ancestors to hear him.

The second he heard the shouting outside his door, Raji hit the save command and plucked the flash drive from the computer. There was no time for niceties like ejecting it. He fumbled and nearly dropped it, then slipped the small drive back into the open seam under the lapel of his coat.

Liquida smiled, then stepped back away from the wall. He shook his head. *Stupid man! Will they never learn?* By the time he got to the door, Bruno was coming back the other way.

"Well?"

"Let's go get him," said Liquida.

They marched down the hall. Bruno nodded to his guy and he unlocked the door. Liquida was first in. He looked at Raji. "My friend, I'm sorry but we're going to have to move you to another room to get the Internet connection."

"That's fine." Raji turned to get his laptop.

"No, you can leave it for now. We'll get it in a few minutes," said Liquida. "First we're gonna get some food and some coffee, so you're awake. I wouldn't want you to make any mistakes."

Raji started for the door. As he passed in front of Liquida, the Mexican reached out and took him by the arm. "Here, you won't be needing your coat. It's very warm in the other room. In fact, we're going to have to turn the heat down."

Fareed stopped and looked at him.

"I insist. I want you to be comfortable," said Liquida.

"Sure." Raji took a step toward the closet and started to take off his jacket.

"Boy, those are big glasses," said Liquida.

"Not really," said Raji.

"You must be blind."

"No. It's just that I have a problem with glare from the screen. They're computer glasses. I wear them all the time at work."

"Here, I'll take that." Before Raji could get his fingers near the lapel, Liquida grabbed the coat from his hand, put it on a hanger, and hung it neatly in the armoire. "Let's go."

They started down the hall with Bruno in front, Fareed behind him, with Liquida and the guard taking up the rear. Before they went twenty feet, Liquida said: "I am going to let you go on ahead. I will catch up with you in a minute." He watched until Bruno had Raji inside one of the rooms down the hall; then Liquida turned and went back to Raji's room.

He lifted the sport coat from the hanger in the armoire and started feeling around. It took him less than twenty seconds to find the small hard lump under the lapel and to see the tear in the seam. As soon as he had the flash drive in his hand, he grabbed the computer and took them both down the hall to another room. He knocked on the door.

A few seconds later, it opened. Inside Liquida could see a blue haze hovering just beneath the ceiling.

"What can I do for you?" Leffort slurred the words as Liquida got a blast of secondhand cannabis.

"Time for you to go to work." Liquida pushed his way into the room.

"Please. By all means, come in." Leffort stumbled backward toward the bed and started to giggle. "Can I offer you anything? Glass of wine, truffle, croissant, a Quaalude?"

The room was a shambles. Dirty dishes and empty food containers covered the desk and part of the floor. The top of the bureau had become Leffort's laundry chute, dirty underwear and socks everywhere. The smell of sweat was covered by the sweet perfume of the weed. Two of the bureau drawers were pulled open and filled with garbage. With the sleeping curtains drawn, the clutter, and the smell, the place felt like an opium den.

"Welcome to my humble abode." Leffort took one more step back and fell onto the bed.

"This is a pigsty," said Liquida.

Bruno had taken the entire floor for a week and told the front desk not to bother sending up the maids. Food was brought in by Bruno's people from one of the local restaurants. Another day of this and Leffort would be sleeping with rats.

The story Liquida had told Raji was only half a

lie. If Liquida had his way and everything worked out, they would be out of Paris and on their way south toward Marseilles before the sun came up.

Leffort took another drag on the joint as he maneuvered his head onto the pillow and lifted his white gym-socked feet up onto the bed.

Liquida swept the dirty dishes and garbage off the surface of the small table with one arm and started setting up the computer. "Get over here now."

"Have you seen this one?" Leffort's attention was back on the television set, a porn movie running on one of the pay-per-view channels. "*Lilly's Arch Day Triumph,*" said Leffort.

As soon as he got the computer up and running, Liquida crossed the room. Leffort was in middrag on the joint when Liquida slapped it from his lips and stamped it out on the floor.

"That's good shit. What did you go and do that for?"

"I want you to take a look at this." He held the small flash drive, half the size of a pack of chewing gum, up in front of Leffort's eyes so he could see it. Larry tried to focus.

"What is it? Lemme see." He took the drive between his fingers, examined it for a second, then put one end of it to his lips and tried to suck with his lungs. "No taste at all. What is it?" said Leffort.

"Son of a bitch." Liquida ripped the flash drive from his mouth.

"Suck on that, you're gonna need to break out the Shop-Vac."

"You stupid shit." Liquida grabbed him by the collar and started to pull him up off the bed. After

Liquida dragged him to his feet, together they stumbled into the bathroom. He maneuvered Leffort into place, bumped him with his hip, and let go. Leffort tumbled into the tub. He hadn't hit the porcelain surface when Liquida pulled the curtain closed and turned on the shower full force with cold water.

"Aw shit! Nooooo! God damn! Turn it off! You're gonna fuckin' drown me."

"Try the backstroke," said Liquida. "You keep this up, you and I are gonna go in the other room and play with a pillow. Did I tell you the dream I had?"

Ten minutes later Liquida had him stripped, dried, and covered with a towel, everything except the upper chest and the nipple rings Leffort had installed in L.A. Liquida pushed him out into the room toward the table and the computer.

"What do you want?" Leffort's tone was no longer pleasant.

"I want you to get your ass in that chair and look at this." Liquida handed him the flash drive once more. "Tell me if it's what we're looking for. The targeting software."

"Lemme see." Leffort held it up to the light. "What does that say?" He showed it to Liquida.

"It says Kingston."

"Yeah, but there's numbers after it. What do the numbers say?"

"Looks like two hundred and fifty . . ."

"Two hundred and fifty-six gigs," said Leffort.

"So what is that?" said Liquida.

"That, my friend, is the largest flash drive on

the commercial market. Must have set him back at least a thousand bucks. There's probably something bigger that the government has, but for you and me, that's as big as they get, at least for now anyway."

"So what does that mean?"

"It means it's big enough to hold what we're looking for."

"Yes, but is it there?"

"How do I know? Listen, I need a smoke."

Liquida grabbed him by the few hairs on his chest, pinched one of the nipple rings with the other hand, and started to twist.

"Ow! Shit, that hurts."

"Yes, I know. It was good of you to provide them," said Liquida. "Most people I do this to, I have to bring my own pliers. Listen to me!" He kept twisting.

"Ow! Oh, shit!"

"Get your ass over to that computer and tell me what's on that thing or I'm going to take you out on the balcony and teach you how to fly without wings. Do you understand?"

"Yesss! I understand."

"Good." Liquida let go.

"Oh God!"

The way Leffort said it, Liquida had to wonder if the sick fuck might have actually enjoyed it. Maybe when Leffort was finished with the job, Bruno would give him to Liquida as a project so he could flame up the rings in his tits with a torch.

THIRTY-NINE

Is this your room?"

"Yes." Bruno gave him a cold stare as they sat in the hotel room waiting for the food to arrive. The goon, the one Bruno used to guard the hallway, stood near the door.

Raji looked around appraisingly at the spacious suite, a pair of antique couches, Bruno on one, Raji on the other, facing each other across a low coffee table between. It was a large sitting room between what looked like two separate bedrooms.

"If you have a Wi-Fi signal here, why don't I just get my computer and I can get started?"

"Just sit tight," said Bruno.

"Fine." Raji was more than a little nervous. The fact that they took his jacket from him made him wonder if they had seen the flash drive. If forced to, he could deliver a reasonable facsimile of the targeting software downloaded from an online site where he had parked it the night before he and Leffort flew out of L.A. It was an insurance policy. The online version wouldn't work, but there was no way for anyone to know that until they tested it. It was a precaution Raji had taken just in case. In fact, he had prepared not one, but two levels of deception in the event that they backed him against a wall and threatened his life. They were both designed to buy time.

As the minutes passed, Raji began to relax. If the man who called himself Joaquin had found the flash drive, he would have been in here by now confronting Fareed with it. He took off his glasses and allowed them to dangle from the woven cord around his neck.

A few minutes later there was a rap on the door. Bruno looked at the guard and said something to him in a language Fareed didn't understand.

Raji assumed it was room service delivering the food.

The guard checked the peephole, then turned and said something to Bruno.

"Just a moment." Bruno looked at Fareed. He struggled to lift his prodigious weight from the sinkhole of the couch, leaning with both hands on the coffee table as he did so. He made his way to the door.

The guard opened it just enough to let him out.

Raji tried to see who was out there, but the broad back of the guard was in the way. The guy closed the door and Fareed just sat. He was wishing he could take a shower. For the last two nights he had been sleeping in the same clothes, harassed repeatedly by the blinding beams of flashlights. He was exhausted. Without coffee he wouldn't be able to keep his eyes open much longer.

Another knock on the door. The guard opened it. This time it was Bruno.

Raji put his glasses back on.

Bruno approached from across the room. He was breathing heavily, sweating as usual. The man needed to lose weight and get some exercise. "It appears we're having some problems. It seems there is some difficulty with the Internet. They tell me it is down throughout the hotel. And the desk informs me that they are unable to find a restaurant to provide coffee or food because of the hour."

"So what do we do?" said Raji.

"I guess we are going to have to wait until morning. Hopefully by then the Internet will be up and running, and at least we can get some breakfast. So for now it's back to your room."

Raji shook his head. "You wake me up for this?"

"I am sorry, but it cannot be helped," said Bruno. "We will take care of it all in the morning."

Bruno and the guard led Raji back down the hallway. There was no sign of Joaquin. The suggestion of food had set Raji's stomach to growling. It would be at least four or five hours until breakfast. He was hungry, but at least he could shower, change his underwear, and sleep.

When they got to the room, the guard opened the door and gestured a head nod for Raji to get back in his cell. The second he did, the door closed behind him and the key turned in the lock.

"Bastards!" Fareed didn't linger on the thought. He turned immediately and saw that the computer was still where he left it, on the desk against the far wall. He took two steps toward the armoire, opened the door, and checked for his coat. It was still there in the same place where Joaquin hung it. Raji pressed with his fingers under the lapel until he felt the small hard prominence of the flash drive. He took a deep breath and relaxed.

Raji closed the armoire and walked across the room to his suitcase that lay open on the unfolded luggage rack near the desk. He got out a clean set of underwear and his toothbrush. He was about to take off his glasses when he felt a cool breeze from behind.

He suddenly realized that the air in the room was fresh. He turned quickly and looked toward the window. The drapes were drawn back and the window was closed. Raji turned toward the set of French doors. The drapes were closed. He couldn't remember whether they were open when he left or not. He laid the underwear and the toothbrush on top of his shirts in the open suitcase. He moved slowly toward the French doors.

Before he got there, one of the curtains moved. Raji felt the light breeze as the fresh air from outside ruffled the heavy velour. He stopped in his tracks and stood there for a second. Something told him not to look. Instead he turned as if nothing had happened and walked back toward the suitcase.

His heart pounded in his chest like a sledgehammer. With his head down as if looking for something in the suitcase, Raji glanced toward the curtains. He knew that death was waiting for him out on that balcony. He fiddled in the suitcase, trying to figure out what to do. His mind raced. The window was bolted. The door to the hallway was locked. There was nowhere to go except the bathroom, and once there, there was no way out. Still, the door had a lock, and the key was inside. But to get there Raji would have to pass between the bed and the curtained-off French doors, a narrow gauntlet of less than three feet. He glanced once more at the curtains. If Joaquin was waiting for him there, that's when he would make his move, before Raji could get to the bathroom and slam the door.

Raji needed a weapon, anything to ward him off, to beat him back. He had nothing. He thought about his shoes, but they were rubber-soled. They weren't hard enough to do any damage, and if it came down to a fight for leverage, without shoes on his feet he would be lost. What if somehow he got out of the room and had to run? Without shoes, what would he do then?

Fareed left the shoes on his feet and instead grabbed one of the long white cotton athletic socks from his suitcase. He looked for something heavy and hard to drop inside of it. He kept an eye on the curtains. All he could find was his can of Barbasol shaving cream. It had been put in his checked luggage. The label on the can read eleven ounces. It was almost full. It wasn't as good as a lead sap, but if Raji had enough room to swing it and get velocity, the hard pressurized can could do some damage, enough to keep Joaquin at a distance. And unless he had a silencer, neither Joaquin nor the goon outside could use a gun, not in the hotel. Anyone on the floors above or below would hear it.

Raji edged his back toward the French doors so that Joaquin couldn't see what he was doing until the last minute. He pushed the can into the sock. The heavy cotton fabric stretched around it like a snake swallowing a full meal. He pushed until the can seated in the toe. He gripped the open end of the sock as tightly as he could with his right hand. There were a good six to eight inches of empty stocking between his hand and the can, enough to whip the weight and get it going.

Raji took a deep breath. If Joaquin wanted to come at him now, Fareed would take his chances. He turned and squared his body, facing the curtains, his feet spread about shoulder width.

He took two tentative steps toward the curtains and started swinging the can over his head. Within seconds the length of the whip doubled as the centrifugal force stretched the cotton.

Raji could feel the pulse pounding in his head as he moved toward the bathroom. The canned bolo whistled through the air above his head like a propeller. Fareed hugged the side of the bed, staying as far from the curtains as he could, inching his way toward the bathroom. He knew that if he got too close to the French doors, the weighted sock would tangle in the heavy velour and he would be dead. Joaquin, who probably had a blade, would be on him before he could think.

The curtains moved. Fareed felt the cool air. It was now or never. He was three feet from the open bathroom door. He would have to pull down the singing bolo to make it through.

One more step sideways with his back to the bed and Raji lunged for it. He threw the sock and can into the bathroom, grabbed the door with both hands, and slammed it closed. With his shoulder to the door he felt for the key, found and turned it until it locked.

Raji stood there in the darkness leaning against the door and breathing heavily, waiting for the adrenaline to flush from his heart. His hand felt for the light switch on the wall as his upper back absorbed the punch. An electrical shock passed through his body. Fareed thought he must have been wet when he touched the light. Numbness gripped his fingers, and his knees buckled.

Raji looked on in wonder as the light came on. His eyes beheld the needle-sharp point of the stiletto protruding from his throat. He wondered how this could be since the pain never registered in his brain.

Liquida's blade had severed the spinal column just below the base of the brain. The body was dead, though the eyes might blink and see for a few more minutes. Liquida had no intention of wrestling with anybody. As far as he was concerned, he was following doctor's orders. He was still on light duty until the wound under his arm healed completely.

He pulled Fareed over backward into the shower-tub so he wouldn't bleed all over the floor. Liquida had already lined the tub, everything but the drain, with a blue plastic tarp.

The second Leffort told him that the stuff on the flash drive looked real, Liquida started packing his bags.

As he labored over Raji's body, closing his eyes, retrieving his blade, and draining the blood from the tarp, the little hairs on the back of Liquida's neck were standing up. He could smell the FBI bearing down on him.

He told Bruno to call Marseilles and have them rev up the jet, and to be ready to leave the hotel in less than an hour. A rocket hadn't been designed yet that could get Liquida out of Paris fast enough.

FORTY

It was Harry's watch, though he could barely keep his eyes open. He sat behind the wheel of the small Renault, struggling to stay awake. Harry looked at his watch. It was just after four in the morning. Paul would spell him in two more hours.

The entire exercise was a catch-22. The only way they could search the hotel to find out if Liquida was there was to bring in the French police, and the only way they could do that was to see him and identify him first. At least they now had the benefit of the FBI sketch. A computer printout of Liquida's poster off the FBI website lay on the passenger seat next to Harry. Joselyn was able to produce it using a printer in an Internet café.

For two days they camped in the cold car and saw nothing. Once each day they would drive around the block and search for a new parking space to keep from being ticketed.

Harry's stomach was beginning to growl. He would have killed for a cup of coffee. The sidewalks were dead. There was no one on the street except for an occasional car and driver passing down the rue des Écoles on their way to work or going home from a night shift somewhere.

Harry decided to get a change of scenery. Perhaps it would wake him up. He turned the key in the ignition, started the car, and turned on his headlights. He checked the side-view mirror for oncoming traffic, then pulled out of the parking space and did a U-turn directly in front of the canvas canopy over the entrance to the Hotel Saint-Jacques. He drove to the end of the block and turned right. This area of the Latin Quarter was a maze of one-way streets. The only way to drive around the block was to backtrack. By now they were used to it.

Two more right turns and Harry found himself on the rue Valette, the side street that bounded the Hotel Saint-Jacques on the right-hand corner up ahead. He planned to cross through the intersection of the rue des Écoles and try to park on the other side, where he could lean back in the driver's seat and watch the hotel entrance through his rearview mirror.

Before he got to the intersection, something caught his eye. Harry saw the lights on inside a small café at the corner of the alley just behind the Hotel Saint-Jacques. He had but one thought. Coffee!

He slowed to a crawl and looked for a parking space. There were none. Every spot was taken. The street was dark except for a few lamps that hung from the sides of the buildings. He could cross over the intersection, but then he'd have to walk back and cross the street directly in front of the Saint-Jacques and along the side of the hotel. Paul had given strict instructions that none of them were to go near the place. He had seen what happened to Herman.

Harry stopped the car in the middle of the street. He looked in his mirror to make sure no one was behind him; then he turned the wheel to the right and pulled into the brick-paved alley directly in front of the café. The two front wheels bounced as they crossed the swale into the alley. The car's headlights flashed against the masonry wall of a six-story building perhaps a hundred feet away. The alley looked like a dead end.

The sudden bright lights scared two itinerants leaning over a blue bundle on the ground at the foot of the distant building. Bending over, they both looked back, white faces and stark eyes; they stared for a second into the blinding headlights. Suddenly they both turned and took off. They disappeared into an opening on the left side of the alley at the far end. It looked as if it might be a garage, but the opening was too small for a car. The two men had left their bundle behind.

Harry sat there for a moment looking, wondering what it was that he was seeing. The second he hit the bright beams he realized; there was a shoe with a foot in it sticking out of the end of the blue bundle.

Bruno's two men scrambled down the steps of the passage du Clos Bruneau and clambered into the white van parked at the curb. The second they were inside, one of them slid the door closed.

"Where's the body?" said Liquida.

Bruno translated. One of them answered in Russian as he pointed back toward the steps and the alley that ran behind several of the small hotels, including the Saint-Jacques. Then he pointed and said, "Politsiya!," something for which Liquida did not need a translation.

Bruno said something to the driver, and the man stepped on the gas. The van pulled away from the curb and down the rue des Écoles headed for the A6, which would take them south through Lyon and on to Marseilles, where the private jet was waiting.

Harry had no cell phone. He considered whether to back out and take the car back to his hotel to get Paul and Joselyn or simply go into the café and have them call the police from there. He did neither. Instead he got out, locked the car, and began hoofing it back to the Hotel Claude Bernard. It was only a short block away. Harry was afraid if he took the car, he would have trouble finding a parking space once he got there.

Running part of the way and walking, he took less than three minutes to get to the room. By the time he knocked on the door he was breathless.

When Joselyn opened the door, she was already dressed and had her shoes on. She took one look at Harry and said, "What's wrong?"

Harry had his hands on his knees, bent over, trying to catch his breath. He lifted one hand to point, but he couldn't speak. Finally he said, "Body in the alley!"

"What? Where?"

"Hotel," said Harry.

"Paul!" Joselyn turned and yelled toward the bathroom.

FORTY-ONE

By the time we reach the car parked in the alley, it is still dark. Harry asks me if I want him to turn on the headlights, but I tell him no, not until we get up close and see what is there.

"Why don't you take the keys and stay in the car," I tell Joselyn.

"Why don't you?"

"I'll do it," says Harry. "There's an opening down there to the left. Do you see it?"

I can barely make it out in the dim light.

"That's where they went," says Harry. "I don't know where it goes, but if they come back out, try to stay clear. I'll use the headlights to blind them. Cream 'em against the wall with the car if I have to."

"OK." Joselyn and I step slowly toward the end of the alley as Harry gets back in the car. We can see the long rolled bundle lying on the ground. It is sort of crumpled against the foot of the building. As we draw closer, I can tell, whatever it is, it is wrapped in one of those blue plastic tarps that you can buy in any hardware store in the world.

I can't see the foot until we get closer. Harry was right. As we get within a few feet, I can tell that the running shoe sticking out of the bundle has to belong to a man. It is too big for a woman.

"Maybe we should call the police," says Joselyn.

"In a minute," I tell her.

The bundle is tied with twine. Neither of us has a knife or anything sharp enough to cut it. I am left to find the end and try and untie the knot. I pull my hands inside the long sleeves of my sweater and roll the bundle toward me looking for the end of the twine. Each time I try to roll it, the bundle seems to want to roll back the other way. Lividity has taken over the body, and the blood has settled to the lowest point and solidified, creating a counterweight.

"What are you doing?" says Joselyn.

"I'm trying to untie the knot."

"Leave it alone. Let's get out of here."

"Go and sit in the car with Harry," I tell her.

"Not unless you're coming."

"Watch the alley. Make sure nobody comes in behind us," I tell her.

It takes me a good two minutes to find the knot and to push the heavy cotton twine backward, using my thumb and my fingernails to untie it. Once the knot is undone, it becomes easy to unwind the string from around the outside of the bundled tarp.

As I am doing this I am looking overhead to see if there are any surveillance cameras in or near the alley. It doesn't look like it, but I can't be sure. Using the inside of my sleeves, I pull the edge of the tarp and roll the body out.

The inside of the tarp is covered in blood, some of it clotted, some dried.

Joselyn looks away and covers her mouth with her hand. "Let's get out of here. Why are we doing this?"

"Because I need to know what's going on. Why don't you go back to the car," I tell her.

"No. I'm OK."

The victim looks to be maybe forty years old with dark hair. The body is matted with blood. His flesh is the color of a bleached cotton sheet, pure white. There is a puncture wound in his throat, traces of blood still seeping from it.

He's wearing a buttoned dress shirt and light-colored cotton jeans of some kind. I can see that there is nothing in the breast pocket of his shirt. I feel the pockets of his pants, front and back. They are empty.

"Who do you think he is?" says Joselyn.

"I don't know. There's no identification. No wallet, no watch, no rings. Whoever dumped him stripped the body." I lean over and carefully turn down the collar on the back of his shirt. I don't like touching the body any more than I have to. But it is the only chance I have to find out who he is. There is not a doubt in my mind that Liquida killed him. His shirt collar is covered with blood and there is a hole just under the label, but it is readable: "Kenneth Cole."

"What are you doing?" she asks.

"Can't be sure, but I'm guessing his clothes were bought in the States."

"You think he's American?"

"I don't know." Then something catches my eye. "Do you have a handkerchief?"

Joselyn feels around the pockets of her pants and her jacket. "No, but I have some Kleenex."

"That'll do."

She takes out a small pocket pack of tissues and hands it to me. I take five or six and create a thick pad. "Don't look," I tell her.

I lift his shoulder with my left hand and reach down under the body toward the bottom of the plastic tarp underneath him.

"What is it?" Joselyn has her back to me.

"Looks like a pair of glasses. They must have missed them." As soon as I pick them up I realize why. The neck strap has been pulled free from one of the temple tips, the part of the frame that hooks over the ear. If I had to guess, I would say that whoever murdered him dropped him onto the tarp as he was dying. This would account for all the blood inside the tarp. His heart was still pumping. "I am guessing that Liquida probably tangled his hand in the strap as he was dropping him onto the tarp. The glasses fell off and he never noticed them."

"You're sure Liquida did this?"

"Look at his throat."

"I'll take your word for it," she says.

"That's a puncture wound. Caused by something narrow and sharp. Herman has one just like it in his back. You know anybody else uses a stiletto like that? That's his calling card.

"I'll call the French police as soon as we get back to the hotel. Tell them about the body, give them

Liquida's name, tell them to check the FBI's list for the poster and to search the hotel."

"You think he's still there?"

"No. But the French police, once they have the poster and a name, at least they'll start watching all the airports." I throw the edge of the tarp over the body. "Let's get outta here."

FORTY-TWO

I make the call to the local authorities, not from the room but from a pay phone in the lobby of one of the adjoining hotels. I don't leave my name, but I tell them about Liquida and the poster with his picture and give them the name of his hotel. Even if they don't catch him, I am assuming that someone at the front desk will recognize his picture. They might be able to tell the cops when he left so that the French authorities will know how much of a head start he has.

When I'm done, I hang up the phone and head back to the room. Before I get there, I hear the alternating high-low pitch of the sirens from the French police cars as they arrive in the dead-end alley down the street.

By the time I get back to the room in our hotel, Harry is already there with his bags packed.

"Time to go home," he tells me.

"Yeah, I suppose I'm going to have to call Thorpe and tell him what we found and hope he doesn't turn us over to the French police. If he does, we'll be here for a month answering questions. Thorpe sent me an e-mail. Told me that if we weren't back by late tomorrow he was gonna put us on the no-fly list."

"Nice of you to tell us," says Harry.

"I didn't want to worry you," I tell him.

"Well, then, let's get our asses in gear before he slams the door and locks us out of the country," says Harry.

"Where's Joselyn?"

"She's in the other room checking her e-mail. She looked a little queasy," says Harry.

"Yeah, I don't think she's used to seeing dead people," I tell him.

What I mean is, unlike the two of us who have spent a lifetime getting off on morbid victim photos from various medical examiners in capital cases.

The door to the bedroom opens. Joselyn is standing there with a puzzled look on her face. "Hey, you guys. There's something going on in here I think you need to see."

"What is it?" I ask.

"Something on my computer. I just noticed. Not sure what it is."

Harry and I follow her into the bedroom. We stand looking over her shoulders as she sits in front of the laptop.

"What's wrong?" I ask.

"It's this." She moves the cursor so that the little arrow stops on an item over on the left-hand margin of the screen. "See that?"

The cursor has landed on something called "Specs."

"What is it?" asks Harry.

"It looks like an external drive," she says. "The problem is I don't have anything plugged into my machine."

"Then where is it coming from?" I ask.

"I don't know. I suppose it's possible it could be coming from another room, but that would be highly unusual."

"Why is that?" says Harry.

"It's possible you might pick up a Wi-Fi hot spot, you know, a neighbor's Internet signal. That can travel a little ways. But an external drive, that's usually hardwired. I'm no hardware whiz kid, but I suppose there are drives that work off Bluetooth. Although the range on that would be real short."

"How short?" I ask.

"I don't know, four or five feet. The signal won't pass through a wall. I'll tell you that. Give me a second." She moves to a different screen, the control panel on her laptop, and finds the Bluetooth connection. She toggles it off. When she returns to the original screen, the external drive has disappeared.

She looks over her shoulder at me.

"Turn it back on."

She does, and the drive appears once more.

"It wasn't on your computer last night?" I ask.

She shakes her head. "No."

Then there is only one place it can be coming from. I am looking at the bloodied glasses sitting on the bureau a few feet away. They are still partially wrapped in the tissue where I left them. I pick them up and walk toward the door.

I don't get more than three steps when Joselyn says: "It just disappeared."

I walk toward her.

"It's back."

I look at the glasses. I'd love to wash them, but I don't dare just in case there are prints. Instead I peel off some of the tissue and hold the lenses up to the light. "That's funny."

"What?" says Harry.

"It's window glass," I tell them. "I don't see any correction at all." I look at the heavy tortoiseshell frames and thick temples like two pieces of lumber. When I catch them in the light, I can see that one of the temple pieces is translucent, but the other has something solid inside. "I think I found it. Watch the screen," I tell them. Keeping my fingers on the tissue, I fold both of the temple pieces closed.

"It disappeared again," says Harry.

"That's cute." I open them again.

"It's back." They both speak at once. Joselyn wants to know if she should open it.

"It's your computer," I tell her. "Do you think it's safe?"

"After what we've been through this morning, who knows?" she says. She does it anyway.

When it opens, there are two folders inside, one that says "T Data" and another that says "Notes." She opens the first one and gets a long list of files. They run for pages.

I put the glasses back on the bureau and stare at the computer screen.

"What in the world is this?" says Joselyn. "Look

at the size of some of these. And they're all execution files. See the exe after the dot?"

"What does that mean?" asks Harry.

"That means they're program files," I tell him. "Applications. Software of some kind."

"Could be malicious for all we know. I'm not going anywhere near that stuff." Joselyn closes the folder entitled "T Data" and opens the one called "Notes." Inside is a single file. It is entitled "Intel Notes." "This should be safe. It's a Word document." She opens it.

It is not long; single spaced, it's a little over a page in length. We start reading.

"What in the hell is Project Thor?" says Harry.

"Something having to do with NASA. He mentions it twice," I tell him.

"And what's AHIRST?" says Joselyn.

"I don't know. It could be code name or maybe an acronym. A government program of some kind."

"It sounds more like a government agency," says Harry. "He says he wants the information forwarded to AHIRST immediately. Says it's urgent."

We start to concentrate on the stuff about Mexico, the Yucatán Peninsula.

"This place called Coba, I know where that is," I tell them. I'd had a case that took me down into that area some years ago. It is where I first met Herman. "Coba is an ancient Mayan city. Ruins as far as you can see. It's surrounded by thousands of square miles of nothing but jungle."

"It sounds as if there's something there now," says Harry. "An antenna array and a facility of some kind. From the tenor and tone of these notes, this man seemed to be pretty worried about it."

"That's probably why they killed him," says Joselyn.

"What has Liquida got to do with all of this?" says Harry. "This would be out of his league."

"Not necessarily. Not if he was hired to tie up loose ends," I tell him. "Who knows why he killed the man. Maybe he was looking for this. I have to assume that Liquida is headed for Mexico, so that's where I'm going."

"Just because of this note?" says Harry.

"At this point it's the only lead I have, and I'm not giving up. Nothing has changed. The reason I have to find Liquida is still there. If I don't find him, sooner or later Liquida is going to find me or my daughter, and we're going to end up like that bundle in the alley. I can't ask either of you to risk your lives any further. I recommend you go back."

"Just like that?" says Harry.

"You never wanted to come in the first place," I tell him.

"Yes, but that's when you wanted me to come," says Harry. "Now that you're telling me to go back, I have a sudden yearning to see Mexico." Harry, always the contrarian.

"So I guess you and I are going on to Mexico." I smile at him.

"Not without me, you're not," says Joselyn. "And I suggest we put a move on it before Thorpe grounds all three of us right here in Paris."

FORTY-THREE

When the phone rang, it was just after eleven. Sarah knew that only one person would be calling this late at night. "Can we stop it?"

Adin pressed the button on the remote and stopped the DVD, the movie they were watching in the living room of Sarah's condo.

She leaped across the room and grabbed the phone, but not before it rang one more time. "Hello."

"Sarah. It's Dad."

"Where are you?"

"We're still in Paris. How is Herman doing?"

"Grouchy as ever," said Sarah. "When are you coming back? I'm worried about you."

"Soon. Is Herman awake?"

"I don't know. I'll check in a minute. First I want to know, when are you coming back? Is Harry all right?" Sarah had seen enough of the legacy of Herman's wounds to worry about her father, Harry, and even Joselyn, whom she did not know all that well.

"Harry's fine."

"And Jos . . . ?"

"We are all fine. Not to worry."

Paul was not about to tell Sarah about the body in the alley. That would be enough to make his daughter go ballistic. "I need to talk to Herman."

"Let me see if he's awake. Gimme a second."

Before she could take half a step, Herman hollered from the other room: "I'll take it in here. And do me a favor, watch who you go callin' grouchy, girl."

She laughed, waited for Herman to pick up the phone in the other room, and then hung up the receiver. As Sarah headed back toward the couch and the movie, Adin stood up.

"Your father?"

"Yeah."

"As long as we're taking a break, I've got to go to the bathroom," said Adin. "Don't wait for me. Go ahead and turn it on. I'll be right back."

"I'll wait for you."

Adin slipped quietly down the hall, stepped into the bathroom, and silently closed the door and locked it. He didn't turn on the light because it would trigger the overhead fan. Instead he stood in the dark and listened. The guest bath and Herman's room shared a common wall.

"Yeah, I 'member the place," said Herman. "Ruins in the Mexican jungle on the Yucatán, a ways out of Tulum, as I recall. Yeah, I remember Coba. That's the place you hired me, right? Sure."

Silence for a few seconds, then: "It's been a while since I been down there, but I think I still got some friends in the area. Why do you ask?"

More silence: "I don't understand. You're in Paris. Why would you be needing security in Mexico?"

Herman listened. Adin waited. "You sure you want to do that? Why don't you just call Thorpe and tell him? . . .

"What do you mean, he hasn't followed up?"

I was wearing a headset with a mic, using Skype to talk to Herman through Joselyn's laptop while she and Harry used the landline in the room to book our flight and get a taxi.

I had to be careful what I said to Herman. I knew that the front desk at the condo would be listening. While I wanted the message to get to Thorpe, I didn't want it to get there too quickly. If it did, Thorpe would put us on the no-fly list immediately and we would never get out of Paris.

"How are you doing? How are you healing up?" I ask him.

"Me. I'm fine," he says. "Fit as a fiddle. I'm back on my feet. Why don't I just meet you in Mexico? . . ."

"No!" With Herman you never know whether he's telling the truth or just being stoic. I wouldn't put it past him to jump on a plane tomorrow. "You just get better. Take care of yourself. We'll be fine. Listen, I can't talk long. I'll call you again later. What time is it there?"

It took a second for Herman to check. "Twelve minutes after eleven."

"Do you have something to write with?" I ask.

"Gimme a sec."

I wait.

"Got it," says Herman.

"Wait until noon tomorrow. Then I want you to call Thorpe's office. Make sure you get through to him. Tell him to call the Paris police and ask about the package in the blue tarp that was left in the alley behind the Hotel Saint-Jacques early this morning. You got it?"

"Slow down," says Herman. "I don't take shorthand. Saint-Jacques. Blue tarp."

"That's right, blue tarp. The French police will know what he's talking about. Tell him that the package was done by Liquida. We don't know who it is, but I'm sure Thorpe will find out. Tell him Liquida is no longer in Paris. You got that? Tell him to check the area around Coba. I don't know exactly where, but he can look for a large antenna array . . ."

"Slow down. Large antenna array . . ."

I am trying to keep the information cryptic so that Thorpe will not land on us too quickly, either before we can get out of France or before we land in Mexico.

"That's what I said. There should be a large building there as well. In the jungle. I don't know exactly where. We're guessing that that's where Liquida is headed. And tell him we found some strange-looking software inside the package."

"What do mean? What kind of software? What's it for?"

"We don't know. But maybe Thorpe will. Tell him the French police don't have it, we do."

"OK, police don't have it. You do. You didn't talk to the police?"

"No. We didn't want to stick around. Oh, and

Herman, listen. Tell Sarah not to worry. Tell her
I'm getting closer to home. You can tell her about
Coba, but not too much. You know the area, give
her some details, but tell her not to worry. I'll be
back there as soon as I can."

"Got it. Where can I catch you, assuming I get
ahold of some people to set up security down there?"

"I don't know. I'll try and call you from Mexico
when we get there."

"OK."

"Catch you later." I tap the red button with the
computer's cursor and the Skype screen closes.

FORTY-FOUR

This morning Thorpe was in and out of his office like a jack-in-the-box. His ear to the phone, hand over the mouthpiece, Thorpe was talking to his secretary who was standing in the office doorway. "Get ahold of somebody in authority in the Paris Police Prefecture. Check our computer contacts. We must have a name and phone number for somebody somewhere."

The secretary looked at her watch. "It would be early evening over there."

"I don't care. Get 'em at home. Get 'em out of bed. Tell them it's urgent. I need to talk to someone in the prefecture immediately."

The secretary turned and headed for her desk.

Thorpe went back to the phone. "Where did he go? . . . What do you mean, you don't know? He called you, didn't he? . . . When did he call, what time? . . . Well, damn it, why didn't you call me last night? . . . I don't care. You could have called down to the duty desk. They would have called me at home.

What else did he say?" Thorpe listened as Herman conveyed the message given to him by Madriani the previous evening.

Everything was coming to a head at once. Earlier that morning, information from immigration in the United Arab Emirates had finally come back showing that the Spanish passport with Liquida's picture on it had moved on to Thailand.

Thorpe immediately called Bangkok to have his people check and see when it arrived, whether the passport was still in the country and if not, where it had gone from there. Deep down, Thorpe already knew the answer. His worst fears were being realized. The information from Madriani was correct.

Thorpe's people were already preparing a warrant for Liquida's arrest in Paris when Madriani's investigator called to tell him about the dead body in the alley behind the hotel. It was too late. If bodies were popping up, Thorpe knew that Liquida would already be gone from the hotel. His only hope now was to stop him from getting out of France.

"What do you mean, software? What kind of software? . . . You mean he found it with the body? What was he doing messing with the body? Listen, never mind! If he calls again, you find out where he is and tell him to stay there. Do you understand? And call me." Thorpe hung up. "Susan!"

Two seconds later his secretary was back in the doorway.

"Find out who was on the desk last night at the safe house, Madriani's condo. Tell them I want the telephone records for last night, all the audio recordings from Madriani's phone. Tell them to transmit them over here immediately." When Thorpe looked up, Bill Britain was standing in the doorway right behind the secretary. "What is it?"

"More bad news, I'm afraid."

"That's all, Susan." Thorpe motioned Britain into his office and told him to close the door.

The second Britain got the door closed he started talking: "Our embassy people in Paris just called from the hotel . . ." He looked at his notes. "Saint-Jacques, I think it is. When they showed the people on the desk the poster with Liquida's picture, they recognized him. Said he was a guest but that he checked out very early that morning. According to them, it was about forty minutes before they heard all the sirens behind the building in the alley where the body was found."

"Did they have a passport with a name?" said Thorpe.

"Again, another Spanish passport, only this time the name was Jorge Menold."

"They know he can move around on those things," said Thorpe. This was because there was no visa requirement for Western Europe, the Americas, much of Asia, or the Middle East. For Liquida's purposes, a Spanish passport was almost as good as one from the United States.

"French authorities have already put out the name to have him picked up if he shows at any of the airports under that name," said Britain. "But so far nothing."

"He's not that stupid. By now he'll have a stack of passports like a deck of playing cards, dealing off the bottom as he moves," said Thorpe.

"And there's more," said Britain. "The body in the alley . . ."

"Yes?"

"It's one of our two guys from NASA."

"I knew it," said Thorpe. "I knew it. Tell Susan to get Llewellyn up here right away. We need to talk."

Britain opened the door, delivered the message, and closed it again.

"Which one of the two of them was it?" said Thorpe.

Britain looked at his notes. "According to his U.S. passport, his name was Raji Fareed . . ."

"Software guy," said Thorpe. "That makes sense. Looks like Madriani's man was telling the truth."

"What do you mean?"

"Never mind. Anything else?"

"Fareed was booked into the hotel under an Egyptian passport with an alias," said Britain. "The hotel desk said they never saw him in the flesh. Only his passport picture. It was delivered by another man who brought the passports down in a bundle. They said the guy booked an entire floor of rooms for a week. They checked out a day early."

"How many in all?"

"Seven, according to the desk. Six showed up on the first day. Liquida arrived with his new Spanish passport three days later," said Britain.

"Get copies of all the passports. Make sure the photos are clear. And I want those rooms scoured, anything they find bagged and brought back here, do you understand?"

"Our people from the embassy are already working on it," said Britain. "But I'm not sure the French authorities are going to allow us to take evidence if it relates to the murder in the alley."

"Do it anyway. Check and see if they found a computer. If so, tell our people not to let it out of their hands. Tell the French it's embassy property. Put it in a diplomatic pouch if they have to. Go to the State Department and tell them we need a back-dated diplomatic passport in Fareed's name. Shoot it over there. Tell the French he was on State Department business acting as a courier. If State gives you any trouble, tell them to call the White House. Did you check the hotel to see if there was any sign of Madriani, Hinds, or Joselyn Cole?"

"We checked. No sign. The front desk looked at their passport photos and didn't recognize any of them."

"Have our people check the other hotels in the area and do me a favor, put all three names and their passport numbers on the no-fly list. Do it immediately. And make sure they're not just tagged for additional screening. I want them held with a notation to contact the legat's office at the U.S. Embassy. And tell the embassy to contact my office immediately if they find them."

"I can put them on the list but it won't be updated with the airlines until tomorrow," said Britain. "And without a warrant, the French authorities won't take them into custody. How do we hold them?" said Britain.

"Don't worry about that. Just go out to the airport, get their luggage, give them a ride to the embassy, and keep them there. We'll worry about the legalities later."

Britain turned to head for the door.

"One more thing," said Thorpe.

"Yes."

"What kind of resources and juice do we have down in Mexico at the present time?"

Britain wrinkled his forehead with the thought. "I'm not sure the Mexican government has a handle on what's happening down there right now. We don't have much influence, if that's what you mean. What do you need?"

"I'm not sure yet."

"If you need boots on the ground, my guess is your best bet's gonna be Drug Enforcement."

"Then get ahold of somebody at DEA and tell them I need a meeting, later today if possible. Tell them this comes from the highest authority. The man in the big house at the end of Pennsylvania Avenue."

FORTY-FIVE

Coming in from Paris, Harry, Joselyn, and I decided to steer clear of the U.S. air carriers with connecting flights through the States. We feared that Thorpe might have his net out to snag us coming through U.S. Immigration before we could make our way south to Mexico.

Instead we caught an Air France flight from Paris direct to Mexico City. There we hopped a connecting flight to Cancún. Arriving just before midnight, we rented a car and took rooms for the night in a small hotel just south of the city.

This morning we get up early, grab a light breakfast, and drive south along the Mayan Riviera. The sun is bright. The azure blue sea is beautiful, rolling waves piling up on the sugar-sand beaches as we race along the highway.

We head for the coastal town of Tulum. I have not been there in years. My recollection of the area is of ancient Mayan ruins, walls of white coral stone on the cliffs above the beach overlooking the Caribbean. The conquistadors who first glimpsed them from the sea described them in their journals as alabaster marble palaces. It was a view that sealed the fate of the Mayans, for it inspired visions of limitless silver and gold in the minds of the Spaniards.

For the better part of an hour we drive along the coast highway. There are people on the beaches and the occasional "Tourista" van with vacationers, though not nearly as many as I recall from my trip to the Yucatán ten years earlier. Stories of heads lopped off in resort towns like Acapulco and shootings along the border tend to put a dent in tourism. Ordinarily the excesses of narco violence would cause me to wonder what risk we are taking by coming here. The fact that we are chasing Liquida is its own set of perils, causing any other fears to seem incidental.

Joselyn is sitting next to me studying a tourist map from the hotel. In one hand she has a printout of the notes from the flash drive hidden in the eyeglasses of the dead man from Paris. We still have no name for him.

"It looks like there is a connecting highway going west out of Tulum." She plots it with her finger on the map. "Coba looks as if it's, maybe, I'm guessing about forty kilometers west of Tulum. I'm not sure about the scale on this map."

"I don't remember exactly," I tell her. "It's been a long time. The last time I was down here I was pretty well lost. If it wasn't for Herman, I'd probably be buried in the jungle out there somewhere."

"How did you meet him?" she asks.

"He was working for a security company in

Cancún. We hired an entire team of them for executive protection. Herman turned out to be the only one I could rely on. We connected and the rest is history."

"Along the way he took a few bullets," says Harry. "Herman's a regular magnet. If it's made of metal, you can be sure he's got a piece of it somewhere inside him. For a man with nine lives, he's used up twelve of them."

"If you're keeping score, you must miss him," says Joselyn.

"What's not to miss? Biggest human shield I've ever seen," says Harry. "You bet I miss him. And for a big man he moves pretty fast. At least he did before this latest episode. Who knows now? He may be nothing but a walking comp claim. May have to put him out to pasture."

"Yeah, you tell him that. Just make sure you've got a forty-yard running start when you do it," I tell him. "Harry likes to sound indifferent and cold," I tell Joselyn. "The fact is he and Herman have a lot in common."

"What's that? Yeah, now you're gonna tell her we're half brothers," says Harry. "Same father, different mother. How is it we're the same? Tell me."

"You've got the same selfless spirit. Don't be ashamed of it. You're just a smaller shield," I tell him. "If somebody shot at us, it would be a footrace to see which of the two of them got to the bullet first. Harry's only problem is he's not fast enough."

"Who, me?" Harry sounds hurt.

"Yeah, you."

"Never!" he says.

"Do you remember if there was a hotel in the town of Coba?" Joselyn changes the subject.

"I didn't know there was a town," I tell her. "As I recall, Coba was more of a wide spot on the road. Except for the Mayan ruins, there wasn't much there. Last time I came, I was driving in from the other direction, coming east off the highway between Cancún and Mérida. I passed the turnoff to Coba and never even saw it. I ended up a few miles from Tulum before I realized. I had to turn around and go back."

"So you're telling me it doesn't have a Holiday Inn?"

"Not unless they've done a lot of urban renewal in the last ten years."

"We have to sleep in the car tonight, I got dibs on the backseat," says Harry.

"As long as you don't snore," says Joselyn. "You do, you're sleeping in the jungle."

"We'll find something. As I remember, there were some archaeological tourism lodges in the area. We might not get electricity or Wi-Fi, but they should have beds. The ruins used to draw a fair number of tourists. I don't know if they still do or not. The cenotes used to get some divers as well."

"What's a cenote?" says Harry.

"It's a pool of fresh water. Some are underwater caves. The Yucatán is dotted with them. Similar to Florida," I tell him. "The entire area is flat as a board with a low canopy of jungle. Very dry in places. It has coral underneath with aquifers, subterranean rivers that flow through the porous rock. Every once in a while, there'll be an opening to these underground rivers, a small, deep pool with steep perpendicular sides.

"Floridians call them sinkholes. The Spaniards called them cenotes. The Mayans believed they were sacred. A source of water. They built their cities around them. At one point it's estimated that Coba may have had as many as a million people living in the area."

"You're kidding," says Joselyn.

"No. Not even half of the ruins are excavated. Thieves used to come in at night and dig for treasure. The government tried to keep them out, but the area is so large it's like trying to fence off the city of L.A. Now I'm sure the authorities have bigger fish to fry with the cartels. There is also a lake as I recall, and gators—what the Mexicans call *crocadillos*. I was told to stay away from the lake. I remember it had deep muddy banks. The crocs have been known to take a few tourists who ventured too close to the water."

"I'll keep it in mind," says Harry. "Anything else I should look out for?"

"Yeah. A man with a long sharp knife," I tell him.

"How are we going to find this place? The facility with the antenna array?" says Joselyn. "Assuming it even exists."

"I've been wondering myself. But it might not be as difficult as we think."

"Tell me," she says.

"One thing I remember from the last time I was here were the cellular telephone towers. The jungle canopy out there . . ." I gesture out to the left as we drive south along the highway. "In most places, it's no more than thirty feet high. The cell towers stuck up above it like fence posts. You could see them everywhere. A large antenna array is going to stick out," I tell her.

"So all we have to do is climb a tree," says Harry. "And hope we're in the right place."

"Actually I was thinking more like a small airport," I tell him. "Do you see anything like that on the map?" I ask Joselyn.

"Not on this, but then it's not much of a map," she says. "Wait a second. I thought I saw something . . ." Joselyn turns the map over and looks at the other side. "Here it is. Beaches, cenotes, archaeological sites. ATV rentals. Ultralight flights." She looks at me. "I don't know if you're up for something like that."

"As long as it gets high enough and stays in the air, it's fine by me," I tell her. "Where do they fly from?"

"According to the ad, a place called Playa del Carmen."

"It's up ahead," says Harry. "I just saw a sign a few miles back."

"Let's see if we can find the airport," I tell them.

FORTY-SIX

It was nearly three in the morning when Bugsy began barking. Sarah stirred from a deep sleep, unsure what it was.

The dog had his nose right up against the bedroom door that was closed.

"Bugsy, go to sleep!"

But he didn't. Instead he barked again. This time Sarah heard a faint knock.

"Quiet," she told the dog. She got up, threw on a robe, and opened the bedroom door. Bugsy took off down the hall like a shot. Sarah followed more cautiously down the dark hallway. There was another light rap on the front door as she approached the living room.

Bugsy stood there like a statue, looking at the door and growling. The safety chain was latched. Sarah, in bare feet, moved silently toward the door and peered carefully through the peephole.

"What in the world?" She slid the chain off, grabbed Bugsy by the collar, and opened the door.

"What are you doing here? Do you know what time it is?"

"Sorry," said Adin. "I hope I didn't wake Herman." He was whispering. He reached out and touched Bugsy on the nose. The dog immediately picked up the familiar scent and relaxed. "I didn't want to ring the bell, but I had to talk to you. It's very important."

"Can't it wait until morning?"

"I'm afraid not."

"What is it?"

"I don't want to stand out here in the hallway and talk."

"Then I suppose you better come in."

Adin stepped inside, and Sarah closed the door. There was something strange about him. It was the way he was dressed. He was wearing dark slacks, a black turtleneck slipover jersey, and a navy blue blazer. It was a strange outfit for the middle of the night.

"Are you going somewhere?"

"I am. I'll be leaving in just a few minutes."

"Where?" asked Sarah.

"There's no time for that now. Listen to me. I have to tell you something."

"Come in and sit down. I'll turn on some lights." Sarah started to turn toward the living room.

"No." Adin grabbed her arm. He was still whispering. "Listen! I have something very important to tell you. And then I need your help."

"Sure, if I can," said Sarah.

"First I have to tell you the truth. I am not who you think I am."

"Excuse me?" said Sarah.

"Part of what I told you is true, but not all of it. I am with the Israeli government, that much is true. But I am not with the Israeli Security Agency, and I didn't come here to be trained. I'm assigned to the Mossad, Special Operations, Israel's foreign intelligence agency. I came here to gather certain information and to send it back to my handlers in Tel Aviv."

"What are you telling me? That you're a spy?"

"It's not a nice word, but the answer is yes."

"Why are you telling me this?"

"Because I need your help."

"That's not a good way to get it," she said.

"I know. I'm sorry. I didn't have time to sugarcoat it. It's a long story. There are things I cannot tell you. I'm just going to have to ask you to trust me."

"Go on," said Sarah.

"Do you know where your father is at this moment?"

"Why? Why do you want to know?"

"Because I suspect he's in a great deal of danger. I know you've talked to him in the last few days. I was here when he called. Listen, I may be able to help him."

"How?"

"If you tell me what he's doing and where he is, I can help. Trust me. Tell me, when you talked to him, did he ever say anything about something called Project Thor?"

Sarah thought for a moment, then shook her head. "No. I don't think so. I would have remembered that. What is it?"

"It's a highly classified weapons research program. The U.S. government, the Department of Defense, and NASA have been working on it for almost ten years. I can't tell you much. But I can tell you this. The system has the potential to kill millions of people. Also, from what we now know, it appears that your government has lost control of the program. It may be in the hands of others."

"If this thing is so highly classified, how do you know so much about it?" asked Sarah.

"We had someone on the inside. That is, until two days ago. He was working on the project. What you might call a mole. As long as he was there we believed that we had some kind of a handle in case anything went wrong. The problem is that two nights ago he was murdered. His body was dumped in an alley in Paris."

Sarah looked at him.

"The same place your father was," said Adin.

"How do you know?"

"There is no time for that now. I know he called you because I overheard part of the conversation. From the little I picked up, it sounded as if he might be on his way to Mexico. Is that where he is now?"

"I don't know," Sarah lied. "Why should I trust you?"

"Because if you don't, a lot of people may die. If we're right and your government has lost control of Project Thor, that means that by now the items in question are probably in the hands of another government. If so, there is a good chance that Project Thor will be harnessed and turned against either the United States, Israel, or both. If it works, it has the potential to kill millions of people. If it doesn't work, if they get it wrong, it could wipe out life on the planet."

"What are you talking about? What is this thing?"

"Your father doesn't have a clue as to what he's gotten himself involved in. You have to trust me. I need to know where he is."

"Son, in order for that to happen, you're gonna need to take us into your confidence." The baritone voice came from the shadows in the hallway. Herman stepped out into the muted light of the entry. "The last time I looked, trust was a two-way street." Apparently he had been standing there for a while, dressed in a robe and a pair of slippers. "Lady asked you a question. You want information. So do we. What exactly is this thing? This Project Thor?"

FORTY-SEVEN

The operator answers one question for us. There are no other airports south of Playa del Carmen along the Mexican coast, nothing north of Belize. According to him, there are some small landing strips in the jungle, but he doesn't recommend going near any of them except in the most dire emergency. He is sure that some of them are used to run drugs up from South and Central America—what he calls "the Coca Highway."

"Wonderful! How about flying me over Coba?" I ask him.

"I could, I suppose," he says. "But why would you want to go there? You can get much better pictures along the beaches. I can fly you over Tulum and you take some magnificent photos of the temple above the beach," he tells me. "If we get lucky, you see porpoise, maybe a whale or two."

"No, I want to see Coba," I tell him. "I'm willing to pay."

"How much?" He gets a glint in his eye. The eternal question.

His usual flight along the coast above the beaches is ninety-nine dollars for twenty-five minutes. He pulls out a flight chart of the area, and we look at it together. The question for me is whether the little bird with two of us on board has enough range to get to Coba and back. He says it does, but he can't guarantee how much time we would have in the air over Coba once we get there.

"That looks like more than forty miles each way." He takes out a pair of calipers and measures the distance. "Forty-three to be exact," he says. "Eighty-six miles round-trip. That's a lot. Even with extra fuel, I would not be able to give you more than ten minutes over the area."

"That's OK."

"Figure two hours' flying time. For that I would need at least five hundred dollars," he says.

I whistle. "That's pretty steep."

"If I have motor problems above the beach, I can always land on the hard sand along the water. Over the jungle is another matter," he says. "I am putting my airplane at risk. That's the best I can do. Take it or leave it."

"Will you take a credit card?"

"Visa?"

I nod.

"From an American bank?"

"Yes."

"I can, but there will be a five percent service charge," he says.

I agree to the terms before he raises the price even more.

He takes my credit card and hands it to the girl sitting in the office so that she can call and get the charges approved.

He goes to gas up the plane while I talk with Harry and Joselyn out by the car.

"You're really gonna go up in that thing?" Harry is looking over the top of his sunglasses at the flimsy ultralight parked on the apron along the edge of the runway.

"I thought you were going," I tell him.

"I might take a bullet for you, but I'm not going near that."

"You think it's safe?" says Joselyn.

"I don't know. I'm told they leave divers behind in the ocean all the time down here. They forget to count heads," I tell her.

"Let's hope the pilot remembers you're behind him," says Harry.

"I won't have to worry if Visa has cut us off," I tell him. "Of course, we'll be sleeping in the jungle and bathing in a cenote with the gators."

Joselyn shivers and hands me her camera. "Don't talk like that. Here. It isn't the best, but it'll work. Just point and shoot," she says. "If you see anything that you think looks like the description in those notes, take some pictures."

The tiny camera is only ten megapixels with a three power magnification on the lens, but Joselyn tells me that she can download the photos to her computer and doctor them from there. If we're lucky, we might get enough detail to see what is happening on the ground.

Before I know it, the Mexican pilot is back with a receipt for me to sign and a thin plastic helmet that looks like it's more for show than anything else. He hands me some cotton.

I look at him.

"For your ears," he says. "It's very loud."

He is right. I feel as if I am strapped onto his back with a screaming lawn mower engine chasing me down the runway. The push propeller whips the air two feet behind me as the tricycle landing gears tries twice to leave the ground only to come back down hard, each time at an angle across the runway. It jars my lower back. On the third attempt, the front wheel lifts off followed by the other two, and we are airborne.

We climb slowly with the small engine straining behind me. The pilot noses into the onshore breeze coming in off the ocean. The feeling of being in the air with a flapping fabric wing overhead and nothing below me except my feet on a metal rung is not something I would recommend to the nervous flier.

For the first five minutes we follow the coast south as we gain altitude. The houses of Playa del Carmen and the rolling whitecaps piling up on the beaches below take on a miniature appearance as we climb. We clear the town to the south, and after a couple more minutes the pilot dips his right wing. We cross over the highway and head southwest out over the jungle.

He is right about one thing. The ground below us looks ominous if for any reason we have to put down. Except for the occasional blue cenotes and the dull gray marshland around them, the blanket of green beneath us is nearly unbroken. The only human habitations and signs of life appear to be along the highway. The few sparse roads leading into the interior of the jungle go no more than a few thousand feet before they dead-end. After that there is nothing but jungle for as far as I can see.

We fly for almost twenty minutes with nothing until I see a road that looks unpaved winding below us. Trekking its way through the bush, it goes a few miles and ends. What it is doing there I haven't a clue. From this altitude, no more than maybe five or six hundred feet, there are no signs of life on or near the dirt track. I suppose small houses, concrete mud huts, could be tucked away under the trees along the edge of the road, but if they are I can't see them.

We fly on farther another ten minutes when I see a paved road in the distance. The pilot leans his head back toward me and yells above the screaming engine: "*Es* the Tulum-to-Coba highway."

I nod. I wonder how far we are from Coba.

He pushes the little plane forward until it crosses the ribbon of pavement below us. I watch as our winged shadow follows the road west.

I begin scanning the green velvet jungle below, looking for anything that might qualify as a large facility with an antenna array. There is nothing, only a few bald areas where the jungle has been scraped clear for structures that are no longer there, mostly right along the highway. There are a few houses and ramshackle buildings, small settlements.

A few miles farther on I start to see them: the line of cellular towers reaching out into the distance casting their tall shadows over the top of the green canopy, what I remembered from my last trip along the two-lane highway from Coba.

"You see the lake in the distance?" he yells back at me. "That is Coba. We are almost there. I will do a flyover. You want to take some pictures?"

I nod. I have the little camera in my hand, but so far nothing to shoot.

He begins to descend a little. I tell him no, to maintain altitude. This way I can see farther into the distance, my eyes straining for any break in the jungle.

"You scared?" He glances back toward me.

"No."

He notices that I am looking in a different direction. "What are you looking for?" He yells back. "Something special?"

"I'll know when I see it," I tell him. "Have you flown in this area before?" I ask.

"Not often. A few times," he tells me. "People who do the digs on the ruins sometimes like to get pictures from the air. That way they know where to dig. You see over there?" He points off to the right. "Those little hills?"

"Yes."

"They are not hills," he says. "They are Mayan ruins under the jungle. Some perhaps temples or ball courts, maybe palaces. May have been there a thousand years. Covered over by the jungle."

"When was the last time you flew here?"

He shakes his head a little. "I don't know. Maybe three . . . four months. I don't come here often."

"I am looking for a place that is supposed to have a large antenna array. You know antennas, like television. Perhaps a big dish. Supposed to be a new facility of some kind here in the jungle."

He looks back at me over his shoulder, squinting his eyes. "Who are you? What are you doing here?"

"Tourist," I tell him.

"That is no place for *turistas*," he tells me.

"You know where it is?"

He nods.

"Take me there."

He shakes his head no.

"I just need to see where it is," I tell him.

He points off to the northwest. As we approach the area over the archaeological park at Coba, he banks to the right and flies for a few seconds until we find ourselves back out over the highway. It crosses an intersection, another paved road going due north. "There are many cenotes there. There used to be a small village. The landowners, the people with homes, have all been driven out. It is the cartels," he says. "They cleared the jungle and made a landing strip, put up a big metal building of some kind. And what you call *plato*, umm . . ." He makes a cup with the open extended fingers and the palm of his right hand. He turns it up toward the sky and holds the flight stick with his other hand.

"A satellite dish?"

He nods. "There are three of them. Very big. Bigger than any I have ever seen before. One of them is the size of a large building. It's no television?" he says.

"No. We could fly just a little ways up that road," I tell him, "then we could turn and go toward the coast if you like."

He shakes his head. "If I had known what you were looking for, I would not come," he says. "Why do you want to go there?"

"I was told about it by someone."

"Who?"

"A man in Paris," I tell him. "Do you have any idea what they're doing there?" I ask.

"No. And I don't want to find out. Last time I flew over it, it was by mistake. They shot at me from the ground. No small stuff," he says. "No pistols or rifles. Machine guns spitting out bullets of fire."

"Tracers?"

He nods.

"Antiaircraft fire."

"*Jess.* They hit my wing. Punched holes in the fabric. Almost set it on fire. I was lucky to escape. I had to dive down just above the trees. I will not go near there again," he says.

"How far up the road?" I ask.

He shakes his head as he starts the turn toward the coast. "You crazy if you go there," he says.

"How far?"

"Kilometers, maybe twenty, perhaps a little more. Like I say, they forced the people from their homes. There is nothing there now except the big metal building and what you call the antennas. I am told that no one drives up that road any longer unless they are bringing materials or supplies. A man I know went up there in his truck a few months ago. He never came back."

"Why doesn't your government do something?" I ask.

He just shakes his head. "I don't ask," he says. "Sometimes it is best not to know."

FORTY-EIGHT

Sedrick Fowler was a political party animal, the kind Thorpe detested most. Managing partner of a powerful law firm in Boston and courtier to three presidential administrations, Fowler and his connections in national politics went back forty years.

Those who knew him well called him Foul behind his back. His religion may have been liberal, but he didn't slum in the wards with the unwashed masses.

His law firm had a long list of billionaires and gold-plated corporate clients. Between stints doing good works in government, and for a substantial fee, he could get regulatory agencies to bend and the IRS to genuflect. The mere mention of his name could seal an international trade deal and give your company a generational monopoly on government contracts. The by-product of all this nuclear influence was a radioactive amount of political cash. It fueled the revolving door to power, kept the donkey greased between campaigns, and fed the illusion of the party of the poor, money available for Foul's friends and benefactors.

To Thorpe he was just a high-class fixer and bagman. But for the moment, none of that mattered. Fowler was now the gatekeeper, and there was no way to get around him. He was hardwired into the White House as the president's chief of staff. He had Thorpe on a string like a yo-yo coming and going from meetings, railing at the bureau, and demanding to know why they couldn't find the two NASA scientists. Now one of them was dead, and Thorpe had questions of his own.

He had requested this morning's audience and thought they would be meeting alone. Instead Fowler had invited Henry Janda, a four-star army general and director of the National Security Agency. NSA was the government's master code breaker. It was their job to gather signals intelligence, to listen in and read the communications of others, and to make sure they weren't doing the same to us.

"Have a seat. I don't have much time. I apologize for the hour, but it was the only time I could build you into my schedule."

It was six o'clock in the morning. Much of the West Wing was still dark.

"I appreciate your seeing me on short notice," said Thorpe.

Fowler looked up at Thorpe from behind his big desk. "You know General Janda."

"Henry."

"Zeb."

The two men exchanged tight smiles. The fact that the FBI was out of the information loop on critical details involving Project Thor had strained the relationship between the two agencies.

"You called the meeting. I assume you have something for us." Fowler leaned forward in his chair and put his beady eyes on Thorpe.

"We have a lead. We're checking it out. We'll know more in a few hours."

"You found Leffort?"

"Not yet," said Thorpe. "But we may be getting closer."

"Where is he?"

"If the information pans out, he may be in Mexico," said Thorpe.

Fowler leaned back in his chair and shot a glance at General Janda. "What the hell's he doing there?"

Janda shook his head.

"How good is this information?" said Fowler.

"We think it's solid. It would help if we knew more," said Thorpe.

"Where in Mexico?" Fowler ignored the appeal for information.

"That's what we're working on," said Thorpe. "In the meantime, it might help a great deal if we knew who the other man was, the one who's dead. Raji Fareed?"

The darting look in Fowler's eyes as he glanced at Janda told Thorpe what he needed to know. This was one of the items they weren't talking about.

"He worked for NASA," said Fowler.

"It looks as if he was also working for somebody else," said Thorpe.

"What do you mean?" Janda couldn't resist.

"It seems that he was keeping notes," said Thorpe.

"What did you find?" Fowler nearly came across the desk.

"We didn't find anything. Not yet. But someone else did."

"Who?"

"We intercepted some communications." Thorpe looked at Janda as if to drive home the point; mess on our turf and we'll crap on yours. "According to the information, your man Fareed was equipped with some fairly sophisticated computer media, a concealed micro flash drive in a pair of glasses. Not something you could whip up yourself. From what we're told, this device would require the expertise of a pretty sophisticated spy shop, and not the kind you find in your local mall. It works remotely and has enough storage capacity to hold most of the secrets of the Western world, and then some."

"Do you know what's on it?" said Fowler.

"What was characterized as machine language by the person who found it. Computer software, as well as some notes written in plain English by Fareed indicating very clearly that he was working with someone else, somebody for whom he was writing these notes."

"Who?" said Janda.

"We don't know," said Thorpe. "But I thought perhaps you or Mr. Fowler here could enlighten us. It might help if we knew what we were up against."

"This flash drive, do you know where it is?" said Fowler.

"We're looking for it now."

"Who has it?"

"We hope to know more in a few hours." Thorpe

put him off. He wasn't about to give him Madriani's name or to oversell what the lawyer had said on the phone to his investigator until Thorpe knew more. "Bureau agents are about to descend on the other party to these communications shortly. We should have more information then."

Thorpe had left instructions for agents to question Herman Diggs at the FBI safe house and to find out where in Mexico Madriani was headed. The two men had used cryptic terms to describe the location. Apparently Madriani and Diggs were familiar with the area because both of them had been there on business some years earlier. Madriani must have assumed that the FBI was listening. He fed in all the details he could about the flash drive and what was on it but skirted the question of where he and his companions were going, perhaps out of fear that the bureau might have Mexican authorities find and detain them once they arrived. For the moment the only one who knew that was Herman Diggs.

Adin rented a van, and he and Herman sat up front. Sarah and the dog shared the jump seat in the back. There were twelve large sealed cardboard boxes behind her, each one with a label on it in a language Sarah couldn't read. She had warned Adin that it was impossible to book the dog on a flight to Mexico. Even if they could get him on the plane, Mexican customs would quarantine him the minute they arrived.

He told her not to worry about it. He would take care of the dog. They couldn't leave him behind.

There was no one left in the condo to take care of him. She could have called her uncle in Ohio, but Adin wasn't allowing any phone calls out. The minute word got out they were planning on leaving, the FBI would be camped outside the door. Adin seemed to know what he was doing. Somehow he had looped one of the security cameras at the rear entrance so that nothing showed on the monitor at the front desk when they walked out. His only hitch, the one thing he hadn't planned on, was Herman, who was now playing hardball.

Sarah knew that her father was in Mexico, but she didn't know where. The details he had discussed with Herman, and Herman wasn't talking, not until they got to Mexico. The thought that Paul and Harry were in trouble was enough to get him moving.

And Adin didn't have time to argue. From all appearances, he was on some kind of a schedule, though neither Herman nor Sarah knew what it was.

He tried to leave Sarah behind, but she was having none of it. She told him he would have to tie her up and shoot the dog; otherwise, the second he walked out she would call the front desk and have him arrested. If he tied her and gagged her and left the dog, she would make enough noise that Bugsy would bark and wake the entire floor. Sarah suspected that tying her up wasn't a problem, shooting the dog was. Whatever, it worked.

"I take it we're not going out of Dulles," said Herman. The sun was just beginning to peek over the horizon as they headed south down I-95. "If you are, you're goin' the wrong way."

"You're right," said Adin. "Relax, we have a little ride ahead of us."

"Do you mind telling us where we're going? I assume you're not gonna drive to Mexico."

"We're going to Hampton in Virginia, Langley Air Force Base."

"Why there?" said Herman.

"To catch a plane."

"I don't get it. You want to avoid the government, yet you're going to try and fly out of a military base?" said Sarah.

"Except for the two of you and the dog, it would have been a piece of cake," said Adin. "Those boxes back there were my ticket to fly. They are documents under the seal of the Israeli embassy here in Washington. Call it a diplomatic pouch. I am carrying courier credentials from the embassy. There is a tarp back there. I hadn't planned for this, but you, Herman, and the dog are going to have to get under that tarp and remain still until we get through the gate. It should work. I did a dry run yesterday, and the guards at the gate didn't bother to open the van or check the boxes. They know they can't open them, so they just looked through the driver's-side window and counted them. They signed off on the lading and let me through. When I left ten minutes later, they figured the van was empty. They do that again today, we're home free."

"What about the plane?" said Herman.

"It's taken care of," said Adin. "An Israeli Air Force KC-130 will be waiting for us. It's a flying gas tank, used for aerial refueling. It has the range to reach Europe, North Africa, or, for that matter,

South America. I hope we're not going that far?" He looked at Herman who wasn't saying anything. "When we get to the side of the plane, you'll be loaded aboard with the freight. Don't move until I tell you. When I do, move fast. There's a ramp at the rear of the plane under the belly. It will be down. Get up the ramp as fast as you can. There won't be much room inside. The cargo area is taken up by two large stainless-steel fuel tanks. There is also a very large wooden cargo crate up front. Don't go near it! You will have to move between the two tanks up toward the front of the plane. Get in front of the tanks and stay there. Make sure you can't be seen from the open cargo ramp. And don't go up into the crew compartment until I get on board. We don't want any of the military guards to see you moving around in there. They may stop the flight and decide to search it. Any questions?"

"No," said Herman.

"Sarah, do you copy?"

"Yes."

"Can you handle the dog? You're going to have to keep him on a tight leash. If he gets loose and takes off, we're dead."

"I can do it," said Sarah.

"If you want me to take him, I can," said Adin.

"I assume you have other things to do," said Sarah.

"I'll be trying to keep the air force loadmaster busy while you guys get on board. After you're on, we'll bring the boxes."

"Just out of curiosity," said Herman. "What's in them?"

"Nothing. Blank paper and binders," said Adin.

"So the flight is just to get you down to Mexico?" said Herman.

"That and a few other things," said Adin. "I'll tell you more when we get in the air."

Israeli intelligence had known for some time that Bruno Croleva was hired by the Iranian Foreign Intelligence Service to perform logistics on the final theft of Project Thor.

The Mossad took one of Bruno's people and sweated him for information. Isolated and confused, sleep deprived and tormented, over a period of days the man was reduced to a pitiable set of basic human requirements, all of which were rationed out by those questioning him. They soon learned that Bruno had decided to make an offer to a man named Liquida, someone with connections to the Mexican drug cartels to join him on Project Thor. The man didn't know if the Mexican had accepted, but the offer was generous and the assumption was that he would.

In the meantime, Bruno had disappeared. They had to assume that he had gone to ground in preparation for the mission.

Adin had been planted at the FBI to gather information on U.S. surveillance surrounding Thor. The Israelis had assumed that the bureau would be the lead agency on counterespionage efforts surrounding the program. What he discovered was that the FBI knew nothing of the project. The Mossad was about to break off Adin's assignment and bring him home when he picked up rumors of an attack by a man named Liquida on a woman named Sarah

Madriani. They sent him back to work, and within days Adin discovered that the bureau was using Madriani's father as bait to lure Liquida into the open.

Adin had no idea of the connection between Madriani and Liquida. What's more, he didn't care. All that mattered was following the food chain: Madriani to Liquida, Liquida to Bruno. Adin could only hope and pray that he was getting close, and that he had enough time.

FORTY-NINE

It's possible he was a double agent," said Janda. "We don't know." The general and Fowler finally decided to throw Thorpe a bone, what information they had on Raji Fareed. "We had him under surveillance. We thought we had him covered, but we lost him in France."

"Who were you using on the ground?" said Thorpe.

"Military intelligence and CIA," said Janda. "We thought we had plenty of resources. Somehow they both got away."

"Funny how that happens," said Thorpe. "Who were you using here in the States, for surveillance, I mean?" This was a sore point, and Thorpe knew it. Neither the CIA nor the military could be used legally within the territorial borders of the United States to conduct intelligence against U.S. citizens.

"We're not discussing that," said Fowler. "Suffice it to say that we were doing our job."

"We knew what we were doing," said Janda. "The

reason I say Fareed could have been a double agent is not only his background, Iranian father and Israeli mother. We have photographs of him meeting with handlers from both embassies."

"Did it ever occur to you that maybe he knew you were following him?" said Thorpe.

"He was playing a dangerous game," said Fowler. "That's probably why he's dead."

"How long did you have him under surveillance?" asked Thorpe.

"Two years," said Janda. "We have reason to believe he was a deep plant, a sleeper. He could have been activated more recently by radicals, but we don't think so."

"Why wasn't the bureau informed?"

"That's above your pay grade," said Fowler.

"Yet you allowed this man to have access to highly classified information and to leave the country," said Thorpe.

"That's enough," said Fowler. "Your job is to find Leffort and to make sure we get any and all classified information back, including this flash drive. What about computers? Did the French police find a computer in Fareed's hotel room?"

"No. We checked. If there was anything there, whoever killed him took it," said Thorpe.

"Find that flash drive," said Fowler. "Do you understand?"

"Yes."

"Then, unless you have more information for us, we won't detain you any longer."

Thorpe got up, took his briefcase, and left.

They waited for the door to close behind him.

"I don't trust him," said Fowler. "He's not a team player."

"He's old enough to remember Watergate," said Janda. "If you recall, all the team players in that event went to prison."

"You're not getting cold feet, are you?"

"No," said Janda.

"In case you're worried, let me remind you that we're not stealing money and we're not trying to fix elections here. You know as well as I do that this was our one chance to take down the major terrorist cell in Europe. We know they were the people one notch above Bruno Croleva in this thing. They've been the eyes and ears of more terrorist acts than we can count. What we were doing was on a need-to-know basis, and Thorpe didn't need to know."

"I agree," said Janda. "I'm on board."

"Good!"

"It's just that if the media gets wind of any of the details of Project Thor, it's going to be more than just a major international embarrassment. These are serious treaty violations. You know and I know that the president's gonna be looking for cover, claiming that he never authorized anything. They're going to be looking for a fall guy," said Janda. The way he said it made Fowler wonder if he was auditioning for the role. The thought had crossed Fowler's mind more than once.

Project Thor was a direct violation of international treaties prohibiting the militarization of space and the extension of weapons of mass destruction as part of space-based warfare.

Thor was a black box program of DARPA, the

Defense Advanced Research Projects Agency. It was undertaken only because defense agencies realized it was just a question of time before some other government stumbled on what was now becoming obvious.

Weapons of mass destruction on a scale previously unknown were already there and available, just waiting to be harvested. The Rand Corporation and others had done research and rendered reports some years earlier finding that the concept was not feasible. Not because it couldn't be done—the science and technology were already there—but because it couldn't replace a nuclear strike force in terms of deterrence. They were still thinking inside the box, in the terms of the Cold War. Since then the world had changed. Deterrence was not an issue if your goal was to wipe an adversary off the face of the earth and to avoid accountability for the act.

They were the perfect weapons for asymmetrical warfare. If properly deployed in a preemptive strike, the damage would be so devastating that no thermonuclear device, no matter how powerful, could compare. Best of all, they could be used without fear of retaliation. There was no way to trace them back to the nation that launched them. It was the perfect cover.

What no one knew, other than a few people at NASA and a handful of leaders at the highest levels of government, was that the United States was already three years into the testing phase. Two potential weapons were already deployed, something Raji Fareed and his handlers could not have known.

It was Leffort, the trader of secrets, who had

changed the telecommand codes at NASA and severed the telemetry links to Project Thor. The weapons that had been on a taut leash for so long were no
longer under the government's control. If the world
were to discover what was happening, the public
panic and political fallout would be cataclysmic.

Adin drove past Richmond on toward Williams-
burg, then swung around Langley Air Force Base to
avoid the main gate. He approached the base from
the south on State Route 167 where there was much
less traffic and where he had gained access the day
before.

A short distance south of the gate, he pulled off
the road into an industrial area on the tidewater and
parked. They all got out, Adin, Sarah, the dog, and
Herman. Sarah held Bugsy on a leash. Adin opened
up the back of the van. They folded up the jump
seat in the back and pushed the boxes with their
diplomatic seals toward the front where they could
easily be seen by anyone standing outside the driver's window. They made a wall with the boxes and
arranged the tarp behind it.

Sarah and the dog got in first. Adin got Bugsy
down on his stomach and petted him a little until he
relaxed. Herman got in, and Adin covered all three
of them with the tarp.

"Next stop is the gate. Stay still and keep quiet."
He closed the back of the van and locked it. If the
guard made him open it, Adin had no idea what he
would do next. This had never been part of the plan.

Back in the driver's seat he started the engine,

swung a U-turn, and drove back out to the road. He took a deep breath and turned right. Half a mile up, he saw the concrete gatehouse with the guard standing outside. There were two cars in front of him in line. Adin pulled up behind them, stopped the van, and got his paperwork ready. There was a clipboard with the embassy's diplomatic lading slip, along with official documents all in triplicate, stamped with the embassy's official seal.

One car was through. The second took only a moment, an officer with an ID. The guard saluted and waved him through. Adin pulled the van up and stopped.

"Good morning." Adin smiled at him, then handed the clipboard to the guard.

The guard looked at it. At first he seemed a little puzzled, then he saw the day pass clipped to the top sheet. The embassy had obtained it through Israeli military connections with the U.S. Air Force. It was the magic key. "This is a little unusual, isn't it? Don't you guys usually fly this stuff commercial?" said the guard.

"Usually," said Adin. "But we had a military tanker coming in for refueling, so I guess they figured may as well use it."

The guard stuck his head in the window and counted with his finger until he got to twelve. "Looks like it's OK." He tried to peek over the boxes. "Just the twelve boxes, right?"

"That's it."

The guard signed off, tore the top sheet off, and handed the clipboard back to Adin. "Have a nice day."

Adin smiled. "Thanks," he said and drove through the gate. To his passengers in back, he said, "Stay down. We have one more stop to make before we get to the plane." He took the curving road around to the right, passed the huge B-52 on display, and a half mile up he turned left on Laurel. He followed it to the large commissary where it ended in a T intersection in front of the building. He turned right and threaded his way through the short blocks to Holly Street. There ahead of him was a single chain-link gate, the last barrier between the van and the concrete apron leading to the runway.

He stopped at the gate, and a guard came out. He checked the paperwork, didn't bother to look at the boxes, and opened the gate.

As he drove through the gate Adin saw an entire wing of fighter jets, F-18s, parked in a separate area off to the right. He assumed that this was part of the Air National Guard unit stationed at the base.

Two A-10 Warthogs were parked closer in on the apron. Just beyond them, farther out toward the runway, was a KC-130 with four large squared-off propellers in desert camo colors. It bore the Israeli Air Force marking on the side, a simple white circle surrounding the blue Star of David. Adin sighed a deep breath when he saw it. Almost home.

One of the flight crew was standing outside near the open ramp under the tail section talking with a U.S. Air Force officer. The Israeli pointed toward the approaching van, and the American turned and looked.

By the time Adin reached them, he already had the window down and the clipboard out. He pulled up next to the two men, handed the clipboard to the American, smiled, and said, "Do you want to count them?"

The guy just glanced through the window, looked at the boxes, checked the paperwork, and said, "I'll take your word for it." He tore off one more of the forms for his records and asked the Israeli crewman if they needed a hand loading.

"We can handle it," said the Israeli. "You could do us a favor, though. The driver is a military attaché from the embassy. He's going to be flying out with us. Could you park the van and hold it? They'll be sending somebody down to pick it up later today."

"No problem," said the American.

"Go ahead on back. I'll drive over to the hangar and give you the keys when we're done," said Adin.

"I can wait," said the guy.

"I'm afraid it's gonna take a while. There's some things I have to discuss with the crew before we load up and take off," said Adin.

The Israeli crewman looked surprised. But he didn't say anything.

"Well, if it's gonna take a long time, I'll head back," said the American.

"Catch up with you at the hangar." Adin smiled.

As soon at the guy walked away, Adin looked at the other Israeli and under his breath said, "I've got some passengers."

"So have we," said the Israeli.

They spoke for a second, and Adin pulled the van around, backed up to the foot of the ramp, and told his passengers in the back to hang on. He hit the gas and backed up the ramp until the rear of the van edged into the open belly of the plane. He stopped, put the van in park, and jumped out.

By then the other Israeli was already at the back of the van. Adin unlocked the two back doors and they swung open. Except for a few feet exposed under the two open doors at the side, Sarah, Herman, and the dog were completely shielded from view by anyone outside the plane.

Adin pulled the tarp off them and Bugsy jumped. His eyes immediately fixed on the other Israeli. Adin grabbed him as he lunged, snagged his collar. "Easy! Easy! Heel!" He struggled to calm the dog and hold him in the van. He grabbed him by the muzzle to keep him from barking as Adin peeked through the crack at the hinge of the rear van door.

The American airman had turned around to see what the commotion was. He stopped for a second and looked. When he didn't see anything, he turned again and headed once more toward the hangar.

Adin watched him go. "Now!" he told Sarah. "Move."

Quickly she stepped down from the van and up into the plane. Herman followed her. Adin took the dog by the leash. Once inside he gave Bugsy to Sarah. "Hang on to him and don't let him bark."

"How do I stop him?"

"Just like this." Adin took Bugsy's muzzle with his hand and held it firmly but gently.

"He'll let me do that?"

"Yeah, if you show him who's boss," said Adin. He smiled at her.

She took the dog up the ramp and was immediately confronted with what was in front of her.

It wasn't until then that Adin noticed the configuration inside the plane. The twin fuel tanks weren't there. He turned to the other Israeli. "Where are the tanks?"

"It's all right. We have a single tank up front, centered under the wings. We'll have enough range. Besides, you're going to need what's in those other containers." There were two large metal boxes balancing the load, one of them the size of a double shipping container but not quite as high. It had a drop-down door facing the open ramp.

FIFTY

Back at the airport in Playa del Carmen, I question the pilot as to exactly what he saw during his single flyover of the facility.

It has been several months, and he can't recall all the details with precision. From what he remembered seeing, the area was fenced off and there appeared to be some fixed guns, though he can't recall their precise location. He was scared, trying to maneuver the small ultralight to dodge the bullets.

What he remembers most was the large satellite dish. "I almost flew into it," he tells me. "It was very big. Bigger than this building." He is talking about the hangar in which we are standing.

"Excuse me?"

"No, I swear it," he says.

Harry is looking at him as if it's a fish story.

"It saved my life."

"Why do you say that?" says Harry.

"Because when I flew toward it, they stopped

firing. I realized they didn't want to hit it. So I kept going. But sooner or later I had to go around it or over it. That's when I realized how big it was. It sat on top of its own building," he says.

"That would have to be a commercial broadcasting dish," says Harry. "What would they be doing with that?"

"I don't know."

We decide to stay the night at a motel on the coast in Playa del Carmen. We now know how far the distance is to the location of the facility. As the crow flies not far, by car perhaps an hour.

"So what do we do?" says Harry. "Let's assume your man is right, that what he says is up that road is there. I'd say we're at an end." Over dinner at a small restaurant overlooking the beach we talk.

"I think we need to know for sure," I tell him.

"When are you going to know for sure, when they shoot you?" says Harry.

"What if we call Thorpe and try and get him to bring in the Mexican police and all they find is some narco lab, or worse, what if it's a Mexican government facility? It could be a prison for all we know."

"With that kind of a dish," says Harry, "I doubt it."

"Maybe it's a defense facility of some kind. What then? They'll scoop us up and send us home and that's the end of it. Liquida will be gone until he comes back to hunt us on his own terms. Everything we've done to this point will have been for nothing."

"You heard what the man said," says Harry. "They fired at him with antiaircraft weapons."

"The Mexican government might do that if you

overfly an area that's restricted. The pilot has no idea what it was. He was assuming it had to do with one of the cartels. He may be right."

"I'm sorry, but I think we ought to call Thorpe," says Harry. "How about you?" He looks to Joselyn for a second.

"I don't know. I don't mind admitting I'm scared."

"There. See?" says Harry.

"But Paul's right about one thing. We're only going to get one bite at this. I think we need to be sure of our information before we call Thorpe."

"How do we do that, walk up and knock on the front door?" says Harry.

"I think if we can get in close enough, we'll know. How big would you say that hangar was we were standing in?" I ask him.

"I don't know," says Harry.

"It had to be at least a hundred feet wide and almost as deep."

"Bigger than that," says Joselyn.

"If he's right, that's one hell of a satellite dish," I tell Harry.

"Let's call Thorpe and tell him about it," says Harry.

"Not until we see it," I tell him.

"It would be good if we could send him a picture," says Joselyn. "Tell him the location. He would have access to satellite intelligence. A good analyst with high-quality photographs might be able to tell what that dish is for."

"See, women are smarter than men," I tell Harry.

"Not if survival counts for anything," he says.

"Have another glass of wine," she tells him.

* * *

"What do you mean, they're gone?" Thorpe shouted into the phone.

The agent on the other end swallowed hard. "We rang the bell and nobody answered. We got the front desk to let us in and the unit's empty. They left some of their clothes, but the girl and the one you wanted us to talk to, this Herman Diggs, both gone."

"You checked the building?" said Thorpe.

"Top to bottom."

"What about the security cameras?"

"We looked. There's nothing. They didn't leave by the front door. We know that. Video of the back door shows no movement. According to our notes, there was supposed to be a dog. It's gone as well."

"Where's the kid?" asked Thorpe.

"Don't know," said the agent.

Thorpe cupped his hand over the mouthpiece of the phone and looked at Bill Britain, who was seated across the desk from him. "Where's Hirst?"

Britain shook his head.

"Find out if he showed up for work today," said Thorpe.

Britain plucked his cell phone from his belt and headed out into the other room.

"Listen," Thorpe said as he went back to the agent on the phone. "Get a key and check Hirst's apartment. Do you have a cell number for him?"

"Yeah."

"Give it to me," said Thorpe.

The agent gave it to him, and Thorpe jotted

it down on the notepad on his desk. "Call me the minute you get into his apartment." Thorpe hung up. He immediately dialed the cell phone number written on the pad. It rang three times and the insipid voice came over the phone. "This is Adin. I'm away from my phone. Leave a message and I'll get back to you." Thorpe slammed the receiver down on the phone.

Two seconds later Britain came back in the room. He was shaking his head. "Hirst was supposed to be in a meeting at ten this morning. He never showed up," said Britain.

"Damn it," said Thorpe. "I knew it. We should have taken him down when we had the chance."

"We wanted to net his handler," said Britain.

"What happens when you get greedy," said Thorpe.

The FBI had been aware almost from the beginning that Hirst was a plant. They knew he was no trainee. Some footwork on the part of one of the CIA's own moles inside Israeli intelligence identified Hirst as a thirty-two-year-old Mossad agent named Yoni Shahar. He had spent eight years in the Israeli Defense Forces as a member of the elite S-13, Israel's counterpart to America's Delta Force. Shahar had been recruited to the Mossad and had performed a number of overseas missions. One in particular had resulted in the assassination of a high-level Iranian scientist, a nuclear physicist reputed to be working on Iran's atomic bomb project.

"You think he knew we were onto him?" said Britain.

"Yes."

"You think he's got Diggs and the girl?"

"They all disappear on the same day." Thorpe looked at him. "What do you think?" He had promised Madriani that his daughter would be safe. Now she was gone.

"Why?"

"I don't know. But he's been hanging out at their apartment. Took her to the range. Cozied up to the dog. He wanted something. The question is, what?"

"Maybe he was lonely," said Britain.

"Man like that doesn't get lonely. And he doesn't get distracted. He lives for his work."

"It's possible he was after the same thing we are," said Britain.

Thorpe looked at him.

"Liquida," said Britain. "It's possible."

"Why?"

"Liquida gets around. Maybe he killed a high-level Israeli. A contract on some VIP. The Israelis aren't as forgiving as we are. They have a long history of tit for tat," said Britain.

"It's possible." Thorpe thought for a moment. "Or maybe you're right."

"What?"

"Maybe he is after the same thing we are," said Thorpe.

"What do you mean?"

"Project Thor."

"What. You think . . . ?"

"Sure. Fowler and the administration have blinded us. We don't know what Thor is about because Fowler won't tell us. Hirst shows up on our doorstep when—a few weeks before I get the phone call to go over to the White House. I get there, they want to play liar's dice. What if the Israelis already knew about Thor?"

"If they already knew about it, why would they send Hirst?"

"Because they knew something we don't. Maybe there was a piece they were missing and they thought they could get it here. Something we were supposed to know, if we were inside the loop, which we weren't. The people who sent Hirst must have been mightily disappointed," said Thorpe. "Because we don't know shit."

"If so, he picked up the threads pretty fast," said Britain. "Hirst or Shahar or whatever the hell his name is, he's on a better trajectory than we are. If he's got Diggs and the girl, and Diggs knows where Madriani is. Madriani's got a line on Liquida, and Liquida's with Bruno. Hirst is gonna have a front-row seat to whatever is playing."

"And we're going to be sitting here picking our noses," said Thorpe.

"You think he might have killed them? The girl and Diggs, I mean?" said Britain.

"No. If he extracted the information, he'd just leave them. No reason to harm them. They all left together. The girl wanted out of here anyway. She wouldn't have been hard to convince. Madriani's tracking Liquida. Now Hirst has his daughter. That gives him a trump card," said Thorpe. "Madriani's in Mexico. The question is, where? That's where they'll be going."

"Let me check the airports." Britain started to get up from his chair.

"Do it . . . No! On second thought, don't."

"Why not?" said Britain.

"Because he wouldn't go out that way. He's got the dog." Thorpe looked at him. "Unless he shot him. And if he did that, he may as well shoot the girl, in which case he'll never get anything out of Diggs. I know the man. No, if Hirst took the dog, it was because he had a way to get him out."

"What do you mean?"

Thorpe thought about it for a moment. A boat was too slow. The only other aircraft . . . "Check El Al," said Thorpe. The Israeli national airline had been known to cut corners for their government on sensitive military and political matters in the past. "Otherwise check for any MATS flights. Military air transport. Not ours, theirs," said Thorpe. "See if there were any Israeli military flights in or out of the area around Washington since last night. If they're still on the ground, hold them. All flights. If they're in the air, see if the air force can pick them up on radar. If they're over U.S. airspace, see if we can scramble fighters to bring them back."

Britain was headed for the door.

Thorpe stood up. "And see if any of the MATS filed flight plans." Thorpe knew it was a long shot. Hirst would never leave a flight plan behind, but maybe his pilot did. Sarah Madriani was gone. He pounded the top of his desk with a closed fist. At the moment he could have killed Fowler with his bare hands. "What in the hell is Project Thor?"

FIFTY-ONE

Joseph-Louis Lagrange was an eighteenth-century French mathematician who determined that two large orbiting bodies in space could create gravitational pockets in which a third object, smaller than the first two, could become trapped and held in place.

According to Lagrange's mathematical formulas, five such Lagrange points were created by the gravitational pull of the sun and the earth. Another five such points existed as a result of the competing tug of gravity caused by the earth and the moon.

All of this, of course, was mere theory until American and Russian scientists, during the early years of space exploration, verified that all five of the solar and lunar Lagrange points actually existed. Some were stable. Some were not. Those with stability have proven useful over the years as places to park geosynchronous satellites where they can be held in place with little or no maintenance.

Lunar Lagrange Point Two, or L2, was one of

the less stable of these points. In order to hold an object at lunar L2, regular periodic maintenance is required. Without such maintenance the object in question will either be spun off into space or crash into the moon. For this as well as other reasons, lunar L2 is generally not deemed useful as a location for parking satellites.

However, for Larry Leffort and Project Thor, L2 offered immense advantages that far outweighed its gravitational instability. L2 is located on the back side of the moon. An object placed in an elliptical halo orbit at L2 could be maintained as if in a raceway at intense velocity. It would be visible from the earth for only short periods each day at the outer edge of its elliptical flight pattern, during which time maintenance could be performed to hold it in place. During the rest of the time, an object at lunar L2 would be completely concealed from the earth by the face of the moon. Unless someone was looking for it or knew it was there, the chances of observing it were not great, especially if it was held in this pattern for only a short time.

Leffort smiled as he settled in behind the control desk in the jungle enclave north of Coba. He looked at the array of four large computer screens in front of him to check the progress made since his departure from his office at NASA's Caltech facility in California. In less than ten days, the scientists at Coba had done a fine job. But then the software and classified information that Leffort had given them was spot-on.

Leffort had delivered to them access and complete control over two test weapons.

These Near-Earth Objects (NEOs) had been carefully selected and harvested by NASA from among the hundreds that had been identified in the last decade as possible earth impactors and therefore potential hazards. They had been further whittled down based on size, composition, and velocity. In the end they had settled on two relatively small iron-core asteroids, each one approximately twice the size of a school bus.

During the initial trial phase, tractor rocket motors had been attached to each of the asteroids and tested. The results far exceeded anything NASA could have expected. In less than a year, each of the asteroids had been nudged and guided into a pattern in the inner solar system that made it clear to NASA that maneuvering the objects with precision in space was entirely feasible.

Beyond this, the telecommand and telemetry software that would allow the asteroids to be parked at the L2 location behind the moon had been computer tested with a high level of reliability and assurance. NASA was confident this could be done.

The space agency was about to move the objects back out and dispose of them in a collision course with the sun when suddenly they lost control of both impactors.

Leffort had introduced a virus into the JPL computers that controlled the rockets and the experimental gravity tractors. The software controlling the telecommands was the key to the kingdom. Leffort notified Bruno that the scientists in Mexico, using the software Leffort had supplied to them, now had control of the system.

At first NASA didn't know what was happening. They knew it was a software failure, but they couldn't be sure of the cause. And while it ran a wrinkle through their experiment, the test was largely concluded. There was no real reason to pursue it. Over the next several months they would have time to find it and fix it. But there was no real urgency.

The two asteroids were moving at speeds incomprehensible to the average person, in excess of forty thousand miles per hour. This was more than twenty times the speed of the fastest rifle bullet on Earth and more than twice as fast as the manned missions to the moon.

Trying to relocate the two missing asteroids in the vastness of space using the narrow focal range of their telescopes was like trying to find a speeding needle scanning the sky through a drinking straw. NASA knew there was no chance of an accidental impact with Earth based on the last telemetry readings before they lost contact. Both asteroids were on a harmless trajectory out into space beyond the solar system, because that is where they were last seen.

But in fact, control had been taken by the telecommand and telemetry station that was now up and running in the jungles of the Yucatán.

Construction of this facility had been financed by Middle Eastern powers that were now awash in oil money. It had taken place during a period when the Mexican government was distracted and under a virtual state of siege by the drug cartels. Mexico was ripe for the plucking, and adversaries of the

United States, the Great Satan, were well aware of this.

For thirty million dollars, the Mexican government was happy to lease two thousand acres of useless jungle to a telecommunications research lab financed by petro dollars from abroad. The promise of future jobs and potential revenue left the Mexican government to pay little attention given the other crisis they were now facing. The few Mexican officials who sought entry to the burgeoning facility in the jungle were either paid off or disappeared. Despite U.S. concerns, not all of the problems confronting them from Mexico were on their immediate southern border.

The earth survived in a veritable shooting gallery of rocks streaming through space at tens of thousands of miles per hour. Some of these objects were the size of large cities. A few were the size of states. Conservative estimates placed the number of possible extinction-level objects in near-Earth orbit at more than one thousand, of which to date scientists had located and identified only a small percentage.

The potential for destruction was catastrophic. Major collisions with large asteroids were known to have caused extinction-level events in the planet's history. It was, in fact, an irony to Leffort that the antenna array erected in the Yucatán jungle and the building from which he was now working sat less than a hundred miles from the center of one of the largest asteroid strikes in global history.

Sixty-five million years ago, the Chicxulub asteroid, estimated to be six miles in diameter, slammed into the western Caribbean just a few miles off the

Yucatán coast. It created a crater one hundred and ten miles in diameter, believed to be the largest impact structure on the face of the earth. The heat generated by the collision vaporized entire forests. It ejected mountains of material into space. Much of this would have ignited into incandescence upon re-entry into the atmosphere, superheating the air and setting off monumental wildfires around the globe.

The Chicxulub impactor was believed to have buried itself in the earth's crust in less than a second, creating seismic sea waves thousands of feet high. It is also believed that it was the effects of this asteroid striking the earth that spelled extinction for the dinosaurs.

It was only natural that nations would deploy their science to find ways of warding off such future threats to man's survival. Soon a proliferation of acronyms abounded—NEAR, NEAT, NEOSSat, and NEOwise and the Torino Scale—all created for measuring the size and potential for impact of each threat.

From there it was but a question of time before some enterprising soul saw the potential for arresting the threat only to transform it into history's ultimate weapon. Harness an asteroid of the right size and composition, temper its velocity and guide it with precision, and your enemy could be wiped from the face of the earth as if swatted by the hand of God.

Leffort mused at the constantly changing state of the world and the narrow-minded vision of its "leaders" with their rigid timeworn concepts of geopolitics.

Decades earlier the United States had studied and dismissed the use of NEOs as potential weapons of mass destruction. The studies concluded that the kinetic energy stored in these missiles of nature far surpassed the destructive power of anything man-made, including the most devastating nuclear warheads. Yet they waddled in their own ignorance. They dismissed NEOs on grounds that they couldn't be fashioned to fit the prevailing stratagem of the moment, the Cold War concept of MAD—Mutually Assured Destruction.

The defense experts operated on the assumption that the time needed to harness and hurl meteors and asteroids at selected targets on the surface of the earth, while scientifically possible, would cost too much and take too long to be a feasible and effective deterrent to those adversaries that already possessed nuclear arms.

They put the studies on the shelf to collect dust and waited. Since then the world had been turned upside down by the concept of asymmetrical warfare.

Acts of insurgency now used methods of attack and civilian terror no longer confined to conventional battlefields. The dread of nuclear-tipped missiles over Manhattan was replaced by the threat of dirty bombs or nuclear devices smuggled in the hold of a ship or on the back of a truck. The use of subnationals as proxies of terror to mask acts of war by sponsoring states became the norm. Rules of restraint based on deterrence, the old fear of massive retaliation, had gone the way of the goony bird.

In such a world, the veiled promise of nature's

own instruments of destruction could not go unnoticed for long. DARPA and the Defense Department dredged up the old studies and dusted them off. Suddenly they realized the risk. The science of steering objects in space was a known technology mastered by a growing number of states. Streaking fire across the sky, an iron asteroid sufficiently large to survive Earth's atmosphere, whether by cataclysmic impact with Earth or by atmospheric burst, would deliver more death and destruction in a moment of time than any preemptive nuclear strike. And in the sign of the times, all of this could be carried out under cover of an unfathomable act of nature.

FIFTY-TWO

Surprise came from the first large steel container up forward in the belly of the C-130. As the plane lifted off from the runway and began to climb out over the Atlantic, a hatch up on top suddenly popped open. Sarah heard it and looked up, but she didn't see anything.

They were crouched on the floor against the side of the plane—Sarah, Herman, Bugsy, and Adin. A few seconds later a man appeared, looking down at them from over the edge of the container.

Bugsy barked at him and lunged to the end of his leash as Sarah struggled to hold him.

"Easy," said Adin. He petted the dog and looked up. "It's only Teo. I was hoping it would be you." He glanced up at the man. "You can eat him later," Adin told Bugsy.

"Who else would it be?" said the man.

"I could think of at least a half-dozen colonels, all of them younger than you," said Adin.

"Yes, but none of them as good. It's getting a

little warm inside," said the man. "Do you mind if we join you?"

"What if I said yes?" Adin smiled up at him.

"Then to hell with you." Wearing military fatigues and combat boots, the man looked considerably older than Adin, maybe in his late forties or early fifties. He climbed down using the red cargo netting suspended from the inside wall of the plane. Regardless of his age he was quite fit, short, and stocky, his face tanned as if he'd lived his life on a golf course in Palm Springs. His balding forehead was etched with craggy lines and deep furrows. His most memorable feature was his beaming smile. "This the young lady you were telling me about?"

"What has he been saying?" said Sarah.

"Allow me to introduce you. Sarah Madriani, this old man is Teo Ben Rabin. Colonel Ben Rabin to some. But you can just call him Uncle Ben," said Adin.

"Only behind my back," said Ben Rabin.

"And do yourself a favor," said Adin. "Don't believe anything he says."

"Nice to meet you." Sarah smiled, nodded, and shook his hand.

"Teo, I'd like you to meet Herman Diggs."

Ben Rabin stepped gingerly around the dog, keeping a little distance. "I like to keep all my fingers," he said.

"Mr. Diggs is our navigator for this trip," said Adin. "By force of character, you might say. He refused to tell us where we were going unless we took him along."

"A man after my own heart," said Ben Rabin. "Shalom. Welcome aboard."

Herman nodded and shook his hand.

"Are you feeling all right?" said Ben Rabin. He was looking at Herman.

"I'm not great in airplanes," said Herman. "Specially with the fuel tank and the fumes, sittin' sideways like this."

"You're looking a little green around the gills," said Ben Rabin. "You want, I will find you a seat up top with the flight crew. The air up there is a little better."

"Might take you up on that," said Herman.

"Give me a minute."

Herman nodded.

"I take it he's not really your uncle." Sarah looked at Adin.

"Only in spirit," he told her. "The colonel is a man with many nephews."

Ben Rabin pounded on the side of the steel container. "You can come out now!" He yelled at the top of his voice. "The rest of my relatives." He looked at Sarah and smiled. "We were beginning to wonder how long it was going to take before we got airborne. It is damn hot in there."

"Makes you wonder what it was like in the Trojan Horse?" said Adin.

"Something like that."

A few seconds later, men began to crawl out over the edge of the steel container, all in camo-green battle fatigues and heavy boots.

"How many did you bring?" said Adin.

"One platoon," said Ben Rabin. "Eighteen was all we could fit. Like sardines in a can."

"What about the other container?" said Adin.

"Equipment. Ground transport, one Desert Raider with a mounted 105-millimeter recoilless rifle, and one equipment trailer. The trailer will have to do double duty," said Ben Rabin. "Transport both men and equipment. Do we know how far we're going to have to go once we hit the ground?"

"I don't know anything yet. We'll have to talk to Mr. Diggs." Adin turned and looked at Herman.

"What are you expecting, World War III?" said Herman.

"Could very well be," said Ben Rabin. "Do you have any idea what we're going to be dealing with when we get down there?"

"Not a clue," said Herman.

"You do know where we're going?" said Adin.

"A general idea," said Herman.

Adin gave Ben Rabin a look as if to say "the blind leading the blind."

By now the soldiers were wandering up and down inside the belly of the plane, working on the two containers, pulling out equipment and arms, loaded backpacks, staging it all in the narrow aisle between the large fuel tank and the two metal containers. Most of the men appeared to be slightly older than the usual soldier, in their late twenties or early thirties, some of them sporting longer hair. Ben Rabin turned his attention to give them a hand.

"Who are they?" asked Herman.

"What do you mean? Oh, them. Just Israeli Defense Forces," said Adin.

"Yeah, and I'm the Pied Piper," said Herman.

"Wouldn't mean anything to you if I told you," said Adin.

"Try me."

"Special forces," said Adin.

"S-13?" said Herman.

Adin gave him a look. "How would you know about that?"

"Lucky guess," said Herman. That and the shoulder patch of the Shayetet 13, the anchor, sword, and shield emblazoned over the bat wings.

"What is S-13?" asked Sarah.

"If your dad is where these people are going, I'd say he's in some serious trouble," said Herman. Then he leaned into her ear and whispered. "Shayetet 13 are naval commandos, cross between the Seals and Delta Force. They don't usually show up for a party unless somebody's gonna get shot."

The news settled on Sarah like ether, but Bugsy wanted to join the soldiers. Seeing all the movement and commotions excited him. He was like a kid who wanted to join the activity. Every once in a while one of the soldiers would lean in and pet him. He didn't seem to mind.

"You can let him go," said Adin. "It's better if he gets their scent."

Sarah let loose of the leash. Adin unclipped it from the dog's collar and let him run.

"You and I need to go up forward and look at some maps," he told Herman. They got to their feet and went toward the ladder leading up to the flight deck. Sarah followed.

"When we get on the ground, I'm going to ask both of you to stay onboard the plane," said Adin.

"We'll have to talk about that," said Herman.

"This is not negotiable," said Adin. "Depending on where we land, we may not have much time. We'll offload the vehicle and a stacked trailer from the other container. That's ground transport for the men and their equipment. Once we're on the ground we'll get going in less than a minute. You're just going to be in the way. It's very likely that the plane is going to have to take off again."

"Why's that?" said Herman.

"Because we won't be landing at an airport with customs and immigrations," said Adin. "It will be an unimproved field. We won't know precisely where until you give us your information. Your background indicates you worked in Mexico . . ."

"How do you know that?" said Herman.

"Never mind," said Adin. "The point is, you know as well as I do what an unimproved field in Mexico means."

"Drugs," said Herman.

Adin nodded. "The pilot is going to want to turn it around and get back in the air as fast as he can."

"Understood," said Herman.

"Good," said Adin. "Stay right here." Adin climbed the ladder up toward the flight cabin. He knocked on the metal door, and someone inside opened it.

Neither Sarah nor Herman could hear what was

being said up in the flight cabin over the din of the four large engines.

A few seconds later, Adin came back down the ladder with a handful of maps. "What's the name of the place we're going?"

"Coba," said Herman. "South of Cancún in the jungle. Twenty miles or so from the town of Tulum on the Caribbean side."

They huddled over the map with Sarah looking on until Herman circled an area with his finger. Coba didn't show up on the flight chart, but an unimproved landing strip off the main highway some distance to the east did. Adin marked it with a pen.

"That's a ways. I was hoping for something closer." Adin's concern was not only the cartels but the Mexican military. Driving a distance on open roads with military hardware was likely to draw attention. The last thing they needed was a firefight at a roadblock with the Mexican army. "Do you know where her father is?"

"In the area somewhere," said Herman.

"Any way to reach him?" asked Adin.

Herman shook his head. "No cell number that I know of."

"Not much to go on," said Adin.

"According to Paul, there's supposed to be some kind of a large antenna array. Somewhere near Coba in the jungle." He pointed to the area on the map once more. "If it's big enough, it should be visible from the air."

Adin nodded.

"Give me a second," said Sarah. "I might have something." She walked back over to the area where they had been sitting and found her purse. Inside was a folded piece of paper. She opened it and looked at it. It was a printout of one of the early e-mail messages sent to her by her father through the FBI. At the top was Joselyn's e-mail address. She handed it to Adin.

He looked at it. "We'll try it and see." He headed back up the ladder toward the flight deck. This time he disappeared inside with the door closed.

"Listen to me!" Herman took her to one side. "When the plane lands, get over there behind that metal container and sit tight. Stay away from that fuel tank," he told her, "in case there's shooting."

"Where are you going to be?"

"I'm gonna be goin' for a ride," he told her.

"You told Adin you would stay on board."

"I told him I understood. I didn't tell him I'd do it." Herman already had his eye on one of the packs lying in the aisle. On top of the backpack was a TAR-21, a Tavor assault rifle, a shortened bull-pup design manufactured by the Israelis and used for both close-quarters combat and longer open field fire.

Physically, Herman was not yet a hundred percent. He was still recovering from the wounds Liquida had inflicted. But a gun would go a long way toward giving him a leg up. No more wrestling with knives, at least not for now.

Herman had seen the short TAR-21s but only in photographs and online. He wondered how a country that was so small could develop such cutting-edge weapons. It looked like a space gun. It fired the same round as the American M16 and was accurate out to the same range, roughly three hundred meters. But the rifle was only half the length of the M16. The Israelis knew that in tight urban combat, in a building where you had to swing the muzzle to fire, short barrels provided the shooter with a lethal edge.

FIFTY-THREE

Liquida had no intention of unpacking his bags. Two days in the jungle facility and he was ready to leave. What he wanted was his money. "My job was to get Leffort and his information here, and to do it on time. I have done that. Now I want to be paid."

"I understand. So do I. We both want payment. Believe me when I tell you, I am as anxious as you are to go, to leave this place." Bruno cast a wary eye, as if the walls in Liquida's sterile room had ears. "But as I have explained to you, we are not yet finished." He was stalling.

"We are as far as I am concerned." Camped in a building with a huge electronic dish over the top of it was to Liquida like placing a neon crosshairs on your roof. He had no desire to look out his window and come nose to nose with a cruise missile.

Whatever was going out or coming in through the gigantic saucer sticking up in the middle of the jungle was none of his business. All Liquida knew was that he wanted no part of it. That and the heavy machine guns, the concertina-wired fences, and the starched military uniforms being worn by some of the people in the building gave him the willies. He had seen prisons with less security. Dying for someone else's cause was not high on Liquida's list of priorities. Bruno had described the facility as a Garden of Eden, swimming pools and guest bungalows. If so, they were hiding them well. What the place really needed was a good bomb shelter.

Bruno rattled on, telling him to be patient, that everything would be fine. Sooner or later they would pay him with piles of cash that they kept in a safe down the hall. "I promised them that you would do one more job for them."

"What is it they want?" said Liquida.

"They have asked me if you would mind disposing of Leffort."

Before Bruno could move, Liquida turned and opened his suitcase. He pulled out his wrapped bag of stilettos. "No problem." For Liquida this would be a labor of love. He would do it for nothing.

"Not now!" Bruno reached over and put his hand over the lace ties on the silverware bundle.

"When?" said Liquida.

"When they tell you."

"Why?"

"Because they need him, at least for now."

"Tell them I can do it now or they can do it later," said Liquida. "But I am not prepared to stay any longer. They do it themselves, I will give them a discount if they like."

"It's not the money," said Bruno.

"If it's not about money, then pay me," said Liquida. "Next you're going to tell me it's against their religion to kill. Tell them they can put on masks, cut off his head, and show it on television if they like. It's no problem. Happens down here all the time."

Bruno put a finger to his lips. "You should be careful what you say." He looked around as if someone might be listening. "Let me remind you that they could just as easily kill the two of us."

"So we are not free to leave, is that it?" said Liquida.

"That's not what I am saying."

"What are you saying?"

"I am asking you to be patient, to use your head. To think." Bruno fixed him with a long hard stare. "Do you understand? Do that and you will be well paid," said Bruno.

Yes, but only if I'm still alive, thought Liquida. "How long before they are finished with Leffort?" he asked.

"From what I am hearing, by morning they should be done. Tonight they are supposed to be very busy. Something is happening."

"What?" said Liquida.

"I don't know. I don't ask. Leffort has no idea they plan to kill him. I do know that. He told me they are going to pay him in the morning. He showed me airline tickets they bought for him. An early afternoon flight tomorrow from Belize to Mexico City and from there with connections to the French Seychelles. He is convinced they are going to honor their bargain. To pay him for the secrets he's given them."

"But you know better."

Bruno nodded. "By morning I am sure they will give us the word. Kill Leffort and our job is done."

Of course, if they were lying to Leffort, they could also be lying to Bruno. Or Bruno could be lying to him. Either way the result was the same. By sunrise Liquida could be sharing a shallow grave with Leffort. It was the one sure way to keep overhead down and loose ends tied up. The question was, how much trust did Liquida have in any of these people? The answer was none. He smiled at Bruno. "Good! Then we shall wait until morning."

"I knew that you could be relied upon to see reason. You have a good sense for business." Bruno clasped his shoulders and embraced him, what Liquida took for the Chechen sign of death.

Whether Bruno realized it or not, Liquida was now working for himself. The first order of business was to find a way out.

The FBI finally managed to track down Adin's flight from Langley Air Force Base. "Better late than never," said Thorpe. "Right from under our noses. That little bastard is bold as brass."

"They didn't file a flight plan," said Britain. "But radar tracked them out over the Atlantic heading due south. They were picked up again three hours later by Pensacola Naval Air Station on the Florida panhandle. By then they were out over the Gulf in international airspace. It was too late to stop them. But they tracked the heading south-southwest."

"Mexico," said Thorpe.

"What it looks like," said Britain. "We may be able to narrow it down."

Thorpe looked at him.

"Southcom, Southern Command out of Miami, had one of their AWAC flights loitering over the central Gulf track the C-130's IFF signal from their transponder," said Britain.

"I'm surprised the Israelis had it turned on," said Thorpe.

"I guess they didn't want to get shot down," said Britain.

IFF stood for "identify, friend or foe." It was a system of encrypted data sent by a plane's transponder to provide radar data and identification as part of the early-warning air defense system.

"You can bet they'll turn it off before they reach the Mexican coast," said Thorpe.

"Yes, but by then we may have a fix at least as to heading. It gives us something to work with," said Britain.

"What about the girl and Diggs?" said Thorpe. "Anybody at Langley see them board the plane?"

"No," said Britain. "But there was no real reason for them to check. It was pretty much hands off. Hirst had it all well covered. According to the flight documents, they picked up a load of fuel and twelve boxes under consular seal from the Israeli embassy."

"So nobody was watching," said Thorpe.

Britain nodded. "Right."

"He thought of everything." Thorpe sat silent for a moment. "So what do we know?"

"We know Hirst and whoever else is on that plane

is headed for Mexico, but we don't know where," said Britain.

"We can be reasonably certain that Madriani and his two companions are there, along with Liquida," said Thorpe.

"That is, if anything Madriani has told us is accurate," said Britain.

"I think what he's told us is dead-on," said Thorpe. "The problem is he hasn't told us enough. No cell phone calls from him, right?"

"Nothing," said Britain. "The last communication was an e-mail from Paris. That and the telephone call he placed to his daughter and the investigator in the condo."

"According to the transcript of the phone call, we should be looking for a large antenna array somewhere in the Mexican jungle," said Thorpe, "but where?"

"What about Intel Sats?" said Britain.

"The CIA?"

Britain nodded.

"I thought of it, but unless we can narrow it down, at least give them some kind of a reliable vector from that plane when it crosses over into Mexican airspace, their analysts could be looking at images for days. Something tells me we don't have that kind of time," said Thorpe.

"What do we do?" said Britain.

"Let's hope that Israeli pilot keeps his transponder turned on," said Thorpe. "In the meantime, get ahold of drug enforcement. Tell them we're going to need help. Boots on the ground. The Mexican army, the judicial police, the whole nine yards. But only people they can trust. Any kind of political or law enforcement juice they have with the Mexican government, tell them we may need it all."

It was a helpless feeling, throwing himself on the mercy of another agency, and burning whatever goodwill the bureau may have amassed with a foreign country. Whatever was happening in Mexico was beyond the reach of the U.S. government unless they were prepared to go to war.

Thorpe picked up the phone. It was not going to be a pleasant conversation. He would have to call the White House and tell Fowler that the bureau had lost whatever information they might have gleaned from Herman Diggs and that the Israeli government appeared to know all about Project Thor.

FIFTY-FOUR

We decide to time our reconnaissance of the road north of Coba for late afternoon, to drive slowly, and if need be, to wait until dark to take a closer look.

Harry and I select a pair of hundred-power binoculars from a local sporting goods shop. We buy a half-dozen bottles of water, put them in an Igloo container filled with ice, and pick up two large hunting knives for defense along with a handful of road flares, anything that might come in handy if we need help. We would buy guns but we can't.

Possession of a firearm or even a single round of ammunition by a foreign national in Mexico will net the visitor a long and harsh prison term. Mexico is a testament to the failure of gun laws to curb bloodshed. It has among the most severe firearm restrictions in the world. Yet the country has become a veritable war zone of gun-fueled drug violence. Any Mexican teen with a trigger finger can buy a fully automatic assault rifle and bandoliers of bullets for a few pesos from black marketers. The fact that the transaction is illegal means only that the dead victims are all law abiding.

Since guns are not available to tourists, Harry and I have to make do with what we can find. We settle on two rubber-sling spearguns from one of the dive shops in Playa del Carmen. All the while Joselyn is laughing. "Why don't you get the mask and flippers and finish out the outfit?"

Harry is in no mood for humor. He throws one of the spearguns onto the front seat and nearly ends up sitting on the tip as he gets into the car.

By three thirty we reach the highway intersection at Coba. I turn, and we head north. We turn off the air conditioner and open the windows so that all of our senses are alive as I drive slowly up the road. Within two miles, the absence of any other traffic becomes obvious to all of us.

"Get the feeling we're in the land of the dead?" says Harry.

We pass occasional mud-brick huts and small concrete houses, all of them abandoned. Some have their windows broken out with their front doors off the hinges. A few show the scorch marks and black soot of fire.

To Joselyn it reminds her of some of the test sites in the Nevada desert, what she calls "atomic city." "All that is missing," she says, "are the mannequins strapped to posts along the road."

Harry and I are in the front seat. Joselyn is in the back, her head almost on my shoulder as her eyes give the road the thousand-yard stare. The three of us strain constantly to see what is up ahead.

Each curve brings us to a near stop until I can creep around and see what's there. The foliage is so thick that it crowds the road in places, growing over the edges of the asphalt as if to reclaim the offending ribbon that runs through the jungle.

We come to an intersection with a dirt road off to the right.

"Stop!" Harry is halfway out of the car before I can hit the brake. "If anything happens, don't wait for me." With the speargun in hand, he runs cautiously toward the dirt road as Joselyn and I sit in the hot car with windows open, my foot ready to hit the gas pedal to pick him up if I have to. He disappears down the dirt road, and a few seconds later comes back and waves me forward. Neither Joselyn nor I have to ask what Harry is doing. We all know that the road of death is likely to be a dead end. Without saying it, the thought of a vehicle getting behind us and blocking our retreat is ever present.

From the look of it, the pavement has not seen much in the way of recent traffic. There are sizable chunks of rock in the middle of the road.

Harry gets back in the car. "It's OK," he says.

About a mile farther on we pass several abandoned and wrecked cars along the shoulder.

"Slow down," says Harry.

"I'm doing ten miles an hour," I tell him.

"I know. Slow down." Harry tightens his grip on the speargun, though what he is going to do with it if we run into trouble I'm not sure.

I tell him to watch where he's pointing the thing. He tells me to keep my eyes on the road.

Several of the wrecked vehicles have the brown-rusted hue of burned-out metal, their tires gone as if eaten by fire. A light pickup truck, or what is left of it, appears to have been shot to pieces. The driver's door panel is filigreed with enough holes that it looks like a lace doily.

"Pull over," says Harry. He wants to check it out.

I pull in front of the burned-out pickup and put the car in park, but I leave the engine running. Harry and I get out.

As we approach the burned-out vehicle, we realize that the passenger compartment is not empty. Slumped across the narrow bench seat is a partially burned and decomposed body.

FIFTY-FIVE

Part of DARPA's mission, along with the Department of Defense, was to anticipate new weapon systems and to study and explore them before they could be developed and used by adversaries against the United States. It was for this reason that the Defense Department drew NASA into the web on Project Thor.

If they could prove that the concept of using Near-Earth Objects as weapons was feasible, the plan was to publish the findings. Once it was known to the world, it would become infinitely more difficult for any nation to use asteroids in a preemptive strike against a foe and to hide their actions behind the blind of nature.

Any unexplained catastrophic impact would be followed by a thorough investigation, and the possibility of devastating reprisals would act as a deterrent once more. At least that was the theory. Now they had created a monster. Worse, they had lost control of it.

The information Leffort traded away gave up mastery over the two iron-core asteroids. More damaging was the fact that this transfer of knowledge had been grasped without difficulty by the talent pool of scientists assembled at Coba. Where these people had obtained their training Leffort did not know, possibly Europe, perhaps the United States. It really didn't matter. The fact remained, they knew their business. They could easily build on what they had been given.

So far they had managed to park and conceal the two asteroids at the lunar Lagrange point without any real assistance from Leffort. The problem he had now was to keep them away as he prepared the final targeting software for the asteroid's final trajectory around the moon.

Leffort was not at all comfortable doing this. The problem was that the targeting software was not his product. It had been developed by Raji and his crew, none of whom were present. The software was designed to deal with fine-tuning as to deflection, the timing and angle of entry into the earth's atmosphere, which would be critical for targeting.

Because it was not part of his turf at NASA, Leffort had not spent much time familiarizing himself with many of the aspects of final targeting. His specialty was the selection, harvesting, and macro movements of the asteroids in space. When he turned his back on Raji in Paris and allowed him to be killed, Leffort didn't realize the box he was putting himself in. Raji's death suited his purposes because Fareed's portion of the payment would be wired into Leffort's account. But now he had to perform. If anything went wrong, Leffort knew he would be held responsible. They would kill him in a heartbeat, or send the Mexican in to do it.

Over protests by several of the other scientists, Leffort cleared everyone out of the small control room. He wanted the others out so that he could do the final preparations and make the last lunar course corrections to escape the Lagrange point without a crowd looking over his shoulder. He promised that he would review everything with them in fine detail when he was done.

The last thing Leffort needed was people who knew what they were seeing if the telemetry readings on the monitors revealed that something had gone wrong.

He locked the door to the room and went to work. Leffort reached into his pants pocket and took out a plastic pill container. He popped the cap and took two of the pills, a double dose of slow-release amphetamines that helped focus his mind.

He spent the next several minutes checking the software to make sure it was properly installed. Then he began the procedural checklist. Ordinarily this would be a two-person job, one person reading the checklist while the other verified that each of the command codes was properly entered into the computer. Twice he lost his place on the checklist and had to go back to reconfirm the proper command sequence in the computer.

Twenty minutes later he was finished. He checked both clocks, the one on the wall and the one in the computer. The computer clock controlled the mission schedule. Timing was critical. There existed only a small window of about six minutes in which a launch for accurate targeting could be made. Once past the window, Leffort would have to wait twenty-four hours for the next rotation of the earth. It was, after all, a moving target, not only rotating on its axis but also moving through space at more than sixty-six thousand miles per hour.

He kept his eyes on the computer clock as it counted down to single digits. He watched it reach zero and waited two more seconds before he pushed the entry key on the computer.

The endless list, long chains of numbers, began racing up the screen as the software took over.

The motor on the mammoth satellite dish outside began to turn, making subtle adjustments in the orientation of the antenna. It would link up with the antennas on the rocket motors attached to A-1, the smaller of the two asteroids, on its next loop out beyond the edge of the moon. Within seconds the command codes would be fed into the microprocessor linking the four rockets, and the asteroid would be tipped from its balance point at lunar L2 and begin its journey.

Using lunar gravity and its own velocity, the asteroid would slingshot around the lunar surface in the same way NASA had done with its orbiters on moon missions.

The iron-core asteroid would begin its journey of nearly 240,000 miles. By the time it was picked up by astronomers on Earth, it would be too late to even think. Moving at more than 600 miles per minute, it would reach its target on the North American continent in just over six and a half hours.

Given its mass and velocity, a direct hit was not only unnecessary, it was inadvisable. If an impact was to look like a naturally occurring event, it would not make sense to strike a city center. Anywhere within a twenty-mile radius would be enough to level and incinerate almost all of the metropolitan area.

An elevated level of dust in the atmosphere would surround the earth for a few months, but would not, according to the calculations, result in anything approaching a nuclear winter.

The purpose behind this test was not unlike Trinity, the early Alamagordo tests of the atomic bomb. Leffort's clients had to be sure they got it right before bringing the second weapon closer to home and risking self-annihilation. The people paying him had to know how much dust and rock would be ejected. They wanted to have some sense of the heat that would be generated, the volume and the range of any fiery ejecta that gravity carried back through the atmosphere. They had to know how far fires would spread, as well as the effect of the ground shock waves as the impactor mostly vaporized and buried what was left of itself a mile deep in the bedrock at ground zero. In the end, all that would be left would be a vast crater.

It was the similarities of the desert with its geologic characteristics so much like those of their homeland that gave Leffort's clients the idea—setting up in the jungles of Mexico and targeting the area around Phoenix and Scottsdale in the state of Arizona would make for the perfect test.

Once the first asteroid was proven to work, they would know with a high degree of confidence what to expect when they launched the second, the larger of the two asteroids, into the desert just outside of the city of Tel Aviv in Israel. It was to be the fulfillment of the promise to wipe Israel off the map.

Leffort was confident that with enough practice and the right space rock, he could penetrate the earth's atmosphere to create a supersonic shock wave that would level everything beneath it—a blast similar to the Tunguska event.

On June 30, 1908, a sudden flash of light, brighter than the sun, followed by an ear-shattering shock wave, struck the area over the Tunguska River in a remote region of Siberia. It leveled trees, stripped their foliage, and set wildfires over an area of more than eight hundred square miles. Virtually nothing was left standing.

It has been estimated that the offending meteor may have been no more than thirty to sixty feet in diameter. Scientists believe that it never actually impacted the earth but disintegrated in the skies above. Its mass coupled with its extreme velocity caused a massive shock wave as it collided with and finally exploded in the thickening atmosphere of the earth. Had it occurred over Manhattan it would have destroyed the city and killed almost every living thing in the five boroughs below.

Leffort watched the telemetry readings on the large left-hand screen as the rockets fired up. Within seconds they began to nudge the asteroid from its raceway behind the moon. Everything looked smooth until suddenly . . .

A hundred and twenty miles above the Mare Orientale, a largely featureless plain on the southeast rim at the far side of the moon, the rear lateral thrust rocket attached to A-1 began to vibrate. It shimmied and sent the asteroid into a yaw as it began to tumble.

The rocket was programmed to fire for a minute and forty seconds. At fifty-seven seconds a large amorphous section of iron, what rocket engineers at NASA had called the dorsal fin, tore itself free from the asteroid and began to spin toward the surface of the moon.

Leffort watched in horror as the telemetry data began to pile up on the screen. Something had gone badly wrong. He wasn't sure what it was, but A-1 had given up any semblance of equilibrium. The readings for yaw, pitch, and roll all exceeded acceptable parameters for anything close to controlled flight. From all the readings, A-1 was nothing but a tumbling iron anvil in space. Caught in the moon's gravity, flung like a stone from a blind man's sling, it could end up anywhere.

Leffort stood there paralyzed. There was nothing he could do but watch as the numbers stacked up. With each passing second, the blood in his veins grew hotter. All he could do was turn off the monitors. The minute he opened the door, they would want to know what was happening. Dark screens would be a dead giveaway. Leffort's mind raced. All he wanted now was to survive, to get away from them.

A quarter of a million miles away, beyond the edge of the moon's southern hemisphere, the tumbling train of iron finally ceased its twisting tails of fire. The three remaining rocket motors shut down, though by now the tumbling asteroid was a perpetual motion machine.

Moments later a silent ball of fire erupted on the dusty plain below as the errant engine and the two tons of iron to which it was attached slammed into the surface of the moon. From space it looked like a pebble in a pond as the shock waves spread out into rings of ground matter rippling up, forming a new crater near the southern edge of the Orient Sea.

FIFTY-SIX

Liquida would have to leave most of his luggage behind. He grabbed a few things from his suitcase, including an extra stiletto from the bundle in his bag. He put one of the knives in a scabbard that was sewn inside the lining of his light jacket and slipped the other into a separate sheath and slid it into his pants along the side of his hip.

The prefabricated metal building was designed like a fortress, steel walls with small slits for windows in some of the rooms, none of them large enough to crawl through.

Liquida's room didn't even have that. It had only an air-conditioning register high on the wall pouring cool air into the room. There was a larger rectangular return duct in the ceiling that sucked the warm air back through the system.

The oversize commercial air-con system was one of the few concessions to comfort in the facility. Liquida assumed it was necessary to maintain cool temperatures for the electronics, banks of large industrial computers housed in a room down the hall. Beyond that was the control room where Leffort worked. Armed guards were installed at several locations along the corridor. The entrances and exits were all sealed by solid steel doors, each one controlled by an electronic passkey.

Bruno hadn't given Liquida a key. When Liquida asked for one, Bruno apologized, claiming it was an oversight, and told him he would get him one as soon as he could. But the key was never produced.

Earlier in the day when Liquida made a bid to take a walk outside, he was turned back by one of the guards. He was told that without a key he was not allowed to leave the building. Liquida didn't press the matter. Instead he went back to his room. He poked around carefully, looking for hidden camera lenses. He didn't find any. At least they didn't have him under surveillance. It was while looking for cameras that he realized his only way out was through the air-conditioning register in the ceiling.

He put on his jacket, stood on a chair, and found the catch on the hinged metal vent over the register. He opened it, dropped the covering vent down so that it hung open from the two hinges, and pulled out the rectangular fiberglass filter.

Liquida stepped down from the chair and looked for a good place to hide it. A cheap particleboard cupboard that served as a closet rested against one wall. He slid the thin rectangular filter behind it and walked back to the chair in the center of the room.

He looked up. The opening into the sheet metal

duct system was easily large enough for Liquida to fit through. It was a good two and half feet wide, and at least eighteen inches deep. He had shimmied into much tighter spaces before. The only problem now was, the partially healed muscles under his arm from the knife wound given to him by Madriani's detective, the big black guy Liquida had killed in Washington. This was still painful and weak.

Liquida grabbed a spool of heavy thread from the sewing kit in his luggage. He took a stick of chewing gum from a package in his jacket pocket, popped the gum in his mouth, and pulled out a good length of thread from the spool. He looped the thread over itself several times until he had four strands, each one about fifteen feet long. Then he snipped the end of the thread with his teeth. He passed one end of the four-strand thickness around the top slate on the back of the light metal chair, then tied the ends of the thread together so that the entire fifteen feet formed a single continuous loop. The other end of threaded strands he passed through his belt. He tugged on it to make sure it wouldn't come free.

Then Liquida stood on the chair and took a deep breath. He chewed the gum. It was better than breaking his teeth on a bullet. As he reached up with his hands inside the frame of the register, he felt the first twinge of pain under his arm. He didn't wait. Instead, with a pull from his arms and a healthy jump from his legs off the chair, Liquida hoisted his upper body up into the opening in the ceiling.

He felt the sharp pain, the tearing of scar tissue as the muscles under his arm reminded him of the slashing cut. He paused, his weight on his chest just inside the sheet metal duct, his legs dangling into the room as the sweat dripped off his forehead.

Liquida breathed heavily and chewed on the gum as he waited for the searing pain to pass. It took almost half a minute to subdue the agony before he could move.

Slowly he slid his hands forward and pulled his body along the inside of the sheet metal tunnel. Each move was a new experience in pain. Finally everything but his toes was up inside the metal ceiling duct.

Then slowly he reversed the process. He shimmied backward, pushing himself back over the hatch in the ceiling until only his head and shoulders remained over the open register.

With his right hand he reached back and fished for the end of the threaded loop under his belt. He found it and pulled it free.

Liquida took up the slack in the thread and pulled on it gently until all four legs of the chair cleared the floor. Slowly swinging the chair like a pendulum, back and forth, he made three full passes toward the wall near the head of the bed. On the fourth pass, he let out the thread and dropped the chair so that it landed neatly with the back against the wall.

Liquida smiled to himself as he nibbled through the four strands of thread. Once he had severed them he pulled the continuous loop from the back of the chair and reeled it in until all of the thread was in his hands. He balled it up and stuck it down the neck of his shirt as the forced air from the conditioning system whistled past his ears.

He reached down and lifted the vented register cover closed. He took the chewing gum from his mouth and stuck it to the metal edge of the frame around the louvered vent, then pulled it tightly closed. The gum sealed the cover in place. Anyone looking in the room now would think Liquida had simply vanished.

At a point roughly a hundred miles north of Havana, the flight engineer on Adin's C-130 radioed to the base in Israel. He asked to have an uncoded message sent to Joselyn Cole at her e-mail address, making an urgent request for information using Herman's name. He needed to know Madriani's location as well as the precise location of the antenna array and the facility in the jungle. It was now two hours later and they had heard nothing.

Forty miles out, the pilot turned off the plane's transponder. He dropped down to wave-top height and hugged the water, trying to stay below ground radar.

Twenty minutes later the C-130 crossed over the white-foamed breakers and sugar-sand beaches of the Mexican Riviera. The pilot nosed the plane up to clear some low-lying cliffs and the buildings on top of them. They were just south of the island of Cozumel on the Yucatán Peninsula.

Herman sat up front behind the pilot looking out the windows for any landmarks that seemed familiar. "You're too far north," he told them.

The pilot dipped the left wing and took a heading due south.

Herman could see the coast highway out in front of them through the plane's windshield. The white sand beaches and resorts along the water's edge raced by beneath the belly of the plane. "Just follow the highway," said Herman.

Every once in a while the pilot would have to pull the nose of the plane up to avoid a building or the fronds of an occasional tall palm tree. The shadow of the large four-engine plane rippled along on the beaches and bluffs beneath them as they flew.

Eight minutes later the reflection of the sun on the white coral facade of the ruins at Tulum appeared just above the nose of the plane.

"There!" Herman pointed over the pilot's shoulder. "See those ruins up ahead?"

The pilot nodded.

"Off to the right there should be a paved road, two lanes as I recall, into the jungle. It connects with the main highway between Cancún and Mérida. It's the road to Coba. After that I don't know," said Herman. "I'm afraid you're on your own."

"Nothing more specific?" Adin was in the chair next to him.

"The area around Coba is all Paul told me," said Herman. "Whether he had more information I don't know. Nothing back on the e-mail yet?"

Adin looked at the navigator who doubled as the radio operator. The man shook his head.

"We'll just have to look," said the pilot. He dropped the starboard wing and edged the plane toward the right. Moments later they picked up the narrow thread of light-colored asphalt leading into the jungle, the two-lane highway to Coba.

"What have we got for a landing strip?" asked the pilot. "Anything in the area?" He was talking to the navigator seated to the right of Herman and Adin at a kind of desk. The man was scanning a computer screen looking at charts and global positioning satellite (GPS) maps.

"Looks like one unimproved short strip, but it's quite a ways out," said the navigator. He did some quick calculations using the computer's keyboard. "It's halfway to Mérida," said the navigator. "Off a federal highway. Mexico one-eighty, it looks like. It's a long way from Coba."

"Great," said the pilot. "Somebody better tell Uncle Ben we've got a logistics problem. Tell him to get up here."

"I got it." Adin unbuckled and headed back toward the cargo area.

"What's the problem?" said Herman.

"Nowhere to put down," said the pilot. "We can't run the jeep and the trailer loaded with troops and munitions on a public highway. Not that far. We'll end up in a firefight with the Mexican army."

Herman nodded.

"We'll have to look for something else," said the pilot. "There's bound to be other strips, but they're not always marked on the charts."

"Places prepared by the cartels," said Herman.

The pilot nodded. "We may have to shoot our way in and out. I'm going to pull up to seventy-five hundred feet and level off in just a couple of minutes, as soon as we get some more eyes up front here to help us look. Tell some of the guys in the back to strap themselves on the ramp and lower it a little so they can see what's behind us, in case we missed anything."

Herman got up and followed Adin out of the flight cabin and down the ladder.

FIFTY-SEVEN

Liquida began the painful shimmy like a snake through the ducting, pushing with the rubber toes of his running shoes, pulling with his hands as best he could. He tried to make as little noise as possible, though the constant roar of the air conditioner sucking air through the return would have swallowed almost any sound coming from the vents.

He was moving away from the control room and the space next to it with the banks of computers. As he approached the next register, Liquida pulled the stiletto from the sheath in his coat. He used the sharp point to part several openings in the glass fibers of the filter so he could peek through the slatted metal vents down into the room below.

There was a long counter that separated the room into two sections. The door to the main corridor outside was closed and, if Liquida had to guess, it was locked. It wasn't a solid-core wooden door like the one to Liquida's room. This one was steel with a sensor on the wall so it could be opened with an electronic key card.

A man was seated at a desk against the wall on the left side of the room behind the counter. Liquida could see the back of his head as the guy worked over what looked like a set of books.

Against the opposite wall behind him was a large industrial safe, double doors, thick tempered steel that looked to be at least eight inches with two large cylindrical stainless-steel bolts protruding from each of the two open doors. Inside were stacks of cash, what looked like greenbacks, U.S. currency, enough of it to fill a small van.

Liquida wondered how many people worked here. Whoever they were, they weren't taking their salary by check or in pesos. And neither was he.

With the ramp on the belly of the Hercules C-130 partway down, the noise from the four roaring Allison turboprop engines was deafening. Sarah had to cover both ears with her hands as wind swirled through the cargo hold. Herman held on to Bugsy's leash as the three of them huddled against the side of the plane in front of the smaller cargo container.

Every once in a while Sarah would crawl to the corner of the container and look toward the back of the plane to see what they were looking at. All she could see from where she knelt was an endless green carpet of jungle. She felt the plane gaining altitude. She crawled back to Herman, petting Bugsy with one hand on the way.

"Good luck finding a place to land," shouted Herman.

She nodded. "What if they can't find one?"

Herman shrugged a shoulder and gave her a face like he had no clue.

"You think they'll try to parachute?" she asked.

Herman shook his head. "Not into that." What he meant was the jungle canopy. Anybody jumping into an area of dense foliage like that was asking for trouble. Most, if not all, would get hung up in the trees. Those who didn't break bones or get killed in the fall would be easy targets for anybody on the ground with a rifle.

"Sarah!"

When she looked up, Adin was at the top of the ladder looking down from the flight deck. He waved them up and motioned for her to tie off the dog.

Sarah looped Bugsy's leash through the cargo net on the side of the plane and tied it. She settled him down into a prone position on deck and petted him, then followed Herman up the ladder.

Once they were inside the flight compartment, Adin pointed out through the small windshield in front of the pilot. Off in the distance were two looming white dishes, one of them large enough that it looked like a giant parasol someone had dropped in the jungle.

Adin looked at her. "That has to be it." He glanced at Herman.

"When Paul said antennas, I was thinking more along the lines of a series of towers," said Herman.

"No." Adin shook his head. "You see the smaller dish?"

Sarah and Herman squinted out toward the windshield and then nodded.

"That's a radio telescope," said Adin. "It's not real big. Not as large as the ones in Puerto Rico, but it's enough to see out into space."

Herman gave him a puzzled look. "What's that got to do with it?"

"It's what we're looking for," said Adin.

"What do you mean?"

"Trust me, that's it," said Adin. "Look off to the left." He took Herman by the arm and pointed. "You see that clearing next to the buildings?"

Herman squinted and then nodded.

"Pilot says it looks like a landing strip. Can't tell if it's paved from this distance, but it should be enough for us; that is, if it's long enough."

"You're not gonna try and land there, are you?" said Herman.

Adin nodded. "It's our best bet. If we get on the ground fast and off-load, they'll never know what hit them." He took a couple of steps forward and tapped the pilot on the shoulder.

"If that's the place, you're out of your mind," said Herman.

Immediately the plane's wing dipped. The C-130 made a deep banking turn, dropped altitude, and veered off to the left.

Sarah lost her footing. Adin grabbed her and held on until the plane leveled off. It circled away from the two massive dishes in the jungle and took a heading south toward Coba.

"Get your guys ready!" The pilot yelled over his shoulder to Teo Ben Rabin, who was seated behind him. "We're only going to get one shot at this. I'll approach low in over the trees," said the pilot. "They gotta be ready to move the second we hit that runway."

"Got it," said Uncle Ben. "Excuse me." He pushed past Sarah and Adin and headed for the cargo bay.

"I want the two of you to get down behind that first cargo container in the center aisle. When we land, I want as much metal between you and whatever is around those buildings as possible. That'll be the safest place for now," said Adin. "If we start to take fire and they hit the fuel tank, get out of the plane fast. Don't go out the ramp," said Adin. "You'll never make it. Use one of the forward cargo doors and keep the plane between you and any incoming rounds, understood?"

Sarah nodded. "Where are you going to be?"

"On the Jeep," said Adin. "I'll be OK. Worry about yourself," he told her. "It was stupid of me to allow you to come."

"Worry about that later," she said.

"You watch her," he told Herman.

"I can take care of myself," said Sarah.

"Why don't you land somewhere else and try and buy some time?" said Herman. "Now that you know where it is, what's the rush?"

"I'm afraid we don't have any time," said Adin. "It may be now or never. You understand what I said about getting off the plane?"

"Got it," said Herman.

"You're in charge of her and the dog. I want them alive when it's over." He looked at Sarah. "Take care of yourself. Stay down low." She was trying to put on a brave face, but she was scared. He could tell by the look on her face.

What Herman didn't tell Adin was that he had climbed up into the container where Ben Rabin's men had first hidden. While Uncle Ben's men were busy looking out the ramp at the back of the plane, Herman jobbed two nine-millimeter Berettas and four clips of ammunition from a duffel bag stashed inside the container. He would have preferred to take one of their nifty Tavor rifles, but he figured it might be missed.

To Herman's thinking, if he and Sarah could stay alive long enough, there would be plenty of opportunity to pick up loose weapons off the ground from some of the S-13 men who didn't make it. Herman didn't think much of their plan to land on the field. To him it was suicide.

FIFTY-EIGHT

In his heightened state of fright, Leffort wasn't sure what he was hearing at first. With the iron asteroid out of control and the monitors in the room all dark, his mind was seized with thoughts of escape. The noise went on for several seconds before it even registered in his brain.

When it did, it hit him like a shot of adrenaline. The sound was muted by the solid steel door of the control room and the heavy insulation in the walls and ceiling around him. But there was no mistaking what it was. An alarm pierced the silence in the hallway outside, the buzzing Klaxon on the wall.

Leffort was sure he had triggered it. Either the result of the unbalanced telemetry data being fed into the computers or the fact that he had powered down the large monitors on the wall—something had set it off.

There was nowhere to go. Leffort was trapped in the room with two armed guards outside the door. Someone pounded on the other side. Finally despondent, he picked up his card key and unlocked it from the inside. When he heard the electronic bolts snap open, he waited for several seconds. Leffort expected the guards to storm in and take him, but they didn't. He opened the door a crack and looked out.

The corridor was a sea of pandemonium. The Klaxon horn on the wall blaring in his ears was deafening. Guards were running in every direction. Two of the scientists Leffort had thrown out of the room were standing there gesturing frantically as they spoke.

Leffort stepped out and closed the door behind him. "What is it?"

One of them who spoke English looked at him wide-eyed. "Radar warns of a large unidentified aircraft."

"What?"

People racing by were bumping into the two men. One of them, the one he was talking to, tried to edge toward the closed control room door. "I must get inside to take some readings."

"Where was the plane? How far out?" Leffort changed the subject.

"Very close," said the man. "One of the guards outside saw it. Only a quick glimpse but he said it looked like a military plane."

"The Mexican government?" said Leffort.

"We don't know. They have ordered all technical staff to the underground bunker." The alarm was the signal to battle stations. "The rest have already gone. I was waiting for you to open the door." He reached for it.

"Never mind!" Leffort blocked him with his body. "I'll grab the printouts, lock up, and meet you at the bunker."

The man smiled. "Good. Thank you. You are a prince." He was still genuflecting toward Leffort as the two of them disappeared into the sea of human chaos flowing down the hallway.

Leffort stepped back into the room, closed the door, and tried to collect his thoughts. The printer was off. He had never turned it on. For a man who was an agnostic, Leffort was beginning to believe. If there was a God, surely he had intervened.

He stepped out and closed the door to the control room behind him. This time he made sure it was locked. Then he headed down the hall the other way, away from the bunker and the other scientists.

The shock of the blaring sound was sudden and loud enough that Liquida banged his head against the sheet metal ducting above the pay room.

He didn't know what the alarm was, but he figured there was a good chance Bruno or someone else had discovered him missing from his room.

He watched through the louvered vent as the man at the desk below him stood up and listened for a moment. First the guy turned and looked at the locked door to the hallway outside. When he turned to glance at the open safe, Liquida moved. The guy started gathering up his papers and books on the desk.

Using the stiletto, Liquida quickly popped the

catch on the register cover. He allowed the vent cover to swing open and pushed the filter out of the way.

The thin flat filter floated toward the floor like a leaf. As it brushed past the man's shoulder, the accountant looked up just in time to catch a glimpse of Liquida's sinister smile. The Mexicutioner descended on him headfirst with his arms straight out as if to embrace his victim with the point of the stiletto.

The bookkeeper threw up a hand to ward it off, but he was too late.

Liquida fell on him. The needle-sharp tip of the blade slipped smoothly into the right side of the man's neck as if the wound were a ready-made sheath. With all of Liquida's weight behind it, the stiletto buried itself to the handle in the victim's upper chest just inside the clavicle.

The shocked man broke Liquida's fall, and they both collapsed onto the floor. The two of them lay sprawled, the bookkeeper pulsing a river of blood as Liquida wiggled the blade in the wound. The tip had either punctured the upper chamber of the heart or severed the aorta. Either way the man would be dead within seconds.

Liquida waited a few counts for the convulsing body to become still. Then he got to his knees, stood, and pulled the stiletto from the deep wound. Liquida wiped the blade and his bloodied hand on an unsoiled portion of the victim's pant leg.

Without another thought, he turned his attention to the open safe behind him. For the first time Liquida realized that the stacked wall of greenbacks

inside the two yawning steel doors was nearly as tall
as he was and four times as wide.

He walked across the room and grabbed one of
the enclosed bundles from the top shelf. They were
five-dollar U.S. banknotes, all of them vacuum
packed in plastic. Liquida could tell from the way
it was packaged, as well as from the residue of white
film on the shrink-fitted wrapper, that it was cash
from one of the cartels. No one else in the world
bundled bills like that. They had to protect their
money from seawater, chemicals, and fuel during
storage and transit. To Liquida the narco seal of ap-
proval was better than a certificate from the U.S.
Treasury. He knew it wasn't counterfeit and no one
would have a list of the serial numbers.

What better way to launder it than to transfer the
narco dollars to Bruno's clients, who in turn would
wire excess oil revenues into a cartel account overseas. In the meantime, Bruno's clients could use the
narco bills to meet their payroll in the jungle. It was
the perfect symbiotic relationship.

The second shelf was stacked with tens. The shelf
below it held twenties.

Liquida worked his way to the floor of the safe.
It was stacked at least three feet high with bundles
of hundred-dollar banknotes, each one a tight plastic brick. The safe was at least two feet deep and
four feet wide. If true to form, each plastic-wrapped
brick of hundreds would contain ten thousand dollars.

Just like the post office, the cartels had to weigh
everything for transport. Otherwise overloaded

planes would nose into the jungle and their jury-rigged diesel-powered semisubs would be littering the seafloor. Liquida knew from his work with the cartels that a million dollars in hundreds would weigh just under twenty pounds. He had no idea how much money was in the bottom of the safe, but it was more than he could carry without wheels.

His worst enemy now was time. Keeping one eye on the door to the hallway outside, Liquida searched the cabinets under the counter. He found a stack of heavy canvas bags, each one the size of a twenty-five-pound sack of flour. They were cash bags without lettering on the outside. Each one had a tie string stitched near the open top of the bag.

Liquida quickly filled four of the bags with hundred-dollar bills and tied them closed with double knots. He lifted each by the tie string until he was satisfied that the thick canvas tie would hold the weight of the bag without breaking.

He went back to the cadaver on the floor and stripped the dead man's belt from his pants. The alarm outside was still blaring. Liquida fished for the guy's electronic key card and found it in his pants pocket.

He went back to the money bags and made a separate loop from the remaining ends of the ties on each of the bags. He threaded the leather belt through the loops and then buckled it. He hoisted the load over his shoulders so that the bags were evenly balanced, two in front, two behind, roughly eighty pounds total. It was heavy. The weight swayed as he moved, but Liquida could handle it.

What he couldn't do was take his eyes off the safe. He had barely made a dent in the bottom stack of bills. He set the load down and grabbed two more canvas bags.

FIFTY-NINE

As they came in low over the trees, wheels and flaps down, the pilot could almost feel branches scraping the belly of the plane. He feathered the engines to try and keep the noise down.

Suddenly a flock of birds flew up in front of him. Several hit the windshield, feathers and blood flying. Fortunately the plane wasn't going fast enough to break glass. A few of the birds went through the props. The pilot pushed the throttles forward for more power. The four large Allison engines roared as the plane nosed up.

"Shit!" The pilot shook his head. "If they didn't know we were coming, they know it now." He eased back on the throttles once more. He could see the runway ahead of them now. It was paved and long. At least that was good news.

He glided in over the last set of trees, goosed the engines, and aimed for the end of the runway. The plan was to hit the ground as quickly as possible, reverse the props, gun the engines, and stand on the brakes while the loadmaster in the back was lowering the ramp. If they hit it right, the drop-down door on the second container would fall at the same time. The Jeep with its recoilless rifle would be on the runway before anyone knew it. Adin, with two of the commandos riding in the back, would open fire on anything that moved. Ben Rabin and the other men would push the ammo trailer onto the ramp and allow gravity to do the rest. In the meantime, two of the commandos would drop out through the forward cargo door on the port side while the plane was still moving, cross the runway, and set up two squad machine guns for covering fire.

The plane passed over the first threshold markings on the runway. The pilot pushed the yoke forward. Suddenly the portside window on the flight deck exploded. Pebbles of glass sprayed the pilot's face as bullets whizzed past his nose, punching holes and blowing out dials in the instrument panel above his head.

A second burst of fire riveted the side of the plane, thumping the metal. The screen in front of the navigator exploded as the twenty-millimeter rounds sliced through the plane, blowing the man out of his chair and cutting him in half. Electrical shorts ignited flames in the wooden panel behind the screen. The aluminum in the plane began to burn as the flight engineer grabbed a fire extinguisher and began to spray.

"Keep it out of my eyes!" screamed the pilot. He struggled to control the plane as he tried to wipe blood from his face using his shoulder. The wheels on the undercarriage hit the ground hard, jamming the pilot's lower back into the seat. It threw the flight engineer to the floor.

The pilot reached over and reversed the props, then pushed the throttle controls all the way forward. The plane nearly stood on its nose as it slowed. The pilot pressed on the brakes, his gaze fixed on the runway, when suddenly his eyes widened in horror. Coming head-on, the propellants' exhaust was almost invisible as the rocket-propelled grenade smashed through the windshield and exploded inside.

The plane veered to the right. The guard with his rocket launcher still at his shoulder stood at the edge of the runway smiling for almost a second before the windmilling prop on the outboard engine sprayed him like chum into the open air.

The plane's forward wheel rolled into a swale at the edge of the runway, then ran off the pavement. It buried itself in the deep gravel at the edge of the concrete.

The plane came to an abrupt stop with the four Allison engines racing in reverse. Ground fire, including tracers, poured into the two starboard engines from the buildings along the right side of the runway. One of the engines started to smoke, then sputtered and died.

"Could have warned him 'bout that," said Herman. He grabbed Sarah by the arm and tried to pull her along behind him as they crawled low in the center aisle. She was anchored by the dog next to her. Bullets rattled against the plane, punching holes in the aluminum fuselage. Herman could hear them hitting the other side of the steel container, but none of them seemed to come through.

Up at the top of the ladder, the aluminum bulk-head to the flight deck was perforated with so many holes that it looked like lacework. The exploding grenade had peppered it with shrapnel.

Sarah jumped and Bugsy barked at the jarring clang as the heavy steel door on the second container dropped onto the deck of the cargo bay. A second later, the Jeep, its engine revving, shot out of the container and down the plane's rear ramp.

The Hercules was stopped with its nose pitched down at an angle. This set the bottom of the ramp at a sharp angle to the concrete runway. The Jeep went airborne before it hit the ground. When it did, one of the commandos was jolted off the back of the vehicle. Sarah saw him go flying. She held her breath. He bounced and rolled like a rubber ball, landed on his feet, and started to run.

At the same instant two of the other commandos dropped out of the forward cargo door on the other side of the plane and disappeared.

Sarah looked back for the commando who had fallen from the Jeep. She watched as he took three strides before he was spun around and cut down by a swarm of bullets that sparked and chipped the concrete all around him. Sarah lay staring in shock as the man's body continued to take hits, his life snuffed out in front of her eyes.

"Son of a bitch!" Just as Herman said it, a stitch of bullets penetrated the side of the plane in the gap between the two steel containers. Instantly four neat holes appeared in the stainless-steel fuel tank. Three of them started hemorrhaging high-octane aviation fuel into the cargo bay. "Time to go," said

Herman. "Stay with me and stay low." Crouching down, he moved toward the open cargo door on the other side of the plane. When he looked back, Sarah was still lying on her stomach staring out the back of the plane at the dead man on the tarmac. Herman skidded across the aisle on one knee and grabbed her arm as if in a steel vise.

The pain broke her trance. Sarah shot him a glance.

"It's too late to help him," said Herman. He jerked her up onto her knees.

"Ow!"

"Sorry, but you gotta stay alive." Herman gave her a look to kill.

Suddenly she smelled the aviation fuel. Sarah nodded. "Go. I'm right behind you."

Herman got to the open door. A second later, Sarah and the dog were huddled up close behind him. Herman pulled one of the pistols from inside his belt under his shirt and cycled the slide to chamber a round. He looked out the door. He could see no incoming fire on this side of the plane. All of the rounds seemed to be coming from the buildings on the other side.

Every few seconds a tracer flashed by overhead and disappeared into the jungle in the distance. Rounds ricocheted off the concrete in the narrow gap under the belly toward the rear of the plane.

The reversed propellers created a virtual wind machine, all of it blowing in their direction, ahead of the wings. Herman was getting ready to jump when he looked down to his right and saw the body crumpled on the concrete a few feet away. The commando's squad automatic weapon, the SAW machine gun, lay beside the man. One of the commandos made it, at least far enough to get away from the plane. The other one didn't. He had gone to the rear where the belly of the plane had lifted up because of its nose-down position. At that location, there was no defilade behind the plane. It made him an easy target.

"As soon as you get out, move toward the front of the plane but stay flat on the ground," Herman yelled over the roar of the engines. "Keep the plane between you and those buildings. And keep your head down." As soon as he said it, Herman dropped out from the door. He landed on his feet, turned back, and grabbed Sarah by the waist as she crouched in the door. She jumped and he eased her out onto the ground.

Bugsy jumped from the plane. The noise of the engine and the sudden wind from the whirling prop scared him. He jerked on the leash and ripped it from her hand. Instantly he was gone.

Sarah looked over Herman's shoulder and yelled: "Bugsy!" But her voice was swallowed in the din of the engine. She watched as the dog raced across the runway ahead of the ricocheting bullets. She couldn't believe that they were actually shooting at him. For the first time she wanted a gun, something with which to strike back.

Herman tried to push her to the ground. Sarah would have none of it until she saw the dog disappear into the trees at the edge of the jungle. For a moment Sarah thought she might cry. Then she remembered the dead man on the tarmac.

She got down flat on the ground. Herman got down next to her.

"You OK?"

She nodded. "I'm not leaving without him."

"Worry about staying alive," said Herman. He looked around, trying to figure out their next move.

"What do we do now?"

"Sit tight," said Herman. "Stay here."

"Where are you going?" Before she could turn to look, Herman was gone toward the tail of the plane. He hugged the side of the fuselage as he approached the spinning props. The wind nearly peeled him off the metal. One of the engines on this side was already smoking.

The incoming fire seemed to diminish. Now there were only occasional bursts and single shots that could barely be heard over the roaring engines. Herman wondered where Adin and the Jeep had gone.

He got down on his hands and knees and scurried with the pistol in hand toward the dead commando and the SAW machine gun. Under the belly of the plane Herman could see several men in uniforms with assault rifles moving on the other side coming toward them. Between the approaching hostiles and the plane was a chain-link fence with a gate. The three armed men were maybe seventy meters beyond the fence.

Just as Herman reached the automatic weapon, a hand grasped his shirt. He looked down. The commando wasn't dead. Herman came face-to-face with his open eyes. The soldier gestured toward his legs. He was wounded in both thighs and couldn't walk.

Herman nodded, handed the machine gun to him, and grabbed the web harness at the back of his neck. "Ready?"

The guy nodded.

Herman dragged him twenty feet behind the belly of the plane where Sarah lay prone on the concrete.

The wounded soldier rolled onto his back. "Where is the colonel?"

Herman had to read his lips over the massive noise from the engines. He shook his head. "Don't know." He hadn't seen Ben Rabin or any of the other commandos since the Jeep took off. He assumed they were still inside the plane. Herman fished in the guy's backpack. He got up close in his ear and asked him if he had a medical kit. Herman wanted to stanch the bleeding from the wounds in the man's legs.

The smell of fuel was becoming pungent as it dripped from the belly of the plane and ran into the concrete swale underneath. Herman took one look at the overheating engines. The plane provided cover for the moment, but he knew they couldn't stay there for long.

SIXTY

Leffort hugged the walls on the inside of the corridor as he listened to the massive gunfire outside. The place was a goddamn war zone. All he wanted now was to find a car and get as far away as he could.

The buzzer was still ringing in his ears, though someone had finally turned it off. The gunfire outside seemed to ebb.

With it Leffort began to move more quickly down the hallway. He crossed an intersecting corridor and saw an open doorway on the other side. There was a janitor's large rolling trash bin in the hallway outside, one of those rectangular canvas trash bags on wheels. He moved cautiously. The last thing he needed was to run into one of the guards and find himself ushered to the underground bunker. They might as well put him against a wall and shoot him now.

Leffort peeked around the open doorway. Inside the room was a long high counter, an empty desk against one wall and an open safe against the other. He arched an eyebrow and glanced at the sign over the door. It was written in a language he didn't understand, some kind of script that looked as if it was written upside down and backward.

The room appeared to be empty. "Hello!" He waited to see if a head might pop up from behind the counter. It didn't. Leffort stepped inside. There was a closed gate in the middle of the counter. He walked toward it.

Leffort didn't see the blood or the body sprawled on the floor on the other side until he was a few feet from the gate.

He stopped dead in his tracks and looked around. His gaze wandered back to the blood on the floor, then caught the windows on the far side of the room. Two of the narrow slits looking out over the runway had been shot out. The venetian blinds in front of them were ripped to pieces. Leffort's wheels began to turn, dead man, stray bullets, open safe. The conclusion was pretty obvious. To Leffort it spelled opportunity.

He glanced over the edge of the gate and looked both ways. Except for the dead man, the room was empty. He reached over and felt for the latch. It had to be there somewhere. It was.

He opened the gate and walked quickly toward the safe. A smile spread across Leffort's face as he approached the two open doors. The safe was filled with money. He glanced back over his shoulder one last time to make sure he was alone and that he wasn't dreaming. There were no voices, no footsteps out in the hallway, only the occasional sound of sporadic gunfire outside, which for now buoyed his spirits. As long as they were busy out there, they wouldn't be coming in here.

Leffort's attention was so fixed on the cash in the safe that he nearly tripped over the six buff canvas bags on the floor in front of it. He looked at the dead man lying on the floor, then back to the bags. "If that isn't poetic justice," said Leffort. He didn't have to guess what was in the cloth sacks. It was nice of the guy to bag it for him. The only question was how much.

He tried to untie at least one of the bags to find out. The double knot was too tight. Leffort knew there was no time to screw around. He looked at the stacks of bills in the safe, then went over quickly and examined them. It didn't take him long to realize how the denominations were organized and to discover the sizable void in the hundreds on the bottom shelf. His admiration for the deceased was growing by the minute. Unlucky the man may have been. A fool he was not.

Leffort tried to lift the bags using the leather belt they were attached to. The load was heavy. He got it up on one shoulder, but by the time he got all six bags through the gate in the counter, he was struggling and having second thoughts. He dropped the load and started dragging the sacks on the floor behind him.

At the door he checked both ways and saw the cart. Leffort laughed and shook his head. The man had thought of everything—except a bulletproof vest.

He pulled the load out into the hallway, closed

the heavy door behind him, and started lifting the bags into the rolling trash bin.

From the room across the hall, Liquida couldn't thank him enough. Everything had been going swell until the bullets started flying. They punched holes in the cabinets under the counter and had Liquida crawling around on his hands and knees out the door. He had been forced to leave the money behind and was beginning to wonder if he would ever get back to it.

He watched as Leffort struggled with the bags. The man was a wimp, a certified candy ass. If Liquida had had more time, he would have strung the bastard up by his nipple rings and let him hang for a few days over hot coals. As it was, he was in a hurry.

The problem with the load was that it was all strapped together by the leather belt. Leffort couldn't lift the whole thing high enough to get it all into the bin at one time. He leaned over and unbuckled the belt and started to slip it from the loops in the ties at the top of each bag.

He cleared one bag when his right hand suddenly went numb. Leffort looked at it, then tried to massage it with the other hand. There was a pain, a hitch somewhere high up in his back. He wanted to reach for it but his arms were dead, only a tingling from his shoulders to his hands. He tried to say something but he couldn't. It was the strangest feeling. His mind seemed clouded. He looked down through a foggy gaze and realized he'd grown a third foot—his right, his left, and a middle one that wasn't there a minute ago. He chuckled almost whimsically as blood ran from the corner of his mouth and dripped onto the floor.

He had no sense of anything below his neck. And yet he was standing there, supported by what he didn't know because he couldn't feel his legs. It was as if he was weightless, floating in space, when suddenly he tumbled upside down into the bin. He didn't seem to mind. It was like the ultimate anesthetic. Someone had tickled the crazy bone in his brain. For Leffort this was something new and different, the ultimate out-of-body experience. He gazed up into Liquida's eyes and suddenly realized that the feeling of warmth on his back was his own blood. Leffort smiled, and everything went dark.

"I hope it was good for you," said Liquida. "Because I certainly enjoyed it. It could have lasted a little longer, I suppose . . ." He talked to himself as he wiped the stiletto on the canvas cloth along the side of the bin, then threaded the bag back onto the belt. Like Santa with his sack, he lifted the load of cash and headed for the door.

"Rebel Two, this is Rebel One, where are you?" Ben Rabin spoke into the small mic on the headset fastened to his combat helmet.

"Rebel One, I am in the defilade behind the brick building at the end of the runway." Adin spoke to him from the shadows behind a small blockhouse just off the runway under the trees. The guards had fired at the speeding Jeep but missed. "They are moving on you, three of them that I can see," said Adin.

"We got 'em," said Uncle Ben. "One sniper up on the flight deck, the other at the top of the ramp."

"Give me the word, I'll take out the twenty millimeter," said Adin.

"There are two of them," said Ben Rabin.

"I know the other one is behind the plane. I don't want to risk losing the artillery until we take out the dish," said Adin.

"Roger. We go on the count of three?"

"Give me a few seconds." Adin looked at his loader on the back of the Jeep.

The guy swung the tube of the recoilless rifle until it was perpendicular to the back of the vehicle.

"I'll back up. Give you a window. Whatever you do, don't miss," said Adin.

"I won't."

"On your count," Adin spoke into the mic again. He started the engine on the Jeep.

"One, two, three." Before the last syllable cleared Uncle Ben's lips, two sharp cracks echoed from the plane. Two of the standing bodies beyond the fence fell.

The Jeep skidded into reverse. It cleared the corner of the small brick building and stopped. A second later, fire erupted from the 105-millimeter barrel. As the round streaked across the runway, a third shot could be heard coming from the plane. The last guard approaching the C-130 fell as the explosive round struck the twenty-millimeter antiaircraft gun in front of the large building. It erupted in a ball of fire as bodies and shards of steel flew into the air. Secondary explosions of live ammunition filled the sky as the surviving guards scurried from the sandbagged emplacement.

Adin pulled the Jeep behind the buildings as the field came alive with the sounds of battle once more. Fire poured into the crippled Hercules again as the plane took the brunt of the reprisal. Adin waited only long enough for the loader to put another round into the recoilless rifle. "Hang on."

He raced out from behind the brick building toward the crippled plane, gunning the Jeep with both hands on the wheel and his head down.

The movement drew small-arms fire as they sped across the field.

A few seconds later the trailer rolled down the ramp of the plane. It hit the twisted end of the ramp and turned over on its side directly under the huge tail of the plane. Ben Rabin's men poured out of the belly of the plane like fleas, taking cover behind the trailer and opening up on the building with everything they had.

The Jeep cleared the front of the plane as Adin got a fix on the other twenty-millimeter gun. "Do you see it?"

"Got it," said the loader. Just as he said the words, the spray of heavy tracers bent away from the plane toward the Jeep. The recoilless rifle belched fire as the recoilless round streaked on a flat trajectory across the distance. It hit the sandbags directly in front of the heavy gun and exploded, sending sand and bags into the air as shrapnel killed the gunner.

"Got him," said the loader.

"No, you didn't." Adin could see the guards pulling the gunner from his seat. Another guard climbed up and got behind the gun. "Hit 'em again!" yelled Adin.

The loader raced to get another round into the rifle as tracers began to snap and streak over their heads. Adin sensed that they had but seconds before the Jeep would be nailed by the heavy twenty-millimeter rounds. He had to move or the Jeep and its vital recoilless rifle would be destroyed.

Adin punched the accelerator and took a sharp turn to the left. The loader hung on for his life as centrifugal force nearly flung him from the back of the vehicle.

They headed for cover behind the plane, hoping for another shot. Adin couldn't risk losing the recoilless rifle until he used it to take out the two satellite dishes, his primary goal of the mission.

Heavy fire poured in on the C-130. With the Jeep gone as a target, the twenty-millimeter tracers zeroed in on the outboard starboard engine of the plane. The heavy rounds blew the spinning prop apart, sending the massive blades into the air. Seconds later the engine exploded. Fire erupted all along the wing as the inboard engine went up.

The heat of the explosions drove Herman and Sarah back away from the airplane. Herman dragged the wounded commando out onto the open tarmac away from the left wing and the violently gyrating propellers of the two remaining engines. It was only a question of time before the massive fuel tank inside the plane exploded. Herman tried as best he could to maintain cover as the dense black smoke of the burning plane began to billow over the field.

We could hear the crack of gunfire punctuated by the bass thump of occasional larger explosions. Suddenly, as we came around a bend, we saw smoke.

"Slow down," says Harry.

"I want to see what's happening," I tell him. I hit the accelerator and he hangs on.

"Be careful," says Joselyn.

Just as she says the words, I round another bend and find myself staring at a brick guard kiosk in the middle of the road. The heavy iron drop gate is down, but no one appears to be in the hut.

"Hang on!" I pull forward and do a sweeping turn in front of the hut in case we have to pull away in a hurry. The guardhouse is empty. I turn off the engine and grab the binoculars.

A few seconds later Harry and I are out of the car. I am standing perched with my toes on the threshold of the open driver's-side door looking over the roof of the vehicle through the hundred-power field glasses.

"What do you see?" asks Joselyn.

"It's a plane. It's on fire," I tell them. "Sons of bitches are shooting at it. Oh shit!"

"What is it?" says Harry.

"Lift the barrier!" I tell him.

"What? Where are you going?"

"Just do it!" I toss the binoculars to Joselyn, jump behind the wheel, and start the engine.

Before Harry can lift the gate, the car is spitting

gravel from the back tires swinging around in a full turn. He lifts the balanced metal pipe. I pull forward and he jumps back in the car. Before his door is closed we're moving again.

SIXTY-ONE

Adin saw the three of them huddled like orphans on the naked tarmac, Sarah, Herman, and the wounded squad machine gunner. He wondered where the dog was, worried that he might have gotten left on the plane. But it was too late now.

"Ready?" He yelled to the loader on the back of the Jeep.

"Do it!" said the man.

Adin spun the Jeep around one more time and headed back toward the twenty-millimeter gun. If he could knock out their last big weapon, Ben Rabin and his men might have a chance to advance on the building even under the withering small-arms fire.

The two remaining props spinning in reverse blew a wall of thick black smoke across the runway ahead of the plane. Adin used it as a screen to close the distance on the twenty-millimeter gun.

By the time the front of the flying Jeep emerged from the wall of dense black smoke, they were less than sixty meters from the sandbagged gun em-placement.

Adin swerved to the left and hit the brakes as the gunner swiveled the barrel of the recoilless rifle and took aim.

The gunner sitting on the back of the twenty-millimeter tripod saw them at the last second. He tried to bring the muzzle of the gun to bear, his thumb over the trigger as the flash of the explosion blew him out of the chair. Boxes of twenty-milli-meter cannon rounds exploded inside the ring of sandbags.

The loader on the recoilless rifle was yelling and screaming, hanging on with one hand as small-arms fire tattooed the metal on the rear of the Jeep. Before Adin could hit the accelerator, two AK rounds ripped into the man's chest, blowing him off the back of the vehicle.

Adin turned. One look and he knew the man was dead. He hit the accelerator and raced toward the screen of the smoke as bullets flicked off the concrete, chasing him across the runway. One of them snapped past his ear and hit the windscreen in front of him. The bullet shattered, sending shrap-nel from the copper cladding into his forehead and cheek. Adin turned the wheel just a little. He changed course to force the shooters to reacquire their target. The adjustment gave him the time he needed to blow through the wall of smoke. Once behind it he jogged again, this time to prevent a late shot from tracking him blindly through the screen.

The massive shock wave rocked the Jeep as the fuel tank inside the plane exploded. Shards of aluminum and steel were blown into the air. A mushrooming black cloud roiled upward and rolled open in a ball of orange flame three hundred feet in the sky.

Adin saw the three of them pulling back from the flaming wreck, Herman pulling the wounded SAW gunner away from the spreading fuel-driven fire as Sarah struggled under the weight of the machine gun and the heavy ammo bag to keep them both out of the flames.

Under the end of the burning plane, Adin could see Ben Rabin and his men fighting to right the ammo trailer before the massive tail section collapsed onto it.

He turned the Jeep toward Sarah and Herman and raced across the concrete runway. The vehicle skidded to a stop right next to the three of them.

Adin set the brake and jumped out. He grabbed the wounded soldier by the feet. Together he and Herman loaded the man into the back of the Jeep under the barrel of the recoilless rifle. Adin took the machine gun from Sarah and handed it to the wounded commando and asked him if he could still shoot.

The man smiled and nodded. He set his back against the bolted rifle mount and steadied the machine gun over the left rear wheel well of the Jeep.

Adin put Sarah in the back behind the right seat, told her to lie flat and keep her head down. "Can you drive?" He looked at Herman.

Herman glanced at the stick shift, standard four-speed ahead with a fifth gear for overdrive. "Sure. What are you gonna do?"

"I'm going to be working the rifle," said Adin. "We need to take out the two big dishes," he told Herman.

"Let's do it." Herman jumped behind the wheel, released the brake, and started feeling the controls to get used to them. "Tell me when you're ready."

Hirst climbed on the back and loaded one of the self-propelled rounds into the recoilless rifle, then closed the breach. There were only three more re-coilless rounds left in the Jeep. The rest were in the ammo trailer. Adin tried to peer through the smoke but couldn't see what was happening under the tail of the plane. "We'll take the big dish first." Then he told Herman to hit it. "Go!"

Ben Rabin struggled with the heavy metal trailer, trying to tip it back onto its wheels as the flames burned from the plane's tail section over their heads. The Israelis desperately needed the two mortars stored inside the trailer. They couldn't get at them because the compartment where they were stored was buried under the trailer.

Ben Rabin had been hit twice in the upper body, through-and-through flesh wounds that hurt and bled. But there was no time to worry about them. Four of his men were already dead. Three more were wounded. There were only a dozen of them left including himself.

He tried to guess at the number of troops firing back and estimated their force to be at least three times the strength of the Shayetet. Normally that might give an enemy almost even odds except for the fact that the Israelis had lost the element of surprise and were now stranded out on the naked runway.

What they needed was some way to close the distance on the building under the large saucerlike dish. But the seventy yards of bald concrete between the burning plane and the building was a killing zone. Two of his men had already died trying to cross it. Without cover, the withering fire raked the surface of the concrete all the way across the runway and into the brush five hundred meters away on the other side.

The enemy kept bouncing rounds into the up-turned bottom of the trailer. Sooner or later they would hit something hot inside and the entire ammunition train would go up, along with it most of his men. Ben Rabin needed something to turn the tide; otherwise they would all die here on the tarmac.

"What are they doing here?" asks Harry.

"I don't know, but Herman I couldn't miss," I tell him. "I'm sure it was Sarah on the ground next to him. I only got a glimpse, but I could tell it was her."

"Doubt if there would be another duo like that," said Harry.

"Who would bring them down here?" asks Joselyn.

"I'll be sure and ask the minute I catch up with them," I tell her.

"They must have been on the plane," she says.

"That's what I am thinking."

The sky in front of us suddenly erupts in a billowing black cloud. A second later the shock wave jolts the car.

"Shit!" says Harry. He peers through the windshield with an expression of fright.

We race along the road, my heart pounding as we speed toward the runway down on the flat about a half mile away.

"I'm going to stop up ahead and let both of you out," I tell them.

"No, you're not," says Harry. "You want, you can let Joselyn out, that's fine."

"Screw you," she tells him.

"No sense all of us getting killed," I say.

"What are you going to do?" asks Harry.

"I'll know when I get there."

"You don't even know what's going on," says Harry.

"It's easy enough to tell friend from foe when they're shooting at your daughter," I tell him.

"You don't have a gun."

"No, but I have a rental car," I tell him. "I'll drop the two of you off and you can tell Hertz that I'm sorry."

"You're not listening. We're not getting out," says Joselyn.

"You're crazy," I tell her.

"So are you," she says.

"I'm not going to argue with you," I tell her.

"Then shut up and drive," she says.

"Listen to the lady." Harry is busy stretching the band to load up the speargun.

"What are you gonna do with that?" I ask.

"At least I can harbor the illusion I've got something to shoot back with."

"Do me a favor." I glance back over the seat at Joselyn. "If you're not getting out, at least get down flat on the floor behind the front seat."

On this point she does not argue.

I press on the accelerator and we rocket past a line of parked vehicles along the side of the road, all of them empty, security pickups and small sedans with light bars overhead.

"I guess we can assume that all the occupants are out there trying to kill the people on that plane," says Harry.

"That would be my guess."

Harry tries to scrunch down into the footwell on the passenger side.

I check my seat belt, pull it tight, and brace myself.

"Don't you think you're going pretty fast?"

"You're the only woman I know who would be worried about speed when a firing squad is about to shoot us."

"You're still going too fast," she says.

"Momentum is our friend."

A glance at the speedometer tells me I'm clocking a hundred and ten kilometers an hour, something just south of seventy miles per hour.

"Try not to hit anything solid," says Harry. "The secret is to keep moving."

"I know."

"The minute we stop they'll riddle the car with bullets and kill us all." Harry's happy thought for the day.

"It sounds like you've done this before," I tell him.

"Little old ladies in crosswalks," he says.

We rocket through an open gate. We are by it so

fast that I can't tell if there is a guard in the kiosk or not. Up ahead I see the smoking plane, billows of flames as the entire fuselage is now engulfed. Bullets are flying. There is no sign of Sarah or Herman. With all the smoke I can't see a thing on the other side of the plane.

My eyes focus on the firing line ahead of me, soldiers in uniform kneeling behind a row of sandbags. There is so much noise and commotion they don't even see us. Their eyes are riveted on the victims out on the runway.

"Hang on!" I yell.

SIXTY-TWO

The oil-laden smoke now lay like a pall across the runway. Herman picked his location carefully, then stomped on the accelerator and drove the Jeep headlong into the drifting black cloud. As soon as he cleared it, he spun the vehicle around, turning to the right. This gave Adin with the recoilless rifle a clear shot from the back end as the man with the squad automatic weapon laid down covering fire from the left side.

The second the Jeep stopped, the SAW opened up. The gunner stitched .30-caliber rounds along the top of the sandbags seventy meters away.

Two of the guards who didn't get down fast enough ended up taking bullets in the chest and the head. The others ducked.

Sarah covered her ears with her hands in an effort to keep the explosive rattle from the machine gun from blowing her eardrums.

The covering fire gave Adin the time he needed to zero in on the large parabolic antenna.

To blow a hole through the massive reflecting dish wasn't enough. Adin wanted to nail the smaller boxed antenna that contained the high-end electronics where the radio waves were concentrated and received.

He took careful aim as bullets snapped by his head, then pulled the lanyard and watched as the round streaked across the distance, exploding as it struck the apex of the metal frame holding the antenna in front of the huge concave dish.

Sarah saw a series of sparks spit from the shattered black box as the recoilless round fried the electronics inside. "Go!" Adin dropped to his knees and slapped the side of the Jeep over the back wheel well. He smiled at Sarah and held up one finger. "One more to go."

Herman popped the clutch and raced back through the smoke to the relative safety behind the smoldering plane. He didn't stay there long.

Hirst quickly reloaded. He was now down to two rounds. The gunner in the back changed out his triangular magazine under the machine gun.

Herman looked over his shoulder. As soon as he got the all-clear sign from Adin, he circled back. This time he popped out of the smoke at a different location. In less than a minute they took out the other antenna, but not before two rocket-propelled grenades streaked past them.

The guards were beginning to take notice, zeroing in on the Jeep. Both Adin and Herman saw them coming down the line carrying boxes of grenades and shoulder-fired launchers. They knew if they could take out the only remaining vehicle, the Israelis on foot could be chopped up at will.

Instead of heading back toward the burning plane, Herman drove toward the far end of the runway beyond the range of the RPGs. They stopped and checked their ammunition: a single recoilless round and one more magazine for the SAW. They loaded up and debated how best to use them.

The first two or three I blindside while they are still down on one knee. We roll over them like speed bumps. The car barely slows. In the rearview mirror I can see the bodies writhing on the ground behind us.

The next ones I hit are standing up. The first two go airborne up over the roof. The third one hits the windshield and shatters the safety glass on the passenger side of the car. I roll over a few more and we start to lose speed.

"Pick it up," says Harry.

I can feel the tires getting tangled in body parts. I pull to the right to clear the underside of the car and let the next few go.

Our reward is to be shot at from behind as I hear the flat thud of bullets pierce the trunk of the rental car.

"Everybody OK?"

"Good!" says Joselyn.

I look over.

Harry nods.

The strange thing is that none of the men I hit

see us coming until the bumper is into their legs and they are bent sideways over the hood—deer in the headlights.

If it was a game for points, I'd have to take a handicap. They have no chance to get the muzzle of their rifles around. Most of them can't even see us bearing down because the man standing next to them is in their way.

I pick up speed and plow back into the line. The first three I hit, the impact sends them flying over the sandbags. I floor the accelerator and take out some more. Two bullets pierce the back window from behind, shattering the glass. One of them takes a piece off the rearview mirror. The other goes through the windshield.

Harry smashes out the glass in front of him with the butt of the speargun so he can see. The whole time he's doing this he has the spear aimed at the side of my head.

"Watch the point!" I tell him.

"Watch where you're going," he says. "You hit those sandbags we're all dead."

While we're arguing, something whizzes between our heads leaving a vapor trail, a taste of aluminum in my mouth, and the smell of burnt rubber. I look at Harry and suddenly there's an explosion somewhere behind us.

The next guy I hit lands up on the hood of the car. Rifle in hand he reaches inside the broken windshield. Harry shows him the business end of the speargun. The guy smiles at him and rolls off the right side of the hood. He bounces on the road away from the car and strangely enough lands on his feet as if nothing has happened.

Ben Rabin watched as the first body flew up into the air. It spun like a rag doll and fell to the ground. Three more suddenly followed. Then an entire line of bodies, like grass being clipped in a mower, flew over the roof of the moving vehicle, flailing arms and legs.

The car seemed to pull away from the line and gain speed, then plow back into the assembled rifle-men behind the sandbags.

Ben Rabin wondered if the driver was drunk. If so, and if Uncle Ben survived the rest of the day, he was prepared to spring for another drink or an entire bottle if the driver wanted it. He shouted for his men to hold their fire. He didn't want them killing whoever was at the wheel. He couldn't believe what he was seeing.

He picked up the wireless headset. "Rebel Two, this is Rebel One. Come in. Rebel Two, this is Rebel One. Come in, where are you?"

When the crackling headset in the Jeep sounded, Adin, Herman, and the wounded SAW man were sitting at the end of the runway making final preparations for a run at the building.

Adin grabbed the headset. "This is Rebel Two."

"Where are you?"

"Far end of the runway," said Adin.

"We need to move now," said Ben Rabin. "Can you see what's happening?"

"No."

All of a sudden an explosion erupted behind the sandbags.

Adin looked up. "Is that you?"

"No," said Ben Rabin. "They're doing it to themselves. There's a driver, ran a vehicle through them. Bodies flying everywhere. But we have to move now before they regroup."

"What do you want me to do?"

"Catch them in a pincer from their right flank," said Ben Rabin. "We'll squeeze from this direction."

Adin grabbed a pair of field glasses from the glove box in the front of the Jeep and checked to see what was at the near end of the sandbags and the chain-link fence. What he saw was a small blockhouse with a slit in it, what looked like a light-machine-gun installation, protecting this end of the roadway leading to the front of the buildings.

"You got it. Give me thirty seconds to get in position."

"Roger. Out," said Ben Rabin.

SIXTY-THREE

By now the incoming volley of fire into the trailer and the area around the plane had died down. Ben Rabin looked up and winced at the smoldering tail section over his head. A few more minutes and the steel supports holding it to the fuselage would start to give. Half a ton of hot metal would fall on the overturned trailer.

"Take all the ammunition and grenades you can carry," he told his men. "Get ready to move."

They started stripping the trailer of anything they could reach, bandoliers of bullets, bags of grenades.

Ben Rabin grabbed two satchel bags filled with C-4, along with a roll of det-cord and two electronic and six pencil fuse detonators. He handed one of the satchels to his sergeant and draped the other over his shoulder. He looked at his watch. "Grab your weapons and follow me."

Ben Rabin broke cover and ran toward the gate in the chain-link fence. Eleven other soldiers followed him. He watched in amazement as the red sedan continued in the distance driving down the line, rolling up the enemy's left flank. The driver had a perfect angle. No more than a single soldier, maybe two, could turn and draw a bead on him at a given moment. The car was moving so fast that by the time they turned, the vehicle was on them.

The driver missed a few of them. The survivors lined up and fired toward the back of the vehicle as it sped past.

Ben Rabin and two of his commandos aimed their assault rifles from the shoulder and fired. They dropped the guards who had escaped becoming hood ornaments before they could pull off any more rounds.

Liquida, looking for a vehicle, had worked his way to the end of the complex of small buildings. He found nothing and began to suspect that he was going the wrong direction.

Hauling the heavy money bags was wearing him out. He was breathless and sweating and beginning to wish he had used the cart into which he had piled Leffort's body.

Occasionally he got a glimpse of the mayhem outside through the various doors in the complex. With the electronic key card from the man in the pay room, Liquida seemed to have access to everything he needed except a car.

He picked up an assault rifle from one of the dead guards who had stumbled back into one of the buildings and died near the front door. The clip was mostly empty, but it still had three rounds. Liquida didn't plan to use it unless he had to.

He sat for a moment and rested; he felt the weight of the bags and wondered how the hell he was going to get away. Suddenly there was an explosion outside. It shook the building.

Liquida dragged himself to his feet and went to the door. He looked through the blown-out plate glass opening. One of the double doors was missing, reduced to a pile of glass pebbles under Liquida's feet.

He glanced down the street. A small concrete pillbox at the end of the road was belching black smoke. Chunks of fractured concrete littered the pavement around it. Liquida watched as a low-slung Jeep drove slowly past the smoldering wreckage and turned toward him, heading down the street in front of the building.

He stepped back into the shadows inside the door and watched as if in a daze as the Jeep cruised by. The breeze from the slow-moving vehicle blew curling white tendrils of smoke from the barrel of the recoilless rifle. As he looked on, Liquida was in no doubt as to the existence of the afterlife. Otherwise how was it possible that the man he had killed in a parking garage in Washington three months ago could today be driving a car in the jungles of Mexico?

His eyes remained riveted on the Jeep and its driver. The vehicle pulled sideways in the street as the gunner on the back opened up with a machine gun. The Jeep sat there. Liquida got an even better look at the man behind the wheel. There was no mistaking him. There couldn't be two that looked like that, the one they called Herman Diggs, Madriani's investigator. What was he doing here? More to the point, how was it that he was still alive?

Within seconds Ben Rabin and his men vaulted over the sandbags and opened fire into what was left of the confused guards. Mangled arms and legs lay everywhere. The speeding car had left a trail of carnage and chaos that unnerved the remaining defenders. Some of them threw down their weapons and gave up, while others ran.

Ben Rabin could see the black smoke from the blockhouse at the other end of the street three-quarters of a mile away. He could hear the distinctive automatic fire from the SAW. He wondered who the driver of the red car was and whether he was still alive.

His men started to round up the guards. Ben Rabin handed the satchel bag to his sergeant, nodded toward the huge satellite dish, and told him to take it down. "Find the control room. Gather any papers, laptops, data drives—whatever you can find—and get it ready for transport. And find the technicians. Get them all together. They don't know yet, but they'll be joining us for the trip back home." In the meantime, Ben Rabin had to find a phone or a radio. By now the backup C-130 should be waiting for them in Belize.

Resistance seemed to stiffen at the other end of the road. Flurries of rocket-propelled grenades whistled past the Jeep. Adin sensed they were down to hard-core fanatics, the handful of guards who would fight to the death rather than give up.

He told the commando to stick to short bursts on the SAW. They were running low on ammunition.

He tapped Sarah on the leg and motioned her toward the back of the Jeep. "Time for you to get off," he told her.

"Why?"

"Between here and the end of the road it's liable to get hot," said Adin. He was worried that if one of the rocket-propelled grenades ripped into the Jeep, she could be seriously wounded, or worse.

He grabbed a pistol from a box in the back of the Jeep, a Glock 23 with a fifteen-round clip. "I'll catch up with you," Adin yelled to Herman.

Herman looked back and nodded. The Jeep moved on down the street.

Adin took Sarah by the hand and walked her toward one of the buildings. "You'll be safe inside until we get back." They crossed the small strip of grass and headed toward the door, Adin with the pistol in his hand to make sure they would have no problems.

"Wait here." He peeked inside. It was a small lobby. The building had taken the brunt of some of the fighting, window glass on the floor. One of the doors was missing.

He checked inside, took a couple of minutes, and found the place was empty. "Come on in."

Sarah stepped over the broken glass.

"We'll look for Bugsy when I get back." He smiled

at her. "We'll find him, I promise. He won't go far. He's a good dog."

"I know he is. I just want him back," she said. Sarah started to cry.

He wiped her cheek with the back of his hand. "Don't think about anything now. Just sit and relax."

She laughed. "How can I? That's easy for you to say. This is probably all in a day's work."

He gave her a serious look. "No. This is at least two days' worth of work." They both laughed.

Sarah had seen enough violence in a few hours to last her a lifetime.

"Here, take this." He handed her the pistol.

"What about you? Aren't you going to need something for protection?"

"I'll be fine."

"No, really." She tried to press the gun back into his hand.

Adin looked down and lifted his left pant leg a few inches. Strapped to his ankle in a holster was a small snub-nosed revolver.

They were still laughing when Sarah looked over his shoulder and saw him. At first she just stood there with a quizzical look on her face.

"What's the matter?"

"Look out!"

Before the words cleared her lips, the shot rang out. The explosion of the Kalashnikov reverberated through the room as Adin flung himself into Sarah. They landed in a heap on the floor.

Liquida tried to line up for another shot, but the guy was on top of her. He moved for a better angle. As he did, the wall behind him came alive with bullet holes as the blast of gunfire echoed through the room. At first he wasn't sure where the shots were coming from. Then he saw the gun in her hand pressed to the floor by the weight of the man's body.

A second flurry of shots, one of which nicked his shoulder, told Liquida he'd had enough. He fired another round from the rifle as he retreated out through the back door, the way he had come in.

Sarah pulled herself out from underneath Adin and fired two more well-aimed rounds at Liquida's fleeting shadow. "Are you all right?" She turned and looked at Adin. He wasn't moving. There was blood on the floor. She rolled him over and looked into his face. She put her cheek to his nose searching for breath and felt for a pulse at his throat. There was nothing. She knew that the spark of life that had danced so freely in those large brown eyes had been extinguished. He was dead.

Sarah knelt there looking at him. She wanted to cry but she couldn't. She tapped the muzzle of the gun on the polished stone floor as rage crowded out every other emotion. Fury filled her as she raised herself up and glared at the dark hallway and the wall with the two shadowed bullet holes.

With purpose she walked toward the rear of the building, squeezing the pistol in her hand. She saw drops of blood where Liquida had gone. Sarah knew she hit him. Now she would track him into the bush and kill him. She was not without caution, but anger filled her every pore. Her body was awash in a sea of adrenaline.

SIXTY-FOUR

The wounded soldier leveled the barrel of the machine gun at the wrecked red sedan as it raced toward them. Finger on the trigger, he was trying to save the last few rounds. He would wait until the car was on top of them before he opened up.

The Jeep blocked the road. At the last second, Herman held up a hand. "Hold it! Don't shoot."

The commando eased off on the SAW.

"I know them." Herman smiled as he saw Harry through the broken windshield. He looked like Poseidon holding a trident in his lap.

As the car pulled up next to them, Herman realized that the fire engine red exterior was not all paint. The driver's-side window came down. Herman was left staring at the stern and angry face of his boss.

"Where is she?" I ask.

"She's OK," says Herman. "She's in a building back there for safekeeping. Adin is with her."

"Who the hell is Adin?"

"That's right, the two of you never met," says Herman. "A young man. Nice guy."

"I'll bet. So tell me, is he responsible for bringing her down here or are you?"

Herman swallows hard.

Joselyn is behind me with her hand on my shoulder. "Relax!" she says. "You've killed enough people for one day."

"I'm just getting warmed up," I tell her.

"Don't say something you're going to regret. She's OK and that's what counts."

"We'll talk about it later," I tell Herman. "Where is she?"

He points up the road behind him. "Third building on the right. How you doin'?" He looks at Harry.

"Better than you at the moment." Harry smiles. "See you later."

We pull away and drive toward the building.

"Cut him some slack," says Harry. "If you lived with your daughter and tried to tell her no lately, you would know it ain't easy."

"What are you saying?"

"She's a lot like you."

"Hold your chin up just a little higher and ask a couple more questions, I'm sure he can hit you dead center," says Joselyn.

"OK, enough," I tell them.

"He's in a bad mood," she says.

"You think he's bad now, wait till he talks to his daughter," says Harry.

* * *

Liquida lugged the money as far as he could. He wasn't going to run any farther. He stashed the bags behind some brush and started dripping false blood spoor down the path leading to the small lake behind the complex.

The area was dotted with deep cenotes, some of them with sheer cliffs, walls fifty feet high. In other places, surface lakes bubbled up in the otherwise dry jungle where thick, deep mudlike brown cement ringed their shores.

Liquida dripped blood almost to the edge of the water from several different directions along three different trails so in case she got lost she could still find her way to the lake. If there was one thing that was certain, it was that Liquida wasn't going back to those buildings or anywhere near the landing strip. He could hear explosions in the distance, not rifle fire or artillery. Whoever won was busy blowing the place up, carefully timed detonations. To Liquida this spelled one thing—the military hand of government. And he didn't care which one. They were all bad.

He stanched the bleeding from his shoulder with a handkerchief, then carried the rifle into the bushes and waited. Liquida checked the magazine. It was empty. He had one round left in the chamber. If he couldn't kill her with that, then he shouldn't be in business.

Sarah tried to keep her head, to recall everything Adin had taught her about the pistol and how it fired. The Glock had no external manual safety.

She pressed the magazine release on the side and checked the clip. She had only six rounds left plus the one in the barrel itself.

It was the problem with the small light handgun. It was so fast and easy to shoot that you could squeeze off fifteen rounds in a matter of seconds and not even know it. She slid the magazine back into the handle and pushed it home until it clicked into place.

Bracing the gun in both hands, Sarah moved cautiously down the trail as she followed the drops of blood. She could hear explosions in the distance and began to wonder if she had made a mistake. It might have been wiser to go after Herman, tell him what had happened.

Then Sarah steeled herself and said no. Liquida had killed both her girlfriend, Jenny, and now Adin. He had tried to murder her not once, but twice. Adin was an innocent victim. She knew he was dead only because he had been standing too close to her at the wrong time. She knew that if she didn't find Liquida now, he would be gone.

In her own mind, he had passed from the realm of the human to a lower form of life. Killing him was like flushing an amoeba. He was diseased in the way a rabid animal was and required killing for the same reason. She couldn't believe she was having such thoughts, that she could harbor such hate. A year ago she had been in college, but so much had happened in that year. She shook off the thought and looked down the path.

The jungle growth was low, the trail covered with overhanging brush. In places, Sarah had to stoop to get under it. Suddenly something snapped off to the right. She stopped, her eyes trying to penetrate the dense foliage. It was as if she could feel hands coming out of the brush at her. A noise to the right—she turned and fired, squeezing off two quick rounds. She listened and heard nothing except the pounding of her own heart. She could feel the surging blood at her temples.

Sarah looked down the path and saw a continuous trail of blood. She began to wonder if she had wounded him more seriously than she thought.

Again she heard the snapping of brush off to the right. She knew he was there. She turned with the pistol and aimed toward the sound, but this time she didn't fire.

Liquida could hear her footsteps as she moved down the trail, snapping twigs and dry leaves under foot. She would never make it as an Indian scout. He sat on a rock and listened as she came closer.

He tried to gauge how far back she was. Then he picked up another stone and tossed it back up the trail and across to the other side. A second later he heard two more shots. By now she must have been sweating blood.

He sat calmly on the rock and listened as she crunched down the track toward the lake. He waited a few seconds and threw another stone. She fired again and then *click*.

Liquida smiled. He checked the one remaining round in the rifle. It was time to go to work.

* * *

Sarah stood stone still on the trail and trained her eyes on the traces of blood to where they ended twenty feet ahead at the edge of the lake. It was as if someone had dripped it along the path using a paintbrush. She silently slipped the magazine with the two remaining rounds back into the handle of the pistol. The slide on the top had been held open after she had fired the single round in the chamber. She knew he would hear the empty click. He was somewhere off to the left. The last stone he threw nearly hit her.

She steadied the pistol with both hands and kept her thumb on the slide release the same way Adin had shown her at the FBI range. As soon as she pressed it, the slide would spring forward and carry the first of the two rounds from the clip into the chamber. From there, in less than a second, if she could get a clear shot, she could pump the two rounds into him. She tried to envision the silhouette targets from the indoor range—center mass, chest high.

Liquida was about to step out onto the trail when he heard the thrashing in the brush behind him. He turned to look and before he could move, the Doberman was on him, flashing teeth and dog breath. The animal seized his arm, the sharp canines ripping into his flesh.

Liquida tried to fling him from his arm. The dog hung on like a bear trap, growling and kicking up dust as he pulled with his hind legs. Somehow Bugsy had lost his leash running through the brush. Liquida got a grip on the rifle with his left hand, finger on the trigger; he tried to steady it but the dog was in too close. He couldn't get the muzzle of the barrel on him. He kicked the animal in the stomach, and the dog bit down harder all the way to the bone.

SIXTY-FIVE

Sarah heard growling and thrashing in the brush. She pointed the pistol toward the noise and waited.

"Bugsy! Here, boy. Come here!" She knew from the sound, like a parent knows a child. She tried to coax him out, but he wouldn't come.

Suddenly there was the sound of a shot, close, no more than twenty feet away. The dog screeched.

Sarah saw red. She held the point of the pistol chest high and fired into the brush. With the second shot, she heard a deep groan and suddenly everything went quiet.

She stood there on the trail looking at the bushes and listening. She waited a few seconds. "Come on, Bugs. Come on out." But the dog didn't come. There was no sound, no movement in the brush.

She waited, what seemed like forever, and then slowly began to inch her way down the trail toward the lake. She called the dog again but heard nothing.

She reached the edge of the mud, the soft shore, with her back to the water. She held the gun out, even though she had no more bullets. She wanted to close the slide but couldn't remember how. She pressed the slide return on the side, but it didn't work. If Liquida stepped out now and saw the slide was back, he would know that the gun was empty.

Sarah remembered the snub-nosed revolver strapped to Adin's ankle, but it was too late. A second later Liquida crashed through the brush with the butt of the rifle over his head. He came at her swinging it like a club.

She saw the mass of blood on his left side as the rifle came down on her shoulder. It drove her to the ground as she dropped the pistol in the dirt.

Liquida pounded on her back with the butt of the rifle as if driving a post into the ground. He dropped the gun, descended on her, and pulled out the stiletto. He straddled her back and pushed her face in the dirt. Taking the handle of the blade in both hands, he raised it above his head like an Aztec priest in a ritual sacrifice.

Harry was forty feet away when he saw the flashing blade in the air just as Paul, like a heat-seeking missile, hit Liquida from the side. Madriani drove his shoulder through the Mexican's upper body, sending both of them skidding into the mud at the edge of the lake.

They lay crumpled in the muck, both dazed by the blow for several seconds before Liquida rose to his knees. When he stood, Harry could see that the knife was still in his hand.

Before Paul could get to his feet, Liquida was on

him, the slashing tip of the blade searching for its target. The glistening point buried itself in Madriani's right arm as Liquida drove him back to his knees. With his foot he kicked Paul in the stomach and pushed the lawyer over backward into the water. Liquida landed like a panther on Paul's back and tried to drown him, all the while cutting and slashing with the blade.

Somehow under the water Madriani found the Mexican's feet and pulled. Suddenly Liquida found himself upended, thrashing about on his back in the shallows. He slashed out with the knife and missed. Madriani backhanded him hard across the face, the bones of his knuckles ripping the flesh under the Mexican's right eye. Before Liquida could recover, Paul's hand came back the other way as a closed fist and caught him on the cheek on the other side.

The blow rattled Liquida's brain but not before he sliced the front of Madriani's shirt open, drawing a line of blood across his stomach and chest.

The two of them engaged in a death match as Joselyn reached Sarah lying in the dirt at the end of the trail. The speargun that Harry had clutched all afternoon, now that they needed it, was left in the car.

Paul and Liquida fought in a slow death spiral, dancing for position in the water. Madriani had come to a knife fight empty-handed, and Liquida intended to make the most of it. He smiled as he watched the rivulets of blood flowing from the shallow slash across the lawyer's chest. What he didn't see were the two hooded bumps on a log floating just at the surface of the lake as it drifted in behind him.

Madriani stood motionless, his back to the shore. Suddenly a flash of white water erupted behind Liquida. Before he could even flinch, the jaws of death bearing a hundred razor-sharp teeth slapped shut around the Mexican's hips. The crocodile and his bloodied prey twisted and thrashed.

Liquida screamed and slashed out with his knife. The thin sharp point snapped as it struck the armor-hard scales on the back of the beast. The crocodile rose up and rolled over, taking Liquida beneath the waves. As the roiling surface settled, all that could be seen were bloody bubbles of air as they burst forth from the surface of the lake's dark waters.

SIXTY-SIX

Four and a half hours after the final shots were fired in the jungle near Coba, a single errant asteroid somehow slipped undetected into the inner solar system. It had happened before, close calls with potential impactors, but this one was far nearer and more dangerous than most.

News accounts of the mysterious fire in the sky over the southern United States received sparse coverage in the world's media. Less than two inches appeared on one of the inside pages of the only major daily in Phoenix, Arizona.

Scientists at NASA were still gathering data and analyzing the potential for disaster. A few members of Congress renewed their calls for more funding to scan the skies, the first step toward avoiding any future catastrophic event.

But most leaders, including those in the White House, assured the public that there was no real reason for concern. There was, after all, a far greater chance of winning the lottery than being killed by an asteroid.

Near disasters were always something that government leaders sought to downplay, especially if their own incompetence and possible corruption were contributing factors. It was one of the time-tested reasons for classifying otherwise public information. People in positions of power always had to survive; otherwise the world might turn upside down. Doctors merely buried their mistakes. Presidents shoveled them by the ton into the constantly sucking and massive dark hole of national security.

Fortunately the asteroid merely skimmed the earth's upper atmosphere before skipping out into space, a close call, but no harm—colorful fireworks that illuminated the evening sky over the American Southwest.

What the newspapers and even the American government didn't know was that Lawrence Leffort's attempt to peddle secrets to a foreign power, and to test the deadly results in the desert of Arizona, was doomed from the inception.

Even without the failed rocket mounts, the iron asteroid that Leffort and his colleagues had so carefully harvested and sequestered behind the moon never had a chance of reaching Earth. The reason was that the final targeting software from the flash drive in Raji Fareed's jacket had been intentionally scuttled by the man himself.

Fareed was an Israeli agent, a longtime sleeper in the space-age catacombs of the American empire. He had been sending information to Tel Aviv for years. It was how Israeli intelligence became aware of Project Thor. And they were not alone.

For decades America's technologic crown jewels had been plundered by government and industrial spies and peddled by presidents who pocketed million-dollar speaking fees after they'd left office. The entire concept of a global economy embraced by both major parties was a naked excuse by political leaders and their Wall Street buddies to hollow out entire American industries and sell them abroad. American workers were left behind to squabble over the crumbs from diminishing social programs.

Of the few items of value in Fareed's Paris hotel room, the only one that counted was the curious pair of spectacles with the wireless flash drive, the ones that Bruno's men left on Raji's body when they dumped him in the alley. Along with Raji's notes, the glasses contained the accurate targeting software. It was the reason Fareed wanted so desperately to get online, so that he could transmit the data to his handlers in Tel Aviv.

As it turned out, the information never left America. The spectacles rested in the bottom of Joselyn's purse and there they stayed until one afternoon when she crushed them under the wheel of her car. She smashed the flash drive with a hammer in the garage of the house she shared with Paul in Coronado, San Diego. It was bad enough knowing that NASA and the American Defense Department possessed the secret for bombing the earth with missiles from space. Joselyn had no intention of making it easy for the information to propagate.

And oh yes! Minutes after the croc tasted Liquida, while he was still deciding which parts were appetizers and which were entrées, the dog Bugsy crawled from the brush into Sarah's lap. He had been shot in the side by the Mexicutioner but only grazed. He cried and whimpered but survived. Now he lives in the house with Sarah. This spring he sired three pups. Sarah kept the pick of the litter. She named him Adin.

ACKNOWLEDGMENTS

Many people, both family and friends, provided encouragement and support in the writing of this book.

Most of all I wish to thank my assistant Marianne Dargitz, who for years has provided not only her energy and unflagging support for my work but also her encouragement to guide me during difficult periods. Without her constant efforts none of this would have been possible.

I also wish to thank Josh Davis of Tech Help in Bellingham, Washington, for particular assistance on the technical aspects of this book, especially for his expertise on matters relating to computers and advice on the application of flash drives and Bluetooth technology.

Among others to be thanked are my publisher William Morrow and all the people at HarperCollins without whose unstinting care and love of publishing nothing would be possible. Most of all I wish to thank my editor, David Highfill, who has been a friend and constant source of encouragement and patience; editorial assistants Gabe Robinson and Jessica Williams, who fielded my phone calls and handled so many technical aspects during the transition from paper to digital editing; my agent, Esther Newberg of International Creative Management; and my New York lawyers, Mike Rudell and Eric Brown of Franklin, Weinrib, Rudell & Vassallo, for their constant attention and guidance to the business aspects of my publishing career.

Finally, and not least, for their caring interest, love, and constant encouragement, I thank Al and Laura Parmisano, who have been there for me always during good times and bad; my friends Jan Draut, John Garrison, Mike Padilla, and Jim Bryan; and for her constant and unconditional love, my intelligent, beautiful, and wonderful daughter, Megan Martini, who for me makes all things possible.